WHIMS OF GOD

WHIMS OF GOD

M. A. AIKENS

Plum Lane Books

This book is dedicated to my devoted husband, Bill, who saved me in ways he can't possibly know.
To Misty, the goddess of reading.
To Kelie and Barbara, my whims.

And to all those creatures of special design who assisted in writing this book.

TW: This book contains themes of abuse, assault, murder, and suicide that some might find disturbing.

The author would like to acknowledge the hard work provided by her editors:
Michael Garrett at manuscriptcritique.com
Karen Sanders at karensandersediting.com
and to her cover designer, Jessican Bell, at jessicanbelldesigns.com

For inquiries related to this book and others, contact Margaret Aikens/Plum Lane Books at:
www.margaretaikens.com

First Printing, 2023

One

A single piece of paper weighs 4.5 grams. Abby used five sheets to tell her story, yet the weight of the words made it immovable. In an instant, everything changed. Our childhood, once lustered, became dull and tragic. Our memories darkened; our innocence dimmed.

That is how this story begins. It is also how it will end. In between, I'll purge our sins and secrets, asking for forgiveness and the understanding that comes in the aftermath of truth. How much understanding you grant will depend on how much of this confession you care to believe. In the end, I can only hope you quietly accept the reasons behind the terrible things we all did and the secrets that forced us to do them.

Those reasons are strong.

Our secrets are horrific.

And may God forgive me... I have my regrets.

Many subtle but historic events occurred in 1976. That year, Jobs and Wozniak offered their *Apple*. NASA's first shuttle raged in the skies, and Dolly Winthrop wore the crown as Bayport, South Carolina's first and only Bicentennial Queen.

Dolly's appointment held little importance against the impact of spaceships and fruit, but her placement upon a tissue-wrapped float offered a connection I desperately craved. Dressed as a mermaid, she wore a long auburn wig that looked very much like my own head of hair. Outside my mother and me, I'd never seen another redhead roaming the wild. Bayport was your average fishing town full of shrimpers and women in pantsuits. There was nothing relatable about them as they were mostly brunettes or blondes or buttercup blondes with blue eyes but no redheads. Not even fake ones.

They didn't even carry red hair dye at Linden's department store. Mama Nash suggested Mother use honey and cinnamon ground into a poultice. Didn't work on her grays, but it tasted terrific on toast, so we ate it.

"There she is," I shouted, skirting aluminum chairs. "I see Dolly, Mama Nash. I see her. Oh, look at her costume. Isn't it bright? And her hair. Oh, Mama Nash, just look at her hair."

"That half-naked belly is what I'm looking at." Mama's eyes narrowed tightly on Dolly's plump breasts. "And what's she got on her tits?"

"They're just shells, Mama Nash. Flag-colored ones like the mermaids wear."

"I ain't never seen no mermaids wearing no flags on their tits. And her belly is bare to the world."

"Bathing suits show more belly than that, and they only painted the shells for the bicentennial year. They're probably white or green underneath."

"Don't care what color they are underneath. This ain't nothing but filth." Then she called Dolly a Jezebel and dragged me down the street to her car.

"It's not filth," I screamed as she stuffed me into the scalding back seat. "It's a costume, and I'm going to wear one just like it at Halloween."

Mama leered in the rearview mirror as we climbed Oaks Bridge toward Frogcreek. "You ain't wearing nothing that belongs on a tidal creek whore. Good Christians don't do that, Sarah Thorn."

In the six years she was my babysitter, I never once challenged Mama Nash. Her beliefs were pragmatic. A saintly mix of Christian sobriety and regional folk magic she divined in her youth. We shared long talks and agreed on most everything, so there was no need to question her means. However, that day, with exhaust blowing through the broken windows of that busted-up Ford, bravery won over caution, and I made the mistake of testing the waters of Mama's mercurial mood.

"Dolly's not a tidal creek whore." I burst up, gripping the back of her seat. "Gossips say you can't be a Christian when you're dressed up in muumuus doing rootwork all day. They say you fed your husband and daughter to hogs in Lou'siana, and you can't be a Christian because you're a witch."

That woman nearly crashed that car with both of us in it. She skidded over, dangling one fatty arm on her seat. "God, I worship. Rootwork, I practice. And you ain't wearing no get-up like that when you ain't nothing but nine years old, and I'm still able to whip your behind."

"You can't whip my behind 'less my momma says you can."

And that was when I learned the back of Mama Nash's hand was far less appealing than the gentle stroke of its palm. It was swift and shocking, like being slapped with a belt dipped in jasmine.

"Show your momma that cheek," she said. "Ask her if it's okay I whip that."

I screamed, smelling the vinyl baked in the sun and wanting to yank every fuzzy gray hair she owned. The tears ended once we got to Mama's house, and I saw my best friend, Abby, was there. Mama called her *sunshine at dawn*, referring to the summer-kissed tint of her skin. She was the perfect shade of copper. Naturally darkened beneath warm Southern suns, she held an ethereal glow reminiscent of goddesses cast in dark bronze. She was beautifully crafted but exotically strange for a town full of shrimpers and pantsuits.

Abby's father, Buster, was not beautifully crafted nor branded with epithets conveying sweet charm. He was a detestable butcher whose father raised him with the staple of cruelty common in men who loathed anyone smarter and more innovative. Part of Buster's ancestral breeding was isolation. He feared all things outside the blood-stained shop on Branch Street and envied sociable citizens who found his drunken tirades irritating. Mama Nash was one of those citizens.

Buster called her a witch, accusing her of committing unspeakable barbarism against those she considered displeasing. And although rumors about Mama's questionable past spanned farther than Buster's malodorous shop, Buster nattered the most.

While Buster never allowed his daughter around Mama Nash, Abby's mother, Ida, brought her whenever Buster was off selling turned meat from his butcher shop's truck. I was selfishly glad when he did. That was the only way I could spend decent time with Abby, and if people got sick, then so be it.

Abby and Alicia were licking honey from Mama's beehives when I wandered up. Alicia was Mama's granddaughter and, by all accounts, the meanest child in the world. She enjoyed teasing me for my pink, freckled skin and for not having a father, which, obviously, was impossible since I walked and breathed every day. He died before I was old enough to know what a father would mean in my life, and I was unaware that Alicia's torments were born of her lack of masculine affection in her fledgling years.

I once overheard Mother and Mama discussing how Alicia's daddy ran off, leaving Mama's pregnant daughter to fend for herself until she died. The pain of that fact showed on Alicia's face whenever the mention of mothers arose. Her black eyes went darker, and she tightened her lips, trapping emotion behind the trembling grip of her chin. That expression was why I never used Alicia's circumstances as weapons against her, no matter the beatings she gave me with mine. I was never told not to. Just didn't seem right, so I didn't.

She wouldn't have had such good ammunition if I'd kept my stupid mouth shut. I often made the mistake of confessing I saw fireflies in daylight and heard the cries of the sun as it set. Heard it clear as day. Long, sizzling whines made me leap toward the riptide behind Mama Nash's before Abby yanked me back, holding me tight as I wept.

"It cries like the moon," I'd say between sobs. "But the moon only cries when it loses its stars, and the sun only cries for itself."

While Alicia used my notions for petty tortures, Abby indulged them with me. We danced in clouds of fireflies and listened to the words of the trees.

"What do they say now?" she'd ask, and I'd sandwich her tiny frame between me and the oak's craggy trunk and relate the magical stories of trees to the only other person who allowed my instincts to breathe.

After feeling left out of such whimsical fun, Alicia pounced, saying I was stupid, a baby, or a liar. My reactions varied according to the intensity of Alicia's usually gruesome mood and my propensity to overshare an interest in things that didn't exist. Still, it vented frustrations of the woes I suffered, so I endured the after-effects of Alicia's brutality with dramatic, Oscar-worthy flair.

"Alicia's teasing again." I stormed to the porch where Mama was stripping fresh corn. "She says trees don't talk and fireflies at the tide pool aren't real. She's stupid and can't even read big kid books like everyone else."

"Ain't Christian to raise your pride over others, Cherie."

Stomping a foot, I reiterated my dominance over Alicia through literary prowess. "Speaking the truth isn't raising my pride. Abby and I finished *Charlotte's Web* in two days. *Two days*, Mama Nash. Alicia's the same age as us and still reads baby books in the dummy class. She's jealous, and that's why she's so mean."

"Girl's mean because she's hurting inside," she said, gathering me close to her breast. I loved Mama's breast. It was impossibly deep, with swells that bulged from the top of her bra, glistening like gold when she'd sweat. I loved the necklace that covered it, too. It was full of gator teeth, interspersed with some kind of bean that made wonderful clicking sounds when she walked. I always played with it. Flipping it, clicking it. Imagining poor creatures floating in moss-shadowed bayous, gumming their prey in the mud.

"You still mad I called you a witch?"

"'Course I ain't mad. You had yourself a spell, baby. Ain't no different than anyone else."

"Don't mind when I get like that, Mama Nash. I know you didn't feed your husband and daughter to those nasty hogs. Mother yells at folks when they say it. She tells them your husband and daughter died from weak blood, and they should mind their own bitter tongues than to go wagging them off at a good woman like you."

Mama smiled, rocking her chair. "Your momma is warmer than sunshine, Cherie. Always do as she says."

"She tells me to write, but writing bad dreams seems stupid to me. Not like it stops them."

"Ain't meant to stop them. Purging on paper is better than leaving them be."

"My head hurts when it happens sometimes, and I see things I don't always like. It's like my heart opens up and sucks in the world."

"Only special people see God's earthly details," she said, kissing the divide in my braid. "You're blessed like that."

"Don't feel very blessed. Ladies at the parlor tell Mother there's something wrong with me. They call me names when they think I can't hear."

"Damn nags." Mama scowled, tucking me close. "Don't listen to them."

"Hard not to listen when they whisper so loud."

"They're nags." Then Mama lifted my chin, adding, "There's a purpose for you, and you'll fill it one day. But for now, keep your gifts between you and your shadows."

Tugging the black velvet pouch on her wrist, I said, "Throw bones for me, Mama. Tell me my purpose right now."

Mama opened the pouch, spilling small bones onto the porch. They scattered with dull ticking sounds on the boards, one propping on the toe of her canvas flat.

"That means you're somebody special, Cherie. Set off as God's blessed whim."

That wasn't true, but I liked it.

"I see grand and magnificent things for you, child," she said. "People, places, and crowds holding signs. Your stories will 'waken the world.'"

"The world?" I gasped, shifting my rump on her generous thighs. "How, Mama Nash? How?"

Mama smiled, turning again to the bones. "You'll be the voice of the broken. The keeper of secrets and the wing from a butterfly's back. Your purpose is to give what's needed, Cherie. The world will listen and love you for that."

I stared between Mama and those obviously misguided bones. "Those things are broken. It can't be my purpose to have people listen to me. Alicia sure doesn't. Mother doesn't listen when I tell her I don't like peas, and Abby only listens when I cry."

"Trust what I say, child. Those bones are spilled right."

"Throwing bones scares people, Mama. I don't think you should do it willy-nilly like that."

"Ain't nothing wrong with helping God in His efforts."

"Efforts with what?"

"With the world," she said. "And the people what's in it. Good and the bad."

"Abby's daddy must be one of the bad ones." I pressed into her, curling corn husks over my thumb. "Know what folks say at school, Mama Nash? They say Buster beats Ida because Abby come out a girl. Is that true?"

"No, that ain't true," she said, and we both watched Abby dancing in the sun with her black, wavy mane at her back. "Our Abby come out special. All of you did."

"Mother says we should feel sorry for Buster because of what his daddy did to him."

"Cry for the child locked up in that well. Curse the beast what come out."

"Can I curse Alicia?" I asked, sitting up. "Can I make her fall in the riptide or get stung by your bees?"

"Don't be wicked. You need one another to help you manage your struggles."

"Alicia will struggle with meanness," I said, falling back to her chest. "Meanness and reading big words."

"'Licia will struggle with love."

"What will Abby's struggle be?"

"Abby will struggle with patience," she said.

"Abby's got to be patient with a daddy like that. What will my struggle be?"

Mama looked at me, and a shadow fell over her face. A moment of darkness, like clouds veiling over the sun, and she said, "Your struggle will be that you live."

These were my learning tools. In our world, *Dick and Jane* jumped from bridges and deserved their stinging gashes because they didn't listen to the world around them told through nature and hints from God. At the end of Mama's sermons, as we watched the Bible waving overhead and the alligator tooth necklace clacking at her breast, she'd smile, clustered with pride.

And we'd smile back, knowing some honey-oozed treats lay behind the doors of the little gray shack that always smelled of flowers, food, and sweet ocean air. Mama fed us from the bellies of her bees, from the honey rich with love and mixed by the hands of the closest thing we knew to God's own touch. She'd lead us to the back of the yard, to the tide pool, where we'd splash and play, learning to love, hate, and live. Mama lined us up, braiding Abby's dark tendrils into my fiery red with Alicia's brown in the center, and she'd call us God's whims.

Mama said we all struggled so much even God couldn't define our plans, so He moved us together according to the tragedies that chased us and the needs we'd face in their wake.

"Whims," she'd say, pulling us into her arms. "You're all just whims of God."

Two

Three weeks after Dolly's boobs got me slapped, the whole county was covered in mumps. The onslaught was vicious, claiming Bayport's pubescent spawn like a curse thrown down from the heavens. Mama opened her home to those frail angels whose parents found themselves caught between the work of a shrimper and the ills of a child.

Shrimping work always won out.

"This one's dead." I waved for Alicia and Abby, inviting them to gawk at our newest ailing acquisition. We teetered on discarded beehives, peering through windows in Mama's back room.

"That boy ain't eleven." Alicia shoved the curtains aside. "Legs barely fit on the bed."

"Who says he's eleven?" Abby asked.

"Grandma did, but he looks way bigger than that. Damn mump kids spoiling the house."

"They're not spoiling anything," Abby said. "That's not even your room."

"That's my napping bed, though," I whined, resting my chin on the sill, "and I don't want mump breath staining my sheets."

Abby scolded us both. "Be proud Mama's helping this boy. Good Christians open their doors, and that's all Mama's done."

"Good Christians get their kids shots." Alicia sniffed. "Island folk spread cooties faster than horse shit around here, thinking doctors are giving out palsy. None of us got the palsy from shots."

Adding to the confusion, I said, "Mother said boys' peties fall off when they get the mumps."

"Peties...?" Alicia lurched back. "Lord, now we've got peties falling off? What's that woman filling you with?"

"Heard it last night with my very own ears. Mother was on the phone with another nurse, and she said boys put ice on their peties because that's where the mump germs take root."

"Good glory." Abby prayed to Saints Joseph and Jude before nudging me hard in the ribs. "Go in there, Sarah. See if his petie fell off."

"Are you nuts? I can't go in there looking for that. What if he wakes up? What if he's dead?"

"Princess is scared." Alicia snickered, pinching my arm. "You scared of dead boys or looking at peties?"

"I'm scared Mama will finish her biscuits and find me poking around in that room."

"Those biscuits take hours." Abby pushed me again. "Go on, Sarah. Look for his petie or see if he's dead. Mama should know either way."

"He does have nice comics," I said, noting the colorful books on the bed. "I can do that."

With each foot in my accomplice's hands, I slid through the window, falling to the floor in a heap. Dead Boy just lay there, lace curtains licking his cheek.

"He's breathing," I whispered back to the girls. "Don't think he's dead."

Alicia upped both thumbs while Abby wiped away pretend sweat.

"Girls!" Mama's voice snapped outside, sending me scrambling beneath Dead Boy's bed. "Get your tails outta that window."

A slap burned the air, and although unsure if it hit a backside or Mama's likened hand, I knew the sound well enough to quickly avoid its source. Abby and Alicia slinked from the window, leaving me trapped beneath Dead Boy's bed. Mama's screen door slapped shut in the kitchen, and her worn terry slippers scraped in from the hall.

"Wake up, child. Restore yourself." Mama laid a tray on the floor by my face. There was a white china bowl and spoon, a cup of cool water, and jars of blossom honey seasoned with rose hips inside.

"I'm cold," Dead Boy whimpered. "And it hurts."

"I know it does, baby. I know."

I'd never witnessed such sadness before. He was so alone, so frightened. At times, a name would skitter across his lips as if calling for someone he couldn't quite reach. It was a soulful need, the anguish unforgettable.

After Mama returned to her biscuits, I slid from under the bed, and Dead Boy looked at me, brown eyes wide and blinking. "Who are you?"

"Nobody," I said, hoisting the quilt from his lap. "Just came to look at your petie." He was fully intact. Swollen and sad, but his privates were fully intact. "Still there. Must not be sick enough yet."

"I'm plenty sick." Dead boy slapped my hand. "What're you doing in here?"

"Came to see if your petie fell off like I said. Sort of surprised to find it's still there, seeing how sick you look. My mother's a nurse, so we got shots. You didn't get shots?"

"We don't believe in medicine like that."

"You're island folk, ain't you? Only island folk don't use doctors. What's your daddy do?"

"He's a shrimper."

"Mine too," I chirped. "Then he died in the war. He wasn't island folk, though. Island folk are stupid."

Dead Boy lifted his sweaty blond head. "This old woman here lives on an island. Bayport's nothing but islands."

I bent closer and got in his face. "This here's Frogcreek, boy. It ain't no island 'cos it's stuck on Grainger. Grainger's the island, and it's stuck to Sweeton's Island, and that's tied to mainland, and that's where I live, so I know Frogcreek ain't no island. And that old woman's taking care of you so your trashy family can pick the sea while you lay here sweating all over my napping bed. So, I'd be more respectful if I were you because that's Mama Nash, and she's special, and she'd throw a curse on you hotter than Hades itself."

His eyes narrowed down into little black slits. "You talk too fast, and you're mean."

"Least I'm not crying from not having shots. Got the chills too?"

He nodded. "Can't seem to get warm."

Pressing my hand to his head, I gasped at the heat. "How could a body shiver cold when it's so blamed hot?" Lifting a corner of the blanket, I said, "Move over."

Dead Boy blinked, stunned.

"What're ya, dense shrimper's kid? I said move over."

The bed creaked as he inched back, letting me ease beside him. I dug an arm beneath his shoulders, twining our bodies and smoothing the blankets.

"What's your name?" he asked.

"Sarah Haley Thorn. What's yours?"

"Ethan Scott Bennet."

"You smell like honey, Ethan Bennet."

Ethan smiled. "Will you stay with me, Sarah?"

"I'll stay with you, Ethan," I said, kissing his cheek. "I'll keep you warm."

That was the first time I'd slept with anyone besides my mother. The gentle embrace of it, the smell of honey on his seasoned breath, and the warmth of his fevered skin scored a memory I'd never forget. That was the first of many embraces we'd share and the start of a love story that would span the whole of our lives.

All Southern children share the splendor of unforeseen bonds. It is inborn, a natural occurrence of pressure and time, growing pearls of kinship within fragile shells. This inherent connection fused three girls with the shrimper's son, who survived his ordeal with the stoic bravery of a shorebird hooked at the wing. Physically, Ethan healed. But he suffered a furtive tragedy bruising his heart. It showed on his face when he stared at the shoreline or studied the stars in a velvety sky. There was a dark spot in him. An undeclared brokenness and still-bleeding wound. A quiet limp in his soul.

With alliances forged, our foursome invaded every corner of town, turning Bayport's sidewalks and storefronts into endless kingdoms of childhood games. Riding his Schwinn over Oaks Bridge onto mainland, Ethan plucked us each like a rose. Abby came first. She'd lie about deliveries or burdens for school, then she'd dash over Branch Street to meet Ethan at The Waterfront Park.

Ethan had a brotherly fondness for Abby. Their ties were implicit. A quiet connection of hard-scrabble lives and general parental neglect. They hugged when they met, smiled, and laughed. Ethan was careful with her, arranging her hips on his handlebars before racing through summer-baked streets to pluck me. The rhythmic whir of the playing card clipped inside Ethan's spokes blended with car horns and tires as he darted through the traffic clogging Ribaux and North. That sound and the chirp of Abby's delighted squeal forever infected the caves of my ears.

"Hop aboard, Shakespeare," Ethan said to me. "We have castles to conquer and monsters to slay."

I straddled his seat, molded my chest against the arc of his spine, and absorbed the honey-sweet scents of his skin. Everything about him was natural to me. Ethan carried the world in his blood and bones like saplings risen from roots. The comfort of that—the natural wildness of warm skin and breath—drew me closer in a much tighter hold.

Flaunting her independent nature, Alicia refused Ethan's offer of a bumpy bicycle ride and met us at whichever location suited our day. Those places varied by weather or adult intervention, but we never failed to fill every hour. We ran on beaches or sat by Mama's tide pool, eating honeycombs and splashing our feet. Sometimes, we met at Shell Beach in Port Royal or Shoreline Cemetery, chasing between faded headstones. Mostly, we played at Bayport's most infamous abandoned house, Branch Street Castle.

Large and bordered by water on two sides, the castle was an old antebellum mansion the city couldn't decide whether to keep or kill. It sat at the dead end of Branch Street, draped in overgrowth so high the house was barely visible from the turn to Oaks Bridge by the park.

Slinking through its fractured portals, we opened a fantasy world of knights and lonely princesses. Ethan swung an oar overhead, pounding up the cobwebbed stairs, shouting, "I'm here to slay your monsters!" then we'd squeal and hide, waiting for rescue.

Still, other times, we'd stir like monkeys through the castle's solarium, trying to clear the thorny vines from the greenhouse trapped in its middle. Ethan always objected, telling us it wasn't safe. Dutifully, we listened. He was taller and older and gave us a sense of endearing protection I think we all needed.

We spent three scorching summers running those streets. Through bicycles, growth spurts, and small minor wars, our attachments always endured. But friendship was no barrier to time, and as childhood morphed into that terminal infection of age, the threads of our bond became worn. Ethan exchanged playtime adventures for trawler work out on the sea. His family's shrimping demands required laborious attention, and, loving the Atlantic more than anything else, Ethan was quick to comply.

Alicia's skepticism grew with her chest. She buried herself in volunteer needs, cleaning at Shoreline and guarding the beach, but her sarcastic wit never changed. Brazen in thought and solitary, her opinions teetered between toilet humor and unwanted critiques of my jotted-down dreams. She was rigid, arrogant, and cursed more than most trawler captains leaving the docks, but she couldn't deny the virtuous mercies she shared with the weary and poor.

Although Abby matured, her home life retained its vile inhumanity at the hands of her father. The Mills were the typical small-town cliché, living in a shanty behind the butcher shop's lot and holding a loathsome regard for social involvement as families like that sometimes do. It was something Abby suffered like a bad taste in her mouth.

Shame and embarrassment curved her features more than any expression I'd seen on her face. Her father taught her to be ashamed of her deeply tanned skin and the womanhood she tried to avoid. Abby kept herself covered in homemade shirtdresses, flapping the heat from the fortress of fabrics she wore. By eleven, she created elaborate stories to explain the chronic succession of bruises and cuts. By twelve, she denied them outright. Ida's mousy defenses did little to end her husband's attacks, and after surviving her own brutal beating, which hunched her shoulder and fogged her left eye, she escaped with Abby to visit her family in Florida.

Thus heralded the summer of my unbearable pains. Nightmares tortured my sleep, writing filled my waking hours, and the need for oblivion darkened my thoughts. Suicide was impossible as I couldn't leave Mother in a town lacking anything follicly red, but even love couldn't silence my mind. The riptide at Mama's became a convenient alternative to flaying my wrists or dangling my body from a low-hanging branch. I'd stand at its edge, listening to calls from the buoy bell's cries, and weep, fighting the demons infecting my mind.

Every woman I knew became the gatekeeper for my mental collapse. Mother soothed me, Mama prayed for me, and even Alicia held my hand once or twice, but none compared to Abby's assuasive efforts in my daily routine. Her soft-hearted nature and understanding of my mental revolt offered my turmoil a soft place to fall. My needs were self-ish, but without her, insanity rallied unchecked. Each day was a battle for lucid resolve, so I waited, running to Branch Street and pacing in front of the butcher shop's walk.

Week after week, month after month, I prowled the walk by those filthy store windows until her bright, golden eyes graced the door.

"Abby?" My breath hitched when I saw her, and I rushed inside, jerking her into my arms. "Mama said you'd never come back, but I knew you would. I just knew."

"You shouldn't be here, Sarah. Mama won't like it, and she just left the shop."

"Mama was here?" I asked, peering back. "Mama never comes to the shop."

"She was checking on me and won't like knowing you popped in here too."

"Oh, I don't care about her. It's been awful while you were gone. Just awful. When d'you get back?"

"Last night," she said, and I noted the changes twisting her face. Her eyes were less bright, her smile less wide, and the chirp of her laughter fell to a breath.

"Need a phone call?" I asked, dipping to capture her eyes. "I can pretend to be one of the lunch ladies from school again. They can order some lard for delivery and get you out of the shop for a while."

"Thanks, but I have work to finish here first."

"How about Lola Crabbe? Or her husband, Seymore? If I drop my voice, I can—"

"No Lola and Seymore today. How are you?"

"Terrible. Started my monthly, and Mother had to show me how to use those pads. Mama kept putting warm pots on my belly, and Alicia—"

"It's time, gal." Buster scuffed from the littered back room. He was pale, round, and dirty. Like the gelatinous ooze that collects in the bottoms of bait wells once the water drains out. That was what his presence dealt. That was what he was. "Get into that Perlick and stack this last load of crates."

Perlick was the freezer's manufacturer. Twenty years before, the walk-in appliance adorned the kitchen of a local statesman who lost his position to a squandering life. Envious of anyone wealthy and bold, Buster claimed the freezer at auction, trucking it home and taping the politician's name on the door to embarrass the family. But when the town saw the idiocy Buster scrawled on his sign, the only person embarrassed... was Buster.

"Harley Freidman jamed his meat into this Perlick heer wonse. Now his meat onlee jams inside me!"

The sign made no sense and was a grammatical gaffe, but it entertained the town, nonetheless.

"Hear me, gal?" Buster kicked the crates by his feet. "Get inside that Perlick and finish them crates. And don't open that door but a crack."

"Yes, sir." Abby followed his directions but stopped at the freezer to stare at the door.

"Abby?" I dipped closer, touching her arm. "You okay?"

"I'm fine." She shivered, tilting her body and curbing inside. "I can do it."

"What you doin' here, gal?" Buster propped himself on the counter, resting an elbow beside gherkin jars. "If you're lookin' for that Nash witch, she's already gone."

"Mama Nash isn't a witch, and I came to see Abby."

"Did you, now?" That old dogfish grinned, sucking a bone between rotted teeth. "Might not be safe letting you visit my shop. Folks say you suffer thoughts of the damned."

"Don't suffer anything except fools who beat up their wives."

Unaccustomed to mouthy women, Buster wasn't sure what to do. He crooked a lip before delicate whimpers turned our attention to a brown wicker cradle by the door. Abby lurched from the freezer, collecting the bundle out of its nest, cooing and soothing as I moved in to look.

"A baby?" I asked, folding the blanket from two chestnut eyes. "Ida had a baby again? When?"

"Four months ago," Abby said. "Momma pushed him out at her sister's house in Eustis. Isn't he sweet? Name's Edward."

"He's perfect, Abby. But Ida shouldn't have more babies. Mother said it wouldn't be safe."

"Not like she had any choice." Abby placed a pacifier inside Edward's mouth before laying the boy in bed. "That's why we left last summer. Better that way."

"Told her to get rid of that thing," Buster said.

"If she did that, you wouldn't have your boy now, would you?" Abby faced Buster with fists at her sides. "You got your boy, and Momma got a beating that clouded her eye."

"Maybe she should'a done what was asked."

"Maybe she should've done what was right."

The two fell silent, trading ominous, unblinking stares.

"Don't argue with him." Taking her elbow, I urged Abby toward the Perlick again. "Let's unload crates, then we can play. Ethan and Alicia are fishing at the beach, but—"

"Ain't going near that freezer no more." Buster threw an arm in my way. "Abby can do it alone."

"No need for Abby to do it alone. Let me pass."

"Girl needs to learn how to work."

"Abby knows how to work. Stacking crates inside the doorway was good enough while she was gone. Keep doing that, you old goat."

"Ain't doing it halfway when I got a gal who'll do it for full. Loading crates ain't hard."

Crossing my arms, I said, "Well, if it's so easy, go in there and do it yourself."

Buster's eyes floated to the Perlick's closed door. Even at thirteen, I knew the rising tincture of fear. I'd seen it in mirrors and windows and my mother's shocked face when I ran to her bedside, swearing monsters were calling for me.

"Folks say you suffer thoughts of the damned too, Buster," I said. "Everyone knows what your daddy did when you were young. Made you afraid of tiny, dark rooms."

"I ain't afraid, little gal."

"Prove it." I shrugged. "Step into that freezer. Show me you're not afraid."

Mocking Buster Mills was a hazardous act. He didn't confine his disdain for the supposedly weaker sex within the walls of his alleyway home. It extended, reaching like fingers from old rotten trees, waiting to shatter their nests.

"He's right," Abby said, tying apron strings at her waist. "Shouldn't be here anyway. Your mother and Mama don't like it."

"Wouldn't be saying that if *he* wasn't here."

"Yes, I would, Sarah. Now go."

"All right, but only because you're asking me to. Buster can't stop me from seeing you here or anywhere else in this town."

Whirling defiantly, I darted down Branch Street and rounded the alley to the back of the shop. Empty crates towered beside the shop's office door, and I curled beneath them, waiting to see Buster head to their house adjoining the shop's gravel lot. Only took a minute before the back door kicked open, and Buster stepped out. He took an uneven drag from a bottle of whiskey, swiped a filthy arm on his chin, and then staggered into the house. Assured he was gone, I raced to the shop, finding Abby opening crates by the Perlick's closed door.

"Ta-dah." I threw my arms out before hopping inside. "Told you that tub of chum couldn't keep me away."

"Damnit, Sarah." Abby rushed to the meat cases, ensuring the office door remained tightly shut. "What if Buster comes back?"

"He won't. Not if that bottle holds out." Frigid air melted from the Perlick's frayed seals, and I bristled, rubbing goosebumps pebbling my arms. "That freezer need new gaskets or something? Feels like the arctic's leaking in here."

"Feels cold because of that fever you got. Always get one before your mind takes a turn."

"I don't have a fever, and there's nothing wrong with my mind. Mother took me to doctors in Charleston while you were gone. They made me sleep in a dark room while they watched my nightmares. Couldn't even get up to pee."

"Watched your nightmares?" she asked, pressing a hand to my head. "Why'd they do that?"

"Beats me. Mother gave them my notebooks, and they said I had an imaginative mind that wandered into my sleep. One doctor said I was willful and Mother should paddle me more. Damn doctors. Got ice cream after, so it wasn't too bad."

"What about headaches? Still fighting those?"

"Got one right now," I said, flicking the box cutter trapped in her fist. "Want help opening crates? I'll hook hams in the Perlick if you want."

"Hooking hams is the last thing I need. It'll be hell if my daddy finds you in here."

"What're you so nervous about?" I asked, tipping closer to her. "Buster bleaching hens in the dry sink again?"

"He doesn't want anyone in the freezer with me. Not anymore."

"Stupid old drunk," I mumbled, stepping to Edward. Silent and sleeping, he resembled a chipmunk snuggled in reeds. "Must be fun having a baby around."

"With Edward, it is." Abby smiled, touching his ear. "Sure does sleep a lot, though. And my land, does he love to eat. Seems I'm always washing a bottle or two."

"Bottle washing is the momma's job, Abby. Why isn't Ida doing all that?"

Abby paused, looking at Edward with all the tenderness of sisterly love. "She's not been right since we left last year, so it's best tending to Edward myself."

"Whole town had your names on their tongues when you left. Stella Clarke was opening the bank and saw Ida running with you down Ribaux to the bus station. She told my mother Ida's eye was nearly popped clean out. What'd he hit her with this time?"

"Washing paddle," Abby murmured. "Every time she passes a mirror, she cries."

"Guess I would too." I sighed, caressing Edward's pink chin. "Wish I had a brother like this. Or a sister. Either would be nice."

"We are sisters, Sarah. Not blood like Edward me, but we're sisters in everything else."

"All right, then," I said, kissing her cheek. "Sisters help when they're stuck doing chores." Then I turned to the Perlick door, grabbed its handle, and flung it back to the wall. "Open Sesame!"

"No, Sarah. Wait—"

"Don't be scared, scaredy-cat." Plumes of frost bathed my legs, and I reached for a box, bumping the door as I crouched. "Dang it, why's that safety latch so dad-blamed sharp? Feels like it's got pointy teeth." I fingered the L-shaped tear in my shorts. "Got a rip in these new pants too. Mother will have my head if she sees."

"Oh, Sarah." Abby moaned, and her eyes seemed to melt as they closed. "Didn't I tell you not to open that door? Didn't I tell you to leave?"

"Stop worrying so much," I said. "I'll tell Mother I snagged it helping Mama straighten her fence. Not like the world will end."

"But it might." Abby's breath caught, and she trained her eyes on my hip. "Blood sisters."

"Blood sisters?"

"Yes, Sarah. Blood sisters. Don't you want to be sisters with me?"

"Sure. But let's do it later, okay? My head still hurts, and the heat makes me woozy."

"We're doing it now." All at once, she lifted the box cutter and opened a trench in her palm. "Remember this, Sarah."

"Have you lost your mind? What're you so—"

"Hold still." Before I could stop her, Abby dipped my shorts and swiped the box cutter blade on my hip. "Blood sisters."

"Holy Christ!" Shocked at the sudden bloodletting, I watched as she slapped her palm to the split in my skin, grinding her wound into mine. "That burns like the dickens, Abby. You want to bleed us all out?"

"Remember," she said, trembling hand seizing my face. "We're blood sisters now, and if anyone asks, that's what we'll say."

"Could 'a warned me first." I was slightly annoyed at the lava flow staining my shorts. "Or done it the way you did yours. Felt like Buster took a bite out of me."

"He didn't. Now, go before—"

"Damned gals ain't got one lick o' sense." Buster curbed through the doorway, marched to the Perlick, and kicked it shut with a thud. "Didn't I tell you to stay out of my shop?"

"She didn't set foot in the freezer, Daddy. Did you, Sarah? Tell him you weren't inside that freezer today."

"Didn't go inside your smelly old Perlick. Only opened the door."

"The door?" Buster inched closer, taking my arm. "Did you see it?"

"See what, you old crab?" My mind was ablaze, fueling anger, rage, and the irresistible need to strike out. "The fuzzy ground round you keep in the back? Yeah. I saw that."

"No, she didn't," Abby said. "Sarah's leaving right now and not coming back. Right, Sarah?"

"No, that's *not* right. I'll go where I please, and this tub of shit won't stop me."

"Tub of—" Buster spat the bone from his mouth. "What'd you call me, gal?"

"Sarah didn't call you anything. Didn't see anything either. Even if she did, she'd forget by morning. That's how she is."

Dismissing Abby's defenses, I clipped both hands to my hips. "I called you a big... tub... of... *shit*."

Buster exploded, spitting out curses, twisting my arm, and wrangling my body like a worn cotton doll. "Did you see it, gal? What'd you see in that room?"

Abby's panicked cries filled my ears, but with my headache rising and trembling hands balled, my senses couldn't mirror the world. My mind had gone dark, my vision narrowed, and my body collapsed in his grip.

No one really faints in the South. We suffer the vapors, the swoons, or maladies of hysteric distress, but no one ever says the word *faint*. Except for Mama. Mama called it just what it was... *She fainted.*

"You're at The Waterfront, Cherie. You fainted from the heat in that shop."

"Fainted?" I coughed, arching my back against the slats of a bench. "From heat? How'd I get—"

"I carried you here." Ethan's fishing pole rattled as he helped me sit up. "Alicia and I heard the ruckus and ran to the shop. Found you spilled on the floor. Buster was flat against the wall, covered head-to-toe in scratches."

"She okay?" Abby scowled, bending with her face matching mine. "He only shook her a little."

"Pitched a fit in Buster Mills's shop," Alicia said. "Princess got what she deserved."

"Hush up, 'Licia." Mama pointed to Ethan. "Give me that water there, boy."

Ethan wrestled the canteen from his pack and passed it to Mama.

"Want me to get her mom really quick?" Ethan asked. "I can run to the hospital. Tell her to come."

"You ain't telling her nothin'." Mama pressed the canteen to my mouth. "Drink this water, baby."

"Be thankful me and Ethan were fishing downtown and not at the beach like we planned." Alicia propped her foot on the bench. "No telling what would have happened if we didn't hear that ol' bull shark yelling at you for breaking pickle jars on the floor."

"Pickle jars?" I asked. "The ones by the register? They broke?"

"Hell yeah, they broke," Alicia said. "Juice and gherkins all over the walls. Glass everywhere. And there was Buster, trembling like a June bug on ice. You wrecked that shop good and hard."

"Didn't wreck his stupid old shop. Only went to see Abby."

"Was you in that Perlick today?" Mama tossed a glance toward Abby. "Was she?"

"No, Mama Nash. She stayed in the shop. Didn't go near that freezer at all. Isn't that right, Sarah? Tell her I'm right."

"I guess so. I mean—" Memories of something deeper survived, but I hadn't the energy to ferret them out. "Maybe I was just in the shop."

"Maybe?" Mama inched closer. "You don't remember?"

"Some I remember, some I don't. Like, maybe I dreamt it."

"Well, someone remembers." Mama raised her brow toward Abby. "Tell me what happened in there."

"Nothing, Mama. I swear. Sarah came to the shop and Daddy told her to leave."

"And did you?" Mama turned her attention to me. "Did you leave like Buster said?"

"Not right away. I remember hugging Abby and Buster squeezing my arm, and then... then—"

"Then what?" Mama's eyes narrowed tightly on mine. "What happened then?"

"Daddy told Sarah to leave," Abby interrupted, wringing her hands. "Sarah didn't, so he got mad and shook her. I tried stopping him, but he wouldn't listen to me."

"Did he hurt you?" Ethan squatted with a hand on my knee. "Is that why you can't remember breaking those jars?"

"I didn't break any jars."

"You did, Sarah." Abby nodded. "I saw."

"Leave her be. God blinded this girl for a reason. Best we don't press her now." Mama inspected me, mopping my face and scowling at the stain on my shorts. "What's that blood on your hip?"

"My hip? Oh, that's from, that's from..."

"A box cutter," Abby chimed in. "That's a box cutter scrape. Right, Sarah?"

"Box cutter?" Mama sneered at Abby again. "Did Buster do more than rattle her brain? Already warned him about beating you. Won't take no time to add more to the list."

"No, Mama Nash. Daddy told her to leave the shop, but Sarah wouldn't."

"That don't explain no blood on her hip."

"Blood sisters." Abby displayed the wound in her palm. "Remember, Sarah? I cut my hand and put a tiny cut on your hip. Then we mixed the blood. See?"

"That don't make no sense," Mama said. "Why cut her hip and not her hand like you done?"

"Miss Sheila would see a cut on her hand, so I made the cut on her hip."

"That true?" Mama lifted my chin. "Tell me right now. Is Abby twisting what happened in there?"

Accepting the story was easier than mining the truth, so I shook my head and said, "No, Ma'am. I'd swear on a stack of Bibles she's not."

"Don't swear on something like that. It ain't Christian." Mama grunted onto her feet before asking Abby, "Buster was scared?"

"Yes, Ma'am. He surely was."

"And crying?"

"Like gulls in a storm. Whined about glass on his back. Hid behind the counter. Cried about being in the dark too. But it wasn't dark, Mama Nash. Not even a bit."

"Was to him." Mama sighed, straightening Abby's bib on her dress. "Come see me tonight. We got honey to make. And keep our Sarah out of the shop. Her mind ain't ready for that."

"Yes, Ma'am." Abby squinted, watching Mama plod through the park. Then she sat beside me and said, "Stay away from the shop, Sarah. Please?"

"How will I see you?"

"Pretend to be Lola or the lunch ladies like you usually do." She smiled sweetly, kissing my nose before standing again. "Need to get back to my crates." Then Abby waved as she left, trading winks with Alicia before crossing the street between cars.

"Better now?" Ethan took a seat at my side. "Need help getting home? Shouldn't walk by yourself if you're sick."

"She ain't sick," Alicia said. "Just screwy is all."

"Sarah's not screwy. Stop talking like that."

"Just because you like her doesn't mean it ain't true," she said. "You're always watching her when you think we can't see. Sneaking around corners, hiding in trees. Wouldn't be here right now if you didn't see her running into that shop this morning."

"Ethan likes me?" I flushed, looking at him. "Is that true?"

"I like everyone." Ethan frowned, kicking his foot at Alicia. "Talking about people like that isn't right. I've seen people touched in the head and Sarah's not like them. Not even close."

"The girl says trees talk and fireflies shine on the beach." Alicia twirled fingers by each of her ears. "Nuttier than elephant shit."

"Better call Abby nuts too," Ethan said. "She says the same things."

"Abby plays along with Sarah, but that's different from thinking it's real."

"Stop talking about me like I'm not even here." Dipping my waistband, I thumbed blood from my still stinging wound. "And I don't need you walking me home."

Ethan plucked leaves from my hair. "Did you really rip up Buster's shop?"

"Who says it was me?"

"Abby did," Ethan said.

"Buster too." Alicia pulled a packet of Grizzly from the fold in her sock and sat down. "First thing out of his mouth was '*Look what that crazy gal done.*'"

"Well, he's a liar. Old fart made that mess after drinking all day. He's blaming me so I'll stop helping Abby in there. Abby'd get a whippin' if she didn't agree."

"That's what I think too," Ethan said. "Bum's halfway into a bottle of rotgut by noon every day and it's half past three o'clock now."

"Why would Buster throw jars at his walls?" Alicia tucked a plug of tobacco into her cheek. "Abby'd get her teeth knocked out if she did that. That only leaves Sarah right here."

Ethan shrugged. "Could have been Ida."

"With that clouded-up eye?" Alicia scoffed. "Wasn't Ida."

"Well, it wasn't me," I said, shaking Ethan's empty canteen. "Not sure there's much left."

"That's okay." Ethan took the canteen and stuffed it into his bag. "Want me to walk you back home?"

"Think I'll sit here a while."

"You sure? We can stay if you want."

"No, we can't." Alicia hacked, hurling rust-colored spit on the walk. "We've got fishing to do."

"Don't worry about me," I said and managed a smile. "Go fish with Alicia before it gets dark."

Ethan gave in, collected his gear, and helped Alicia with hers. They pushed inside crowds along The Waterfront's path before Ethan stopped, dropped his poles, and dodged through the swings toward me.

"Alicia's right," he said, falling in front of my knees. "I do like you, Sarah. More than Alicia, more than Abby. Something about you just pulls me in. And no one will hurt you again. Not Buster or anyone else. I'll swear on Mama's King James. That's a promise I'll take to my grave." Then he planted a kiss on my cheek before darting away to the path.

That was the summer our childhood died. With a heartfelt promise from a boy on his knees and a kiss to my upper right cheek, it was gone. Over the next four summers, Ethan's bike sold, Abby's bruises lessened, Alicia's virtues advanced, and my writing greatly improved. We matured, trading lighthearted antics for soft pluming age and the vastness of futures unknown.

Three

Abby and I lay on the beach behind Mama Nash's, enjoying the strawberry-pink cassette player Mother gave me for my seventeenth birthday. Edward giggled beside us, filling buckets Abby crafted from milk jugs and straws.

"Edward is special," my mother would say, referring to his quietness and soft, soulful ways. Larger than most five-year-old boys, Edward was slow to walk and talk and held an almost pathological attraction to his sister's naturally gilded eyes. He touched them, kissed them, and laughed loudly when Abby brushed their silken edge on his cheeks. He was the link that strengthened the chains of our bond, darling and innocent, and Abby rarely left him behind.

That section of the beach was desolate compared to adjoining stretches of shore. But for the pitching clang of the riptide's buoy bell and occasional travelers circling the lot, that thin slice of earth was the loneliest place in the world. Abby and I made it our own, building oyster shell barriers and castles of sand with Sargassum ribbons on top. Those were the moments I felt truly free, dispensing the torments of my traveling moods, letting my raptures unwind.

Aerosmith's melodies buzzed from the speakers, and I snapped my fingers and wiggled my hips, devouring their force like a drug.

"Does it have to be so loud?" Abby reached over, forcing the volume knob down with her thumb. "I know your mind craves violent impact sometimes but keep that noise down when you're out here with me."

"My mind doesn't crave violent impact."

"Yes, it does. Colors, sunlight, and everything loud. It's like your body goes right up in flames. You write more too. And you're meaner."

"All right, your highness." The breeze caught Abby's hemline, and I tugged it. "Aren't you hot wearing that shirtdress out here? Why not borrow one of my suits? You're a pretty girl, Abby. Nothing wrong with showing it off."

"Nothing wrong with modesty either." She huffed, poking the fleshiness that bulged from my top. "That bikini has more business draped on a squirrel than tied around you."

"That's the point," I said, tickling Edward's ribs so he laughed. "Why'd you bring Edward today? Buster drinking again?"

"Daddy drinks every day. You know that. And I'm not leaving Edward in that smelly shop when the lunch ladies or Lola call for deliveries, and we can get out. Make sure they know I thanked them, all right?"

"Lola and the lunch ladies will all know you thanked them," I said with a smile. Then I slid my sunglasses over my nose and lay back. "Edward's almost five, Abby. Shouldn't he be talking more?"

"Edward's precious just as he is," she said, ruffling her brother's dark curls.

"Being precious isn't enough. Buster knows he wasn't born right. Didn't help to have Ida push him out in that shack you were flopping at, either. That was no place to have a baby. Ida told Mother what happened."

"Edward was stuck. That had nothing to do with having a baby in a shack. Now stop talking about it. You know I don't like it recalled."

"Can't believe Ida came back after the beating she took. If a man beat me while sticking it in, he'd be pissing out blood once he finished."

"Stop cussing so much." Abby shielded Edward's tiny ears. "We don't need Edward's first word to be bullshit or ass."

A group of four boys broke through the pines by the lot. They were boisterous and loud, volleying a football overhead as they walked.

"That's Ethan Bennet," I said.

"Where?" Abby tightened her eyes on the group. "Which one?"

"Tall one in the cut-offs. If he'd turn around, I could get a good look at his ass."

"That's not Christian, thinking like that. Mama said so."

"Well, Mama's not here now, is she? And if God didn't want us thinking like that, he shouldn't have made Ethan Bennet so damn easy to stare at. Would you look at him, Abby? He's tall as a boat mast and wide as a stern. Must be four years since we've laid eyes on that boy. That'd make him, what? Nineteen?"

"Probably. Last time I saw Ethan was when you tore up Daddy's shop."

"Didn't tear up that old shop."

"Did too."

"Did not."

"Did too."

One freckled boy sauntered up close. "You two look like a checkerboard game. Who's jumping next? Black or red?"

"Better than being trawler trash," I said. "Now move. You're blocking my sun."

"Trawler trash?" Ethan crouched, handing Edward a small wooden horse. "Only Sarah Thorn could say those words with such conceit. How ya doin', Shakespeare? Still pitching fits?"

"Still hearing gossip about you is more like it."

"Oh, yeah? Who's telling lies about me?"

"Bethany Nelson. She told Mother you got drunk and jumped naked off the parkway into Johnson Creek, dragging her behind with her brand-new patent leathers still on."

"I told her to take her clothes off."

"Her father's First Baptist's minister, you fool. Clothed or not, she's hardly the bridge-jumping type."

"What about you, Shakespeare?" He winked. "Are you for or against the ritual of bridge jumping?"

"Naked or clothed?"

Ethan dipped, kissing the crescent-shaped scar on my hip. "As nature intended, Miss Thorn."

"Ethan Bennet!" Abby heaved, blazing a hand across Ethan's head. "Keep your lips to yourself."

"Geez, Abby." Ethan winced, rubbing the lump on his skull. "Didn't mean anything by it. Just fooling around."

"Well, you find Bethany Nelson to fool around with, but leave Sarah alone. What'd you want anyway?"

"Came to play with Edward. Toss the ball back and forth. Maybe look for some shells."

"Not today." Abby tucked Edward close. "He didn't sleep well last night, and he's tired."

"Told you she wouldn't let us." Freckled Boy juggled the ball. "May as well have that kid tied to a tree for all the fun she lets him have."

"Better not be talking about Abby like that," I said, sitting up.

"Who else would I mean? Poor Edward can't have any fun without her. Guess the apple doesn't fall far from that rotten bunch."

Abby shrank at the *rotten bunch* insult, and I pictured ten-thousand ways to beat that boy's face. "You're Ethan's big brother, right? Evan?"

"What if I am? You gonna tell Mama Nash to curse me with a face full of zits?"

"Too late for the zits." I stood, snapping my suit bottom and dusting my hands. "Someone should teach you some manners here first."

"Don't, Sarah." Abby reached out. "I don't mind nasty words."

"Well, you should. Especially coming from someone like him."

"There goes that trawler trash comment again." Ethan laughed, catching the football and hurling it back. "Careful, big brother. Don't want to end up like old Buster Mills."

"That skinny shrimp doesn't scare me," Evan said. "Why, I've hauled catch ten times her size, and sharks so mean they could have—"

And before Evan knew what hit him, *I* was hitting him. Down on the sand, face slapped, fists balled, and nails scoring flesh in a relentless defense I was sure he'd never witnessed from my gender before.

"You talk about Abby like that again, and they'll need dogs to find your ignorant ass."

Then I exploded his nose with my fist.

Ethan crowed, hauling me off at the waist. "Holy hell, you're a foul-mouthed little thing."

"Not as foul as your brother, Ethan. Maybe now he'll think twice before shit-talking Abby."

Evan struggled back to his feet. "That shit right there is why everyone thinks you're crazy, Sarah Thorn. Always screaming and fighting, and everyone knows what happened in Buster's shop four years ago. What *really* happened, I mean."

"Sarah fainted because it was hot," Abby said. "Mama Nash would tell you the same."

"Mama Nash would lie for this girl." Evan coughed, hawking gobs of blood to the sand. "Sarah Thorn didn't get her way and threw a tantrum like she's doing right now. Buster told her to get out of his shop, and she tore that building apart. She's spoiled and got the whippin' she deserved."

"Say what you like about me," I said, feeling Ethan's grip on my arm. "But talk about Abby like that again, and I'll make sure Shoreline has one more party to give. You understand, Evan Bennet?"

"Something tells me he does." Ethan spun me around, and I faced him. I'd never been so physically close to a man before, and although I'd never experienced chest hair brushing my skin, I immediately knew I liked it. "Wanna see if my petie fell off?"

"No need." I snickered. "Bethany Nelson told me it's there, and Holly Winstead said the same, along with a Winn Dixie cashier and two cheerleaders I know."

Ethan ghosted his lips on my ear. "My reputation's sorely misjudged."

"Is it?" I breathed. "Really?"

"Uh-huh." He nodded, grazing his stubble-lined jaw on my cheek. "But you keep wearing little red bikinis like this one, and I may have to prove it's not."

Then he cracked a hand across the flesh of my sun-kissed backside and ran laughing down the beach with his group. I fell to the sand, a gelatinous puddle of goo. My hands shook, my eyes lost focus, and my breath was so tight I had to cough just to get it to move.

My skin pricked alive, spreading perfect warmth throughout my chest, down my arms, and lower, into places Mother forbade me to speak about outside of private medical concerns. But I couldn't help what I felt. It was a rush of bodily hope. The reach of one soul to another. A wanton, lingering need.

Four

Curling into bed between cool, cotton sheets was a nuisance I rarely indulged. Sleep was a bother for me. A hindering annoyance and a giant waste of time. I'd spend hours in bed, writing or reading, staring at ceiling fans, or counting the flowers that papered my walls.

As with other quirks of my fate, my nocturnal exploits snared Abby too. She'd tap on my window or stalk our front porch, waving at me through the screens. And I'd throw off my covers, slip from my bed, and trespass the hallway splitting the house. The floorboards presented a minefield of squeaks, requiring cotton-soft footsteps and long-legged sprints. Then I'd scoot through the kitchen and open its door to meet Abby by the streetlights outside.

Midnight was a haven for us, and we'd angle the sidewalks leading to the most secluded parts of Shell Beach's primordial stretches. Tall seagrass and sun-bleached logs adorned the shoreline, broken only by the shadowy presence of a boat run aground in the distance. We'd wait to see flashes from fireflies we chased, and I'd spread my arms and look to the heavens to wait for their fluttering touches.

With my pale skin glowing and red hair ablaze, I'd glide and twirl among their groupings, reflecting moonlight off the high white muslin of my gown. I'd take Abby's hand, and we'd slip and sway with the tide, unseen by neither man nor beast until, one night, the beast strode in, and Buster called out for his daughter.

"Don't be scared," I said, yanking us behind sea oats. "I'll jump out

34

and tell him you're gone. Once he's turned, you run through the dog-woods for home."

"He won't believe you. He'll find me. He'll hurt you."

"Only thing he's fit to hurt is his liver. I'll distract him, and he'll go somewhere and pass out. Maybe this time he'll do it in a nice salty marsh."

Abby smiled, a slow curving feature in one corner of her perfect mouth. "Who's your whim, Sarah Thorn?"

"You're my whim, Abby Mills. And I'm yours." Then I hugged her before darting out.

"Abby's not here," I said, bouncing in front of Buster's hulking frame. The man carried the sourness of low tide and mud, and thick sprigs of hair straddled his head like legs splayed out on a spider.

"Hey, crazy gal. What you doin' on this beach all alone?"

"Taking a walk, and I was just going home."

"Lots of footsteps denting this sand," he said, pointing his bottle of Jack at the marks. "Abby's here, ain't she?"

"No, but I wouldn't tell you if she were."

"Keeping secrets ain't proper, gal. Didn't that witch teach you better than that?"

"Only ignorant gossips think Mama's a witch."

"Gossips are right. Killed her husband and daughter, and everyone knows it. Sacrificed their flesh to raise the devil himself."

"They died from weak blood. Mama said so. And the only devil in this town is you, Buster Mills."

"You love my little garbage girl too," he said. "Edward come out slower than slugs, but he's a boy. Not Abby, though. That gal ain't nothing but trash."

"Don't talk about Abby like that. Abby's beautiful. Mama said she's sunshine at dawn, and God gave her copper skin and golden eyes to prove it. She's a whim of God."

"She's God's garbage." He reached out, floating a hand through my hair. "But you're sweet, ain't ya? Got eyes green as the sea and marsh-mallow skin like your momma. Bet you got some fight in you too."

"Lay a hand on me and you'll be battling curses till the heavens burn out. Mama Nash will make sure of that."

"Old witch cursed me once," he said, dipping close. "Didn't quite take."

"Mama's curses never forget. They're dark and cunning, and you'll be choking on blood once they come."

"Got yourself a brave mouth on you, gal." Buster tossed his bottle aside and closed the space between us. "Mouth like that should show respect for a man like myself. And respect from a woman starts on their knees."

"Why should horse shit get any respect?" I laughed. "All it does is stink up the dirt."

He slammed me into the sand so hard I thought my head would snap off. I slapped him, kicking, bucking, and smelling the stench of his sulfuric breath. The things he said were predictably vile. Things about my mother's breasts, her smell, and how she walked like she was tempting him with the natural swing of her hips.

Just as my energy began losing hope, the beach echoed with an ear-splitting *snap*, and Buster Mills, the butcher of Branch Street, fell to the sand like a heap of netted fish.

"The hell off of her, you rotgut son of a bitch," was all I heard over the rumblings of thunder as it battered the shore. "Sarah?" Ethan lifted me by the arm. He was shirtless and sweating, clutching a broken oar in his hand. "You hurt?"

"Don't think so," I said, straightening my gown. "But you hit him, Ethan. You knocked him out cold."

"So what? Filthy prick needed his ass kicked. Felt good too. Like clubbing a tuna."

"How do we move him?"

"We're not moving him, Sarah. It's not like we've got a forklift around."

"Rain's coming in," I said. "We can't leave him like this in the rain. What if he drowns?"

"What if he does?" Ethan shrugged, taking my elbow and pulling me toward the boat. "We'll be helping God in His efforts."

Ethan's gait was a formidable trod. He didn't veer, didn't look back, and didn't answer when I asked who owned the boat to which he was dragging me. He threw the oar to the sand, lifted me up, and set me onto the boat's tilted deck. He followed, took my hand, and led me down through the hatch. The space was tight, heated by gas lamps, melting chilly wisps that crept through the boat's aged planks. The odor was earthy. Not musty nor foul, just damp.

"Whose boat is this?" I asked, settling by his feet. "Looks cozy."

"It's mine. I'm fixing it up. Then I'm sailing off the edge of the Earth."

"Well, that's dramatic." I sniffed, tilting a box full of cans. "What's with the chili and soup? You living in here?"

"Had a fight with the folks," he said, snatching the box. "It's not a big deal, and it's certainly nothing to sneer at."

"Nobody's sneering at you. There's just nothing here. Only pillows and quilts. How come—"

"Would you be quiet?" Ethan stretched over me to peer out the hatch. "I saw his fat ass getting back up."

Never having been educated in the finer points of the male physique, Ethan Bennet's bared chest offered quite the lesson in sensual presence. Sculpted and tawny, it was a prime example of what nature could do to a body conditioned at sea. I wanted to touch it. To press my lips against his skin, trailing my tongue over muscle and hair, tasting sweat, salt, and...

"He's gone," Ethan said. "Stumbled somewhere and passed out. I'll take you home once the rain stops." Ethan snapped a towel from a nail on the wall, scrubbing it over my head. "Being out there in the middle of the night is a stupid, risky thing to do. You should be home in bed."

"If I slept better, I would. Abby and I play down here until I get tired. Sometimes I sit up and write."

"Writing would have been safer than traipsing all over Shell Beach. What were you doing out there?"

"Chasing fireflies. We dance in them out by the oats."

"Stop lying about those fireflies, Sarah. Abby's the only one who fell for that crap, and it's a damn mean thing to do to her. Knock it off."

The thought of Ethan watching me, his honey-sweet scent and scrape of his hands in my hair, turned every mundane movement into a wild, coaxing seduction. I knuckled the floorboards. They were old but sturdy enough to support what I hoped would be vigorous physical movements.

"Would you touch me, Ethan?" I asked, looking over my shoulder. "And let me touch you? I want to know what you're like."

"What I'm *like*?" Ethan hitched back. "You talking about sex with me, Sarah?"

"Yeah. I'm talking about sex. Is that so bizarre?"

"A little, since you spent our childhood calling me horrible names. Why am I so interesting now?"

"Well, to be honest, I never thought of you as anything more than legs, arms, and really gross jokes. But since you kissed my hip the other day, I can't get you off my mind. Just thinking about you makes my temperature rise, and I can't stop staring at your chest."

"Well, I can't stop staring at your chest either," he said, tipping close. "*If* we're being honest and all."

"So, see? We're stuck here anyway, right? Makes perfect sense that we should."

Ethan dropped the towel and scratched the back of his head. "There's dangerous logic buried in there, but—"

"C'mon, Ethan," I said, yanking his arm. "Let's do it. Let's have sex on this boat."

Taking a moment to think, Ethan shrugged. "Okay."

"Really? You want to?"

"Hell yeah, I want to." He reached for his waistline, unzipping his shorts. "It's disturbing how excited you are."

"Oh, I'm excited. I'm really, really excited." I handed him blankets, helping to smooth them all out. "Show me everything, Ethan. And make it special. I want you to make it special for me."

"I pity the bastards who didn't make it special for you. What'd you do afterward? Cut off their balls?"

"No balls to cut. You're my first time. I wanted it special and figured it would be with you."

"First time?" Ethan stalled, and the color drained from his face. "First time for what?"

"First time having sex. Everyone says you're good at it, and after that day on the beach, I figured you be the best man for the job."

"Best for the job?" He repeated, raising his brows. "You mean you've never done this before? You're a virgin?"

"Well, don't say it like that. It sounds mean when you say it like that. And anyway, so what if I am?"

"So, a guy doesn't just go ripping through virgins, Sarah Thorn."

"Ripping through virgins?" I shrieked. "Last week, you were kissing the scar on my hip, and now you're ripping through virgins?"

"Last week, you were half-naked, looking like you'd already done this. Now you're a virgin in a white muslin gown. There's no way I'm touching that shit."

"How do you go from licking my hip bone to the Virgin Mary in one dirty thought?"

"Because I can." He sighed, raking his hair. "Ever use a tampon?"

I gasped, horrified. "Shut up, Ethan. I'm not telling you that."

"That means you haven't."

"I swear, you're the filthiest damn..." the rest came out as a furious mumble.

Ethan scratched his chin, studying my hips like a gift he wasn't sure how to use.

"Well, Ethan? Are we doing this or not?"

"Just give me a minute. I'm not sure what to do with you yet."

"What to do with—" My hands went straight to my hips. "I'm seventeen, Ethan. I'll lose it to someone eventually. May as well be right here, right now, with you."

"Well, thanks for the vote of confidence, Miss Thorn. Glad to know I'll do in a pinch."

"Oh, don't be such a baby. You're here, and I'm here; if you don't do it, someone else will. There are other boys, you know."

"Oh, yeah? Well, it's reassuring to know you'd lie down with any mongrel you find on a beach somewhere."

"All right," I said, flipping my hair. "Hollis Miller. I'd do it with Hollis Miller."

"Hollis Miller?" He blanched. "That prickless wonder? You'd have better luck losing it to a jellyfish. Who else you got?"

"What about Walter what's-his-name? Broke his leg, jumping off the Whale Branch bridge. I bet he's big."

"Walter Salinger? Yeah. He's big, all right, and his tits are roughly the size of yours. You'll be lucky to find his dick at all."

Thunder disrupted my protest and sent Ethan to peer out the hatch. "Sounds like the sky's falling in. I'll take you home when the rain stops since I have no intention of doing the nasty with you."

There was no way I was leaving that boat with my female appointments intact, but with Ethan hellbent on being a gentleman, my choices were limited. Looking around, I considered my options and selected the most expedient route: sudden, visceral lust. Taking advantage of Ethan's distraction, I shimmied the gown from my arms. I knelt there, fists clenched, heart hammering, and ivory breasts damp with the rain.

"Turn around, Ethan," I whispered. "Look at me now."

"Look at what?" Ethan turned quickly and froze. His lips parted, and I saw the drop in his throat as he swallowed, but the only things that moved were his eyes. They tripped over each part of me, soaking in the features of a body changed by time, nature, and the efforts of genetic design.

"My God, you're a beautiful thing," he said. "Are you sure, Sarah? You sure?"

"Yes, Ethan." I nodded. "I'm sure."

"All right." He coughed once, reached behind me, and patted a quilt. "Lie on these blankets. Floor's hard."

"What about rubbers? Mrs. Wilburn in health class says we should use rubbers because sex brings nothing but blisters and brats."

"Mrs. Wilburn opens doorknobs with tissues. I'm positive I don't have blisters, and there's no chance of brats from me, either. Got sick, remember? Doctors said I can't make babies."

"Does that make you sad?" I asked, hearing the trip in his voice. "Not sure what I'd do if I couldn't make babies."

Ethan shrugged, tucking pillows under my head. "No sense worrying about something I can't change, but it's probably different for girls."

"Probably," I said, settling back. "Have you really done it before? Gone all the way with a girl?"

"A few times, but not like this. Not with a girl like you."

"You mean with a virgin?"

"No, Sarah." He dipped, angling my chin in a kiss. "I mean with a girl like you. Now, close your eyes."

I did as he asked, feeling the glide of a single finger tracing the swells of my breasts. My hands clenched, my voice went deep, and I ached in places I never knew I could feel. Warm, wet streaks covered my right nipple, followed by the sting of a tiny bite as he sucked it under his teeth. My stomach clenched, and sharp sensations hit my groin like a thunderclap, arching my back and choking my breath.

Ethan...

"Lift your hips," he whispered, tickling my panties away.

There was a soft sigh, and the tick of a zipper as Ethan kicked off his shorts and rested gently upon me.

My eyelids fluttered open, and I stared at him, noticing hints of gold in his eyes. He was sweating, braced above me, and his body shook as if terrified.

"Sarah." My name was a whisper, barely a breath. "You ever see the horizon after storms out at sea?"

"From beaches at Mama's sometimes. Why?"

"Seeing them on the water is better," he said. "The sky glows orange with milky white clouds underneath. Like heaven burst right into flames."

Tracing the line of his jaw, I smiled. "Sounds pretty."

"There's nothing like it. When we were little, my daddy told Evan and me if we worked really hard, he'd take us out there to touch it, but then he'd just laugh and call us stupid. That hurt like hell knowing something so beautiful was so damn close, and we'd never be able to touch it. You look like that now. With your hair spread over your shoulders like that. You look like heaven on fire."

"And you're shaking because it frightens you now?"

"No," Ethan whispered, sliding his lips over mine. "I'm excited because now I can touch it."

And there, wrapped in gaslight and the soft weaving rock of a storm, Ethan Bennet pushed his hips into mine, and my body was no longer my own. I marveled at the grace of it. The language, the movement, the sweet pain of the ache. There was so much to gather, so much to feel. I couldn't define the sensations.

Soft, silky noises, touches and breaths, subdued furies, and an indescribable need to answer the smallest of movements with the deepest of touch. And when he did as I asked and moved just right, answered my begging and whispers for more, my soul awakened for the very first time, and my body raged alive.

Love happens quickly at that age. When shared lives melt into an embrace so tight that to pull from it makes the heart itself burn to ash in its absence, love comes in, brings it to life, and saves it.

We continued that summer and into the next that way, meeting at the boat and making love under moonlight. Ethan grilled fish over fires, listening to my recitations of Faulkner and Woolf. I wrote every day while Ethan tended the boat, and we laughed and played as if no other world existed outside our own.

But for the nightmares I had, it was paradise. Ethan held me when they came. He'd press for details about why I had them, and I'd answer with flippant excuses cloaked in humorous appeal. I didn't want him to know how I was. Confessing too much would kill the innocence we'd found. The love. But paradise wasn't tamed by the raptures of children, and as youthful boys do, Ethan Bennet broke my heart, and so, as youthful girls do, I punished him for it.

It was just after my eighteenth birthday when it all went to hell. I sold my first story to a Charleston-based publisher called Veritas. They were independent, looking for new talent, and made a good fit for my pulpy short stories. After showing the acceptance letter to Abby and Mother, I drove to Shell Beach to find Ethan. He'd taken work as a charter boat hand, tending excursions stretching days at a time. He called the dock, telling them he'd return that morning, so I knew he'd be waiting alone at our boat.

"Don't go bragging about the fish you caught." My voice carried beneath the shadowy pines. "It'll never beat what I've hooked, Ethan Bennet. Not in a million—"

I stopped, and my limbs seized at the sight of Ethan and a shirtless girl wrestling alone on the sand.

"Ethan?" His name died as it fell from my lips. "Ethan, why?"

"Jesus, Sarah." Ethan burst up, grappling the girl in his arms. "Don't—"

"Don't—?" I watched the blonde break away, cackling and pointing before leaping through oaks toward the street. "Ethan, why?"

"Wait for me, Sarah," he said, trading glances between me and the blonde. "Please? I'll tell you why I was gone if you wait. Wait for me, please."

But I didn't wait. I ran. I ran from our childhood. I ran from that boat. I ran from the agony of every broken promise left beaten and bruised on that beach. Panic welled in my chest. Ethan hadn't followed. He hadn't chased. He only asked me to wait. Then he left through the trees to find her.

Ethan Bennet killed my heart.

That was my first lesson in learning how a wounded heart bled. The trauma was sudden, but the pain was slow, and since spite was my nature, forgiveness wasn't forthcoming, but Ethan's punishment certainly was.

Five

"Your brightness is gone, Cherie." Mama dented the edge of my bed. "And E'Tan's feeling bad, too."

Mama never pronounced Ethan's name with any sort of clarity. No matter how she tried, it always came out with a decidedly French articulation.

"I never liked that boy." Mother was far from being a snob, but she did have particular aspirations for me that didn't include tangling body parts with a shrimper's son. "You can do better than boys with bad reputations, Sarah."

"That ain't one bit of true, Sheila Thorn. E'Tan's a good boy. Just carries secrets like everyone else."

"That's a load of crap, Mirabella." Mother employed Mama's Christian name in evaporating patience. "She's barely eaten or slept since that day, and I'm tired of seeing her slogging around in that chewed-up t-shirt and shorts."

"We all have secrets, Cherie. Can't shame E'Tan's unless we shame our own."

"Well, why don't you fess up Ethan's big, fat secret, Mama?" I said. "I'm sure it'll fix everything."

"Can't do that, baby. That's E'Tan's secret to manage."

"Well, his secret should have managed to keep her shirt on." I scooted from the bed. "I'm going to the beach."

"God sends us who we need, child. Remember that today."

That was when I saw Mama's bones at my feet. "Don't waste your bones on me, Mama Nash. I already know my future, and I'll make sure Ethan Bennet regrets hurting me every day he breathes."

Heavy thumps hit the porch, and we fell silent as if hiding from arrest.

"Better not be that shrimper's kid again." Mother careened from the room, pounding her way down the hall. "Getting tired of him beating my doors."

"Don't care one bit if it is," I said. "Ethan Bennet can go straight to hell."

"Watch that spite, girl. Didn't raise you to be cruel."

"Cruel, Mama?" I threw an arm toward the yard. "Your golden boy had a naked blonde stuck to his chest two weeks ago. You can lecture me about cruelty once you've lectured him."

"That secret you're holdin' ain't better than his."

"That secret's between you and me," I said. "And if you love me, you'll keep it that way."

Enraged by Mama's betrayal, I ran down the hall to escape through the kitchen's back door. Ethan was always her favorite, and she'd defend his antics as if common sense wisdom ended at the base of his skull.

"He's just a man," she would say. "God doesn't make men too bright."

And I'd reply, "Then why'd He make them at all?"

When I arrived at the beach behind Mama Nash's, the sun had just kissed its horizon. Sandpipers skittered as I stood on the shore, kicked off my sandals, and dropped my keys in the sand.

"Softly," I murmured, pushing into the waves. "Neat and serene." Cries from the buoy bell rose with its pitch, matching the water as it pulled my knees, thighs, and hips...

"*And where are we now, Cherie?*" I recited the poem Mama had taught us, warning that terrible spot. "We're *playing beneath the sea*," we would say. "*And why should we be careful there when we play beneath the sea?*" she'd ask. "*Because death lives in the waves,*" we'd say. "*Beyond the ocean deep. God blinks inside the fireflies, and His tides lay us asleep.*"

Then I threw out my arms and started to fall in the waves.

"It gets better, Sarah Thorn!"

A voice carried over the wind, and I turned, finding a wall of a man standing on the shore, peeling the shirt from his back. He was tall and wide with washboard features and chest hair spreading from shoulder to shoulder like the wings of a raven in flight.

"Your mom said someone broke your heart, and you'd be wild as the devil and twice as mean. That true?"

There was no chance to answer before he kicked off his jeans, leaving him standing in nothing but an obscenely tight pair of dark gray underwear.

"Hey," I shouted, watching him march through the surf. "What're you doing getting naked like that?"

"I'm not naked. Still have my underwear on."

"Come near me, and I'll gut you like a marlin," I said.

"Well, that'll just draw sharks. Then we'll have them *and* the riptide to deal with." The man stopped beside me and smiled. "Nice to meet you, Miss Thorn. I'm Blake Bradley."

"This beach is private, mister. You're trespassing here."

"Can't be trespassing if I was invited."

"No one invited you. And how'd you know my name?"

"Well, the name I got from the letter you sent two months ago. The invitation came from an interesting woman wearing gator teeth on her neck."

"Gator teeth?" I scanned the beachfront, expecting to see Mother and Mama waving at me from the house. "Did you follow me here?"

"Only halfway. Almost lost you taking that bridge." He laughed and nudged at the buoy. "Good thing I came when I did. Looks like you're trying to drown yourself."

"I'm not trying to drown myself."

"No? Then what are you doing standing by a riptide? Washing your hair?"

"I was enjoying the surf until you showed up. Who are you, anyway? Some sort of lifeguard?"

"Nope. Some sort of editor. Guess your mom was right about that mean part, huh?"

WHIMS OF GOD ~ 47

I tipped closer and sneered. "My mother wouldn't tell you something like that."

"She sure did. Right after gator tooth woman drew me a map to her house."

"Well, I don't believe you," I said, splashing away. "You're trespassing, and I'm going to call the police and have you hauled from this beach."

Then I dropped some choice curses and took wide, sloshing leaps back to shore. Blake Bradley wasn't impressed. He just fell to the water, enjoying the waves as if dropped from some lofty kingdom.

After snatching my sandals from their half-buried spot, I scraped through the sand for my keys. "Damn keys. Where'd they go?"

"You won't find them," he shouted.

"Find what?" I shouted back.

"Your keys. That's what you're looking for, right?"

"They're here. Just dropped them a minute ago."

"Well, they're not there now."

"And how would you know?"

"Because I took them myself."

"You took them?" I asked, standing and shading my eyes. "You took my keys? What for?"

"Because your mother and her friend told me I should. I was at your house earlier, but you ran outta there like your ass was on fire. They said I should take your keys because you're a runner when you're sad."

"I'm not sad." I reached down, snatching his jeans up and patting them down. "I'm mad."

"No, you're not. Writers get sad and only act like they're mad. You're sad."

"Just where do you get off talking like that?" I said, dragging his jeans through the surf. "You don't know me from Adam, mister."

Blake stood, folded his arms across his rather impressive chest, and recited a Sarah Thorn dossier that could have rivaled a CIA checklist.

"Your name's Sarah Thorn. You're eighteen and have long red hair. Judging from the posters in your room, you like Poe more than Aerosmith and cats more than dogs. You drink too much coffee, and that little shirt you're wearing is probably what you slept in last night. You like candy *a lot*, and your boyfriend just broke up with you."

"I broke up with him."

"Irrelevant," he said, flicking a hand. "You're a writer, which means you have a sense of righteous indignation that's hard to take, but it also means your talent overflows. Your mouth would shock a horny sailor, and your mom and gator tooth woman said I should take you in hand. You're a walking nightmare. I can say what I like to you now."

Fresh out of comebacks, I groaned. "Christ, mister. Where are my keys? Just give me my keys."

"They're in my underwear."

"Bullshit." My eyes dropped right to his crotch. "My keys are not in your underwear."

"Well, if they're not, then my balls sound like wind chimes."

"Dad-blame-it!" I stomped, whipping his jeans to the sand. "Well, will you tell me what you're doing out here stealing my blasted keys?"

"Nobody stole your keys," he said, weaving against the pull of the waves. "I only took them so you couldn't run off. I want you to write for us."

"Who's *us*?"

"Veritas. We bought your *Badlands* story about the priest with the demons in court. My father wasn't sure about you, so I'm here to spy."

"Why should I care what your father thinks?"

"He's MJ Bradley, that's why. He owns Veritas. I'm just the errand boy editor."

"Your father didn't like me?" The thought made me drop to my knees. "Why didn't he like me?"

"Never said he didn't like you, you little idiot. I said he wasn't sure about you. You're young, and he's afraid you're a one-hit-wonder. I told him you're not."

"The confidence is appreciated, mister, but how do you know I'm not?"

"Because it's my job." He rose from the water, fighting the surf back to shore. Blake Bradley walked like a king. Majestic and practiced, with swells at his hips and waves at his back like bowing at the heels of a god. "And stop calling me mister. I'm twenty-four. You make me feel like somebody's uncle. And if you are a one-hit-wonder, it'd be a hit Veritas needs. We need fresh blood, and you're the first to open a vein."

"Should that entice me?"

"I'm hoping it will." Blake dropped to my side, stretching and crossing his legs. "Unless you'd prefer writing for Bayport's prestigious *Gazette* to a bestseller spot in *The Times*?"

"Is that what you're offering? A bestseller spot in *The Times*?"

"The way you write, it shouldn't be hard. Why? Don't you want it?"

"No writer alive would turn down an offer like that."

"So, take it," he said, wiping sand from his chest. "Readers are hungry for stories like yours. They're bored with social lectures, cheap scares, and dull touches under the sheets. They want blood, guts, and sex. That's what you'll give them."

"There are hundreds of writers with stories like mine. Thousands, probably. Why choose my work over theirs?"

"Instinct, aptitude, natural ability," Blake said. "No degrees and no lessons on verbiage. Just damn good stories without all the bullshit. That's rare for someone your age. Where'd you get it? Mom? Dad? Demented grandma somewhere?"

"Nightmares, I guess."

"Nightmares?" Blake looked at me, squinting with the sun in his eyes. "You get stories from nightmares?"

"Since I was eight. Mother made me write them in journals. Now all I do is write."

"Must be difficult, writing bad dreams. Does it ever get hard?"

"Sometimes," I said with a smirk. "But it's what gives me that instinct you want to exploit."

"Point taken." He grinned and propped on an elbow. "My dad's not patient with chances like this, so whatever you choose, choose it fast."

"Your father will wait," I replied, still holding my smirk.

"What makes you say that?"

"Because he didn't send you; you came on your own. If not, you'd have a contract tucked in your jeans, and since I just searched your pants, I know you don't. Which means you're not here to spy. You've come here to beg, and that means I have control."

"Damnit, you got me." He laughed. "But jumping into the ocean to save your life must count for something."

"You didn't save my life, but it does count for something."

"Then it's a deal," he said, settling back. "Now. Tell me about the jackass who broke your poor heart. I'd like to hear more about him."

"Nothing to tell." I shrugged, pulling my knees to my chest. "He didn't really love me. He didn't really want me."

"Well, that's good."

"Good?" I asked, gaping at him. "How do you figure that's good?"

"Because of what gator tooth woman said at your house."

"Stop calling her gator tooth woman," I said. "Her name's Mama Nash. And what did she say?"

"Well, *Miss Nash* says you're supposed to marry me because God tied us up."

"Jesus," I said, burying my face in my knees. "Don't listen to her. She's crazy as hell, and I'm not marrying anyone."

"Oh, yes, you are. I'm going to love you forever. That's what she said. Seemed really happy about it too. Praying and singing, throwing bones on your mom's kitchen floor."

"Her kitchen floor?"

"Oh, yeah." He propped on his elbow again. "She shook that toothy necklace and said God sent me to find you because you're my whim. Whatever that means."

"Just ignore it. She's full of crap."

"She is not full of crap. I'm God's gift. Gator tooth woman says so."

I barked out a laugh. "Mama Nash didn't say you were God's gift. She said you were sent by God. She says that about hurricanes and poison ivy too. I wouldn't brag about it."

"See, there?" Blake smiled, tucking my hair. "I made you mad, sad, laugh, and scream all in one afternoon. We're practically married right now."

"Yeah." I nodded, swirling lines in the sand. "We're practically married right now."

We spent the day together, and I realized how similar we were. With common interests in literature, we shared preferences of favorite authors and books. Blake was impressed, asking questions with a genuine interest no one had shown me before. After the sun went down and he started a fire, we talked about our lives, getting to know one another and enjoying the newness of it. Blake loved Veritas but worried about its future, trying to pull it into a more profitable direction. He talked about family too. Blake wanted a wife, children, and all the trappings that came with a young and rising life. Blake liked things fast. He wanted to win, and I gathered he rarely lost.

Relaxed by the fire, I watched as he tended its glowing embers. He was beautiful. Tall and sculpted with wavy black hair that shadowed his brow when he spoke. His chest was thick and broad, giving me the sense that to lie upon it would be like resting upon the breast of a lion: soft, warm, and just a little perilous.

But his eyes... his eyes shone like nothing I'd ever seen. Bordered in thick lashes, they were blue but blazed nearly clear. It gave him a searching expression of almost constant wonder. As if they could fall onto anyone, ask them anything with no words at all, and get what he wanted from them.

I was drawn to him. Not in the way a broken heart might blindly reach for shelter, but more like finding solid ground after an arduous, frightening leap. There was sanctuary in Blake Bradley. Smart, vibrant, and completely contagious, it would be easy to love someone like him.

So, I did.

I made love to him that night, covered in firelight, breezes, and soft ocean sand. It was beautiful and tender, and Mama was right.

Blake Bradley would love me forever.

Six

Mother liked Blake just fine until the tumultuous vomiting fits in response to my unexpected baby's growing prominence.

Then she got icy.

She worried about our youthful exuberance and my less-than-placid nature, but Blake managed her carefully, promising not to thwart my rising talents and pledging to always be faithful. With assurances planted and Mother's worries settled, Blake and I married soon after. Blake's parents were creative and less strict than my mother, and when we met them in Charleston, I couldn't decide which of their traits Blake had gained most. He carried his father's southern good looks and undeniable charm, but I saw little from his mother, Lena.

There was obvious tension between Blake and her. Lena barely touched her son, greeting him with pecks on the cheek or brushing his hand with her own, but there was no maternal connection. And Blake was unusually timid with her, keeping a cautious distance as if heeding habitual threats. It was a strange relationship, and I was soon to learn why.

As a premier Southern artist, Lena White-Bradley saw beauty in every corner of her world. Known for her depictions of the hauntingly graceful terrain of the Lowcountry, she was equally happy among shrimp nets and trawlers as she was stately, urbane affairs. Lena was delicate and dark, with untamed gray eyes and a stunningly white scar that cuffed her right cheek. A fact of her birth, we never knew why it was there, but she wore it with such pride that it disappeared beneath her confidence like a shield attached to her heart.

Her voice was pleasantly primed with sweet Southern hues, and her sense of humor was delightfully dry. Upon first meeting me by the steps of their Charleston home, Lena spread her hand on my belly and said, "Creation born of creatives. What tragedy hath we wrought?"

I loved her immediately, but sadly, Lena couldn't always achieve the sense she was not haunted. She'd see things and hear things, and MJ fought a constant battle to ride her demons from her. Portraits of his failures painted her skin. Rose-colored scars roamed muscle and veins, trailing the length of her arms. Her wrists were adorned in wide jeweled bands, decorations to hide her attempts. MJ tempered his wife's mania with any number of brown-bottle pills.

When those efforts failed, he turned to sessions with doctors and soft-sided rooms under comical handles like Flintstone or Doe. MJ's devotion to his suffering wife was an endless toggle between darkness and light. Their marriage was a testament to selflessness and gave breadth to the meaning of sacrifice. It was beautiful and tragic, and it would eventually end them both.

Blake and I moved to Charleston two months after we married. The change was novel and, at first, exciting. But there was no golden-eyed Abby, and it held no flirt from Alicia's prickly teases, the fragrant ghosts of Mother's front porch, or Mama's lavender-scented breast.

And Ethan. There was no Ethan.

Although eager at the prospect of motherhood, the process caused a sense of gloom my mind struggled to resist. I vomited every morning and ached along the sinew meant to stretch with each passing day. The battle was constant as my body seemed more intent on purging foreign matter than assembling an act of God.

Seeing my mood falter with the growth of my belly, Blake took me to Bayport again. He stayed with me each weekend and returned to Charleston every Sunday, assuring me all would be well. I'd grown to dislike our minor separations. So much about Blake appealed to me.

There was comfort in his warm neck, wide smile, and the way he held me so closely the only breath I could gather was his.

I spent most days at Mama's tide pool, relaxed against rows of driftwood stumps Blake set up. He padded them with towels, and I'd recline, smiling at fireflies in trees overhead. Blake sat on the grass, taking notes on my work, and occasionally, he'd look at me. But it was a strange and studied expression from a man I was only now coming to know. There was fear in that look, and my husband feared little.

"It gets better, Blake Bradley," I said, splashing my legs.

Blake grinned, fanning pages of notes in his hand. "You're having a high time today. That's why you wrote so much."

"I didn't write. I dictated. And what's a high time?"

"That's what Sheila called it the day we met at the beach. She said you'd be mean as the devil because you were falling from your high time. My mother has them too. She does some of her best work when she's high like that."

"High like that?" I laughed, holding my belly. "You make it sound like she's snorting lines in her studio, Blake."

"That's how you are today," he said, scooting close. "Don't you feel it?"

"I feel like that guy eating dinner in *Alien*. I'm ready to burst. That's what Alicia says."

"Alicia's funny, and I suspect she's a lesbian."

"Alicia's boobs are works of art. If she's a lesbian, the male race should mourn in droves."

"If her boobs are works of art, being a lesbian only makes them more interesting."

"How sweet," I said, throwing sprigs of grass at his face. "Leering at boobs when I'm heavy with child."

Blake laughed and nuzzled my belly. "I'm going to love you forever, remember? Gator tooth woman said so."

"And will you always be afraid of me too?" The question was sudden and unexpectedly sharp. "Considering Lena, I'd understand if you are."

"Is that what you think?" Blake asked, sitting up. "You think I'm afraid of you?"

"When I reach for you, sometimes you pull away like you do with her. Like you're afraid to get close."

"I don't mean to be distant, but I worry for you."

"Worry?" I blinked at the circling gulls overhead. "About what?"

"Nightmares, honey. The intensity you have when you work. I've seen it before."

"With your mother?"

Blake nodded solemnly. "Yes."

"How was she when you were young? You never talk about her. Were you close?"

"We tried to be, sure." He juggled two pebbles, tossing them into the pool. "She made a corner for me in her studio. Gave me lessons every day. We'd go to art shows and galleries, talking to agents and buyers. She was so confident then. Utterly fearless."

I smiled, stroking his hair. "Must have been wonderful."

"It was," he said. "Until it all stopped."

"Because she—" unsure what to say, I paused.

"Went nuts?" he asked with a smirk.

"Don't talk about Lena like that."

"Well, that's what happened, isn't it?" He sighed, choosing more stones from the grass. "Nightmares came first. She'd wake up screaming, eyes wide as saucers. Terrified. I held her and told her nothing she saw was real. She usually calmed down after that."

"So you helped her."

"Not for long." Blake threw another stone, harder this time, so it splashed. "Two weeks later, she tried killing herself."

"The scars," I said. "How'd it happen? And when?"

"On my twelfth birthday. We'd just had a party. Everyone came to the house. My friends, my parents' friends. Big ta-doo at the Bradley abode. Once they left and we'd gone to bed, I heard Mother whispering outside my bedroom. I got up to help her like I usually did, but Dad locked the door from outside."

"MJ wouldn't let you come out?"

"Can you blame him?" Blake asked, throwing more rocks. "I fiddled with the lock till it opened, and that's when I found her collapsed in the hallway with a paring knife jammed in her wrist. I tried shaking her, screaming at her. But she wouldn't wake up. An ambulance came. Took her away for a month."

"Can't imagine being without my mother," I said. "Did you miss her?"

"I missed what she was. The last time I hugged my mother, I mean really held her; I was twelve years old."

"Did you want to hold her?"

"Every son wants to hold his mother. They might not admit it. May not even act like they do, but they do. Lena stopped letting me after that night. Dad took her to doctors and therapists for years. None help as well as the meds."

"Must be lonely living like that," I said.

"Dad manages. Not much more he can do."

"I don't mean MJ, Blake. I mean Lena. Everything she does is so scheduled. Sleeping, eating, medications, and work. It's like MJ traded his affection for doctors and pills."

"And what did my mother trade?" Blake sat up. "She traded us, Sarah. She chose imaginary monsters over her husband and son. She fights doctors, throws away pills, and denies anything's wrong. Hell, she'd choose that paring knife over us if we let her."

"What about hospitals?" I asked, wary of pushing too much. "Places where Lena can be helped. Understood."

"We've tried them. She's good for a while, but something happens, and she throws out the meds or locks herself in that studio. You can't help someone who thinks nothing's wrong."

"No wonder MJ's so watchful of her."

"She's left him no choice. And he loves her, Sarah. Like I love you. That's why I think we should talk to someone."

"That's not the same thing," I said, caressing his chin. "Mother took me to doctors when I was young, and they weren't concerned. I just need to write."

"But the things you see, the nightmares you have. Writing doesn't stop them, and with the baby coming—"

"I'm not like Lena, Blake. Don't be afraid of me. Please?"

"I'm not afraid of you, honey," he said, cupping my chin. "I'm afraid *for* you. There's a difference."

Pressing my forehead to his, I whispered, "But they hurt me exactly the same."

Blake's was experience run aground, and from that experience, he knew better than I the terrible price of pretending a bending mind can't eventually break. Because no matter our denials of them, they can break. They do break.

Two days later, we lay at Bayport Memorial, cradling our new son between us. He'd come early. The effect of a womb turned hostile; they induced as my blood pressure rose too high to support my growing guest. But despite the tumult of a difficult birth, our baby was healthy and blessed with incredibly capable lungs. We named him Michael Benjamin, Michael after Blake's father and Benjamin after mine.

Mother cried when she saw him. Gathering Michael into her arms, she held my father's picture and said, "This is your Grandpa Ben. He was a strong and brave Marine. His chest was wide, his eyes were brown, and his hands were broad like spoon oars."

Barely three when he died, I wasn't old enough to recognize my mother's heartbreak in my father's absence, and I couldn't remember her crying. Seeing it then, as she held what life she gleaned from the man she'd never replaced, I knew her as vulnerable, lost, and alone. Sensing the need, we stayed in Bayport until I was strong enough to return to Charleston. Blake and I cuddled in my teen-sized room, giggling at the efforts of his rugged frame lodged beneath the canopy of my yellow princess bed. I'd press closely, kissing him deeply and feeling my love for him grow by the day.

Two months had passed since Michael's delivery, and I was healing well. When Abby escaped her father's bloody demands, she and Edward visited. At seven, Edward was taller than others his age and far less vocal, but he was gentle with Michael, stroking his hands and delighting in Michael's chirping, infant squeals.

"They'll be as close as we are," Abby would say, placing Michael across Edward's lap. "Like brothers but with different blood."

Abby looked forward to that. She needed the aspects of familial love without all the brutal attacks. Alicia went to school, accepted at the police academy in Columbia. She visited Mama's house, bringing a *Globe* article about a woman who gave birth to an octopus in a bathtub.

"See?" she said, dropping it onto my lap. "Michael's not so great."

Alicia's teasing became an endearment for me. I looked forward to Michael growing up with a woman who formed attachments through scorching wit and what Blake considered an almost valiant nature. Ethan's updates came through small-town gossip. He was in Michigan, attending college for a degree in Naval Engineering. Evan left, too, choosing somewhere in Texas for the same purpose. I never asked for details, not having the patience to endure a recap of Ethan's playboy exploits in my absence. Knowing his whereabouts was enough, and I figured I'd get more gossip as it rolled.

Blake returned to Charleston, eager to begin the life he'd envisioned for us. We'd make love every night, he'd said. I'd write every day, and Michael would grow to love words. It was an innocent wish from a man trying desperately to mold a childhood different from his own. Blake wasn't violated, and he wasn't neglected. His home life wasn't full of instances of gouging, physical pain. Blake's beginning was worse.

His was a world of creation tempered by the invisible monsters Lena held closer to her heart than she did her own son. Blake's scars were bloody, and they opened like geysers when our gaze would meet, and his crystal eyes collected what information they could to answer my curious moods, or my high times too often peaked. It was a pattern just beginning with a routine soon to grow.

Seven

Nothing rivaled Mama's kitchen at sunrise. Coffee rattled the pot while she sat at the little pine table, snapping green beans or stripping her blooms. The air was scented with eggs, croissants, and jars of honey trapping colorful flowers inside. The buds didn't overpower the honey, only enhancing the sweetness with delicate hints and subtle perfumes on the tongue.

Lifting the lid from Mama's cast-iron pot released the buttery steam from her sausage and shrimp. "The smell in your kitchen should be sold as a drug." I claimed a chair and smiled at Michael, who slept in a basket at our feet.

"Get you some coffee with honey," Mama said. "You need the sweet."

"Coffee's not good when I'm breastfeeding, Mama."

"That's a nonsense. I raised you on Folgers, and here you are sassing your mouth."

"Don't take it personally. Doctors say not to, so I won't."

"Doctors ain't nothing. Thinking they know so much cutting people up?"

Wagging a bean in her face, I said, "That temper of yours is why you have such a bad reputation around here. Buster Mills tells everyone you're a witch, and the whole town thinks you fed your husband and daughter to a bunch of hogs. Honestly, Mama, that one's horrible."

"Damn nags never did get my story straight. Men like Buster got no business taking air. I told Ida to put that rabid dog down, but she's too stupid to do it."

"Lord, Mama." I laughed. "When did you tell poor Ida Mills to kill her husband?"

"Long while back. Buster went rabid. Bad men do that sometimes and need puttin' down once they do."

The screen door slapped shut in the front of the house, and a familiar voice thundered in. "This shack's gone to seed, old woman. When's the last time you mowed this yard?"

"Praise Jesus. That's our E'Tan." Mama nearly hit the floor as she stood. "Let me take hold of this boy."

Ethan scuffed behind me, hugging Mama and saying he'd trim the yard. Mama kissed him and offered him breakfast.

"Coffee's good, Mama. Thanks." Ethan tossed his sunglasses to the table before sitting down. "Hey, Sarah. How you been?"

"Good enough," I said stiffly. "How are you?"

"Doing okay." Ethan gestured to Michael. "Handsome boy. Looks like he's got your red hair."

"Got her nature too." Mama handed Ethan his cup. "All meanness and spite, plus he don't sleep very well."

Ethan teetered his chair. "Squirrels were eating your glories again, Mama. Why do you bother tacking those lousy cans to that fence? Every one of those things is rolling out there in the dirt."

"Blamed rats." Mama slipped on her house shoes and snatched her long wooden spoon from its pot. "Sit here and catch up. I'm gonna beat me some rats."

Then she kicked through the door, leaving us mired in rattling pot lids and awkward regret.

"Guess you know I've been at school," Ethan said.

"Mama told me." I snapped another long bean, trying not to sound curt. "Michigan. Right?"

"That's right. Evan left too. He's in Texas."

"What about the business? Your parents?"

"Don't really talk to the folks anymore. Storms and imports are killing shrimping work. Dad left for Georgia. Mom packed up and followed behind."

"I'm sorry, Ethan," I said, finally looking at him. "I know how you loved it. What will you do?"

"Not sure." He shrugged, squeezing the mug between his palms. "Evan and I talked about refurbishing the boats, selling them or something. We'll figure it out." Ethan sipped his coffee and then looked at Michael. "Baby happened kind of fast, didn't it? And the husband? What's his name? *Bob?*"

"It's Blake, Ethan. His name's Blake. Don't pretend you don't know."

"Blake," he mumbled, sipping again. "Gossips say he's your publisher."

"Gossips are wrong, as usual. Blake's my editor."

"Is he good to you?"

"Of course, he's good to me. What kind of question is that?"

"A practical one. You barely knew the guy, and suddenly you're married and have a baby with him. I'm worried, Sarah. I care about you."

"Yeah, well," I shoved from the table, taking the bowl to the sink, "you care about lots of girls, Ethan. Always have."

Ethan spun from the chair and leaned on the counter beside me. "I didn't cheat on you, Sarah. I wouldn't have done that to us. What you saw that day isn't what you think."

"Jesus. Why do bastards like you always say that? *It's not what you think. It's not what you saw.* You blame the very women you lie to."

"I didn't lie to you, Sarah. I never lied."

"You told me you loved me, Ethan. *That* was your lie."

"Just give me five minutes. Five minutes to tell you the truth. I never meant to hurt you like that."

Hoisting Michael's basket, I moved to the screen door and said, "You didn't just hurt me, Ethan. You broke what we were. You broke both our lives."

My drive onto mainland never took longer than it did on that day. Every mile pulled me farther from Ethan. There were fractures in us. Memories and moments we'd never reclaim and beautiful instances my mind would forget. I was never sure if a human heart could love in equal division, but at that moment, feeling the elation of a life trimmed with Blake while mourning the loss of the man who first loved me, I was never more certain it could.

Four years passed before I saw Ethan again. I lived in Charleston in a large white home, ages old and brought to life with paint, plaster, and girded foundations. I found kinship in Lena, a woman whose demons paled my own. I saw our husbands bond over torments suffered by their wives and watched as Blake, terrified and unsure, slowly replaced his marital presence with an array of pills meant to keep me whole.

And inside it all, I wrote.

My books became synonymous with graphic display and licentious passions. I was glorified for abilities critics called *beyond my age* and vilified for creating primal worlds where strong men reigned and women faltered at their feet. I was publicized inside a whirlwind that taught me the riotous mechanics of fame, and Veritas flourished from it. My life blurred, and Sarah Bradley's name was reduced to the initials *SB* for a more marketable device.

Still, a part of me remained. A gift of my birth given by those who first held me. The title I insisted be kept. It was my mother's, my father's, and I was soon to own it last.

Thorn.

Eight

⟨❧⟩

Blake could scald the air in a room the moment he stepped through the door. It was his nature to unwind the business in a room. To fix what was wrong. When he thundered into my office at home, striking the volume on my CD player, I wasn't surprised.

"Guns N' Roses is too much for a four-year-old and too loud," he said.

"They're singing about rain in November, Daddy." Michael giggled, straddling my lap in my chair. "Mommy's on a high time, and music has to be loud so she can come back."

"Mommy should take her pills." Blake raised an eyebrow at me. "Did you?"

"Pills make me tired, and Michael wanted to listen to music."

"Well, he doesn't need it blasting his ears."

Blake's concerns were valid, but I ignored them, turning to Michael again. "And where are we now, Cherie?"

"We're at Mama Nash's. We're playing beneath the sea."

"And why should we be careful there when we play beneath the sea?"

"Because death lives in the waves," Michael said. "Beyond the ocean deep. God blinks inside the fireflies, and His tides lay us asleep."

Michael swayed, giggling as we spun in the chair.

"Teaching poems about drowning isn't practical," Blake said. "Just tell him not to swim there."

"That's not good enough. Mama taught the poem to us too. It helped us remember."

"Well, it didn't work too well, considering the first day we met, you were standing in the middle of it."

And there it was. One of many icy notations precluding the fear that, at any moment, I'd go dark and fall beyond his reach.

"Stop it, Blake. The rhyme's easier to recall than a rule."

"Then write one that'll keep him out of the streets," Blake said, pounding out of the room. "Michael, tell your mother what you did today."

"Michael?" I tugged on his ear. "Were you chasing birds again?"

"Only two. They flew away, and I wanted the feathers they dropped on the grass, but Daddy said no."

"And did you listen?"

"Uh-uh. I pulled Daddy's hand and told him to come."

"And what'd Daddy do?"

Michael shrugged, unfurling feathers clasped in his fist. "He went."

We laughed, and I spun the chair, turning the music back up.

Michael was a godsend to me, indulging my notions as Abby had done. We'd play in the yard, enthralled by oaks and the silvery insects that dotted the skies, and we'd laugh and run in pretended anxious reach. It was within this reverie Michael discovered the passions that made his grandmother Lena such a wonderful toy. Whereas my visions forged into words too broad for Michael's small mind, Lena's existed in tangible patterns and colorful strokes of a brush.

Lena gave Michael her gift of seeing contrasts in life. She'd collect it from sun-ravaged faces of shrimpers who adored her and in the arthritic grip of women braiding seagrass rope in their laps. Beauty knew Lena as its voice, and Michael consumed every lesson she gave. He filled his young days with the glorious tortures of two women whose manias structured their lives. Painting with Lena and running with me inside clouds of lights I knew he couldn't see because there'd be no lights where he'd run.

And I'd feel pain in my heart, sharp and quick, realizing I was raising my son inside madness.

Nine

The first thing Blake saw when he walked into the bedroom was my suitcase spread on the bed.

"Headed to Bayport?" he asked, pulling his jogging shirt off.

"Just three or four days. Water Festival starts on Monday, and Michael wanted to go."

"I saw aspirin in the kitchen last night. If you're starting a high time, you'd better stay home."

"You could come too," I said. "Mother and Mama would love to see you again. We even have Alicia patrolling the streets now, and it's been months since you've been there."

"Can't leave with the New York meetings going on. Just wait until I get back."

"That's what you said two months ago. I'm tired and want to go home."

Michael raced in, tossing books on the bed. "Mama Nash says we're making blossom honey, Daddy."

"Save some for me," Blake said, scrubbing his son's auburn head. "And tell Mama Nash to send up some pralines. I want enough so I don't have to share."

"She won't do that, Daddy." Michael raced back to his room. "Mama Nash only makes them for me."

Blake chuckled and lifted a green satin gown from the bed. "Hey, I remember this gown. It was always so pretty on you. Why'd you stop wearing it?"

"We sleep in separate bedrooms now, Blake. I stopped wearing it when you stopped asking me to."

"We made love last week." Blake sat on the bed before plucking the shoes from his feet. "Or did you forget?"

"Hard to forget something that rarely occurs anymore."

"Separate bedrooms was your idea, Sarah. I never shoved you out of our bed."

"Maybe not consciously, no."

"Am I supposed to decipher that?"

"Nothing to decipher," I said, folding a shirt. "Lena pushed you away, and now you're afraid to get close. Don't need Freud to figure that out."

"Don't need Freud to see you need help either."

"I'm not like Lena, Blake. I'm not screaming with a paring knife lodged at my wrist. I'm not fragile like her."

"Keep ignoring the signs, and you will be."

"Migraines with aura aren't signs. They're headaches. People have those every day."

"What about everything else?" he asked, standing again. "You barely sleep or eat. You see lights in the corners of your office that Michael says you call fireflies. You have nightmares almost every night, don't trust a soul around here except my mother, and your temper's so bad no one dares work with you now. Take a break from the writing. It's becoming too much."

"Take a break?" I turned from the suitcase and cringed. "You want me to stop writing?"

"If taking a break lessens the high times, then yes. That's what I want."

"Well, you're not getting what you want. I'm a writer, and you're not taking that from me as your brand of sick punishment."

"This isn't punishment, Sarah. It's common sense. Even doctors mentioned stricter treatment, better medications."

"Oh, this is punishment," I said, slamming a drawer. "Poor Blake Bradley, with the broken childhood and the broken mother, strapped with the broken wife, he won't dare divorce lest he falls victim to some

Plath-like revenge. Don't worry, Blake. I've never been much of a poet. Our dirty secret will die once I suck in the gas."

Blake slumped on the bedpost. "Don't talk like that, Sarah. C'mon."

"Forget it." I thudded the case to the floor. "When do you get back from Manhattan?"

"Next Friday. Where are your pills?"

"In my purse."

Blake took the bag as we walked to the door. "Call every day, so I know you've taken them."

"I always call, and I always take my pills."

"We both know you don't," he said.

"Well, thank God I have you to remind me."

And Blake never let me forget.

Ten

Rolling into the driveway of my childhood home always made up for having to leave it. It was just a plain blue rambler, but the pink azaleas my father added the year he died gifted me with the image of a woodland cottage raised by a king to shelter his queen in his absence. Mother and Mama were rocking on the porch when we got there.

They resembled the strangest of bookends like that. Save for dead husbands, they had little in common. Mother wound her hair into tightly pinned buns while Mama tied hers into braids. Mother wore dresses cinched at the waist, while Mama donned colorful kaftans and smocks. Mother was tranquil with lighthearted ways, while Mama was forward in hers. Their friendship was a local annoyance they both found amusing.

According to gossip, the only reason a widowed young mother would bring an old Frogcreek woman into her home was if the Frogcreek woman were cleaning it. As a child, I thought Mama was the worst housekeeper alive because in all the years they sat on that porch laughing together and discussing their lives, Mama Nash never cleaned a damn thing.

Michael leaped from the car, balancing a stack of books in his arms.

"I brought new books, Grandma." Michael popped kisses on both women's cheeks before darting away through the house. "Come read them to me."

"Get into our chair, and I'll be there quick as a snip." Mother held her hands out to me. "Got my opinions and gripes?"

"Ignore the nasty ones," I said, handing her papers with my latest reviews. "They're written by frigid old spinsters."

Mama spat in the bushes, mumbling about sin and sex in a flurry of prayers.

"Stop spitting in my azaleas, Mirabella. Girl's just using her gifts."

"Writing filth ain't a gift. And it ain't Christian like she was raised."

"Want me to get you a picket sign?" Mother tipped closer to Mama. "You can call the ladies from First Baptist and have yourselves a picnic on my lawn like they do. How about you do that and stop spitting in my azaleas for once?"

"Don't tie me with those nags, Sheila Thorn. Our girl has a special mind meant for writing special things and not writing filth."

"Sex isn't filth, Mama." I kissed her, sitting on the porch by her legs. "Mother's done it. I did it. So did you, at least once."

"She's got you there, Mirabella. We've all done it. Even you."

"That's a private thing meant for bringing life. Not for men to be leering at."

"Most of my readers are women."

"Jezebels," Mama said, ripping blooms in her lap. "Don't know their own shame."

I sighed and rested my head on her knee. "You're SB Thorn's worst critic, Mama. And still, I love you."

"Got a headache, baby?" Mama wrangled knots from my hair. "Lord, you feel warm too."

"It's a high time," Mother quipped. "She'll be happy as a clam until she's not, then woe the rest of the world."

"Would you two quit blaming everything on my mental state? I'm tired. Been working like a shrimper's kid, and I'm worn to the bone."

"Speaking of shrimper's kids," Mother raised a hand at the road, "ride's here, Mirabella."

"What ride?" I peered through the bushes, watching a rusted Dodge pickup roar down the street. It had more primer than paint, and the bumper bent so low it scraped near the curb when it stopped. "Damn. Is that Ethan?"

"That's him," Mother said, still snipping reviews. "Came home a few months ago with that farty old car. Dirty heap stinks up the whole town."

I poked Mama's thigh. "Get up, Mama. Go out there before he walks up."

"Hush, girl. That ain't nothing but the boy you grew up with."

"The hell he is," I said, scrambling to safety behind Mother's shrubs. "And you two know it."

Ethan trespassed the drive and whistled as he ogled my car. "You stealing cars, old woman? Who's got the Merced—" His foot slapped hard to the porch when he saw me. "Sarah. Haley. Thorn."

"Ethan Scott Bennet."

"You two sound stupid." Mama gathered blooms from her lap. "Help me out of this rocker here, boy."

Ethan reached over, holding her arm. "How ya doing, Sarah?"

"Doing well," I said, spanking leaves from my shorts as I stood. "Great, actually. Work, marriage. Everything in life is just great." The trip in my syntax couldn't bury my lies, so I avoided the topic instead. "Didn't think you'd be here today. Now, I mean. I mean, I don't think about you at all. Ever."

"You don't?" Ethan smiled, plucking spent blooms from my cheek. "I think about you every day."

"You smell like fish guts and look like a homeless man." Never having warmed up to the boy who sullied her daughter's young heart, Mother's opinion of Ethan was brusque. If she knew the truth of me ripping my dress off and begging for sex, she'd have flat-out fainted.

"Sorry, Ma'am. Evan and I stripped trawlers today, and I didn't have time to wash up."

"Pay no mind, boy." Mama stepped from the porch. "Ain't nothing wrong with the smell of a hard-working man."

"Is your husband here?" Ethan asked me.

"Not this time. *Bob* had work in New York."

Ethan laughed. "How about an escort? We can go to the beach and catch up."

"I'd like that," I said. Then our eyes met, and we smiled, and at that moment, I was no longer broken. I wasn't questioned. I wasn't feared. And I wasn't blamed for being a creature born of bedlam. Ethan Bennet didn't know me as fragile.

To him, I was not untouchable.

Eleven

Abby and I planned an afternoon with Edward and Michael at the beach. June's early daylight heated the shore, and I knew the sand would be powdery soft. I made my morning call to Blake, assured him all was well, and when he asked if I'd taken my pills, I lied and told him I did. The deception was common and too practiced to avoid.

Mother approached from the kitchen, giving me a heavy once-over. "That red bikini has seen better days, Sarah. Women with your shape should be careful of what's falling out."

"Half the town picketed stores selling my books down here, Mother. My nipple falling out should be the least of your worries."

Michael held army men up. "Don't forget these."

"No little men," I said, slipping a t-shirt over my head. "I'm not digging through sand for bits of plastic."

Michael spun and ran down the hall as Mother dropped to the couch.

"Geez, are you sick?" I asked. "You're the same color as that ugly tweed couch."

"Didn't sleep well last night." Mother pulled a throw blanket over her legs. "And don't call my furniture ugly."

"Want me to stay? The beach isn't going anywhere."

"Abby won't get another chance if you don't go today, and Michael's been screaming for Edward. You go on."

I crouched, kissing her lips. "There. Now we'll share cooties like we used to."

Mother whispered she loved me as she quietly drifted to sleep.

The drive to the butcher shop was blissful and short. The sun was shining, the wind whipped my hair, and I fired alive with rampant sensations only attainable when my mind slipped its leash. I was on the upward drift of a high time, and it was beautiful.

Buster hulked from the grubby back lot as I parked by the shop. The passage of time did little to change or improve him. He was still dirty and round and couldn't detach from that same bloody apron and shirt.

"Well, if it ain't the queen writer herself," he said, watching me slide from my car. "Got any more dirty books?"

"Go get Abby."

"Can't you ask any nicer than that?"

"I'm not asking," I said. "I'm telling. Get Abby."

"She got inventory in the freezer today. Can't go nowhere till the boxes get done."

Rolling my eyes, I leaned toward the shop's open door. "Abby? Tell your tub of shit daddy you're running with me for the day."

"Abby's making deliveries now." Ida's cowardly moan wandered out. "Maybe come back tomorrow."

"Shut up, Ida," Buster snapped. "You talk too much, and this here queen don't care to hear nothing from you. Do ya, queen?"

"Buster, why are you still alive?" I asked, hearing a chuckle deep in his throat. "I mean it. I've seen jellyfish with more spine than you, and they're littering the beaches in stinking mounds. Why don't you join them?"

Buster stepped closer. "Abby told me what happened in that Perlick back then. I know what you saw."

"Saw plenty in that lousy thing. Moldy pork butt, rotten hens—"

"Know about that scar on your hip too. Abby told me the truth."

"Only you'd notice a box cutter scar on a little kid's hip."

"Box cutter?" He stopped, and his eyes trained right on my shorts. "You think a box cutter done that to you?"

"Momma?" Michael stretched up from the car window. "Can we see Edward?"

"In a minute, honey. Momma's talking right now."

"That day don't stick in your mind at all, does it, gal? Abby said you wouldn't remember what happened in there, and by damn, she's right."

"Still telling lies?" I smirked, tying my hair. "Everyone knows you busted those jars yourself. Sprayed glass all over that floor. Abby said you couldn't even stand. Told everyone you were curled in a corner, crying like gulls in a storm."

"Best watch your mouth with me, gal. Might regret what you say later on."

"My only regret was passing out before seeing you whine like a goat."

Michael leaped from the car, racing past Buster through the door to the shop.

"Hang on there, boy." Buster shoved me, snatching up Michael and straddling him over a hip. "What you doin' running into my store?"

"Brought toys for Edward. We're going to play at the beach."

"Edward ain't got the sense to play at the beach. Don't you know that?"

"Put him down, Buster," I said, walking into the shop. "I'm not in the mood for your bullshit right now."

"Boy should learn not to run through strange places, queen. He could get hurt."

"So could you, old man." Ethan curbed through the doorway. He smelled like diesel and naphtha and wore a greasy brown t-shirt and jeans. "My friend told you to put her son down. I think you should listen, don't you?"

"Buster?" Ida stood at the counter, sliding the bandana off of her head. "Maybe put the boy down like they said."

"Shut that worthless mouth before I pop that other eye, Ida."

"Go to the house, Miss Ida." Ethan gave her a nod, and Ida turned, slipping away to the back. "This piece of shit won't do a damn thing."

"This here's my store, boy. Man can do as he likes with what's his, and there ain't nothing you can do about it."

"Sure, there is." Ethan slid a buck knife from the belt of his jeans, tapping the point on his palm. "We can finish what your daddy started and try that bait well again."

"You Bennet boys think you own this whole town. Don't own shit 'cept for that busted up charter your brother runs down."

Ethan huffed, nudging his chin toward Michael. "What's your name, little man?"

"Michael Benjamin Bradley. What's yours?"

"Ethan Scott Bennet." Ethan gripped Michael's hand in a shake. "Tell me, Mr. Bradley, have you ever heard of scrimshaw?"

Michael shook his head. "No."

"Well, old fat Buster sure has. He was about your age when he left the catch on his daddy's trawler one night. His old man was so pissed off he threw Buster into a bait well full of broken glass and said he was making scrimshaw so his little boy would never forget that fish again. By the time they pulled him out, old Buster had bloody reminders all over his back. Didn't you, *Buster*?"

Buster stuttered, licking the sweat from his thick upper lip. "You don't know nothin'. You Bennet boys don't know—"

"That was mean, Mr. Buster," Michael said. "Your daddy was mean to do that to you."

Ethan sheathed the knife before reaching for Michael. "Cry for the child locked up in that well. Curse the shit what come out."

Michael giggled. "You cuss like my mommy."

"Because she's the one who taught me." Ethan set Michael down before patting his rump. "Now go hug your momma."

I swept Michael up, glaring at Buster. "Touch my son again, and I'll have your balls hanging with Mama's gator teeth. Filthy drunk."

My hands were still trembling when I opened my car door and buckled Michael into his seat. "Don't talk to that man again," I said. "He's a monster."

"You said monsters weren't real. Only in books."

Ethan pressed a hand to my back before opening the passenger door and sliding into the car. "Listen to your mom, little man. Buster's the meanest monster in the world. He's just walking around in people skin. Don't go near him again."

Dipping through Ethan's window, I asked, "What are you doing in there?"

"Hitching a ride in your fancy black car."

"Guess I owe you after saving me again. Where to?"

Ethan looked back at Michael. "Michael, where do princesses and knights go when they're done fighting monsters?"

Michael thought for a moment. "Castles?"

"Damn right. Want to see one?"

"Can we?" Michael smiled.

"Way to start trouble," I said. "That house is probably in worse shape than when we were running through it."

"Since when did you get so cautious, Shakespeare?"

"I'm not being cautious. I'm being responsible."

Ethan grinned, resting his head on the seat. "Since when did you get so responsible?"

We laughed, and before I knew it, I aimed my car toward the dead end of Branch Street, where I'd teach my son the fine art of childhood criminal trespass.

Twelve

Michael whined as we trudged through the castle's side yard. "This isn't a castle. Castles are stone, not wood. And the yard's all messy. Like no one's mowed it before."

"Not all castles are made of stone," Ethan said. "See the water back there? That's like a moat. There's a glass room called a solarium too."

"You never let Abby and me dig in that mess," I said.

"Michael's a boy." Ethan shrugged, yanking boards from a window. "Boys should do adventurous things."

"Like run in the street?" Michael clapped.

"Hell, no," Ethan said. "Running in the street is for wharf rats. You're no wharf rat."

Ethan hoisted himself through the warped window frame, gathering Michael before reaching for me.

We stood in the smaller of two front rooms. The walls were papered in Victorian stripes, cracked and sepia-toned with age. The air smelled of dampness and old rotting wood, and I recalled the room having views of the water and dock with a white picket gate.

"City's been threatening to tear it down for years." Ethan righted a pocket door between the parlor and stairs. "Every month, someone tries swinging a wrecking ball through the place."

"Oh, I hope they don't. It'd make a beautiful home for a family one day. Blue velvet drapes on the windows and polished brass knobs on the doors."

"Repairs would cost a fortune, and no one around here has money like that or the clout to get permits."

"This part's dark." Michael peered cautiously through a long, narrow hall. "What's down there?"

"On the left is the kitchen." Ethan picked him up. "At the end is the glass room I told you about. Want to see?"

"Better not be full of snakes," I said.

"What a little hypocrite. You'll write about blood and sex, but the prospect of a real-life reptile is too much."

"Yes, Ethan. It is."

Ethan shouldered the door at the end of the hall, flooding the space with fresh light. Birds dashed apart, and wide hammocks of vines dangled loosely from transoms above.

"It's still here?" I pointed to the greenhouse, stabbing through growth. "Hard to believe the kudzu hasn't eaten it yet."

"That's hard oak. Glass is gone, but the frame's probably good."

"Looks like heaven," Michael said, waving a fly from his face. "Like where angels would live if God painted with Grandma Lena."

Ethan whispered to me, "Boy's strange, Sarah. Better teach him to fight because talking like that will get his ass kicked all over this state."

"Well, if he starts talking about heaven on fire, I'll give you a call."

"You remember that, huh?"

"Lost my virginity ten seconds after. That's not something a girl forgets. Besides, that comment surprised me coming from you. Felt so sincere."

"It was sincere. You were beautiful, Sarah. Still are."

I thanked him, watching cardinals racing through vines. "Do you still go there?"

"Go where?"

"To Shell Beach?"

"No," he said flatly. "No reason to go, so I don't."

"Not even to think about things?"

"Waking old ghosts isn't something I do, Sarah."

Scraping leaves with my sandal, I said, "Well, what if those ghosts are still there?"

"But they're not." He spoke sharply, looking at me. "They left when you married someone else five years ago. They left with what's strapped to my hip right now."

"Take me anyway."

"We'll go to Shoreline and everywhere else, but we're not going to Shell Beach. The boat's gone now. No need to go back."

"I don't care. Michael needs to see where we played, so we're going, and you're coming too."

Ethan grumbled to Michael as I dragged him back down the hall.

"Don't be like your mother. She's bully and spice and not very nice."

"Mommy's a girl, Ethan. Girls are sugar and spice and everything nice."

"Not your mother," Ethan said. "And not if you don't do what she says."

Thirteen

By the time we arrived at Shell Beach, we'd shown Michael every tree branch and sidewalk where our childhood lived. We tagged headstones at Shoreline, crossed bridges we jumped, and waded small inlet waters we fished. It was sweetly nostalgic but inwardly sad.

"Where are you living now?" I asked. Ethan and I sat on the sand, watching Michael chase after gulls. "Mainland or island?"

"Island, of course. Evan and I found a trailer off the parkway on Grainger. Thing's isolated and has a rusted-out cistern stinking up the front yard, but it'll do for now."

"Something better will come. You've got the charter work, and you'll decide what to do with the boats. At least you have Bayport. I miss it down here."

"Something wrong with Charleston?"

"Charleston's too fast," I said, picking at shells. "Too many people. Too many cars."

"New York will be a culture shock, then."

"New York?" I gaped at him. "Who told you about New York?"

"Ran into your mom at Winn Dixie last month. She told me."

Chuckling, I said, "Bet she couldn't wait to share that news. Especially with you."

"Nearly dumped a wall of Wheaties to catch me before checking out. Is it true?"

I nodded, burying my toes under the sand. "Veritas is growing, and we want to compete with larger houses. That means Manhattan, but I'll come home like always."

"To see me?" he asked with a smile.

"Not how you're thinking. No."

"And how do you know what I'm thinking? Maybe I want to jump bridges or watch Sesame Street at Mama's. You don't know."

"Yes, I do. You're a very predictable pervert. Both of those things you'd ask to do naked."

"Not true," he said, trailing a finger straight down my thigh. "Panties are always an option."

Ethan winked, and I wondered how long it would take for my breath to return after I wrapped it around his tongue.

"You're about to say we have to leave, aren't you?" Ethan asked.

"I think we should, yes."

"All right," he said, helping me up. "But you'll miss one hell of a Sesame Street episode. Michael? Better hurry before your mom's temper goes off. You're only four, and I doubt you've witnessed it yet."

"Four and a half." Michael sprinted with his fingers spread wide. "I'm four and a half, Ethan. Almost five."

"Well, if you want to see six, you'd better stay on her good side." Ethan swept Michael over his back. "Why, did you know she broke some boy's leg once? His name was Walter Salinger, and she pushed him off a bridge."

They were wonderful together and so alike. They consumed the world like food or drink or anything their bodies would need to survive in a place more savage than their natures could abide. They weren't born to the world in which they lived; they were made of it.

We drove into town while Ethan watched Michael napping in his seat. "Kid sleeps like a gator. Doesn't get that from you."

"Blake sleeps like that too. So did you. Must be a male trait."

"Recalling how another man sleeps?" Ethan joked. "That's rather indecent, Mrs. Bradley."

"Indecent or not, whenever I wake up freezing in my room, I remember you stealing the sheets."

"Your room?" He huffed, dusting sand from his thigh. "Do rich people sleep in separate bedrooms in Charleston?"

"If one's a writer with insomnia, yes. Blake can't suffer through that."

"I never suffered. Still have nightmares?"

"Sometimes. Not often."

"What does Blake do about those?"

Hesitating to answer, I said, "He comes in and sits with me."

"Sits with you?" His voice tightened, and I felt his eyes on my cheek. "Does he hold you?"

"There's no need for coddling, Ethan. I'm not a kid anymore."

"That's not coddling, Sarah. That's kindness. Do you still write the nightmares?"

The question was laughable. "Wouldn't have any books if I didn't."

"That's not funny. None of this is funny. Pull over at the end of the bridge."

"Pull over? What for? Why are you grilling me so hard?"

"Because something's not right. Just do it."

Ethan waited until I pulled into Benson's bait shop at the end of the bridge. Then he turned in his seat and began shooting questions at me.

"What'd you mean when you said those ghosts never left?"

"Jesus, Ethan," I said in a breath. "Let's not ruin this day."

"You mean we never left? You and me. Is that it?"

"Everything's different now. I've changed so much. You wouldn't understand."

"Why'd you make me go to Shell Beach?" he asked. "You could have gone alone, taken Michael. You didn't need me there. Why'd you do it?"

"To remember."

"Remember what? Me? You wanted to remember me?"

"All of it. The boat. That summer. How it felt. So much is slipping away, and I thought—"

"Don't let it slip away, Sarah. You and Michael can stay."

"I'm not the same anymore," I said, watching dust rolling over the lot. "Whatever we have, our childhood, friendship, anything we feel right now would be ruined if I stayed."

"Jesus, is that what Blake says about you? He says you ruin things?"

"Blake doesn't say that, Ethan. That's not what I meant."

Ethan slumped in the seat, staring out. "You still love me, Sarah. I felt it every time you touched me today. I saw it in your eyes when we spoke."

"Things are different now. It wouldn't work out."

"You were never supposed to leave me," he said, taking my face in his hands. "Everything that happened was so damn wrong."

Ethan kissed me before getting out of the car. He strode through the lot, back hunched, aimlessly crossing the street.

Michael stirred in his car seat and yawned. "Is that Ethan, Momma?"

"Yes, honey. It is."

"Can we see him again? He was fun to play with, and I like how he talks."

"Yes, baby. We will. We'll see Ethan as much as we can, whenever we can."

"Because we like him?"

"Because we love him," I said, bleeding tears. "We never stopped."

Mother's house was ghostly when I bumped the car up the drive. Quiet and still under rust-colored skies, the porch glowed yellow, and a single light blazed from her room.

"Grandma's still up," Michael said, curbing past me to storm through the house. "We're going to read before bed."

"It's late, Michael. Only one story tonight." After dropping our bags by the door, I noticed Mother's sofa throw piled on the floor, and I folded it twice before draping it back to its spot.

"Grandma's in her reading chair." Michael grabbed books from a basket by the TV and darted back down the hall. "We're reading four books."

"Did you hear what I said? Only one story tonight."

The evening was falling, but I assumed Mother would want coffee on the porch. That was our nightly routine. It started when I was fifteen, and she handed me a cup of Folgers cruelly diluted with milk.

I was filling the pot when Michael stomped into the kitchen and dropped to a chair. "Grandma won't turn any pages."

"She's not feeling well, honey."

"But she could tell me, Momma. She's just sitting there, holding Grandpa Ben's picture."

"The picture?" I turned, setting the pot to one side. "She's sleeping, Michael. She just fell asleep in the chair."

"No, she's not, Momma. Her eyes are still open. Is she mad at me? Why's she just sitting like that?"

"Stay here," I said, kissing his head. "I'll see."

I'd never faced death so boldly before, so when I found Mother seated primly in her reading chair, I froze. Death was nothing like what I thought it would be. There was no violent impulse to scream, nor did I feel the need to close my eyes in a sudden, compulsive revolt. She looked beautiful. Poised and delicate, gazing down at the glossy black frame in her hands. The picture leaned forward as if she'd held it close to her heart, then simply let go.

I dragged closer, admiring the elegant stillness. I'd never been that close to my mother without her touching or speaking to me. She'd take my hand, stroke my hair, or smile with a kiss on my cheek, but she never failed to make her presence physically known, no matter how slight our engagement. And the loss of it now, the lack of it, knowing it would never happen again, was the worst pain I'd ever felt. There was nothing left to do but what I had always done when needing the soothing touch of her hand.

I knelt at her side, told her I loved her, and for the very last time in my life, I cried in the arms of my mother.

Fourteen

I stood at Mother's graveside alone. Everyone else drifted away like little gray clouds between headstones. Blake took Mama and Michael to the car while Alicia drove Abby to the shop. There was a strange mix of earthly events. Mockingbirds crooned, sunlight burned, and squirrels ran, chasing up trees. The world was so ordinary in its movement, unaware of the tragedy endured by its caretakers.

A shoulder brushed mine, and Ethan was there, staring at the hole by our feet. He wore a charcoal gray suit and a striped silver tie, and with hair neatened beyond what Mama would have called *church-combed*, he looked downright elegant.

"Thought she was an angel that day," he said.

"What day?"

"That time, I was sick. My mom put sulfur mud on my chest. Some island medicine shit. I dunno. Your mom busted in, wearing that white uniform, hair falling out of that little pinned hat, cussing like the devil himself."

"Ethan Bennet, my mother never cussed."

"The hell she didn't. Sheila Thorn yanked that crap off my chest, scooped me up, and told my mother she was dumber than shit. Then she bolted out the door, taking me to Mama's."

"I never knew," I said. "Why didn't anyone—"

"She kidnapped me."

"God, Ethan." I scoffed, unwinding tissues. "She hardly kidnapped you."

"Yes, she did. She kidnapped me."

"Ethan..."

"I was almost on a milk carton, Sarah. Holy Christ!"

Using that tissue muffled my laugh. "No wonder she hated your guts."

"Can't hold it against her," he said, tugging me close. "That woman's the reason we met."

Then, with a breath hitched in my throat, straining against the defensive dam I'd created, they came. The tears. A tide of raging, soulful salt, releasing themselves into the embrace of the man who knew the map of my heart better than anyone. I wailed, crumbling against him, floating weightless and independent of my limbs as he sat me on a bench and voices crowded nearer.

"Come with me, honey." Blake lifted me, his face coming into my view. "We need to go home."

"Blake?" I cried, wrapping around him. "You came for me. You came?"

"You're the husband?" Ethan asked.

"I'm Sarah's husband." Blake eyed Ethan's outstretched hand. He didn't bother to shake it. "Who are you?"

"Ethan Bennet. I grew up with Sarah. We played right here at Shoreline when we were kids."

"Uh-huh," Blake said, studying Ethan like a bug he should swat. "Sarah's had a long day, and she's tired. I'm taking her home."

Blake led me back to the car, but Ethan called out, "Sarah's never been much of a crier."

"What?" Blake stopped, looking back. "Sarah will be all right, Mr. Bennet. She just needs to rest."

"You have to hold her. Draw out the pain until the dam bursts. This is just the dam bursting. You should let her feel it."

"If that's what you think, you don't know my wife very well."

Ethan shrugged, slid his sunglasses over his nose, and said, "You've been married five years. I've known her for fourteen. I'd say that's knowing somebody pretty damn well."

Blake gave no response outside a disgruntled *thank you* before turning us toward the car. That moment ignited a war. A battle between a present and past with me staked like a calf between lions. There'd be no map for our strife. No predictable occurrences of judgments and blame. Just mistakes we would make, accusations we'd throw, and two men with crosses to bear.

Blake was quiet, taking the bridge out of town. He was quiet pulling into Mama's long drive, and when he thanked her for keeping Michael so I could rest, he did so quietly. He was also quiet when we dragged into Mother's house twenty minutes later.

And that's when the quietness stopped.

"The man at Shoreline," he said, dropping his keys and my purse onto a chair. "Was that him?"

"Him who?"

"Ethan Bennet. Was that the boyfriend?"

"Jesus, you're doing this now? I just buried my mother, for Christ's sake."

"And I just saw a man groping my wife at her mother's funeral, Sarah. Was that him or not?"

"Yes, that was him," I said. "And he wasn't groping me."

"He was practically rubbing your ass while your son watched."

"What'd you want him to do, Blake? Ignore me? I needed someone, and Ethan was there."

"I was there," he said, stabbing his chest. "I was right the hell there."

"No, you weren't. You were a hundred feet away, watching from a distance like you always do when tragedy strikes. You only came when you had to."

"I took Michael to the car so you could have time to yourself. I thought you could use it."

"You went to the car because you're afraid of me, Blake. Afraid to touch me. Afraid to get close. All you see are pills, doctors, and a disaster you have to prevent."

"I see a woman pretending there's nothing wrong when there is, and you can't do that, Sarah. You can't act like your problems just don't exist."

"Oh, I know they exist," I said, swiping my purse and keys from that chair. "Every time I reach for you and you turn away, I know they exist. Every time you answer my nightmares with pills, I know they exist." I stopped as I opened the door. "Why didn't you leave me in the riptide that day? It would have been a less lonely death."

Blake's voice struck the door as it closed, and I wasn't sure if he was cursing in anger or calling my name from concern. Neither would have kept me at home. I needed the night. I needed the coolness and the anonymity that came from a colorless world. Winn Dixie's payphone still owned its wall beneath overhead lamps in the lot. I parked beside it, rummaging for applicable quarters and dimes in my purse.

"Seven o'clock," I whispered, tapping my watch. "Still time."

Dialing the butcher shop's number came easily, as did ordering two roasting hens and one pound of bacon, thickly sliced. Abby would deliver the order to Mr. and Mrs. Seymore Crabbe on Fripp Island. Mrs. Lola Crabbe always made the call. The Crabbes paid cash via bottle returns and coins scraped together from extra chores done for my mother. With a driveway too narrow for Buster's meat truck, the Crabbes offered cab fare, which Buster greedily accepted for his daughter's delivery, with a heavy tip for an after-hours consideration.

Lola Crabbe made her order that night too. Ida wrote every word, reciting its details to her drunken bastard of a husband. Lola apologized for the hour, then chatted with Ida about how lovely Southern accents were compared to her own midwestern style of speech. Then, as always, Buster accused Ida of bothering his customers, and he yanked the phone, banging it back to its cradle.

This was our game, mine and Abby's. When Buster's hold became too tight, and Abby cried, her golden eyes dipped beneath the slowly drawn shades of those filthy butcher shop windows; when she entered the chill of that freezer to count those damnable boxes of bloody, stinking meat, Mr. Crabbe's wife would call, and she would set Abby free.

The beach behind Mama's was the perfect place for regret, and from that vantage, I was free to render remorse. There was no death without blame, no loss without answer, and no grief without fault. But who's to blame for killing a heart, drained of its weakening beat? Who answers for the wilting nature of age? Only God.

With the buoy bell clanging its sorrowful song, I scoured the galaxy and screamed at deities in their silky black sky, and I mourned every lovely thing I lost. And while waving fists and threatening stars did little to chasten the amusement of gods, I could rob them of one of their pawns. With one dousing leap, I could steal the mind they broke at my birth, ruin the body that ached for release, and deny them a soul come undone. I could steal them away and empty them all, washing them clean of the world.

"Michael." Abby draped over my back, kissed my jawline, and like she'd done a hundred times as a child, saved me from disastrous ends. "Don't leave him alone in this place." Then she took my hand and guided me down to the sand. "Are they here?" she asked, hooking my arm with her own. "Are fireflies here?"

"Over the shoreline." I sniffed, wiggling a hand. "And there by the buoy."

"How many?" she asked. "Tell me."

"Thousands." Fireflies glittered, and I lifted my arms, feeling their wings spark inside golden illuminations igniting all over my skin. "See them, Abby? Do you see?"

"Always," she said. "They're shining like diamonds and rubies tonight."

"Fireflies aren't red."

"Mine are." She giggled and pressed a hand to my head. "Have a fever?"

"Just a headache. It'll pass."

We sat silently before Abby said, "I prayed for you today. Got on my knees with Mama's King James and prayed for God to heal your heart and grant memories of your mother to sustain you."

"Would have been better to ask why He took her."

"God doesn't take people, Sarah. Her heart was too sick and weak to go on, so it stopped."

"Why didn't Buster's heart stop?" I challenged her with a look. "Why take my mother and leave someone like him sucking air?"

"Because it isn't his time. God has a plan, and all we can do is follow along."

"If killing my mother and keeping you tied to Buster's bloody fist is part of God's plan, then He should take another look at His whims down here, Abby. We're not doing too well, know what I mean?"

"Some plans take time," she said, smoothing my hair. "We have to be patient and wait for the signs."

"Is that what you're doing? Waiting for signs before you leave Buster's shop? All you have to do is walk out the door. Not like that bastard would care."

"He'd care if I took Edward, and I can't leave him, Sarah. You know I won't do that."

"So take Edward too. Come live with us in New York."

Abby hitched back. "What would Edward do in a city that big?"

"Play at the park, chase after birds. Same as Michael."

Abby dug a trench in the sand. "Edward needs places that are quiet and still, and cities aren't quiet or still."

"How quiet is that shop with Buster swinging his fists in your face?"

"When was the last time you saw a bruise on my face?" Abby smiled, and I realized she was right. I hadn't. "Last time Buster laid a hand on me, I was twelve. Mama told him if he did it again, hell wouldn't have enough room for all the pieces she'd have to send down. Buster says he's not afraid of Mama, but he is. Ida's afraid of her too. Mama threw her bones and said Ida would go like her sisters all did. Slow, cruel, and eaten with cancer. Buster will die screaming the way he deserves."

"Mama's bones are about as precise as a winter weather report."

"They're better than that," she said, looking right and then left. "Still see them?"

I nudged toward the water. "A few by the buoy. Some by the lot. What do you see?"

"Three by the shoreline. Two by the trees, but they're going to bed with the sun."

"Thank you." I kissed and hugged her and wanted to cry for loving the lie she just told. "Who's your whim, Abby Mills?"

"You're my whim, Sarah Thorn. And I'm yours."

"Always and forever?" I asked.

"Always and forever," she said. "Time to go."

We drove into town, where I stopped a careful distance away from the shop. After handing Abby a trifold of cash, I kissed her once and watched as she rounded the alley for home. Branch Street was empty as I stopped at the light, facing the left to go home. With the twist of my wrist, the car made a right, rolling onto Oaks Bridge and the parkway beyond.

Moonlight guided me along white, sandy paths as I searched desolate corridors and wide, winding roads until I came to a trail at the end of the parkway closest to water. At its end sat a trailer with a view of the marsh. It was isolated and old and had a rusted-out cistern stinking up the front yard.

Fifteen

Cold grass shocked underfoot as I neared the trailer's front stoop. Crickets chirped, and lizards taunted the screens, but no other sounds of an outside world interrupted that diamond-shaped spot. The aluminum door opened with a nearly silent click as I stepped inside, smiling at the tidiness. The counters were clean, dish towels folded, and lemon scents hinted in the air.

Sculpted green carpet decked a narrow front hall, housing a bedroom filled with odd pieces of diving gear that didn't fit Ethan's interests. I assumed that was Evan's room. Down the hall to the left was another door, closed, with slivers of light underneath. The door opened easily, offering a subtle squeak as I curled inside and pressed it back to its frame.

Breezes pushed through the windows, rustling pages of maps on the walls. Near the door sat a plywood desk with aerial photos of islands and design plans of luxury boats weighted with rocks. A kayak and paddles crowded a corner, and across from it all, sleeping soundly beneath white linen sheets, lay Ethan sprawled on the bed.

I felt spectral, approaching him quietly, removing my clothes as I walked. He had such peace as he slept. His eyes didn't flutter, his lips parted only slightly, and his chest moved in an undulation so smooth it could have been run by precision.

"Ethan, wake up," I whispered, dragging a hand down his chest.

Ethan mumbled, and his eyes twitched open and finally focused on mine.

"Sarah? Jesus—" He shot upright, sitting on the edge of the bed. "What're you doing here? What's going on?"

"I'm supposed to be here. I made a mistake, and I love you."

"Sarah, don't do this," he said, raking a hand through his hair. "Don't stand there with your clothes off saying you love me."

"I do love you, Ethan. I just didn't see."

"Didn't see what?" he asked, looking at me. "Didn't see me five years ago, shouting at your mom's front door? Beating the shit out of that boat until my hands were so bloody I couldn't wash the stains out? Is that what you didn't see?"

"Mama says God sends people we need, and we have to be careful to see them. But I didn't know that was you, and I ran to Blake, and I ruined us, Ethan. I ruined everything."

"No, Sarah. I ruined us. If I'd told you the truth by the boat that day, we'd—"

"That summer was perfect," I said, pinning his lips with a touch. "There was no fear and no doubt. We just loved each other. Do you know how rare that is, Ethan? How wonderful it is to be loved like that?"

Ethan raised up, flipping me onto the bed. "Come back to me, Sarah. You and Michael. We can start over again."

I stopped him with a kiss, whispering, "Pretend it's that night. We're on the boat making love, and no one knows. This is all I can give you, Ethan. I can't offer more, or we'll lose what we already have."

Ethan dropped his head to my neck. "Come home every month. I don't care what you say to him. I don't care how you lie. Just get here, Sarah. Anything less would break my damn heart."

I agreed, tears dripping down as he tenderly kissed them away.

We made love that night, forging a routine of secret devotion but understanding that was all I could give. Our affair would become natural to us. As close to the life we were meant to have as either of us would have made it. Over the years, we'd observe the achingly common and frightfully brilliant moments shared by two people who loved once and never stopped.

We couldn't stop.

My monthly trips were a respite, I'd say. I told Blake Michael needed to learn the unwounded lands between ocean and earth, and Bayport would offer that gift. I took my medications, keeping Blake comfortably placid in his empire of words where he replaced his marital presence with writs of prescriptions and the swallow of pills. My childhood home became my own. Ethan built a gazebo in the backyard. We planted jasmine and honeysuckle against the frame where I'd create worlds, sharing with people who'd become family by rights of circumstance.

Mama watched Ethan and me. She'd sneer and scowl and would call it a sin if she ever admitted she knew. But Mama's world was one of practical placement where, when confronted, she'd piously state, "Your secrets are not mine to tell."

Blake would come, sharing the house, my moments of clarity, and sometimes my bed. But his fears were evident, and he'd check for tremors or inquire about flashes of lights I could never confirm as real. And while he was there, as I watched him play with the son he loved so much, as he swam in the ocean and pressed his lips to mine, a flicker of hope would rise, and I'd see him again. A young man on a beach full of passion and handsome, brutal beauty. And I'd feel a painful desire for a man I did truly love, but who thought me too fractured to want.

Sixteen

Blake leaned on the doorjamb of my office, amused. "The health department will remove our child if you don't clean this hellhole."

"Hellhole?" Laughing, I noted disheveled bookcases and lipstick-smeared mugs on my desk. "That's slightly insulting, Blake."

He pointed to the right. "Those French doors have an outstanding backyard view, honey."

"Yeah?"

"There's a whiteboard over them."

"That's for outlines. I need it."

"You'd rather stare at colorful markers than gaze at the Charleston Harbor?"

"Michael draws birds on it." I smiled, adjusting pens in my bun. "That's all the view I need."

"You're a mess." Blake laughed softly and settled into the brown leather chair by my desk. "What'd you think of the queries I sent?"

"Not sure," I said with a shrug. "One was all right."

"Only one? There are ten authors on that list. The editors said six were good."

"Then why ask me? I'm not an editor."

"Your opinion matters, Sarah. The editors just—"

"The editors are shit. They don't communicate with writers; they lord over them. And they don't want to edit a thing. They want to abort darlings and use a red pen. They're fond of red ink. It reminds them of blood."

Blake grinned, crossing his legs. "Can't imagine why they won't work with you, honey."

"Probably afraid of that singular opinion you prize so much. New York will be terrified too."

"Can't argue with that. You have an eye for dark-horse stories, but New York will respect you for it. They already do."

"I'd rather be feared," I said. "Fear leaves a deeper impression."

"Tell that to protestors." Blake winked and pushed from the chair. "Can you be ready by eight?"

"Eight's fine, but I don't think Lena should do this tonight. Ink's barely dry on the discharge papers, and now she's doing a show?"

"The doctors said she's all right."

"The doctors thought she was all right before we found her on the roof three weeks ago too."

He dragged a hand down his face and said, "The woman stopped taking her meds, Sarah. Can't blame the doctors for that."

"Who wanted the show at the house?" I asked, dropping my pen in its cup.

"Mom did. Dad tried to change her mind, but she wanted it there. Galleries are helping. They know how she is."

"Yeah. They know the money too."

"Don't be like that, Sarah. C'mon."

"They're vampires, Blake. Her one agent, the skinny mouth-breather? He dragged a sketch pad into her hospital room last year."

Blake sniggered, rubbing his chin. "He didn't last long after you got hold of him."

"That idiot sneaked a sharpened pencil to a sleeping patient, for God's sake. Bastard's lucky he didn't end up crapping out lead."

Blake relaxed on the doorjamb again. "You're good with her, honey. That's why Dad calls you whenever Mom holes up in the studio like she does. He never knows what she's feeling anymore. Fear, terror, or—"

"It's loneliness," I said. "Women can abide fear and terror. We can even live without love. What we can't tolerate is loneliness. It's loneliness that kills us."

Blake's eyes glued to mine as if he wanted to ask me to explain, but he didn't. He couldn't. Instead, he pulled a little carved horse from his pocket and placed it on my desk. "Michael said Ethan made this. Wood's unusual."

"It's Apitong," I said, palming the toy. "Boat makers use it. Ethan made seven animals, one for each of Michael's birthdays. Edward has some too."

"Ethan's a talented guy." Blake's mocking opinion couldn't hide his disdain. "Building gazebos, carving animals. Michael says you see him a lot when you're there."

"Hard to avoid a man who practically runs that whole town," I said. "Not to mention Mama has him tied to a mower every weekend. We see him there too."

"And at the beach, and sailing boats, and eating out..."

"Along with Abby and Alicia. So what?"

"So Abby and Alicia aren't building gazebos for my wife and carving toys for my son, Sarah."

Tilting my head to one side, I said, "Is there something you'd like to ask me now, Blake?"

"Should I, Sarah?"

"Jesus Christ." I tossed the toy in a drawer and shoved back. "I'm not having an affair with Ethan Bennet if that's what you're driving at, but do you think I'd tell you just because you asked?"

"What will you do once we move to New York?" he asked, swiping the dust from a shelf. "Will you still go there each month, bringing Michael?"

"Probably. I write better there, but I never said you couldn't come too."

"I can't leave for two weeks every month."

"Yes, you can. You don't want to, that's all. If there were an author or contract lurking down there, you'd find a way."

"You're suggesting I stop working?"

"Just saying you should stop using work as an excuse."

"Excuse for what?"

"To not get close."

"Close to what?"

"Close to me, Blake," I said, throwing my hands in the air. "Jesus. Close to me."

Blake flinched, stammering, "That's not... that's not what I—"

"Forget it." I readied my pen, striking through characters I suddenly wanted to kill. "This conversation's old and only pisses me off. Close the door when you leave."

Gathering mugs from my desk, Blake said, "I wasn't going to ask if you were having an affair, Sarah."

"I'm busy, Blake. What is it you wanted to ask?"

"I was going to ask..." he paused, blinking at me, "...are you lonely?" Blake's expression was soft and pensive, and his eyes were so sad that he looked like a child abandoned.

"Why are you asking me that?"

"Are you?"

Dropping my pen, I said, "Asking a woman if she's lonely is the same as asking if she's having an affair. She'll give you the same answer to both."

"And what would that be?" he asked.

"She'll say no to you, Blake. She'll say no to you every time."

Blake only nodded, adjusted the mugs, and then left without saying a word.

Ours wasn't a deliberate dissection of one another, nor were there intentional inflictions of pain. We just lost our way. It was a subtle marital separation where one party stopped reaching out, and the other grew weary of trying. Blake had stopped reaching out, and I'd grown tired of trying.

We pulled into Blake's parents' drive amid a bustling exertion. Caterers primped tables while designers set last-minute flourishes, trimming the expanse of the backyard's neatly groomed edge. Lena's works were displayed through the grounds, brightening lush greenery with flashes of azure and red. Her agents hovered nearby and gnashed smiles at buyers eager to own a creative portion of Lena White-Bradley's surging life force.

"This is too much," I said, dodging valets cornering cars. "Why would she have a show at the house?"

"The series is called *Sky*, honey. Having it outside made sense."

"Well, MJ should have said no."

"Calm down, Rambo." Blake lifted my hand in a kiss. "Let's save bloodshed for protesters."

"No fighting today," I said, smoothing my dress. "Blood stains on satin are too hard to wash out."

We laughed, and Blake took my elbow, pulling me under a vine-covered arch by the drive. "Don't go to Bayport tomorrow. Let's go somewhere together instead."

"Go somewhere?" I huffed, surprised at Blake's tender request. "Where would we go? And when?"

"Tonight. We'll pack a suitcase and figure the rest from the road."

"But we have authors to review, and I've got eight chapters to finish before—"

"Do them after," he said, kissing my neck. "I've made so many wrong turns, Sarah. So many mistakes. Let me make it up to you, please."

"Why now, Blake? Why are you doing this now?"

"Because you said you were lonely, and I know it's my fault."

"I never said that. I never said I was—"

"This morning in your office. I knew what you meant. You thought I didn't hear, but I did." He kissed me again, lingering his lips as he spoke. "I don't want to lose you, Sarah. Please, honey. Let me make it up to you. Give me a chance."

Selfishly, I thought of Ethan and my promise to always return. I'd never broken that vow in two years, but standing with Blake, his voice full of need, I couldn't deny the request.

"I'll have to call Mama," I said. "She's expecting me there."

"Call after the show. This'll be good for us, Sarah. You'll see."

We kissed again before Blake took my hand and rounded the house, where crowds mulled over Lena's pieces. Each display represented a common aerial theme. The first held gauzy clouds over stately blue oceans or a hurricane's darkening threat. Others depicted bright burning suns with deep shades of umber piercing a somber Atlantic.

The last in the series, *The Creative*, was the most moving. There were four portraits of a boy, eyes wide in joyous splendor, reaching for birds overhead.

"That's Michael," Blake whispered.

I smiled. "He's chasing birds."

Each piece was pristine, capturing the essence of what Michael was. An innocent gathering the world in eager hands lifted from pale white sands to azure blue skies melting down. They were masterful. Preservations of life exploding in streaks of blue and pearl-white creams. She painted my soul on canvas.

"Magnificent, aren't they?" MJ approached from a crowd.

"They're perfect," I said, touching a frame. "Did you know about them?"

"No one did."

"Has she come out of her room today, Dad?" Blake asked.

"Once or twice." MJ adjusted his cuff. "She didn't sleep well last night. Sarah, would you mind?"

"Not at all." Pushing between them, I headed inside.

Lena's studio was an oasis of feminine style. Lined in rose hedges, the arched windows stretched from floor to ceiling in gaping passages of blazing sun, drenching the room with bright light. Each indent of the coffered ceiling featured frescos of Lena's design. The faces of shrimpers who loved her. Nets casting from strong, tensing arms preserved in the beauty of their craft. The shades raised high when Lena worked, but when she folded inside herself, fighting the monsters that stalked her, those blinds would draw closed, and Lena fell under dreadful, dark silence.

"Lena?" I called out, skirting around her as she lowered the blinds. "Don't close the blinds today. Everyone's here to see you."

"There you are." She smiled weakly, falling into a loose hug. "That dress is perfect for you. I've always loved you in green."

"What's wrong?" I asked. Her voice was feeble, and I tilted her chin to check the float of her eyes. "Did you take your pills today?"

"Did you?" She laughed softly, raising a brow. "I took all of mine. Blue ones, beige ones. All lined up in neat little rows. My pills keep the demons away."

"There aren't any demons. I already looked. They're not here."

"They're always here," she said, floating a hand over brushes and paints. "That's why Blake couldn't love me."

"That's not true. Blake loves you very much."

"But I taught him not to. The demons came on Blake's birthday, Sarah. I locked his door to protect him. I protected my son."

"No, Lena. MJ locked Blake's door that night, not you."

"They were coming," she said, and her voice nearly hammered the words. "The demons. The monsters. They were coming for Blake. And when the demons wanted to take him, I locked Blake's door so they wouldn't get in. MJ didn't believe me. He didn't believe the monsters were real."

"Lena?" I reached for her gently, holding her arms. "Let's cancel the party today."

"They're inside of us, Sarah. The monsters. The demons. They poison our blood, and they hide in our veins. They spread fear like disease and will come for your son."

"Michael is safe," I said. "He's watching movies with the sitter at home."

"MJ tried saving me, and Blake wants to save you, but he can't." She held me tightly and pressed her lips to my ear. "They're cursed, Sarah. My son and husband are cursed, and Michael will be cursed if you don't stop this now."

Something was wrong. Out of Lena's ordinary stable of mania rhetoric, this was more unbalanced.

"I'm getting MJ."

I turned, feeling slender fingers gripping my arm as Lena pulled me into an embrace so tight I felt the beat of her heart on my ribs.

"You're the light in Blake's darkness," she wept. "The reason he breathes."

"Lena, please." After sitting her on a paint-splattered stool, I turned from the room. "I'm getting MJ."

Reaching the courtyard, I waved toward MJ and Blake.

"What's wrong with Lena?" I asked, watching both men stride the patio steps. "Hasn't she taken her meds?"

"She took them," MJ said. "I gave her the doses this morning, then put the bottle away."

"Well, something's wrong. Her eyes won't focus, she can barely stand, and she's saying strange things. Like she's drunk."

"She took them, Sarah. Hardly fought me at all, and she took the doses all week. I saw her."

"Dad?" Blake's eyes raced toward the house. "Did she swallow them?"

We looked to the corner of the studio where Lena pulled every blind but for one.

Blake cursed, hurling inside. MJ and I followed, rushing past waiters, maids, and people meandering by. We stopped in the hall by Lena's studio as Blake threw open its door.

We found Lena wilted against her easel, the strap of her white silk dress draped down her arm, and her eyes only partially closed. A brush tilted delicately in her hand, ending at a single stroke of Prussian blue paint splashed thick across the canvas. MJ cried out in an anguished moan so striking the birds flew howling from trees. He rushed to his wife, cradling Lena, pleading with her to come back, but she couldn't.

Lena died surrounded by the beauty she created, gripped in the arms of the man who could not save her.

Seventeen

We didn't bury Lena. Blake and MJ followed her wishes for cremation and divided her ashes between two things: the ocean she loved and another odd item of trust she knew would turn heads but wanted, nonetheless. She requested we mix a portion of her ashes with paint and spread it on whatever canvas we saw fit to use. Blake chose the canvas with the Prussian blue streak. He didn't say why, and I didn't ask. I assumed he had his reasons and would divulge them eventually.

He never did.

Blake smeared a curl of paint upon a pallet, removed a portion of Lena's ashes from the cloisonné urn, and mixed them to a deep purple hue. Michael dipped his thumb into the paint, gently smearing the bottom of the canvas where Lena's last stroke had died.

"Don't sell this, Daddy," Michael said in a voice made mature by the moment. "Keep it forever."

"We will, Michael," Blake answered. "We will."

While Lena's first request was simple, the second proved challenging. Fame breeds demand, and for an artist prized in life, the clamor to fill that demand rises tenfold.

News cameras and prying, floating eyes became an escort for each attempted outing. Lena's death became a ghoulish exercise for seedy collectors of the morbidly odd to gather a bit of the artist's last touch. A piece of the body of creation and a photo to prove the moment's authenticity could catch a hefty price from a collector with tastes for amoral exhibits. After a public plea for privacy via the news route, we decided to wait until the notoriety subsided.

As it turned out, we wouldn't have to.

"Where's Michael?" Blake strode into the kitchen, where I was finishing a salad for lunch.

"Reading to MJ by the pool. Why?"

"A fish market on Folly Island called." Blake took a glass to the sink, filled it with water, then brought it to me and sat down. "The manager's friend says he'll help with my mother's ashes as long as we go right now."

"Do you think we should?" I asked, finishing a bite. "MJ's so depressed, and another failed attempt might be too much."

"Can't hurt to try. If it looks like a bust, we'll leave."

"If you say so," I said, sliding my bowl to one side. "Let's go."

We stood as Blake's watch gave a chirp.

"What's that?" I asked and pointed at his wrist.

"Your dose." He juggled my pill bottle from his left trouser pocket and tumbled a pill to his palm. "It's safer this way."

"Safer?" I laughed, crossing my arms. "Safer than what?"

"Safer than letting you take them alone."

"Why can't I take them alone?"

"You know why."

"No, I don't." That was a lie, but I needed to hear it from him. "Why can't I take them alone?"

"Dad never thought my mother would do what she did, so we'll be more careful with you."

"Just who in the hell is we?" I asked, gripping the back of my chair. "There was no we when you decided I needed to limit my writing so my high times would be less frequent. And we don't carry a bottle of pills in our pocket every day, either. So, don't use we to ease your guilt in keeping your wife doped up for your convenience, all right? I'm not your mother."

"And you're not going to be." Blake grabbed the water and held it in front of my chest. "Just swallow the pill."

My temper piqued, my temperature rose, and I recalled distant memories of olive-drab gherkins and glass shattered over the floor. The feeling subsided, and I pinched the pill before flushing it down with my drink.

"You order me like that again," I said, swiping a hand on my mouth, "you'd better do it in a room without so many sharp objects around."

Blake shoved his chair and barged from the kitchen with a stride so deep he could have been chasing combatants. Gone was the lightness he held weeks before, kissing his wife under ivy-webbed shade, promising a more tender start. He was changing into what his father had become, a man lost to a deluge of fear that had become his birthright upon death. It was a familial chasm in which Blake had fallen. The Bradley inheritance of fear.

The fish market was free of usual gawkers, replaced instead by the primal signs of life by the sea. Deep-tanned men, piles of nets, and the awarded tools of a seaborne trade scattered among trawlers and docks. We were the contrast, standing by the car, dressed in funereal attire, wondering what to do next.

"Mr. Bradley?" A lanky man in coveralls emerged from the office across the lot. "Are you Mr. Bradley?"

"I'm Blake Bradley."

"Name's Forrest." The man smiled and tilted his hat when he stopped. "Forrest Gump."

"What?" Blake's cold expression ended the joke. "Now's not the time for a prank."

"No, sir. Not a prank." The man dropped his eyes to his boots and slipped the hat from his head. "I was told I should say that to you. The movie's so popular now, and we're shrimpers, so we thought—"

"Everyone back in the car." Blake snatched Michael's hand. "This is bullshit."

"No, it's not." Ethan emerged from the same door as the man, flagging a hand as he walked. "It was a lousy attempt at humor, and I sent this poor bastard out here to do it. Sorry, John." Ethan patted his friend's arm, sending him back to the dock.

"Apologies, old man." Ethan clipped a nod toward Blake. "My timing never was very good."

"No, Bennet. It wasn't."

Michael tugged Ethan's arm. "Hi, Ethan."

"Hey, buddy." Ethan unbuttoned his suit coat and crouched. "You all right?"

"I'm okay." Michael sniffed and hugged Lena's urn. "I miss Grandma Lena, though. I miss how she painted with me."

"Well, listen," Ethan smiled and tapped Michael's nose, "every time the sun rises and sets, you look to the heavens and paint whatever you see. That'll be like painting with Grandma. Okay?"

Michael gave a slight shrug. "Okay."

Ethan stood, kissing my cheek. "Been a few months, Sarah. Mama sent honey, and Abby says—"

"Want to tell us what you're doing here, Bennet," Blake said.

Ethan grinned, pocketing his hands. "You know, Blake, one of these days, you'll call me by my Christian name, and I'll fall over dead from hearing it."

"Then I'll make sure to speak louder than hell."

"Knock it off," I said, glaring between them. "This isn't a pissing contest."

Ethan smirked before turning to shake MJ's hand. "Nice to meet you, Mr. Bradley. I'm Ethan Bennet. Sorry to hear about your wife's passing, sir. She's done a lot for shrimpers like me, and we love her for that." MJ nodded as Ethan went on. "I imagine in a hundred years or so, these boats will be gone, and the men who ran them will be reduced to some charming Southern myth. But when people see your wife's paintings of a shrimper's kid casting his net against a bright orange sun, they'll know something that beautiful could never have been just a myth."

MJ thanked him, taking the urn from Michael's arms as Ethan led us all to the dock.

"I'm taking you on the water today," Ethan said. "No one will follow or even get close."

"Where's the boat?" Michael swept his eyes toward the docks.

"What do you mean, where's the boat?" Ethan asked. "We're surrounded by boats."

"These are just shrimp boats, Ethan," Michael said.

"Yeah," Blake said. "These are just shrimp boats, Ethan."

"I don't give a damn what kind of boat it is," MJ snapped. "I'm tired and miss your mother. I want to do this and go back to the house."

Blake apologized, draping an arm at MJ's shoulders and walking him to the boat Ethan held.

"She's not pretty." Ethan helped us over planks fastened between the boat and the dock. "Deck is patchwork, and she's stripped to the boards, but the wheelhouse has seats."

The docks erupted in a commotion behind us as vans skidded into the lot and reporters scrambled, flashing their cameras and shouting at us.

"There ya go, Captain Wonderful." Blake gestured to the mob as we entered the wheelhouse, claiming four folding chairs by the wall. "Have any solutions for that?"

"Captain Wonderful?" Ethan laughed, starting the engine with a sputtering roar. "I like that, Blake. And yes. Captain Wonderful planned a blockade."

"One boat hardly makes a blockade," I said.

"Your lack of confidence is insulting, Shakespeare."

"It's not a lack of confidence, Ethan. That's a fact. We've tried this excursion six times. Believe me, one stripped-down trawler won't keep them away."

"You're right about that." Ethan pulled the throttle, picking up speed and hurling the boat toward the bay. "One stripped-down trawler isn't much of a match, so I made a phone call, and I got us ten."

Blake and I gazed over the stern and saw a cadre of shrimp boats, outriggers down, with nets waving like drapes in a gale.

"Ethan, thank you," I said, taking his hand. "Thank you for this."

"Captain Wonderful is happy to oblige."

Michael squealed as we pitched, delighted at the richness between ocean and sky. Dolphins raced at our sides, slick and wet with the sea. Gulls soared overhead, screeching and snatching the fish in our wake.

"Look, Momma. Pelicans," Michael said, pointing through windows empty of glass. "Dolphins too."

"They come for the shrimp like we do," Ethan shouted over the engine's thick drum. "There's nothing better than the Atlantic, Michael. Don't forget that. And don't ever leave it."

"Come on, Daddy." Michael tugged Blake's hand. "Take me on deck."

"I'll take you, Michael." I stood and kicked off my shoes.

"Not now," Blake said, snatching my wrist. "We're moving too fast."

"She'll be fine out there, Blake." Ethan eyed Blake's grip on my arm. "Girl used to run on these things half-naked as a kid."

"Now's not the time." Blake gestured toward MJ. He was fragile, hunched, cradling Lena's urn like a child.

"Daddy's right, Michael," I said, ashamed of myself. "Now's not the time."

We traveled another three miles before Ethan cut the engine, centering us inside the ring of trawlers far from shore. The event was somber. Gulls screamed, water pitched, and each man lined their decks, removing their hats as they prayed.

MJ whispered something too quiet to hear, raised the fine dust of his wife overhead, and with a swing of his arm, Lena disappeared on the breeze. MJ broke down. He'd lost his life's breath. The heart that answered his own turned on him, declaring his efforts a needless concern. Lena hadn't just taken her own life in protest of living; she left her husband with the worst torture those left behind could endure.

He'd wonder *if only* for the rest of what life he had left.

The sun dipped at the docks, and everything was covered in a warm, auburn haze. We stood in the lot, where MJ thanked Ethan before returning to the car.

"Come to my house, Ethan." Michael tapped Ethan's arm. "Dad bought me a hamster."

"Not now, Michael," I said. "Ethan has to get back."

"Your mom's right. I'd better get home before Mama Nash whips me good."

Michael whimpered, hugging Ethan's leg before running to MJ.

"Thanks for the help, Bennet," Blake said. "This certainly was an... ostentatious effort."

"Ostentatious effort?" Ethan laughed. "Why does that sound like an insult framed inside a fancy word?"

"Would you like me to spell it for you? Explain the definition, perhaps?"

"No worries, old man. I've got a dictionary at home. Next time Sarah's in town, we'll figure it out over drinks."

"That's enough," I said, turning to Ethan. "Tell Mama I'll be home once MJ is settled."

"She'll understand." Ethan reached up, undoing his tie. "So, when do we bite the Big Apple?"

"Should be soon," Blake said. "Found an office in Manhattan three months ago, and final meetings for the purchase are set for next week."

"Hard to imagine you living in a big city, Sarah."

"I'm staying in Charleston until Blake finds a place in New York, and MJ can travel."

"That won't take long." Blake touched my back. "I don't like leaving Sarah alone."

"Send her home with me." Ethan shared glances between Blake and me. "Michael too. Mama would love that."

"Sarah can't go running to Bayport every time you people tell her to, Bennet."

"We're not *you people*. We're family, same as blood. And I'm not telling her to run home. I'm suggesting she—"

"Forget it, Bennet. I don't want Sarah alone for too long."

"But being alone in Charleston with a sick man is okay?"

"She won't be alone," Blake said. "My mother's nurses are there."

"She won't be alone in Bayport, either. She'll have all of us."

"Sarah needs certain help, Bennet. Certain... things."

"Blake, don't—" I whispered, seizing his hand.

"What she needs is a break," Ethan said. "Look at her, for Christ's sake. Her hair's pinned up, she's got bags under her eyes big enough to float a trawler, and she looks damn thin."

"Sarah's different now, Bennet. You don't know what she needs."

"I know what I saw on that boat today." Ethan pointed toward the docks. "Sarah wanted to take Michael on deck, and you pounced on her like a gator at feeding time. The woman can't blink without asking you first."

"No, Ethan," I said. "That's not why Blake did that. MJ was—"

"You don't know what Sarah needs. What she's been through."

"Blake, no..."

"I know her better than you think I do. I grew up with her."

"I'm aware of your history, Bennet. Lucky for me, you screwed up."

Ethan stepped nearer to Blake. "You have a problem with me being close to your wife?"

"You're not important enough to be a problem. Men like you never are."

"What's wrong with you two?" I shoved them apart. "Michael's watching you both act like fools."

"Mama's honey's in the truck behind the office, Sarah." Ethan kept his eyes trained on Blake. "Help me get it."

"Let's go," I said.

"Don't be long," Blake shouted as we left. "Dad needs to get home."

I agreed, following Ethan behind the office at the end of the lot.

Ethan tugged off his jacket and slapped it onto the truck's dusty hood. "That bastard's an inch away from being Buster Mills, Sarah. What're you still doing with him?"

"With Lena dying and MJ not well, we're on edge, that's all."

"He's got you pinned to his side like a trophy. It's not normal for a man to act like that. You need to come home."

"I told you, I can't. I have to help MJ while Blake's in New York."

"Why can't Blake help his father? It's his father."

"He's my father too. The man just lost his wife, and Blake's trying to keep the family business from dying before his father does. You should at least understand that."

Ethan slumped on the truck. "How do I do this, Sarah? How do I breathe every day without you giving me the air to do it?"

"This isn't the end," I said, lifting his hand to my cheek. "No matter where I am or what happens, I'll always love you, Ethan. I'll always come back."

But fate would move in, relegating Ethan's face to a memory I couldn't abide, and I wouldn't see him or the home I loved for another seven years.

Eighteen

Each death carries its own wake of tragedy, but the starvation of a soul without its kindred half was a pain Blake's father couldn't endure, and within two months of Lena's passing, MJ Bradley died. MJ's last words on his deathbed were, "Your mother held monsters too close to her heart. It was a burden I couldn't remove."

I'd like to think that, in his final moments, MJ saw a chance to let go of the guilt that haunted him, and those words somehow came as comfort. It would be years before Blake and I spoke of what MJ said that day. The intensity of it scorched across Blake's face, so I never tried. We just took with us the realization that Blake and I had become, with the loss of our parents, orphans alone in the world.

In the coming months, our life progressed beyond the shores of our Lowcountry home. We exchanged the golden vistas of a slower-paced life for a stark and gray version in New York. We moved into a penthouse on the High Line in Chelsea. It was a cold, echoing fortress of a thing with stone floors and white walls, and I found its austere design annoyingly sterile.

Our furniture came within the first week of our arrival. Having familiar items smoothed the sharpness of the place, softening its features with memories of home. We filled the walls with photos of Michael and as much of Lena's work as possible.

Blake named Lena's final painting *Lena's Blue*, hanging it over the mantel. Due to the haunting nature of its birth, the canvas was controversially prized, but Blake refused every offer, saying, "There's no price for this piece. Don't call here again." Then he'd hang up.

On the opposite wall were Michael's portraits from Lena's *Sky* series, *The Creative*. Their brightness and beauty drew the rawness of the room into finer detail, making it less cavernous and more like a home.

Eight months had passed since we last saw Charleston, and I could not make good on Ethan's request to come home. The stress of the move and all the death took a toll on my ever-heaving mind, making my instances of angry rebellion more recurrent. Loosening his grip, Blake left a single pill on my bedside table or in a dish, helping me feel less controlled. But there was no freedom for me in New York. No fireflies in which to run and no moonlight casting its glow. The lack of preternatural allowances left me hollow inside, and I ached for my home every day.

"How d'you like the new office?" Blake asked, setting two boxes of files on my desk. "Room's smaller than Charleston's, but it's quiet enough."

"It's all right," I said, sliding a book to its shelf.

"Just all right?" Blake strode to a wall lined with polished wood cases. "Look at these built-ins, honey. Plenty of space for your things. And that skylight means you'll know the flight path of every pigeon in New York. And what they ate."

"Very funny." I forced a laugh and slid another book to its spot. "That skylight will look like a Rorschach by lunch every day."

"Place is pretty small," he said, walking around. "Looked bigger when we saw it last month."

"Last month, it didn't have my massive desk against the wall and boxes of books on the floor."

"But you wanted this room, didn't you? When we met with the realtor, you said it was good. Am I wrong?"

"This isn't about the office, Blake. I miss everyone. I miss being home."

"It's the change, honey. Doctors said you'll need time to adjust, remember?" Blake leaned closer, rubbing my back. "We'll find another room for your things. An office you'll like."

Blake took my hand, and we left for the living room to sit on the sofa that faced the city outside.

"We don't do this enough," I said, curling under his arm. His cologne was sweet, and I relaxed, feeling his heartbeat against the palm of my hand. "Not nearly enough."

"What's that?"

"Sitting like this. Close, like we used to. It makes me feel better, but we don't do it enough."

Drawing a thumb down my jaw, Blake smiled. "I'll need to work on that, then."

"That's what I want. I want us to work on things, Blake. On us. Let's make this move a fresh start for us both."

"This is a fresh start. New home, new city, new company."

"What about us?" I asked, sitting up. "Let's go somewhere nice. Somewhere open and bright. I want to get out of this city."

"We barely have desks unpacked at the offices." Blake stood, moving to the windows where he pressed a hand on the glass. "We're hiring staff, interviewing editors, and there's so much work to be done."

"We can do that when we come back."

"Hiring can't wait. It's a business, Sarah. That means editors, writers, marketing—"

I slumped, muttering, "You're broken too."

"Don't read anything into this," he said, looking back. "I have to work."

"Lena haunts you, Blake. You'll never let go of memories of her which means you'll never let anyone close. Even me."

"Hiring staff doesn't mean I'm not getting close. It means I'm too busy to leave."

"You're hiding at Veritas. That building, the books. It's safe for you there like Bayport is safe for me."

"Should I ignore everything?" he asked. "Let Veritas die? Throw it away on a whim?"

"Don't you see what you're doing?" I shoved from the sofa to stand at his side. "Lena made you afraid to reach out, but I'm not Lena. There's no need to push me away like you did with her."

"I never pushed my mother away. She pushed me."

"She had to, Blake. You told me MJ locked your bedroom door that night after your birthday party, but that's not what happened."

"I think I'd remember the first time my mother tried killing herself. Details like that are hard to forget. Dad locked me in there so I wouldn't see."

"MJ didn't lock your door that night. Lena did."

Blake's eyes banked to mine. "Mother didn't lock that door."

"She did, Blake. She told me she did."

"When did she tell you that?"

"The night she died," I said. "Lena was afraid she'd hurt you, and that's why she pushed you away. She loved you. She wanted you safe."

"Then she should have taken her meds." Blake sighed and moved to the fireplace with that brilliant blue streak just above. "Can't change what's already done."

"But we can learn from it, can't we?" I eased closer, lifting his hand. "Let me be close to you, Blake. What happened to Lena won't happen to me. I promise it won't."

"You sure?" Blake studied me, placidly searching my face. "Did you take your medications today?"

A lie has only seconds to live. Once spat from the tongue, it's betrayed by the face. The eyes deflect, lips flush red, and the voice raises breathlessly to an inhuman pitch. Blake knew I hadn't taken my pills. He saw telltale tremors in both of my hands, the unfocused drift of my eyes, and the heaving emotions let loose from their cage. The tablets he left in the dish by the stove found their way into toilets and sinks or dropped to the recesses of garbage can bags. Medication became a tyrant for me. A symbol of brokenness I didn't dare face and existence I couldn't accept.

"I wanted to write," I said, dropping his hand and dragging away to my chair. "I can't write when I take them, so I didn't."

"So, you lied about taking the meds?"

"Yes, Blake. I lied."

"Don't tell me what happened to my mother won't happen to you when you're doing the same things. What'd you do with the pill?"

"This isn't a hoarding situation. I just didn't take it."

"What'd you do with it, then?"

"I flushed them."

"Them? How many? And try not to lie again. At least give me that much."

"All of them. All this week."

"Jesus. All week?" Blake dropped to a chair, resting his head in his hands. "What if you hurt yourself, Sarah? What if—"

"Writing is hard when I take them. Pills fog me out, and I can't think straight."

"We'll ask the doctor to adjust the dose or try something else."

"That won't change what they do to me, Blake. My emotions are dead when I take them. I can't remember things, and I don't like it."

"Do you like hallucinations?" he asked. "The nightmares you have? You had one last night. I heard you go into the office."

"How would you know? You were in the other bedroom as usual."

"I heard you typing. I know what you were doing in there."

"What I was *doing* in there?" I pushed from the chair and stood by the windows again. "I was being a writer. When you let me, that is."

"You were writing nightmares, Sarah. *Badlands* came from a nightmare. All your stories do."

I turned quickly and faced him. "And they've all been bestsellers, haven't they, Blake? Everyone knows you, me, and Veritas. And here we are in New York, battling with the big boys. And once you get one more out of me, one more big book that smashes records and makes publishing history, you'll win. So, here." I held both wrists in his face. "Slice it open and bring me a daisy wheel. Let me bleed out your next famous novel. Isn't that what you wanted? To pave the road of Veritas's rise to glory with my dirty little stories. Isn't that what you asked for? Isn't that why you married me?"

"I married you because I loved you, Sarah. I loved you then, and I love you right now."

"You married me because you needed a project. Something to pet and control and—"

"You're going to kill us," he said, rocking with his hands in his hair. "You'll die like my mother, and Michael will be cursed with it, Sarah."

"Cursed?" Lena's final words burned the air. "What'd you say?"

"You'll kill yourself. Then I'll die from guilt like my father, and Michael will never know why. You're cursing us all. Including our son."

Sitting on the table's edge, I said, "That won't happen to us. Lena was—"

"Michael will remember the laughter and spinning in your chair. He'll remember the lights, the colors, and the music, but then he'll remember the screams and the guilt from not being able to stop it, and it'll haunt him, Sarah. He'll feel it for the rest of his life."

There was no more conversation after that. I stood, offered my hand, and told Blake, "Bring me the pill."

SB Thorn died that night. There was no fanfare, no lofty reports of her death. She just faded into the shadows of has-been obscurity where, sometimes, someone might see a worn dust jacket of one of her books and sadly remark, "Whatever happened to her?"

Nineteen

By Christmas, Veritas's move was nearly complete, and we were a fixture in New York's competitive publishing mecca. With three floors overlooking Manhattan, Blake joked we were ready to, "Plot and plan our attack."

Blake was fearless, taking on writers and subject matter poised on the edge of brute shock. We were David aiming slingshots at the hearts of our Goliath rivals, making the name Veritas too weak against its own rise. During a coming-out event at the Veritas offices, Blake stood on a desk beneath a Veritas banner pinned overhead.

He thanked everyone, explaining how Veritas began in a brick corner building in Charleston forty years before. Blake described being a boy and how the smell of leather from the books in MJ's office was the driving force from which his passions grew. And he thanked me, pointing over the crowd as he shouted, "And she's the driving force from which Veritas grew."

Then Blake pulled the banner away to present Veritas's new name, WhiteThorn.

Blake called it a tribute to two women who meant more to him than anything and when he leapt from the desk, saying he'd love me forever, I looked into his adoring eyes and readily answered, "Then I'll give you forever right now."

We were the new darlings in Chelsea, welcomed in closed social circles with Blake's reputation and my notorious SB Thorn moniker making waves in exclusive huddles of whispered conversation. Seeing my discomfort, Blake began a preemptive defense whenever we'd enter a room. Noting the lips cupped close to ears, he'd smile widely and loudly proclaim, "She learned the filthiest parts from me."

That worked to muzzle the mongers unable to comprehend the formidable efforts of a man arrogant enough to love his wife without regret in front of hundreds of people intent on cutting her down. That was something, they learned, Blake wouldn't allow.

We attended Michael's school functions regularly, our pride growing larger with every success he achieved. He bloomed under the reverie of urban habits, sketching the faces of people who spent their days on the street. When he asked to see a shrimp boat to draw or a harbor with views he could paint, we hoped for the best and offered the only place we could think of, New York Harbor.

As grand as it was, with its hurried tugs and bustling exploits of trade, its natural surroundings were meager compared to what Michael was accustomed to seeing, and, holding Blake's hand aboard the Staten Island Ferry, he looked sadly upon the water and said, "There are no shrimpers here. There are no nets and there is no bright green sea grass. There is no harbor here."

Blake gathered Michael, answering, "Your grandmother would say you're being a pest. If you don't see a harbor the way you would like, then draw one the way that you see."

Each week he and Blake ventured to the container dock where Michael sketched longshoremen working the barges. The vessels, large, slow and smelling of diesel, stacked high with steel boxes, and Michael marveled at the Cyrillic, Asian, and Arabic script adorning their sides. Blake discovered in Michael what Lena had seen; maturity of talent in a second chance child. Michael would have the gift of a normal life Blake never had. Michael's days would be calm, protected, and as far from madness as Blake could keep him. That was a silent pledge Blake had made but that fate would not let him have.

"Mama called about presents we sent." Blake brought his plate to the dinner table, setting Michael's down before taking a seat. "Complaining, of course."

"That's a shocker," I said, pouring tea. "What'd she say?"

"That you spent too much on wrapping paper and the Sunday comics were just as good to slap on a box."

Michael laughed. "Mama's too cheap."

"Why'd you ship boxes to your mom's house?" Blake asked.

"Delivery to Frogcreek is dicey. You know that. I always send gifts to Mother's."

"So Ethan can get them?"

"Alicia lives there too. Either one could have gotten them."

Michael chimed in. "I got Ethan's present yesterday. He asked what I wanted for Christmas, and I said—"

"Stop asking that man for toys," Blake said, salting his plate. "Probably bugs him."

"No, it doesn't, Daddy. Ethan makes toys for Edward too, so we have the same stuff." Michael turned back to me. "Can we go to Bayport again? I miss Edward, and Mama was crying when I talked with her."

"Crying?" I asked. "How was she crying?"

"That woman never cries," Blake said. "Probably had the sniffles or something."

"Uh-uh," Michael insisted. "She was crying."

"How'd she sound to you, Blake?"

"Quieter than usual, but she talked about wrapping paper then asked to speak to Michael."

"Did she say anything was wrong? Did you ask?"

"No, I didn't ask. She's an old woman who thinks God runs everything. Even if I did ask, you know she'd just lie."

"She felt better before we hung up," Michael said.

"Why?" I asked. "What'd she say?"

"She made me promise to make good grades and to always do as you say. Stuff like that. I told her I would. Then she breathed like she was smiling or something."

"I'm calling home."

"Mama's not there," Blake said, stabbing beans with his fork. "She's got a revival in Yemassee and needed to go."

"Then I'll call Ethan. Or one of the girls."

"Well, since Alicia's probably working and Abby's not allowed to answer the phone, I guess you'll call Ethan, won't you?"

I stood, slapping a napkin to the seat of the chair. "Maybe I will."

"I wish you guys wouldn't fight anymore," Michael mumbled as I strode to the office.

The phone rang four times before Ethan picked up, and I blurted, "What's wrong?"

"What's wrong?" Ethan chuckled and I heard the receiver shift on his ear. "I've been stripping trawlers since dawn, that's what's wrong. What's wrong with you?"

"Michael said Mama was crying today. Is everything all right?"

"As far as I know, sure. Saw her this morning when I dropped off your boxes. She said you spent too much on—"

"Wrapping paper. I know. Was she okay?"

"Seemed fine to me. She said you need to come home and get naked with me, though."

"Ethan. I'm serious."

"Me too. How about phone sex? Talk dirty awhile. See what happens."

Fighting a grin, I said, "Ethan, please? I'm worried. Was she tossing bones?"

"No, and I was there early. Christmas does this to her, especially with you and Michael gone. When are you coming home?"

"I'm trying."

"There's no trying, Sarah. You pick up Michael and get on a plane."

"Things are complicated right now."

"What's so complicated you can't get home in a year?"

I paused, caught in the secret that bound me to Blake and kept me from the only man who would ever know me as whole. "Work is busy right now."

"Work down here. You write better at home."

"I'm not writing."

"What do you mean you're not writing? What're you doing?"

"I'm editing. At WhiteThorn."

"Editing," he said, and a hiss trailed over the phone. "Since when?"

"A few months ago. Blake needed help, so I took a spot as an acquisition editor."

"What about writing? Did you just give it up?"

"Setting the writing aside while WhiteThorn gets on its legs isn't giving up. Blake respects my opinion, so I offered to help."

"Does he respect the fact you've been writing since you were eight, and Sheila raised you to do it?"

"I did do it, Ethan. Writing takes a toll sometimes, and I needed a break."

"What toll? What's wrong with you?"

"Ethan?" I said, lazily spinning the chair. "Tell me about home."

We talked for an hour. Ethan said Abby was good and Edward was talking more despite Buster's lack of proper care. Ethan helped, taking Edward to the beach or on boat rides, or to do any number of mundane things normal in an un-blighted child. While most teen-aged boys enjoyed beachside waves and flirtatiously teasing girls, Edward was still a child, remaining as innocent at fourteen as Michael was at eight.

Ethan said Mama was still just as feisty and Alicia enjoyed a steady rise within the ranks of Bayport's local police. He also mentioned she was spending time with someone whose identity she refused to divulge.

"That woman's a lesbian," he said. "What a goddamned waste of perfectly good tits."

Although Ethan offered Mother's house to Abby at my request, she refused, so Ethan took the offer instead. He and Evan moved in, adding Alicia to their squatter roles three weeks later. They mowed the yard, tended the house, and made sure Mother's Buick stayed oiled.

When I asked about the trawlers, Ethan said he converted two, with one going to a doctor in Savannah. He planned to pour those gains into refinishing details of others until, as he claimed, they'd be millionaires.

"Millionaires?" I laughed. "From polished-up trawlers?"

"Polished-up yachts," Ethan said. "We're building yachts, Miss Thorn. Great, big, polished up yachts."

The conversation ended with Ethan's usual request I return to

Bayport, followed by my mysterious refusals before softening to despondent goodbyes. Had I known we'd be torn apart that very night, I'd have given a critically different answer.

Twenty

With my concerns for Mama at rest, I returned to the kitchen. Michael retreated to his room to feed his nightly *Rugrats* addiction while the ghostly songs of a Celtic voice melted over the living room walls.

Blake roamed the kitchen, filling two mugs with a steaming dark roast.

"Want coffee?" he asked.

"Sounds good."

"Michael asked about Christmas displays on Fifth," he said. "Want to go? Crowds should thin out in an hour."

I winced, considering the ache in my skull. "I'm not sure."

"Why not?" Blake glanced at the green crystal dish by the stove. The plate sat empty of the pills I dissolved in the toilet that morning. "You feeling all right?"

"Just tired from chasing Michael today."

"Take your meds this morning?"

"Don't I always?"

"We both know you don't," he said and nudged at my wrist. "Let me see."

"I don't have tremors, Blake. I'm tired." Taking the mug from Blake's grip steadied the rising shake in my hands. "Snowplows cleared the streets, and I couldn't keep Michael off the mounds. He was like a greyhound chasing those things."

We walked to the living room and settled into the white leather chairs by the windows. As the sun set in the late evening sky, the buildings grew darker and I sampled my coffee, admiring fractals of orange and blue painting the windows outside.

"They're so bright," I said. "Like colorful shells on the beach. Pretty."

Blake lifted his mug. "But not Bayport pretty? Right?"

"Not like that, no." I smiled, setting my mug on the coffee table. "But why don't we go there for Christmas? It's been a year since we moved, and Michael was asking for Edward."

"For Christmas?" Blake eased from his chair, moving to the windows. "You want to go to Bayport on our first Christmas in New York?"

"They'd love to see us, Blake. I miss everyone, and Michael does too. You never needed connections like that, but we do."

"They don't even know you, Sarah," he said, glancing at me. "You never took your meds down there. You'd play, write, and laugh with them, then you'd come home, and I'd get the angry, terrified woman coming down from her raging mental high. Those people don't know you at all."

"They grew up with me. They know me just fine."

"Do they?" he asked, slamming the coffee mug to the table. "And how well does Ethan know you? Pretty close?"

"We're not doing this now." Pushing from the chair, I rounded the sofa and paced from the room. "Seek therapy for that paranoia, Blake. It's starting to get pretty dull."

"You think I don't hear it in your voice when you talk about him? You think I don't know why you want to go back?"

"I want to go back because I miss them," I said in a turn. "I'm not avoiding the tragedy of my dire existence, and I'm not having an affair with a man living a thousand miles below us."

"That's a lie. You're in love with Ethan Bennet, and you're a goddamned liar."

The look on Blake's face was so bitter, so infused with disdain, it unhinged something in me, and I launched, shoving him back to the glass.

"You know what Mama says about affairs, Blake?" I said, grappling his shirt. "She says men run and women are pushed. Have you pushed me, Blake? Who holds me when I'm scared? When I see the monsters and feel the fear? Who holds your wife when she's screaming at night? Is it you? Or a little gray pill?"

We barely breathed after that. We stared at one another, trembling and trapped in a mutual gaze as tears drained out of our eyes.

"Can we go?" Michael paced in, entranced by the flashes and beeps on his Gameboy. "Let me sit on Dad's shoulders, okay? He's tall, and I'll see more stuff."

"All right," Blake murmured, thumbing a tear from my chin. "Get your boots."

Fifth Avenue was a sea of black woolen coats on the walk. The activity weighed on my already aching head, and the argument with Blake forged a quiet wedge, making the outing more strenuous than it already was. With Michael perched high, we walked among the murmuring crowds, enjoying views of colorful lights, jubilant music, and financially exclusive toys. I brushed in front of Blake, feeling the warmth of his hand cupping mine.

"I'm so sorry," he said, sweeping me into his chest. "I love you, Sarah." Blake dipped, and I reached for his neck, pulling him into a kiss.

That was the pattern of our marriage. A moment of normalcy invaded by cruelty, softened by a warm touch or a whisper of sympathy. It was the template of our strife, and the subsequent healing for the sake of a love spent licking its wounds and a boy who needed us whole.

"Let me down, Daddy," Michael said, wiggling his legs. "It's boring up here."

Blake set Michael on the walk, telling him, "Don't run off, or we'll go back to—"

"Snowplows!" Before Blake could finish, Michael dashed for a landscape of peaks by the curb. "Snowplows were here. Look at the piles."

"We came for windows, Michael." Blake waved at displays full of chattering toys. "Santa's playing drums with his elves over here."

Michael ignored him, scaling the sides of an ice-covered mound. "They're like mountains, Daddy. Almost taller than you."

"I'll get him," I said, cinching the belt on my coat. "Find a display with something more interesting than dirty road snow."

Blake left to search while I tackled the glistening walk. "Michael? That mound is too close to the road."

"But it's an iceberg, Momma. Like the one that hit the Gigantic. The man at the container dock told me the story."

"You mean the *Titanic*," I said, massaging my temple. "Not very smart, playing with icebergs. The captain should have said Mama's poem."

"There wasn't a riptide. Just an iceberg, like the dock worker said."

"If the captain said the poem, the iceberg wouldn't have done that." I knelt, pulling Michael off the mound before tying the scarf to his neck. "And where are we now, Cherie?"

"Don't make me say Mama's dumb poem," he whined. "That's for babies to say."

"Just once to remember where the monsters are, honey."

"This is the city. There are no monsters here."

Blake called for me, but his voice was muffled beneath idling traffic and the rising white noise in my head.

"There are always monsters," I said, holding his arms. "Say it, Michael. Where are we now, Cherie?"

"Daddy?" Michael peered over my shoulder to Blake. "We're at Mama Nash's. We're playing beneath the sea."

"And why should we be careful there?" My vision blurred, and I stammered through skull-piercing pain. "When we... play... beneath... the sea?"

"There is no sea here, Momma. This is a high time you're having. That's all. Come back to me, Momma. Come back to me now."

"Because death lives in the waves," I said. "Beyond the ocean deep. God blinks inside the fireflies, and His tides lay us asleep."

"Momma, no—" Michael twisted, his feet giving way on the ice as he fell.

I heard voices and screaming and saw crimson on white...

...and then all the world went black.

Twenty-One

M eted purrs of machinery ticked into my ears, and I blinked. My eyes wouldn't focus, but I smelled the motley scents of Betadine mingling with faint odors of institutional food and immediately knew where I was.

"Hospital?"

"Praise Jesus," Mama murmured, snatching me up. "Come back to us, baby. Come back."

A strained voice whispered, "Ma'am, hospital rules don't allow visitors to lift the patients. I've already told you that twice."

"Don't tell me what to do with my child."

"Her husband's down the hall. Should I get him?"

"Go ahead," Mama snapped. "And, while you're at it, jump your jiggly, round butt off that bridge out there too."

The voice mumbled about security, and I heard shoes squeaking and leaving the room.

"Mama? I'm in a hospital?"

"You had a spell, baby."

"A spell?" I asked with a cough. "What kind of a spell?"

"Just a spell," she said, kissing me once.

My vision was blurry, and I winced at the faded red streaks on my arms. "What happened to me?"

"Just scratches. I made healing prayers, so they won't even show."

"Scratches? From what?"

"Don't mind that now." Mama rocked me, petting my hair. "We

should have brought the brush with us, baby. Your hair needs a good heavy stroke."

"Us? Who else is here?"

"'Licia come too. Your man called, so we hopped on a plane."

"Did Abby come? Why am I here? What happened?"

"Don't talk, honey." Blake stepped through the door with the nurse. She was short and plump with hips wider than a pelican's nest and lips that barely held any tint.

"Mrs. Bradley needs her IVs checked." The nurse thrust a hand toward Mama. "But that woman got in my way. She was throwing red dust on the floor and rubbing honey on your wife's gums with her bare hands. That's not sanitary."

Mama smoothed the bed sheets and said, "I have special honey back home. Use it to kill pests what get in the way. Want me to bring you a little?"

"Jesus, Miss Nash." Blake pulled Mama away and turned to the terrified nurse. "Don't mind her. She's just being protective."

"She's just making terroristic threats is what she's doing." Alicia flashed her badge from the door. "Grandma's harmless, but I'd move on unless you fancy going bald overnight."

The nurse adjusted her clipboard before stomping away from the room.

"Alicia?" I smiled and reached out. "I'm so glad you're here."

"We missed you, Sarah." Alicia gathered my hands as she sat. "Bayport's downright dull with you gone."

Alicia was a handsome woman. Her features were angular, with dark, deep-set eyes and thin lips, but the perceptibility of her expression always gave her thoughts away. She was an honest person with an honest face, and I knew, with her features twisted in soft aberration, something was terribly wrong.

"Why am I here?" I asked. "Was I in an accident? Who's watching Michael?"

"Where's the doctor?" Blake leaned into the hall.

"Boy, hold your wife," Mama said.

"Is something wrong with Abby?" I asked. "With Edward?"

"No." Alicia banked her eyes toward Blake. "They're good."

"Something's wrong with Ethan?"

Mama looked back. "Boy, I just said, hold your wife."

Alicia stood, and Blake took her spot on the bed. "It's all right, honey." He rubbed my hands while Mama prayed, and Alicia stared at her shoes.

"You have scratches, too," I said, tracing the marks on Blake's neck. "How'd we get them?"

"From you. You lashed out that night."

"What night?" I asked, sitting up. "Was there an accident? What happened? Where's Michael?"

Blake leaned close in a kiss. Not an embrace, but like a blanket. The subtle press of his body on mine. Safe, secure, and warm.

"I love you, Sarah."

"I love you too. Blake, what—"

"Michael," Blake started, floating his lips on my cheek, "Michael was killed ten days ago when we were looking at windows on Fifth. He slipped on ice and fell under a truck as it backed to the curb. You tried reaching him but couldn't. He died, Sarah. Michael's gone."

"Gone?" I pushed on his shoulders, reading his face. "But I was holding him. I was—"

"He fell."

"No. He didn't. Michael said the riptide poem, and my hand was... my hand—" Michael's face barreled into my mind. Crimson on white. Blood on snow. Eyes thrown open in fear. "He fell?"

"You couldn't help, Sarah."

"I let my son fall?"

"This wasn't your fault."

"Why didn't I hold him?"

"There was nothing you could do."

Trapped in the image of an unending reach for a child already fallen, I choked. My breath seized, breaking free in words of heartache and wailed, painful mourning as I collapsed in Blake's arms, and we cried.

Twenty-Two

Mama sat in the corner of my hospital room, mumbling prayers from her aged King James. "That crap's an annoyance," I said, jamming more clothes into the suitcase. "Go into the hallway or bathroom for all I care, but don't pray around me anymore."

"God gives strength during trials. Praying brings us closer to Him."

"If God wants us closer, maybe He should stop killing babies and making trials. How about that?"

Mama eased from the chair, eyes floating smoothly in their little brown pools. "You're stiff today, baby. Best keep those wits."

"After three weeks of hospital food and enough pills to numb the Grateful Dead, I have no wits to keep. Just stop praying before one of us ends up headfirst through that window back there."

"Still spicy, I see." Alicia stepped in from the hall. "Must mean you're recovering nicely."

"What's that you're wearing?" Mama sneered at Alicia's thin blouse and slacks. "I ain't tending no colds for you dressing too light."

"Really, Grandma?" Alicia snickered. "Three layers of thermals with a kaftan pulled on won't make you warmer than me. You look like a Muppet in a getup like that."

I laughed, thankful for the normalcy of spontaneous wit.

"Where's Blake?" I asked.

"Signing your walking papers." Alicia took a chair by the bed. "I pulled the car out front. Our flight's at three-thirty."

"Thank you for coming with Mama. Blake's got no support. Not like family, anyway, and he thinks he doesn't need it."

"He's a loner, our Blake. Likes to keep to himself. Always has."

"He had a difficult childhood, Alicia. Blake's not a bad man."

"Didn't say he was bad. I said he was a loner. Like Bundy or Gacy. Quiet folks like that."

I gave her a chastising look. "Just be kind to him, please?"

"How am I not kind?" she asked, slipping two sticks of gum into her mouth. "I haven't shot the son of a bitch once since we came. That's damn kind if you ask me."

"Hush up 'Licia." Mama took my elbow and eased me down to the bed. "That man's been sweet the whole time we been here. He got us at the airport, and when we told him we were staying at the Holly Days Inn, he said that place wasn't good enough for ladies like us, so he put us in that Plaza place. And it shined, baby. Like a brand-new penny, it shined."

Alicia nodded, smiling at the delighted narration of an innocent. A woman bred under the soft, naked whispers of natural things like starfish in tide pools and riptide disasters. For Mama, New York was a mythical place full of creatures whelped from stone, and she was in awe of their welcome.

"We went to your office," Mama said. "It was messy, so I cleaned it, but the windows were clear, like being up in the clouds. We went to the park, and your Blake showed me snow, baby. He taught me to make snowballs, and we threw them at 'Licia, then he smiled, and I held him, and he cried a little, but I told him to settle his heart, so he did." Mama reached over, lifting my chin. "And when he wasn't with us, Blake was here, whispering so close to your ear, I'd like to die from the love pouring from that man's breath. When you had your bad dreams, grabbing for pens to spill out your grief, he held you that whole time, plucking the papers and giving you more till you got so tired you passed out in his arms. Blake loves you, Cherie. He needs you. Don't never let go of that fact."

"I love him too, Mama. I promise I do."

"All right then," she said, dumping the bag. "Let Mama finish packing this up. You done made a mess of things here."

Mama unpacked my perfectly packed suitcase as I scoured the room for more clothes.

"Anyone talk with Abby this week?" I asked.

"I did," Alicia said. "She says to call as soon as you get home, and she'll answer. Better call Ethan too."

"What for?" I stepped into the bathroom to hide. "He's all right, isn't he?"

"No, he's not all right. He's been calling for days, worried sick. You haven't spoken to him, and I'm tired of fending him off. It's not right, Sarah. You need to talk to that man."

"'Licia. Not our business, child."

"The hell it's not, Grandma." Alicia shoved from the chair. "Ethan's afraid, Sarah. He's worried about you."

"Worried?" I faced her, winding my hair in a braid. "What did you tell him, Alicia?"

"Oh, calm down, princess. I didn't tell him about your lousy fit."

"'Licia. This ain't none of our affair."

"No, Grandma. It's hers. It's her affair. The one we all know about but never admit we see. Well, I do see it. And one half is dying down South while the other is up here doing her goddamn hair."

"You think I don't care, Alicia? Is that it? I care so much that I looked Blake in the eye the night Michael died, and I lied when I said I didn't love Ethan Bennet. I lied to him, Alicia. I lied to the man downstairs right now, fighting to keep his wife sane. I lied to the man who grieved alone, cried alone, and put his son into the ground alone. And I can't do it anymore. It's best to let Ethan go."

"Say goodbye to him first. At least tell him why."

"He doesn't need to know why."

"He does, Sarah. Please."

Mama lunged from the bed. "'Licia, tighten that tongue."

"We can't let this happen, Grandma. It'll kill Ethan if Sarah leaves without saying why. You know it will. Please." Alicia turned back to me. "Listen, Sarah. When Ethan was little, he had a—"

"'Licia!" Mama threw a hand across Alicia's right cheek, the piercing crack of the violent impact looming throughout the room. "Spilling secrets is a sin unless we're ready to spill our own. You ready to spill yours? Mine? Abby's? You still that mouth before God does it for you."

Alicia whimpered, holding her jaw. "Yes, Ma'am."

"Why'd you hit her like that?" I stepped beside Alicia, taking her arm. "She's a grown woman, Mama, and she was only trying to help."

"Grown women know when to tighten their lips. Secrets are God's way of keeping us safe, and when you stray into the business of others, when you tread their secrets, try to pull them apart, I'll slap you down, and I will remind you of that."

The argument ended right there. We never questioned Mama Nash nor challenged her edicts. Her lessons were God's word personified, and she was the guardian of His intent.

Twenty-Three

Tragedy was no stranger to Blake or me, but the death of our child tarnished us both. We were branded, scarred. Mutilated with the disfiguring essence of grief. As we entered our building, greeted with sympathetic whispers of placid-faced doormen, I was surprisingly relieved to be there.

"Everything's ready," Blake said. He held my hand in the elevator, watching numbers flash by the door. "We've made changes to help you heal and adjust."

"Adjust to what?" I asked, looking at him. "To Michael?"

Blake glanced at me, then blinked at the numbers again. "Yes, Sarah. To his being gone."

I couldn't understand what Blake meant. What adjustments could be made to the death of a child? There are none. The death of a child is an affront to nature. It's the thing that weighs us inside while we reluctantly suck in the air meant to keep us moving. It's a contradiction in life. The death of a traveling dawn. It is Eden stopped. There is no adjusting to that.

I closed my eyes as we entered the penthouse, inhaling the scents of a comfortable home familiar in its expanse; the sight of my son and our cherished Lena spread throughout its walls. But when I opened my eyes, the horror facing me had a nearly crippling effect. Nothing but white. No pictures, no paintings, no toys scattered in ruins. No laughter and no life.

Just white.

"What did you do?" I asked, dropping my bags.

"I had to, Sarah. You don't understand."

"Don't understand?" Blake followed as I ran down the hall and threw open Michael's bedroom door. "Blake, no." I moaned at the wearisome space, pounding fists along muted walls where once shrimp boats sailed on oceans. "Everything's gone? You took what was left?"

"Only for now. His things are in storage until you—"

"But you didn't ask me?"

"There was no time. The doctors said it was best if we removed—"

"Michael's things?" I shoved Blake aside and opened the door to my room. There was nothing. No smiles trapped in silver, no eyes wide with joy, nothing to convey my body had once given life. "God, Blake. Why? Those pictures are all we have left."

"We had to, Sarah. You had nightmares about Michael's face. You wouldn't eat or sleep and wouldn't respond to anyone. You screamed and wrote stories. Terrible stories. Nightmares where nothing made sense."

"How did this happen?" I slumped on the bed. "I was holding Michael, and then he was gone? I don't understand how I let Michael go."

"He slipped, Sarah. There was nothing you could do."

"You didn't see what happened. You weren't there."

"I was there. Your hand was on Michael's shoulder, but he slipped."

"How can I not remember?"

"Don't try to remember. Not now."

"And the funeral," I said. "My God, the funeral. You did everything while I was... I was—"

"None of that matters." Blake took my face in his hands. "Everything I did was because I love you. Remember that, Sarah. Always remember I love you."

Twenty-Four

Snow falling on cities is a transformative act. It softens their features, and they lose their grimy textures beneath thick white plumes of falling ice coating their structures like whitewashing muddy children. I'd stare from White Thorn's windows, admiring the chill and bales of froth gathering on cuffs of the city's details. At first, I smiled, but after it was covered, when the cries of the city were muffled beneath buffers of beautiful, feathery ice, I remembered how much I hated it all and how goddamn bloody it was.

"Pill time." Blake strode into my office, rattling the door at his back. He walked to the desk and took a bottle of water from the lower left drawer.

"Stop slamming my door like that," I said.

"I didn't slam it. I closed it."

"Stop closing my door like you're slamming it, then."

Blake husked a laugh, nudging my shoulder with the pill in his hand. "You're agitated. It's the time of year."

"I feel like a Pavlovian dog." Lukewarm *Perrier* wasn't the best, but I swigged it anyway, flushing the pill. "Every time that watch goes off, a pill pops out, and I take it."

"Pavlov's dog was smaller." Blake took the bottle, finishing its contents before dropping it into the little wire bin by the door. "Probably happier too."

"Of course I'm happy. I just swallowed lithium. Isn't that the point?"

"Meds are helping, honey. We need to be watchful this time of year."

"Watchful for what?" I angled around him to sit at the desk. "You think I'm planning some grandiose dive from the roof?"

"This week's hard for us both. The year's been difficult, and we're coming up on... that day."

"Stop saying it like that."

"Like what?"

"That annoying hesitation when you talk about Michael's death," I said. "Like you're tiptoeing around the damned date."

"You're agitated."

"I'm not agitated. I'm tired."

Blake paused, pocketing his hands before saying, "Maybe you should go home for a while."

"And do what? Slog around the penthouse in sweats? No thanks."

"Not the penthouse, Sarah. To Bayport. Maybe you should go home to Bayport."

There was no simple answer to that. I missed Abby and Mama and the warmth of the sun, but thoughts of Ethan's face held me back.

"No," I said, pulling files from a stack by my phone. "I can't go to Bayport right now."

"Why not?" Blake claimed the chair in front of my desk. "Sun, sand, waves. Miss Nash's sausage and shrimp wouldn't be bad, either. A few days on a beach might do us some good."

"Us? Does that mean I can't go alone?"

"That wouldn't be a good idea right now, honey. Not yet."

"Still afraid I'll ditch my pills in the Atlantic somewhere?"

"Am I wrong?" he asked, crossing his legs.

"Dumping meds would be hard since you corralled Mama on your side. I'm sure your occasional updates are terribly enlightening for her."

"She saw you screaming and strapped to a bed last year. That has nothing to do with anything I've said. Later, when you're settled, maybe—"

"When I'm settled?" I asked, folding my arms on the desk. "When does one settle after their child dies, Blake? Two years? Three years? Ten? Is there a timeframe of grief where we clock in and out?"

"I'm doing my best for you, Sarah. I take you to appointments and help with your work. Whatever you've needed, I've done. I'm being as helpful as I possibly can."

"But you're not helping, Blake. John Hatcaden is."

"Provoking me with Hatcaden won't work. You're better, Sarah. Fewer headaches. Less agitation. And we haven't seen tremors or fever in months. The doctors said it would take time after Michael's death for you to—"

"To what? Adjust to the death of my son?" I grabbed more files from the stack. "How can I adjust when you refuse to talk about it?"

"Talking about it would trigger the pain."

"Or help me remember."

Blake blinked at the windows. "If I thought helping you remember would bring Michael back, I would. But some memories are better left buried."

"What about Michael's pictures? His things? You don't let me think of him or talk about him. You change the subject whenever I try."

"This is part of your therapy," he said, still studying the snowfall outside. "You're channeling the emotional process. Redirecting unhealthy thoughts and patterns of—"

"Patterns of behavior?" I scoffed, shaking my head. "Don't bother quoting doctors at me. We see them once a week. If that. All they do is write another prescription."

"The meds are working, though. Aren't they?"

"For you, maybe," I said. "They do nothing but make me into someone else. Someone I don't like. I can't even write anymore."

"Writing on meds is hard for you. You said you can't concentrate."

"I could try without the pills."

"That's not safe, Sarah. You could hurt yourself. The risk is too great."

"So I'm a prisoner now," I said. "An indentured servant. I sit in my nice, gilded office with my nice, gilded pills, then I go home to a nice, gilded cell. Do you have any idea how you sound?"

"I don't care how I sound. I know what could happen if you stop taking your meds."

"You sound like a controlling bastard. That's what you sound like."

Blake burst up, slapping both hands to the desk. "I sound like a husband trying to keep his wife alive because that's what this is, so I don't care how I sound to you. You have a job here. You're good at it. So, I suggest that's what you keep doing."

We stared at one another in what had become a rising contempt over the year since Michael's death. The click of the keyboards, the hushed whispers of the workday advancing outside, and the tick of his watch were all that broke the leaden silence in that room.

"All right." I spun in my chair, hoisting a fat manuscript from a box on the floor. The corners were dog-eared, and it was thick. Heavy. Double the size of a Manhattan phone book. I dropped the ream to my desk with a thud. "My latest addition to WhiteThorn's coffers."

Blake nudged at the blank cover sheet. "No Hatcaden book."

"Why not?"

"You know why not. It's not right for WhiteThorn. We'd be crucified if we published that thing."

"You always said I had an eye for dark-horse books. This is dark-horse."

"No, that's just dark. Too dark. Shouldn't even be reading it."

"It doesn't bother me."

"I don't care, Sarah. Stop bringing it up."

"Then I'll advise Mr. Hatcaden to take it to another publisher. I'll find a struggling house that needs a break and send it to them, but we both know WT needs it."

"We don't need that book. Another like it will come along eventually."

"Not with this message."

"What message?" Blake asked, unbuttoning his shirt cuffs and rolling his sleeves. "The main character's a psychotic prostitute who goes on a murder spree under the sage advice of the demons she sees. She's attacked twice by chapter six and has tortured four men before feeding them to her dogs by chapter eight. Not to mention your murderous prostitute just happens to be a former nun who did some pretty lewd things with her rosary, for God's sake. Can you imagine the press on that thing?"

"It's a story, Blake. Readers will know that."

"Readers will hate it. Women especially. *Badlands* and *Kindred Souls* still get scathing reviews from women. Hatcaden's book is a hundred times worse and has every marker for a publishing disaster. It mocks God, motherhood, sexuality, and psychiatry. You name every socially hazardous topic on the planet, and it's in that book. It's too controversial."

"*Kindred Souls* and *Badlands* were controversial. They still sold."

"They weren't controversial. They were salacious and bloody. Hatcaden's book is controversial." Blake flattened his hands on the desk and leaned in. "You want to go another round with the prim sisters of the Bible belt driving crosses through Bayport's proverbial heart again? Because once they discover the publisher of Hatcaden's bloody treatise was bred under the shelter of their pious wings, all hell will break loose... again."

Pointing to the windows, I said, "Those women complained about every word I wrote, then ran out and bought the next in the series, supposedly, for their husbands."

"Well, they had to have something to burn on their grills."

"The hell they did. They were reading them, Blake."

"So, they were lying when they went on *CNN*, hanging my wife's image in effigy?"

"Through their pearly-white teeth."

"What makes you so sure?" he asked, reclaiming his chair.

"Because they didn't just complain about the books, they quoted chapters word for word. Sex and all."

"This book has more than sex. There's graphic, sometimes violent sex. Not to mention murder and abuse. What the hell are you doing with this thing?"

"What you hired me to do. Pushing a story that'll sell."

"Oh, yeah?" Blake reclined, lacing his hands at his neck. "And what'll Hatcaden do when reporters ask where this story came from? Because that'll happen, Sarah. And that Salinger, Garbo, *I want to be alone* bullshit will only make reporters hungrier to find the guy. What then?"

"I'll make something up."

"Really?" He smirked. "And what will you say?"

"I'll tell them Hatcaden doesn't give interviews. I'll say he lives in an undisclosed facility for the treatment of mental illness."

"And you think that'll work?"

"For a while, it will. After that, who cares?"

"I'll care." Blake stood, pocketed his hands, and paced by the cabinets lining the wall. "That book has an orbit, Sarah. Some people in that orbit know where it came from, and others never should."

"Running from the truth won't make it hurt any less."

"That book isn't the truth." Blake turned. "It's a distortion of the truth. A corruption of truth. And I'm not running. I'm fighting. All I've done is fight. I fight for you, for WhiteThorn, for my father. And now you want me to fight for that book."

"We need this book, Blake. We need it."

"We don't need it, Sarah. You do."

"Maybe," I said. "But I'm doing it anyway. With or without you, we'll see it in print."

"Then do it." Blake strode to the desk, planting a fist on the ream. "But Hatcaden will do no interviews. There'll be no junkets, no dust jacket reveal, and no fanfare book signing bullshit. I don't care how you try to pull it off. It won't happen. Keep this book underground."

"I can't promise something like that. I can't control the buying public."

"You can control what they know about Hatcaden, though. And you'd better." He frowned at the manuscript, fanning its edge. "You identify with her. The character, you admire her."

"Understanding someone doesn't mean you admire them."

"She's abusive, Sarah. Deranged. How can you possibly—"

"It's the struggle, Blake. Mama always said there's a purpose for me, but I can't live like this, so why am I here? That's the struggle. That's what I understand."

Blake reached out, floating a hand on my cheek. "You were young, honey. Mama Nash told you stories to help you understand your moods, the things you saw."

"But there has to be a reason for me. Maybe publishing Hatcaden's book is my purpose."

Blake paused, eyes combing over the smudged cover sheet. He sighed, raised a hand to the back of his neck, and said, "I'll do the edits myself."

"Blake—"

"The staff won't know about Hatcaden, so don't make anyone up. He's a writer and friend, and that's all they'll know."

"All right."

"There're too many *thats* in it. Cut them."

"I will."

"Cut the scene with the pigeons in the parking lot too. That's a darling. Kill it. And the part about dredging the janitor's balls in cat food. That's disgusting."

"It's a metaphor."

"Metaphor, my ass. No man needs to visualize cats gnawing his balls while he's tied to a chair. Hell, that scene made my own balls wanna hide." We both laughed, the first we'd shared in months. "It's too wordy. Weed it to less than ninety thousand."

"Under ninety? Blake, that's—"

"Don't argue, Sarah. We're not paying bills on an overweight novel that will kill us. Cut the damn thing down."

"It won't kill us. It'll open eyes and touch people, Blake. It's going to ravish the world."

"No, honey. It'll *ravage* the world, and WT will lead its charge."

"That won't happen. Trust me. This is right."

"Uh-huh," Blake said, scratching his chin. "There's no title on the cover. What's it called?"

"*Dancing on Third Street.* It's called *Dancing on Third Street.*"

"Catchy." Blake smirked and reached for the door. "Cab's coming in an hour. You going?"

"Wasn't sure that I could."

"Don't do that, Sarah," he said, looking back. "You know I'd never keep you from Michael's grave. I only asked in case you didn't feel like going today."

"I feel all right. I want to go."

"Good. Meet me by the elevators in an hour. Don't be late, or the cab will just leave."

"Blake," I said, rounding the desk. "Don't you think you owe him?"

"Owe who?"

"Hatcaden. You said I'm better. Don't you think we owe him for that?"

Blake rubbed his thumb on the doorknob and said, "My wife just told me she doesn't know why she was born. I don't owe John Hatcaden anything until she does."

Then Blake left my office again.

I couldn't soothe Blake's pain, hearing me question my purpose in life. Blake had a purpose. *I* was his purpose. And he left me to wonder, as I watched him walk away, if having a reason for living wasn't much worse than having no reason at all.

Twenty-Five

⁂

Ten months after Blake's approval, *Dancing on Third Street* made its debut. With an initial print run of ten thousand paperback copies divvied up between bookstores and libraries, our favored dark-horse's reputation rose on eager tongues, breaking free of its reins and straight into the record books as one of the fastest-selling novels of all time. It was controversial. It was protested. And it was lionized. And within two years of its debut, it had sold more than sixty million copies worldwide.

We couldn't bind it fast enough.

Critics both loved and hated it, but everyone called it sensational. The psychiatric field was abuzz with what they described as *an intimate and accurate portrayal of a shattered woman trying to navigate the horrors of her own breaking mind.*

Some called it groundbreaking and innovative. Others burned it. Berkley encased it in a glass time capsule and buried it in honor of its parent, John Hatcaden.

And those prim loudmouths Blake was so worried about? They identified with the book's licentious heroine, Echo Gumson. Echo became an anti-hero to a rising throng of young women feeling lost inside a male-dominated world. She was a dark delegate to the women's movement and a weapon in their arsenal of agenda. Fans made t-shirts featuring the likeness of a frail little blonde with the face of an angel, and large, brown eyes forced open wide in her mania.

Applicable imagery accompanied the likeness, fitting whatever occasion to which Echo applied. From rape centers to sit-ins to protests for equal pay to silly frivolity with a recipe for *Echo Gumson Stew: Add One Bastard, Finely Chopped.*

Her face met us everywhere.

The church didn't condemn Echo Gumson in her journey to find Christ. Instead, they prayed for her kind to have peace in Him. Even Mirabella Nash conceded sympathy for poor Echo's plight.

"Child sees only demons," she said. "What frightful blindness that is."

Reporters hounded WhiteThorn for the whereabouts and life history of John Hatcaden.

"Mr. Hatcaden is an extraordinarily gifted man," I always said in interviews. "He sacrifices for his work and will give no interviews."

It was a joyous game for me. A waltz of cat and mouse exercises tripping through the imagined powers of the press who thought no one untouchable.

John Hatcaden was untouchable.

At one point, for no reason beyond watching mice scatter, I gave an address of 3189 Westward Road. When asked for specifics, I shrugged and said, "You figure it out." They couldn't. Mr. Hatcaden was hiding in painfully obvious sight, and just as Mama often said, those are the secrets to which we are most blind.

It took five years for WhiteThorn to settle from its initial rise upon the wings of Hatcaden's book, and it was still moving. We'd risen to the heights of our industry, but in our golden wake, Blake and I lost what remained of our bond.

The stress of the changes and the already strained condition of our now fourteen-year union was more than we'd expected, and our template of marriage, once broken but navigable, became nothing more than a battlefield we both fought to own.

Twenty-Six

"They'll fall off," Blake said, watching me arrange Apitong animals on Michael's headstone. "Why don't you wait until spring to do this?"

"They're Christmas gifts, Blake. When the snow melts, they'll be lying there anyway."

"Don't get agitated. It's just a suggestion."

"Disagreeing with you doesn't mean I'm agitated. It's quiet here today, and we're lucky it's empty. Can't we enjoy it?"

"Place is empty because it's snowing." He shivered, wrapping the scarf around his neck. "No one comes here in the snow except us."

"Snow keeps people away. No one would see me crying."

"There's nothing wrong with crying, Sarah. The doctors say—"

"The doctors say I should accept the momentum of grief then give me pills so I can't. What sense does that make?"

"None, I suppose." Bending, Blake slipped a card from the box at my feet. "This is from his business, isn't it? Bennet Marine? There's a figure eight on it, and I think that's their logo."

"Probably."

"He's in other states now too. Texas. Florida. Ethan's done well building those yachts, hasn't he?"

"Is that a trick question?"

"No. Why?"

"Because you know I don't talk to Ethan. Not since Michael died."

"You talk to Mama and the girls, though. And the *Gazette* comes in the mail sometimes. Paper says Bennet Marine brought in a ton of jobs and revitalized the whole county. Ethan's been in some magazines too."

"I heard."

Blake tugged his gloves. "He's with lots of women in those pictures. Looks like a different one every time."

"Ethan's always had that reputation. What's your point?"

"I think he's done well. Don't you?"

The conversation was tedious. It wasn't a discussion Blake was trying to have. It was an inquisition. "Yes, Blake. Ethan's done well."

"Why does he still send these? It's been seven years since Michael died."

"For the same reason Mama sends honey. They loved him, and they miss him. I swear you get colder every year."

"I'm not cold. I'm curious," Blake said, and his breath fogged warm on my face. "Have you seen Ethan? Talked to him?"

"How would that happen? I haven't been home in nearly eight years. Ida died three years ago, and I didn't even go to her funeral. What about Alicia's ceremony when she made sheriff two years ago? Did I go?"

"You didn't go."

"So what makes you think I'd see Ethan? I don't even hear about him anymore. Mama and the girls barely say anything."

"Why's that?"

"Ethan probably told them not to," I said, slapping snow from my gloves. "So, see? I haven't seen nor spoken to Ethan Bennet since the night Michael died. The man moved out of Mother's house to get as far from me as possible. He hates me that much."

"That wasn't a selfless gesture, Sarah. Ethan was in love with you and finally gave up."

"Then I guess you have nothing to worry about." I collected the wrappings before cutting through the snow to our cars. "But if I wanted to go home, I would."

"When did I say you couldn't go home?"

"Every time you handed me a pill, it was clear."

"Staying in New York was your choice, Sarah." Blake widened his stride behind mine. "That had nothing to do with me. I only said it was safer if I went along."

"Like that would ever happen. The only way you'd leave this city is on a stretcher."

"Did you forget the episodes you had last month? We could barely hold you down."

"Well, thank God for John Hatcaden's knowledgeable touch and the well-worn shackles on Riverside Drive."

"Those attacks were your fault," Blake said. "You threw out the pills, and whatever set you off went way out of control."

"And shackling me in a hospital was the recommended procedure?"

"You were screaming about Michael, Sarah. You hadn't touched food in three days. What else could I do? Let you scream in that bedroom and starve?"

"That's preferable to shackles and pills."

"No, it's not." We stopped at the cars with Blake swiping snow from his hood. "Why do I meet you here anymore? You only get agitated."

"I'm not agitated because we're at Michael's grave. I'm agitated because my mental state and fidelity are constantly questioned. Maybe I should ask about yours."

"I've never been unfaithful to you, Sarah. Not once."

"Well, of course not. I mean, when would you find the time? And thanks for the fast lay the other night. The charity was appreciated."

"That wasn't charity," he said with a sniff. "I missed you. I wanted to hold you."

"But you don't hold me, Blake. Hatcaden does. If I'm having an affair at all, I guess it's with him."

Then I got into my car and left.

That was the way we were after our sexually referenced arguments. The one where I'd remark on a lack of regular sex, and Blake replied with tedious reminders of intimacy not nearly as impactful as he thought. Not that my husband wasn't gifted in bed. Blake was gifted, beautiful, and remarkably wanton in bed. But he was also afraid to get close, and despite his constant denials, I knew he always had been.

Still, there were those gentle nights when he'd set aside that fear and come to me. His hand brushed my cheek, gently pulling the linens from my body, caressing whatever bared skin appeared first. Those were the times when spite was lost, our defenses lowered, and we'd allow a small truce.

My eyes opened sleepily, and I'd reach for him, gently tangling my hands in his hair as my tongue slipped the threshold of his lips. Then we'd touch and kiss and hold one another so tenderly I could have cried for remembering the times when we didn't use scorn as our only means of speech.

When we made love, we made love.

His mouth followed the swells of my breasts, sucking and licking down to my hips and lower, moving his tongue in motions known only to me until my body struck out, writhing in the ecstasy of my husband's most intimate touch. He'd fall upon me, pushing inside and tying his hips into mine.

Blake...

And sometimes, as our bodies weaved their wonders and his would pulse inside mine, we'd say we loved each other, and it would be true. Because at that moment, we weren't too afraid to reach out and admit we did. Those were the moments when we found our forever.

Those were the times when it shined.

Twenty-Seven

WhiteThorn's building was a mass of movement in the mornings. A sweet-scented world of murmured hums and rhythmic slaps of feet clicking across slick, glossy floors made a pleasant greeting as I marched through the halls.

"Just in time." Blake followed as I opened the door to my office. "Another screwball claiming to be Hatcaden showed up. Legal needs us downstairs."

"Hopefully, this guy's accusations are more interesting than the rest."

"Oh, they are," Blake said, rolling his sleeves. "This Mr. Hatcaden spent time in a psychiatric ward and thinks we disguised a writer as a doctor to steal his life story. Channel 12 is interviewing him next week, and legal wants it stopped."

"Then let legal handle it."

"Not this time. The press is circling wagons, and they'll bleed the story for every last drop. Legal needs at least one of us to confirm or deny accusations."

Dropping my satchel at the side of my desk, I said, "Wouldn't have to deny anything if you'd let me use the writer's real name."

"Revealing the writer means revealing the truth of that book, and I'm not ready to do that. Not yet." Blake turned and reached for the door. "Meet me downstairs before lunch?"

"Wait a second." I tore a pink message slip from its pin. "I need to call home."

"Call later."

"I can't, Blake. This is from Alicia. I hope it's not Mama. She was sick last month, and I haven't spoken to anyone down there in weeks."

"If it were serious, she'd have called your cell and not your office. You know how they are down there. Everything's drama."

"Not this time." I sat in my desk chair and dialed the phone. "This is Alicia's sheriff's number. Something's not right."

Blake perched on my desk with a grin. "Tell Miss Nash to send me more pralines. That dozen wasn't nearly enough."

Alicia answered with, "Sheriff Maynard."

"Alicia, what's wrong? Your message said urgent. Is Mama all right?"

"Grandma's fine."

"Then, what?"

Alicia's shoes slapped the floor as she walked. "Buster's dead."

"Dead?" I looked at Blake, his eyes going wider on mine. "Buster Mills *died*?"

"Yeah, but listen—"

"Holy shit. I know Mama taught us to never celebrate when somebody dies, but even she'd agree Buster's passing was no great loss to the world."

"It's not, but Sarah—"

"Lemme guess," I said rocking back. "Mama finally had enough and helped God in His efforts with Branch Street's notorious butcher."

"No, Sarah. Abby did. She killed Buster two weeks ago. Shoved him into the Perlick and shut the door. Grandma found him the next day. Had to arrest Abby that night."

"Arrest her?" My chair bounced from the wall when I stood. "You arrested Abby? What for?"

"For murder, Sarah. Jesus, I had to. She confessed. Pleaded guilty at the arraignment too. The attorney Ethan hired told her to plead not guilty and claim self-defense, but Abby won't do it."

"What about the Perlick's safety latch?"

"Safety latch?" Alicia's voice hitched. "What about it?"

"That door's meant to be opened from the inside when it's closed. That's what the safety latch is for. Didn't he push it?"

Alicia cleared her throat before saying, "Abby cut it off."

"Cut it off? How? That's gotta be solid metal, and Buster would have seen her do it."

The door banged in Alicia's office, and her voice went pitchy and tight. "Just come home, Sarah. Please? We need you home now."

"Wait a second," I said, circling the room. "This happened two weeks ago? Why are you only calling me now?"

"Grandma said not to."

"And you listened to her? Why in the hell would you—"

"Just come home, all right? The attorney needs to talk to you."

"But I can't tell him anything. I haven't been home since before Michael died."

Rustling scraped the receiver, and a voice shouted, "Damnit, did you hear what she said?"

"Ethan?"

"Get your ass on a plane, Sarah. There's a flight to Savannah leaving at noon. Take it. There'll be a car waiting when you land, and your mom's house and car will be ready. Tell your husband *those people* need your goddamn help down here."

Ethan slammed the phone, leaving me shaken and numb.

"Go home?" I glanced at my watch before resting the phone on the desk. "Right now? For Abby?"

"Sarah, don't do this." Blake stood, clutching my pills at his hip. "Not without me."

"Flight leaves at noon. If I go now—"

"Not today, Sarah. Not now."

"This can't wait, Blake. Abby needs me."

"Then I'm coming too."

"No, you're not." I rifled through folders, choosing unfinished work to stuff into my bag. "Someone has to be here to handle the Hatcaden fraud."

"That's not as important as being with you."

"Stop worrying. Mama and Alicia will help."

"They don't know what you need. Not like I do. There are reasons you can't go alone."

"What reasons?" I asked, hoisting the satchel over my arm. "White-Thorn? Michael? Hatcaden? There are a thousand reasons for me to stay, but only one that can force me to leave. And that's Abby."

The staff watched as I pushed through the door, fording the office in a frantic reach for freedom. Blake strode behind and stopped at the elevators as their doors slid apart.

"Don't leave, Sarah. It's not safe. You don't know what could happen."

"Trust me," I said, tying the belt on my coat. "You'll be happier once I'm not here."

"That's not true. I'm keeping you safe. I love you."

"I know you do, Blake." I reached up, touching his face as the doors slowly closed. "But you've always loved Hatcaden more."

Twenty-Eight

New York's constant roar was never more apparent than when I landed in Savannah. The sweet Southern air and soft lilting song of the voices proved a memorable comfort. Enjoying a February heatwave, I slung my coat and satchel over an arm and inspected the row of complacent drivers gathered like crows on a line.

"Thorn?" A young driver wiggled a placard at me. "Are you Thorn?"

"Yes, but I'm not sure I need—"

"Please, Ma'am. Mr. Bennet says I'm to stuff you into the trunk if you show your, well, your ass."

"My ass?" I huffed, raising a brow. "Show you my—?"

"Yes, Ma'am. Mr. Bennet says I get an extra fifty if you argue."

"Is that right?" I laughed. "Well, it's nice to see Mr. Bennet's amiable means of intimidation still flourish here." Opening my satchel, I removed a cleanly folded fifty-dollar bill, handing it to the pimple-faced driver. "What's your name, and how old are you?"

"Name's Daniel. I'm seventeen."

"Seventeen's young to be driving people from airports, isn't it?"

"I was a deckhand at the marina last year, but my dad died, so Mr. Bennet gave me this job instead. Told him it was illegal, but he just laughed and threw me the keys."

"Sounds like something he'd do. Never be afraid of Mr. Bennet, Daniel. His bark is worse than his bite, and his bite isn't as hard as a spaniel's."

Daniel pocketed the money before giving a passive look as recognition slowly crept in. "Hey, you're that writer, aren't you? The one everybody protested down here."

"Thank you, Daniel," I said, adjusting my satchel and coat as we walked. "It's nice being remembered for something other than talent."

"Yeah. My mom sure hated those books."

"She wasn't alone. Did you read them?"

Daniel blushed, a sheepish expression of embarrassing shame. "Well, a few of the guys and I read *The Badlands* series. They were good, and I liked the sexy stuff. You know, guys doin' stuff to girls? They were creepy too."

"Did you buy them yourself?"

"Nah. They were hard to find once the stores sold out and the library stopped shelving them."

"Where'd you get them?"

"From my mom," he said, angling us through the crowds. We stopped at the limousine, where Daniel opened the door and helped me inside. "She and her church friends read the books, so they knew what to protest about. Mom said you wrote those books for men, but my dad didn't read them half as much as she did. She read them in the bathroom most every night."

"In the bathroom?" I grinned, not wanting to tarnish Daniel's virtuous view of his mother. "Is that a fact?"

"Yes, Ma'am. Said we'd better not bug her while she was reading that smut. That's what she called it, *that smut*. When she came out, she was sweaty and flushed like she'd run a marathon or something. That's how mad she was."

"And you think she was sweating because she was mad?"

"Why, sure. I mean, what else could make a Southern mom sweat?"

"No telling, Daniel," I said with a laugh. "No telling."

The route to Bayport from Savannah was an hour's drive, and as we rolled over Tallmadge Bridge, I rested my head, reveling in the familiar sights and smells of life below the Mason Dixon. Only there in the cellar of the states did one realize some places still cleaved to their deep primal roots. There, the sun still glistened over the waters of an untapped realm. Gulls screamed; their white bellies dipped in placid inland pools. The green of the marshes, adorned with corroded pine trunks, remained as wild and untamed as any place would be had man never crawled from its mud.

The South was a tonic. The colors, scents, and low tide warmth settled my brain, and for the first time in years, my eyes closed without hesitation.

Wrapped inside perfumes of sweet ocean air, I dreamt of dewy beach mornings and boats dipped in moonlight. Ethan's face rose from the back of my mind, and he reached for me, touching my lips and calling my name in a hauntingly desperate prayer, begging, "Stay with me, Sarah Thorn. Stay."

The car lurched to a stop, and I bumped awake, gathering my satchel and coat from the seat. Daniel came to my aid as I opened the door, stretching a leg to the curb.

"Wait," I said, eyes rolling over a stately old home. "This isn't where I'm supposed to be dropped."

"Mr. Bennet told me to bring you straight here."

"Mr. Bennet?"

Raised from her ruin, the castle stood gloriously refurbished. Centered with red double doors, her white clapboard body gleamed against the black shutters and minty green ceiling of the wrap-around porch. Four fans spun lazily, teasing white sheers on the windows inside, while mounds of azaleas lined the front yard, bleeding deep purple hues on the grass.

"Miss Thorn?" Daniel laid a hand on my arm. "What should we do?"

"Nothing," I said, hiking my satchel and coat. "I know why he brought me here now."

After sending Daniel away with an extra twenty, I walked the brick path through the yard. I moved like a frightened cat, taking every porch step with hesitant care. The brass figure eight knocker glinted at me, and I slammed it twice before the door threw open, and Ethan was there.

"Smut writer!" Ethan stood barefoot, wearing frayed jeans, a flimsy gray t-shirt, and his usual stubble-lined grin. "Bayport's prodigal child returns."

I was trapped. Caught in his smile, the line of his jaw, and the flashes of gold in his eyes.

"Ethan?"

"Who'd you expect?"

"No one. I just thought—"

"Well, I tried finding a more fitting escort, but Walter Salinger just went to rehab, and Hollis Miller up and had himself a heart attack on top of some Yemassee waitress named Joy. So, you're stuck with me for right now." He plucked the satchel from my shoulder, dangling it between us. "Traveling light?"

"There was no time to pack."

"Figured as much. Come on in."

Ethan led me to a teakwood bench by the stairs. There was an office to the right, a small parlor to the left, and the once-darkened hallway rippled with light.

"Need a drink?" Ethan set my satchel and coat on the floor. "I've got tea."

"Tea's good." I nodded, looking around. "Tea's fine."

Ethan left down the hall, talking from the kitchen. There was a cadence to his voice. An easy and familiar comfort in the way he remarked on my uppity clothes, twisted-up hair, and the sinful red shine on my nails.

"Here." He practically thrust the sweaty glass in my face. "Still sweet, right? I know those Yankees don't drink it sweet. I trust you haven't defected."

"Sweet's good." I smiled, taking the glass. "I still drink it sweet."

A phone echoed in the office behind. "Have to get that," he said, hurriedly stepping away. "Finish your drink."

Ethan's absence offered a chance to explore other rooms. The house was so pleasant, cheerful, and fresh, like visiting a once ailing friend now gleaming with health. The parlor shone brighter with soft creamy walls, enhancing the red velvet drapes. Wooden floors polished in deep coffee brown, reflected the chandelier's glint overhead.

Memorabilia filled every inch. Pictures of Ethan accepting awards or giving donations hung beside *Gazette* articles showing him sailing on oceans or swimming in lakes. A series of black and white photos chronicled the castle's restoration and Ethan's attendance to a small antique boat.

"Come with me." Ethan's breath was a whisper on the side of my neck, and he took my hand, leading me to the office on the other side of the foyer. Cherry-stained paneling coated the room. There were sepia globes in old, rusted frames and antique pieces of nautical gear tucked inside cases and pinned on the walls. We sat on a black leather Chesterfield facing the windows behind a mahogany desk. Ethan took one end while I took the other, needing the comfort of distance.

"I'm sorry about Michael," he softly said. "You know I loved him."

I nodded, sipping my tea. "Thank you for sending the toys. We put them at Michael's grave every year."

"Hope it's okay to still send them. Didn't seem right to just stop, but if it's a problem—"

"It's not a problem. Make's going there easier."

"All right. I'll keep sending them. If it helps."

"It does."

Unnerving silence gutted the room. A Windsor clock chimed, the ceiling fan *whirred*, and I felt the pressure of questions I didn't want asked.

Then he did.

"So, why'd you just leave me like that?"

"Damnit, Ethan." I set the glass on the floor by my feet. "The driver was supposed to take me to Mother's, but you pushed everything aside to get what you want."

"What I want is an answer. Why'd you just leave me like that?"

"My son died, remember?"

"I loved Michael too, Sarah. And you left me down here without saying a word. Didn't I matter? Did any of it matter?"

"All of it mattered," I said. "I thought cutting it off would be best."

"Best for whom?"

"For you, but I was wrong. And I'm sorry. I'm so sorry."

Ethan eased closer, cupping my knee. "Can't you even look at me now? You're staring at the walls, the windows. Everywhere but right in my face. Why?"

"I feel awful," I said, forcing my eyes onto his. "Leaving you that way was wrong, and I should have said something."

"Then stay with me, Sarah."

"Ethan, don't."

"I've missed you so much. We can start over again."

"Ethan, I can't." Shoving away, I turned to the foyer. "I have to go."

"All right, all right," he said, following me to the bench. "I promise to keep my roguish hands to myself. Now come back to the office, and we'll talk about the weather or fishing and why you can barely look me in the eye anymore."

"You had no business bringing me here."

"I wanted to talk to you."

"That wasn't talking." I wrangled my coat from the floor. "That was an interrogation. I get enough of that in New York, and I need to get to Mother's right now."

"Might be a problem with that," he said, pushing the pocket door back with his foot.

"There's nothing a shower and a strong cup of coffee can't fix."

"Can't fix the power."

"The power?" I asked, clutching the satchel. "What's wrong with the power?"

"Never had it turned on."

"But you said everything would be ready for me. The house and the Buick. You said—"

"Yeah, but I figured you'd rather stay here."

"At the castle?" I flinched. "I can't stay at the castle with you."

"Why not?"

"Because I'm not one of your tidal creek whores, that's why not. Who do you think you're dealing with here?"

"Well, I thought I was dealing with someone I knew, but instead, all I got was some uptight New Yorker with a stick jammed way up her ass."

Shouldering my satchel, I said, "You're still an insufferable prick."

"And you're still a paranoid freak. This isn't what you think."

"Nothing you do is ever what anyone thinks, Ethan. That's part of your indelible charm."

Ethan laughed, watching me bolt from the house.

"That's a ten-minute walk to your mom's house," he said, pointing to an apple-red Mustang out front. "At least let me drive you."

"I'll walk."

"In three-inch heels?"

"I'm from New York. We run marathons in heels up there."

"New York, my ass," he shouted from the castle's front porch. "You're a child of Bayport, Miss Thorn. You can wear all the fancy blue skirts and silky white blouses you want, but you've got mud in those veins. Soft, Southern mud. That means you'll always be one of ours."

Twenty-Nine

Aside from fresh paint on the walls and new blinds on the windows, Mother's house retained its appeal. The ugly green sofa and chairs were still there, biding their time under layers of sheets. Wood grain vinyl replaced the carpet, and the kitchen's faucet lost its *tap-tapping* drip. The rest of the house was rife with memories I hadn't expected to bear. Mother's soft singing poured from the walls, and her laughter floated from rooms.

Burdened with memories beyond my control, I ran through the kitchen and pulled the door so hard that its window broke on the wall. The gazebo stood proudly beneath thick, swaying trees, still round and white but faded in spots where the sun had baked too long. It was quiet inside, and I fell to my knees in an uncontrolled outburst of grief. Pain poured from me, gripped in my hands as they pounded the boards, squeezing old pain from my eyes.

"You're always running from me."

"Ethan?" I spun and glared over my shoulder at him. "Damnit, why can't you stop sneaking around?"

"Following you wasn't sneaking."

"Then stop following me." I shoved to my feet and ran back to the house. "Just leave me alone."

"What's wrong with you, Sarah? Why are you so wound up?"

"I've been on a plane all day," I said, pushing into the kitchen. "I'm tired, and you're chasing me down like a convict."

"So you took it out on the window?" Ethan stopped at the doorway, sliding pieces of glass with his shoe. "Why are you acting like this?"

"Ethan, please." I scraped a chair from the table to sit. "I know you're trying to help, but—"

"Talk to me, Sarah," he said, taking a chair of his own. "Where's that brave girl who used to fight monsters with me?"

It wasn't so much a question he asked as a mystery he wanted to solve. I'd changed. Tightened. Wound myself into a protective coil he'd never seen and couldn't understand.

"She broke," I whimpered. "In a street, in a city far from here, she didn't hold on, and she broke."

"Christ, Sarah." Ethan leaned closer and pulled me into his arms. It was an indulgence of grief that I needed. Unlike Blake, whose treatment of me depended upon a predictable mood, Ethan allowed me to have it. There was no control, and there was no finality. There was just me and Ethan and a moment of luxuriant despair.

After ten minutes of allowing snot on his shirt, Ethan snapped a handkerchief from his pocket and said, "Here, snotty mess. Blow out that nose."

"Hankies?" I folded the fabric, dabbing my eyes. "I didn't know men still carried hankies."

"This one does." Reaching around, he slapped the light switch, and the fluorescent flickered. "We make electricity too."

"Power?" I asked, watching the glow of white overhead. "There's power here now?"

"I called the company and had it turned on." He took a brown paper bag from the floor. "Brought presents too."

"Damn it, Ethan. What's in there?"

"Calm down, potty mouth. Look."

Ethan reached into the bag and pulled out the ugliest pink flannel gown in the world. It had little green clovers and awful lace trim, and I couldn't wait to feel every thread of its hideous softness.

"It's perfect." I smiled and hugged the gown to my chest. "Thank you."

"There's some toothpaste in there and a few groceries."

"I appreciate it. And what I said earlier about not staying with you at the house—"

"Edward's with me."

"With you?" I asked. "He's not staying with Mama?"

"Abby wanted him to, but Social Services barged in and said Mama couldn't provide the special provisions Edward would need. Abby begged me to take him before they dragged the poor kid to some group home in Ridgemont." Ethan stood, stuffed his hands in his pockets, and stared at the glass on the floor. "Special people like Edward can't survive in places like that. Cold rooms. Cold faces. Cold halls. They need a family who loves them. Who'll care for them." Ethan looked back at me. "That's why I suggested you stay at the house. Because Edward's there."

Picking the lace on the gown, I said, "When you brought it up, I thought—"

"Don't worry about it." Ethan smiled, waving me off. "You can see Edward tomorrow. There's a charity dinner at Steadman's Inn tonight, so I had him stay with his doctor. I was hoping you'd tag along."

"To Steadman's?" I frowned, assessing the travel-worn state of my clothes. "This outfit's too casual for Steadman's and hardly right for a dinner party."

"There's time for a shower, and as for clothes," Ethan pointed to a black garment bag hooked on the cabinets behind me, "that's covered, too."

"What's that?"

"What do you think, genius? It's a dress and shoes."

"Looks like a setup to me." Stepping to the bag, I traced the gold stenciled print on its side. "*Abelia's on Branch.* Sounds expensive."

"Stop talking like Mama. And it is a setup. I want to show off my New York smut connection. Go put your gown on."

"All right," I said, collecting the bag before I turned down the hall. "You sure you want to be seen in public with me?"

"Why not?" Ethan followed and stopped in the hallway as I closed the door to my room. "Do you plan a recitation of one of your filthier books?"

"Won't need recitations for an uproar to start." After removing my skirt and blouse, I stretched the gown over my head, enjoying the coolness as it fell down my back. "Guests will rehash rumors I'm a high-priced dominatrix or other lurid gossip. I'm a has-been now."

"Dominatrix?" He chuckled. "Haven't heard that one yet. Should have paid more attention to the protests down here."

"The recluse writer wasted from addiction is my favorite. Makes me sound more cerebral."

"Nah. Dominatrix is better, so I'll keep spreading that one, I think."

"So much for Captain Wonderful," I said, hearing him laugh in the hall.

"Dinner's at nine, so you have a few hours to rest. Give me your clothes, and I'll have them cleaned before we see Abby tomorrow."

With clothes in hand, I opened the door and smiled. "This gown might be ugly, but it feels great on my skin. Even better than Mama's muslin gowns."

"Don't tell her that." Ethan loosened my curls and spread them over my arms. "There. That's how it should be. Loose, wild, and free to strangle small children."

Looking over the hallway, I said, "Everything about being home is so nice."

"Oh, yeah?" he asked. "What's so nice about it? Your favorite part?"

"All of it. The smells. The colors and the warmth." I tipped closer, pressing my chest into his. "And you. I forgot how good it feels being near you again."

"Want to remember right now?" He smiled, drifting a thumb down my throat. "No one would know if we did."

"I would know," I said, stepping back. "And we can't."

"We can't?" Ethan reached out, snatched my clothes, and turned to stride down the hall. "Don't smash your tits on my chest, then tell me I can't take you to bed."

"Ethan, I'm sorry. Touching you comes so naturally, but I shouldn't have done it."

"There are plenty of things you shouldn't have done. Shouldn't have married somebody else. Shouldn't have left me without saying why."

"Leaving was best. I've already hurt you so much, and I don't want to do that again."

"Do you really think we can hurt each other more than we already have? We probably hold a record somewhere for ripping each other's hearts out and grinding them into the floor." Ethan opened the door and leaped from the porch to his car. "I'll be back by eight-thirty. Be dressed."

Ethan was hurting, and that was my fault. For what it was worth, the guilt I was hiding was punishment plenty. I just couldn't tell him it was.

Thirty

After Ethan's heated retreat, I prepared the house for my stay. The bed pillows were flat, so I fluffed them. The Frigidaire was old and clicking, but I opened the door and was happy to find the walls were cold enough to store whatever casseroles I was sure Mama would bring. My cell rattled in my satchel's pocket, and I pulled it out, thinking of everything I'd say to the man on the other end. Blake's pleas were always the same. Concerns over nightmares and the taking of pills.

Our discussions always ended with pills.

"I'm here, Blake," I said, yanking sheets from the chairs. "I'm here."

"How was the flight?"

"Cramped. How's the Hatcaden fraud?"

"Oh, he's found an attorney. Some seedy guy from the Bronx. We're meeting on Monday."

"That should make for an interesting start to your week."

"Probably. I'll call once it's done." Blake sighed. "How are you feeling?"

"Good," I said, folding a sheet. "Tired from the flight. A little hungry, but—"

"No, Sarah. I mean, *how* are you feeling?"

"Jesus, Blake. Did you expect me to leap from the Talmadge on my way into town? I'm fine."

"Without Hatcaden, you'll crash, and it'll be hell when you do."

"Will you calm down? Mama and Alicia are here. If I decide to jump into traffic, I'm sure they'll stop me faster than Hatcaden's pills."

"The meds keep you grounded and your impulses in check. You need them. More than you know."

"Do I?" I asked, husking a laugh. "Considering your mother took a handful of those things, I'd say the impulse control part was lacking." There are thousands of words in the English vocabulary, and the foulest options shot from my mouth. They were purposefully hurtful and painfully cruel. And I hated myself for saying them. "Blake. Jesus, I didn't mean that. I'm tired and—"

"Don't say anything."

"But I didn't mean—"

"Sarah. Just... don't." Blake coughed, dropping his voice to a steady, dismissive pace. "If I don't hear from you every day, I'll come there myself. I'll bring you home, and you won't travel without me again."

"You can't keep me from coming back home."

"Do you think I won't try? I'll call Miss Nash or have Alicia put you back on a plane. I'll do what I have to if it keeps you safe."

"Go to hell, Blake."

"Oh, I've already been," he said. "Every time my wife takes a trip, I get a front-row seat next to hers."

I hung up, throwing my phone at a chair. If there was malice in grief, Blake and I found it. Although we didn't intentionally mean to harm one another, our words became weapons, and our bloody targets each other.

After some wound-licking and considering the cost of divorce, I gathered the dress and brown bag from the kitchen and left for Mother's bedroom. The contents I dumped from the paper bag made me smirk. Black stockings fell first, coiling on the bedsheets like slithering snakes. A matching lace bra and panties fell next, joined by colorful bottles of soaps and perfumes.

Considering Ethan's salacious nature, the garment bag should have contained scraps of lace with spider silk holding their seams, but I was surprised to find a modest black cocktail dress with embroidered lace sleeves.

"Beautiful."

Black silk pumps bulked the bottom of the bag alongside a beaded clutch and a hair comb carved from Apitong wood. Its tines were long, and the figure eight ornament carved from mother-of-pearl told me Ethan made it.

Once I showered and completed my creative female prep work, I was ready. There was a thump on the porch, and I heard Ethan open the door. "Who's ready for clamming?"

"Clamming?" I walked down the hall, jamming the comb into my thick fall of hair. "I refuse to go clamming with someone angry with me."

"If that were the case, we'd never go out," he said, dipping to kiss my left cheek. "We'll settle our hearts tonight, as Mama would say."

"Good plan." I hitched back, admiring his slim, graphite suit. "You're the only man alive who can go from beach bum to Armani model in the time it takes most women to smear on their lipstick."

"And you're the only writer alive who can go from Anais Nin to Jane Austen in the time it takes to bait a hook." He reached for the roses propped on the couch. "Peace offering."

"Robbing Shoreline again?" I held the bouquet, inhaling the flowers' bubble gum scents. "They're perfect, Ethan. Thank you."

"You're welcome. And no. They came from the solarium this time."

"You're doing too much," I said, leaving for the kitchen. "The dress and the comb, especially."

"The dress came from a local shop, and the comb I've had for a while. Always meant to send it with Michael's toys but was never sure if I should."

"Would have been all right if you did."

"Blake wouldn't have cared?"

"Blake wouldn't have noticed." The statement poured out, soft and waning, like minnows escaping gripped hands.

Ethan cleared his throat, taking a seat at the table. "Anyway, it wasn't any trouble, and you wouldn't have complained if Mama or the girls had done it."

"I'm not complaining." I slapped on the faucet, rinsing the stems. "Gifts from you are different than from Mama or the girls."

"They're better coming from me. Did they fit?"

"Did what fit?"

"The panties. Those drawers cost good money, and I should know if they cover your perfect white ass and that little round scar on your hip. That's good manners."

"The panties fit fine," I said, stifling a laugh. "Now shut up about my underwear."

"I'm probably wasting time asking since your memory was always for shit, but did you really get that scar doing blood sisters with Abby the day you ripped up Buster's shop?"

"Never ripped up Buster's shop."

"Everyone thinks you did."

"Does that include you?" I asked, picking spent blooms. "You were the only one who didn't think I tore up that shop and the only one who wasn't frightened of me. Has that changed?"

"No, Shakespeare. Nothing's changed. I've just always wondered about that cut on your hip. How'd you get it?"

"Doing blood sisters with Abby. Can't believe we're still talking about this. I barely remember that day."

"But you remember doing blood sisters?"

"That, I remember. Yes."

"Because Abby told you, you did?"

Looking over my shoulder, I said, "Abby wouldn't lie about that."

"I'm not saying she lied. I'm saying she twisted things you saw sometimes."

"Abby never twisted what I saw."

"Sure she did. You'd make up stories about fireflies on the beach, and Abby chased them with you. You'd say the sun was crying at dusk, and she'd tell you it was going to bed. Abby twisted whatever you saw."

"That's not true." Not wanting to accept my shattered existence, I ignored his assessment of Abby's support. "Tell me about Abby. What's going on?"

"Nothing good." Ethan teetered back in the chair. "According to her, she shoved Buster into the freezer and shut the door after they fought."

"And you believe that?"

"I don't believe she fought with him, no. But what choice do we have? The woman confessed like she couldn't wait to decorate the cell."

"The attorney couldn't get her to plead otherwise?"

"The minute he told her to plead not guilty, she pitched a fit and told us to back off."

I searched cabinets for a makeshift vase, choosing a jelly jar with a chip on its rim. "Abby's naïve, Ethan. You have to explain things plainly to her."

"Can't get plainer than telling her she'll die in prison if she doesn't do what that lawyer says. She doesn't want an investigation at all. According to her, Buster deserved what he got, and she's fine making license plates for a while."

"What about the attorney you hired? Is he good?"

"Oh, he's great. Better than the public defender. Had to threaten her so she'd agree to him, though."

"Threaten her?" I walked the jar to the table. "With what?"

"With Edward. Said I wouldn't sign guardianship papers if Abby didn't take the attorney."

Arranging the roses, I said, "Well, let's hope he's worth the extortion. Who is he? Some offspring of Darrow?"

"Better. Ward Elliot."

"Jesus, Ethan." I cringed. "Ward Elliot?"

"Yeah, Ward Elliot. So what?"

"So the man's barely human."

"Abby doesn't need a human. She needs a Pitbull. Ward Elliot's the best, so I got him."

"The only thing Elliot's good at is warping reasonable doubt into questionable innocence."

"Then Ward is just who we need because I have no doubt our sweet Abby turned her daddy into a freezer pop that night."

"So you think Abby did it?"

"Not the way she tells it, no. My guess is Buster was drunk, got close to that freezer, and Abby saw a chance to get rid of the man."

"Abby wasn't injured?" I asked, fluffing more blooms. "No bruises? No cuts?"

"Not a mark on her."

"Wasn't much of a fight," I said. "What's Mama think about this?"

"Mama says this is God's will and to let Abby do as she likes."

"Do as she likes?" I smirked. "That doesn't sound like something she'd say."

"Better be careful talking like that. That woman nearly slapped my eyes out for making Abby hire Ward in exchange for keeping Edward out of foster care."

Studying the flowers, I said, "What is she thinking?"

"Ward says Abby can plead self-defense, but the girl won't budge."

"Something doesn't feel right."

Ethan cocked his head. "Sarah, don't do that."

"Don't do what?"

"Don't do that thing you do when you think something's going on when it's not."

"Paranoid, you mean?"

"Yeah," he said. "Sometimes you can be a little paranoid, sure."

"Because I think a ninety-pound woman couldn't shove a man three times her size into a freezer everyone knows he'd never go near?"

"If he were drunk, she could have. Besides, who else would have done it? And why?"

"I don't know, but something's not right."

"Well, on that, we agree." Ethan stood, buttoning his coat. "Wash your hands. Time to head out."

I squeaked on the water, splashing my hands in the sink. "It's strange going from writer to editor, Ethan."

"Is it? Why's that?"

"Writers lie to tell their story," I said, snatching a towel. "Editors dig up the truth."

"Which one are you this time, Shakespeare?"

"Depends on what Abby says." I hooked Ethan's arm with my own. "Let's go."

Thirty-One

The Steadman's reedy, blonde hostess proved her attraction to Ethan the minute we walked through the door. Poking one spindly leg through the slit in her skirt, she welcomed us with an annoyingly saccharine voice and a smile like feathers could float from her tongue. Ethan barely noticed, murmuring instructions before guiding us through elegant tables to the private dining in the back.

"The hostess, Ethan," I said. "What grade was she in? High school? Middle? Did you at least wait until the braces came off?"

"Don't judge, Miss Thorn. I recall a certain redheaded seventeen-year-old ripping her dress off and asking for some pretty disgusting things. How could you make me do that to you? Your mom could have thrown me in jail."

"I needed the best," I said. "Ethan Bennet's the best, so I got him."

Ethan stopped before pulling me close at the door. "Just so you know, that first night with you was worth a thousand years behind bars, Sarah Thorn."

Then he kissed me once before breezing us into the room.

The group wasn't terribly large but was bustling enough to fill gaps between white primped tables glinting with crystal. Photographers stood in corners snapping photos and talking with guests. A burly man with a tragic toupee waved at Ethan. He was round and loud, and his galloping trod brought him to us in less than three strides.

"Every tolerable soul with a wallet is here." The man slapped Ethan's shoulder before smiling at me. "Who's our guest?"

"An old friend." Ethan took flutes of champagne from a waiter, handing me one. "Sarah Thorn, Arnold Parker. Don't get too close, Arnold. She's from New York."

"You say that like I'm infectious," I said.

"Well, I wouldn't believe it." Arnold lifted my hand in a shake. "Not with an old Southern accent like that. I can hear it."

We laughed, and Ethan said, "Arnold's a big shot, Sarah. President of Parker Financial and this year's festival organizer."

"Festival?" I asked. "Which one?"

"Valentine's," Ethan said. "Starts next Friday."

Arnold smoothed his tie. "Do you sail, Miss Thorn?"

"No, but we have friends who sail often. Some own crafts from Bennet Marine."

"I'm sorry," Arnold said. "We?"

"Yes." My eyes banked to Ethan. "My husband and I."

Ethan's jaw clenched. "Excuse me, Arnold. I'm sure *Mrs. Bradley* won't mind your company for a while. I see Evan's finally shown up."

Ethan curbed away, leaving an icy stare, a hint of cologne, and a wall of tension thick enough to climb.

"Your name's Bradley?" Arnold was clearly confused. "Ethan said, Thorn."

"Ethan calls me Thorn," I said with a sip. "It might be safer if you did as well."

Arnold continued his dissertations on lavish, beautiful yachts owned by lavish, beautiful people, and I listened intently, honestly interested, but my thoughts obsessed with Ethan. I'd scour the room, my heart thrumming each time our eyes met. Ethan nodded or winked, and I'd return with a tilt of my head or a smile along the edge of my glass. With each look and every passing touch, I felt myself moving further from the truth of my life and into the lie I so desperately wanted to have.

"Holy hell, look who's escaped her wintry abode." A voice split the room, and I saw Evan push through the crowd. Gray highlights tinted his dirty blond hair, but he was still just as tall and as fit. "It's the infamous girl on the beach." Evan pulled me into a hug. "How are you, Sarah?"

"Doing well, Evan. How 'bout yourself? Still shit-talking, Abby?"

"Not after your right hook," he said, rubbing his jaw. "Needed surgery just to breathe after that."

"Better be careful." I teased, displaying a fist. "My aim has improved in New York."

Laughter burst from his chest like a running stampede, and he hugged me. "We've missed you, Sarah Thorn. You call New York and tell them you're not going back."

Evan was wonderful.

A bell rang announcing dinner, and we moved to the table, taking our chairs.

A beautiful woman in a blue velvet dress slid to the spot on my right. Her tanned skin was flawless, and she exuded a threatening manner, twisting her buttery hair and staring at Ethan with the vengeance of a goddess denied. I smelled the man beside her before he even got close. Barrel-chested and sullen, he reeked of various alcohols, stumbling into his chair as he sat.

Ethan tapped his glass, gathering the room's attention. He outlined the scheduled events for the following weekend, gave credits where due, and introduced me as *a carpetbagger come home to roost.* Everyone laughed.

Ethan made a final welcome in a toast to his foundation's launch. He then sat beside me again.

"Why didn't you tell me about the foundation?" I asked.

"Because buying your underwear and drying your tears seemed more important at the time."

"Not as important as running a foundation. What's it for?"

"It's for Edward," he said, swigging his scotch. "People like him are sent to horrible places sometimes, and the foundation will ensure they aren't."

"It's wonderful, Ethan. The foundation, the business. The castle too. The castle's so beautiful now."

"City council called it a dump. Can you believe it? Granted, she was, but only because no one cared for her. Half our childhood lives in that place, and I couldn't let them go tearing her down."

"Abby loved that old house. Probably more than either of us, and certainly more than Alicia did."

"I know." Ethan nodded, swigging again. "I remember."

"I've been worried about Abby and Edward since we moved. I'm grateful you've helped them."

"Well, don't thank me," he said. "Besides Evan, you're the only family I have. I love all of you."

I smiled, sampling my wine. "Alicia said you did something with Mama's house too. Moved it or something?"

"The old place was falling apart, but Mama wouldn't let us fix anything. She said waking the spirits in a settled house was bad luck."

"Only thing settled in that house was the mold."

"Exactly. I moved the old woman to the castle and told her we'd paint her place and have the plumbing repaired. Then I tore that thing down and had a new house built with the same floor plan. Set it farther from the road and put everything back like it was."

Chuckling, I asked, "She didn't know?"

"Not that I could tell," he said, pressing words to my ear. "But if my dick shrivels off, I'll know who told her, so tighten those lips."

Laughter broke from my throat, and I leaned away, gripping Ethan's arm.

"There it is, Shakespeare. There's that laughter I remember so well. Big and bold, like it can't wait to burst from your chest. I've missed it."

"Me too, Ethan. Me too." I breathed, took another sip of my wine, and said, "You never know how good laughter feels until you've lost it. Ever notice that?"

"Is that what happened up there in New York? You lost your laugh?"

"I lost lots of things. Didn't know laughter was one until now."

There was a tap on my shoulder, and I turned, seeing the threatening blonde's open smile. "Mr. Bennet's forgotten his manners," she said. "It's nice to meet you, Miss Thorn. I'm Charlotte Mason."

Charlotte's voice was a sweet, lilting, and menacing thing. Like southern twang spitting acid. The exchange was cordial, but the way she tented her hands, the tilt of her head, and the sneer on her thin glossy lips made it feel more like a threat.

"Are you moving home?" she asked. "My husband and I own Mason Realty, so if you're looking for—"

"Thank you, but no. I'm only here to help a friend."

"What a kind gesture. Who are you visiting? Maybe I know them."

"Abby Mills," I said, giving room as waiters offered our plates. "I'm here to see Abby Mills."

The table went utterly grim. But for the gentle scratching of metal on china and full mouths tumbling food, there were no other sounds in that room.

"You know Abby Mills?" Charlotte asked. "How surprising."

"Not really," I said, arranging my scallops and shrimp. "Abby and I grew up together. She needed my help, so I came."

"I'm referring to your stature, Miss Thorn. The pairing of someone like yourself and Abby Mills is unusual considering the differences in social status."

"Social status?" I sneered, feeling Ethan gripping my thigh. "Have you met Abby, Charlotte? Spoken with her?"

"Miss Mills and I don't walk the same circles, but we're all familiar with the family. These recent events create a lot of gossip, don't they?"

"I wouldn't know. I've never been one to indulge in conversations where topics include the suffering of others."

"Discussing local matters is hardly poor form," she said, rolling capers from the sauce on her cod. "Especially when they involve such terrible brutality from someone as unassuming as Abby Mills. She always was a strange little thing. Pretty enough, but the hair, the eyes, the somewhat earthy look that surrounds her. She never really fit in."

"That's true," I said. "Abby has an exotic appeal unmatched by so many other more ordinary ladies."

"Exotic is the acceptable word nowadays. And that brother of hers. Ethan was kind to take him in, but a bachelor hardly has time for someone like him. He'd be better off in a hospital with nurses and doctors who—"

"Charlotte!" Ethan dropped a fist to the table, clattering dishes and wobbling drinks. "I'm sorry," he whispered to me. "I'm so sorry."

"So, Sarah," Evan spoke up. "WhiteThorn managed *Dancing on Third Street*, huh? That Echo Gumson sure caused a stink. I bet divorce rates skyrocketed after that book hit the shelves. And murder. And vegetarian diets."

The table agreed, recalling the shameless nature and cannibalistic appetite of the novel's infamous heroine.

"Our friend's a psychiatrist," Evan said. "He recommends that book for students of psychoanalysis because it offers a valuable glimpse into a mind under fire. Called that book an incredible work of art."

"Thank you." I smiled, raising my glass. "Mr. Hatcaden will be happy to know."

"I disagree." Charlotte's husband cleared his throat and slid his plate to one side.

"Porter Mason," Ethan whispered. "Maims racehorses when they lose. Tread lightly. He's a bastard down to the bone."

"Well, Mr. Mason," I said, dabbing my mouth, "most people I know disagree with nearly everything I say, but I work with writers, which makes me a seasoned warrior at being disagreed with."

We all laughed, enjoying the pleasantries and my efforts at easing what appeared to be an inexplicable attack from the right.

"Yes, yes," Mason mumbled, downing his mystery drink. "But describing these smut books as art is rather audacious, don't you think?"

Seizing the moment to indulge more blood-lapping, Charlotte sought to clarify who I was to the ignoramus she'd married.

"Porter, you're offending Miss Thorn. She was a writer herself at one time. Mostly horror stories with brutish men taking advantage of women in equally brutish ways. Not my taste."

"My God." Arnold dropped the fork to his plate. "You're SB Thorn. Sarah *Bradley* Thorn? You wrote *The Badlands* series, the books about the priest who put demons on trial and the others with the immortals who licked Christ's blood from the cross. They were cursed for it. What was that series called?"

"*Kindred Souls*," Ethan said. "Sarah started those just after high school. I read them before anyone."

"That was it. My God, I was addicted, and my wife devoured them too. Although, I'm not supposed to tell anyone."

Porter Mason bristled. "But Miss Thorn, the nature of the writing, the grotesque characters and sexualized plots, don't they dilute the craft into something less noble than true art and gifted talent?"

"My husband is right," Charlotte said. "Those stories are from the seedier sects of the literary world, correct? I imagine these so-called writers must have terribly damaged pasts. Look at John Hatcaden. He wrote that Echo Gumson filth and left you to defend it. That man won't dare do an interview, and no one's ever seen him."

"I've seen him." I smiled, licking buttery sauce from my fork. "I've seen John many times."

"He's crazy, isn't he? After all, what do we know about him?"

"We know John's book brought awareness to the suffering endured by those with mental illness. Years ago, families left them in awful places with little treatment. *Third Street* can help change that."

"But he's crazy."

"He's brilliant."

"The man's insane."

"Brilliance is often insanity veiled, Charlotte."

"It's nothing of the kind."

"Christ, lady. What's the difference?"

"The difference is true authors don't write stories that justify abhorrent behavior. Do you think Margaret Mitchell would have approved of Hatcaden's Echo Gumson character?"

"Considering Scarlett O'Hara was raped by her own husband, I'm fairly certain Margaret Mitchell wouldn't be all that surprised by anything Echo pulled off."

"Hatcaden's done nothing but write a filthy novel and made a fortune doing it."

"John Hatcaden opened his mind and shared his nightmares. He invited the world into a private hell only a madman could endure. He's courageous."

"Oh, I remember that." Charlotte snickered, wiggling her spoon. "That's from a speech your husband gave to protestors at the New York Public Library. He was trying to keep his book on the shelves."

"He was defending his author. That was a brave thing to do, Charlotte. My husband is an extraordinarily brave man."

"It doesn't take bravery to defend a cash cow. John Hatcaden didn't see anything worth sharing in a book. Crazy people don't see anything but their own demons. This one happened to make money from it, and you two helped."

"He'd see you clearly enough."

"He'd see a decent woman concerned about his book influencing young minds. That's what he'd see."

"He'd see a whore," I said, coaxing gasps. "He'd see an aging woman in cheap make-up staring at a man she knows she can never have. He'd see money problems from bets on bad horses, a house and cars they can't afford, and a jealous insecurity that could rival Satan's fall from grace."

"You're crazy," she answered, nervously sipping her wine. "And just as disgusting as Hatcaden."

I burst up, gripping my knife and stabbing its blade through her cod. "You ever talk about my husband or Abby Mills like that again, and I'll show you a side of crazy you'll never fucking forget."

Excusing myself, I dropped the knife in her lap as I left.

"Sarah." Ethan followed me down the service hall through the door to Steadman's secluded back patio. Crickets chirped, and the sky was pitch black with only slivers of moon slicing the clouds.

"You just sat there," I said, circling a patch of dwarf palms as I seethed. "How could you sit there and let her talk about Abby that way?"

"Christ. I can't do this." Ethan paced through the patio, shrugging his jacket and pulling his tie. "I can't do this."

"Can't do what? Defend your friends? My God, you just sat there while she—"

"I can't be this close to you and pretend my heart isn't dying. I can't do it, Sarah. I can't." Ethan lunged, pushed me against the patio's wall, and kissed me. And I kissed back, wrapping an arm around his neck, deepening the press of our lips.

We tore at one another. Buttons from his shirt and the lace of my bodice and bra sprayed between us like feathers in a storm. His fingers searched between my thighs, tearing away my panties and freeing me to his touch. Warm lips on my breasts, my back arching into him as I ripped off his belt, opened his trousers and took him in my hand. Ethan groaned, joining us in a single grunting thrust.

Hushed voices poured over the courtyard wall, melting into our muted moans as our bodies collided, claiming, stroking, and feeding ourselves. Heaving breaths lapsed into heavy, sobbing kisses as our hearts remembered it all, and our bodies began to scream. Ethan jerked my hips, cursing along my neck as he plunged into me harder, faster, saying my name as he stilled.

"Stay with me," he whispered. Then he kissed me once more before setting me down on my feet. "Don't leave me again."

"Ethan please," I said. "We shouldn't have done this. It's not right."

"Wouldn't be wrong if you stayed here with me." Ethan swept his jacket out of the grass and draped it over my back. "Don't go to New York. Come back to me now."

A sudden shiver trampled my spine. "Don't say that again. I don't like it."

"Well, nothing's changed with him, has it?" he asked, tucking his shirttail. "Blake doesn't make you feel this way. He never did. I know you want this, Sarah. I know you still love me."

"Loving you doesn't mean I can stay. You have no idea who I am anymore or what you want."

"What I want?" Ethan snatched my arm, pulling me into his chest. "I want you to stop turning away when I look into your eyes. I want you to touch me and tell me you love me again. I want—"

"What you want is a lie," I said, shoving him hard in the chest. "The girl on the boat doesn't exist anymore. And I can't give you that, Ethan. I can't give you a lie."

Skirting around him, I heard Ethan's voice at my back. "Mrs. Bradley, what are you willing to pay?"

"Pay for what?" I turned, tugging his coat. "What are you talking about?"

"Tidal creek whores. How much do they make for servicing big city writers like you? A few hundred? Five? How much am I worth to a woman like you?"

There was pain in his eyes. I saw it. Felt it in my heart. "You're not a whore, Ethan. You were never a whore."

"You come here, you fuck me, you leave. The only thing missing is the goddamn money." Ethan reached for the service door, careening it back to the wall. "I've got plenty of that on my own."

I wanted to scream. I wanted to take Ethan into my arms and tell him the truth of my life, but I couldn't. There are far more terrible things than feeling like somebody's whore. Ethan was lucky to just feel that.

He was lucky he wasn't my husband.

Thirty-Two

Water swirled the drain as I stepped from the shower and heard high-pitched squealing from the front of the house. Unbalanced sequences of whistles and whirrs toggled between short lengths of silence like kids ringing bells on a bike. *The kitchen phone?* That lemon yellow rotary was installed the day my mother and father purchased that house. It hadn't been used since Ethan lived there, so the fact it was ringing lent testament to ageless design. I snatched a towel from the shower rod, raced from the bathroom, and grabbed the receiver on its third tinny ring.

"Hello?" I answered, juggling the phone. "Who is this?"

"Smut writer!"

"Ethan. Why are you calling this phone?"

"You wouldn't answer if my number popped up on your cell. Thank God for Mr. Bell's antiquated technologies."

Swallowing laughter, I said, "What do you want?"

"Calm down, Shakespeare. What's your plan for the day?"

"I plan to see Abby and Edward, then I'm going to Mama's."

"Perfect. Old woman's coming with us, so I'll be there in an hour and pick you up too."

"No, you're not. I'm going alone."

"Why take that Buick when you can ride with me?"

"Because, unlike you, I don't care what a car looks like as long as it runs."

"What about clothes? I was grabbing yours from the cleaners before picking you up."

"The cleaners deliver, Ethan. Always have."

"Have it your way." Ethan chuckled as he hung up the phone.

Tightening the towel, I grabbed my coffee and overcooked toast, settled into Mother's reading chair, and prepared to call Blake.

He answered without greeting. "Sarah?"

"I'm here, Blake. It's me."

"You sound rested. How'd you sleep?"

"Mattress is old, but I managed. How's legal?"

"Usual route. Guy's story fell apart after claiming he wrote *War and Peace*."

"*War and Peace*." I laughed and stuffed a bite of toast into my mouth. "That's more ambitious than writing *Third Street*."

"It was," Blake said, and I heard the scrape of the balcony door open at home. "Channel 12 nixed the interview. It'll be finished by Friday."

"Are you at home? I hear traffic on the—"

"Have headaches today?"

The question gutted me, and I dropped my corner of toast. "No, Blake. No headaches today."

"What about tremors?"

"Do we always have to talk about that? Can't we talk about work or the weather or anything else?"

"Ignoring the signs means waiting until you fall, and it'll happen, Sarah. It always does."

"Not this time. Being home makes it stop."

"High times happen no matter where you are," he said. "Call me tomorrow when you wake up."

"I'll try."

"You'll do it, Sarah."

"And if I don't?"

Blake paused. "Then I'll be there on Friday to bring you back home."

This time, Blake hung up, no conclusions reached as our battle of wills waged on.

A knock rattled the front door. Heavy rapping and a loud, angry voice hit the walls.

"Unlock this door; bit of awful."

"Mama Nash!"

My excitement raced faster than my feet down the hall. There was one more knock before I opened the door and found Mama brooding at me from the porch. Aside from the pickled wood cane at her side, she looked nearly the same. Her dress still billowed in bright rainbow hues while her braids, seasoned with white, still dangled like vines on a fence.

"Ain't never been a girl like you," she said. "A bad, spiteful, ruinous girl."

My arms wilted as she shoved me aside and came in. "You're not hugging me?" I asked. "It's been eight years, and you're not hugging me?"

"Been eight years 'cos of you," she said, easing her bulk to a chair. "No one told you to linger in that city up there."

"What'd you expect? The book kept me busy, and with Blake breathing down my neck—"

"Don't blame that poor man for your rotten mess."

"My mess?" I shrieked, slapping a hand to my chest. "Well, you had a part in that mess, Mama Nash. Or are we conveniently forgetting your role?"

"That ain't no mess at all. God tied you for a reason, and that ain't what I'm talking about."

"Then what?" I asked. "What made you so mad you can't wrap your arms around me? What?"

"E'Tan," Mama said, leering at me. "That's the mess what I'm talking about."

"My mess with Ethan goes back fifteen years."

"Then leave it there." Mama fondled my hand, urging me down to her knees. Her touch was like feathers, and she soothed my cheek and fingered my hair in her usual comforting way. "I know you're hurting, baby. I know you're lonely, and your man has a wall on his heart thicker than tabby shell, but you shouldn't be here alone."

"I'm not alone," I said, kissing her palm. "You're here. So's Alicia. I'm better when I'm down here with you."

"Your man knows what you need, baby. And he loves you." Mama smiled and lifted my chin. "So don't start fires with anyone else. Those are rages you'll never put out."

"I'm not starting anything." I shrugged, standing and clutching my towel. "Alicia told me to come, so I did."

"Uh-huh." She nodded, switching her cane between hands. "And now E'Tan says you won't see him today."

"Oh, that's pathetic. Calling you to tattle on me. You didn't beat Ethan enough growing up, Mama Nash. Not nearly enough."

"He ain't tattled. He *told*."

"Call it what you like. I don't need Ethan to see Abby today. I'll take Mother's car and go there myself."

"Here's what you're going to do." When Mama started a sentence that way, I knew I'd already lost. "You'll settle your badness with E'Tan, and then you'll dress in the clothes I got from the cleaners and come with us to see our Abby. After that, you're having lunch with E'Tan and Edward. And you'll keep your hands to yourself."

Mama brandished advice with the subtlety of trawlers ramming their hulls. Her voice was calm and measured, but it was just a quieter version of a painful spank.

Mama brought my freshly laundered clothes, minus, I noticed, my panties. Had I not known who possessed the items last before the laundry, that could have been an oversight. I had no choice but to go without them, so, as requested, I dressed in ten minutes without the benefit of underwear.

The ride was informative. Mama rendered gossip while Ethan and I sat across from each other, gawking, grinning, and probably picturing each other naked. It was what we did. He looked good too. Feigning maturity in a tailored blue suit and red power tie, smelling like coffee, ocean, and pricy cologne. A captain of industry but still such a brat.

"Only you would take a limousine to a jailhouse," I said.

"Had to. Can't take that old work truck, and Mama says the Mustang is evil."

"'Tis evil. Killed too many creatures in that cursed thing. Squirrels, rabbits, and that poor little dog we ain't supposed to talk about. Bad spirits now."

"It's not the car's fault Ethan can't drive, Mama. He's probably aiming on purpose."

"Don't be wicked. E'Tan can't help it, but I don't care for that ungodly car."

Ethan tugged Mama's ear. "Our Mama deserves a luxurious ride. Don't you, old woman?"

Mama beamed, reaching over to pat Satan's knee. "My E'Tan's a good boy. He's a very good boy."

"Your E'Tan's a suck up," I said.

"A suck up?" Ethan smiled, tilting his head. "Tell me, Sarah. Is it true what they say about women up there in New York?"

"Depends on what you've heard. Something disgusting, no doubt."

"I heard they don't wear their panties."

"Ethan." I flushed, pinning my legs at the knee. "That's not true."

"Are you sure?" Ethan grinned, stretching each little word as it fell. "Because I could have sworn—"

"Jezebels." Mama sniffed. "Don't know their own shame."

"They surely don't," Ethan said. "What about you, Sarah? Do you think women who don't wear their panties are Jezebels?"

"Sarah thinks you're being a wise ass. That's what she thinks."

"That's not being a wise ass. *This* is being a wise ass." Then he looked right at Mama and said, "Sarah's missing something."

"No. I'm not."

"Are too."

"Shut up, Ethan. I am not."

"What's this you've lost?" Mama asked.

"It's special to Sarah." Ethan slipped something white from his coat, clutching it tightly in his fist. "It's a personal, delicate thing just for her." That man slid into a grin so evil he could have challenged a spot down in hell. "Ladies should be more careful with their delicate bits."

"Still a bastard after all these years," I said, fighting the temptation to laugh. "The worst in the world. A bastard every step of the way."

"A bastard?" Ethan's smile morphed into a sneer. "You really believe that, don't you?"

"Believe what?"

"That I'm a *bastard every step of the way.*"

"Lighten up, Ethan. I was making a joke."

"That was no joke. Calling me a bastard is becoming a habit with you."

"The fact you've got my intimate property gripped in your hand proves the point, doesn't it? Not to mention blaring knowledge of your past exploits."

"Past exploits?" he asked, sitting up. "You know, it's amazing how you can't seem to recall the good times we shared, but the crap you remember like it happened last week."

"Memories like that tend to stick. Know what I mean?"

"Yeah. I know." Ethan reached over, slapping the comb on my lap. "You dropped it last night. The other thing is in my breast pocket. Cleaners called, and I picked it up before getting Mama."

"The comb?" I blinked, watching the trinket glint on my skirt. "You had the comb?"

"Yeah, Sarah. The comb."

"But I thought—"

"I know what you thought." Ethan slid back and buttoned his suit coat. "You know, you don't own the right to heartache, Sarah. And you sure as hell don't corner the market on making up for past sins. Think about that, then come back and tell me who's a bastard."

Mama traded glances between Ethan and me. Then she wiggled a hand near the comb and said, "Beauty like that ain't as strong as it seems, Cherie. I imagine it could break easily if pushed too hard or pulled too much. Losing it once could mean you shouldn't have had it at all."

"Yes, Ma'am." I nodded, fixing the comb in my hair. "Yes, Ma'am."

"Child," Mama winked at me, tucking her chin, "who said I was talking to you?"

Bayport's jail was precisely as I'd imagined. Metal tables and chairs, cold cinderblock walls. Depressing, lifeless, and dull. And sitting there, waiting for Abby to come, was akin to waiting for the snow to fall. It was dim, desperately gray, and the only sounds I heard were whispers and shuffling that echoed enough to make it seem more desolate than it already was.

"Abby's been here for two weeks?" I asked, scraping a wobbly green chair from the wall. "And no one bothered to call?"

"Alicia tried," Ethan said, pointing at Mama. "But Mama yanked the phone from her hand and said there'd be hell to pay if she tried it again. Abby was crying, begging us not to."

"Worrying too much ain't right for a heart like yours." Mama smoothed her hips as she sat. "Too much on your mind as it is."

"My state of mind isn't up to you, Mama. Stop trying to control everyone."

"Looks like Abby's content to sit here and rot," Ethan said. "Mama's not helping the situation going along with whatever Abby wants."

"Stop trifling, boy."

"How's he trifling?" I asked. "Ethan's trying to help."

"Keeping Edward with us is enough. No need for that fancy attorney." Mama's eyes pinned to the door, watching Alicia enter with Abby. "Take those chains off her, 'Licia."

"Stop yelling, Mama," Abby said. "It's a rule."

"Twenty minutes is all I can give." Alicia opened Abby's cuffs and lingered a moment before nodding at me. "Glad you're home, Sarah. We'll catch up at Grandma's this week." Then she squeezed Abby's shoulder and turned to head out the door.

Even dressed in prison drab and surrounded by iron bars, Abby looked entirely at ease. She was smiling and healthy, with her hair tied in back, her shoulders dead-straight, and her face utterly free of concern.

"What happened?" I stood, pulling her into my arms. "Tell me what happened that night."

"Can't talk about that," she said, kissing me once. "It's been so long. Just sit here and visit before Alicia comes back."

"Visit with you? You're accused of murder in a death penalty state. You want to die in prison for that piece of shit?"

Ethan opened his coat. "Whole town knows how Buster was, Abby. Change the plea, like Ward said. Think of Edward."

"This is about Edward." Abby brushed a hand down my arm before moving to stand behind Mama. Something had passed between them. A lie. A secret. A soft understanding they'd never betray. How Abby smiled, and how Mama pulled Abby's hand to her shoulder, holding it tight in loving assistance of something unknown.

They were lying.

"What're you hiding?" I asked.

"Ain't hiding nothing, Cherie. God's plan working out."

"Oh, yeah?" I husked a laugh before looking at Abby. "Keep listening to this old woman right here, and you'll end up with a needle pumping poison in your arm. That what you want?"

"Edward needs to be safe, Sarah. You don't understand."

"I understand you're lying."

"Tread carefully, child. Best watch those wits."

"My wits are fine, Mama, and you know it."

"They might teeter if you keep going on like you do."

"Were you there, Mama?" I asked. "The night Buster died. Were you there?"

"Holy Christ, Sarah." Ethan shoved a chair as he walked. "What do you think she did? Drag the son of a bitch into that freezer herself? Beat him with her cane?"

"That's why they didn't want me here, Ethan. They knew I'd see through the lies."

"Sarah, please," Abby said. "Fighting takes strength I don't have anymore."

"Bullshit. You're hiding something. I can feel it."

"There ain't no secrets here, child. Best not to challenge God's will."

"God's will, Mama Nash?" I leaned closer, gripping her chair. "My son's dead. My marriage is in ruins, and my best friend's trying to kill herself by lethal injection. God's will is the last thing I'm worried about. Maybe He should be careful of mine."

Thirty-Three

The car barreled toward Mama's house, racing over Oaks Bridge as I fumed.

"Abby'll come around," Ethan said. "She'll see what she's doing is wrong."

"Not with this woman running the show. Isn't that right, Mama Nash?"

Mama shrugged. "Abby says she hasn't the strength to fight. Best we accept that."

"That's a lie, Mama. And you can tell Ethan, Alicia, and every gossip on Branch Street not to listen to me, but that won't change the fact that you're lying."

Mama turned to the window, changing the topic to something less dark. "Look at that, baby. Look at my beautiful house."

We wound between rows of moss-heavy oaks, entering wetlands with cordgrass and pine. Gone was the broken gray shack where I'd grown, replaced with a light-yellow house with forest green shutters and a gray-shingled roof on its cap.

"Ain't it sweet?" Mama smiled at Ethan with dreamy regard. "My E'Tan is such a good boy."

"Oh, he certainly is," I said, crossing my legs. "Tell me, Ethan. Is it bad luck to tear down an old house?"

"Sarah." Ethan's eyes darted between Mama and me. "Don't do this right now."

"Don't do what?" I shrugged. "I'm just asking about Mama's new house."

"Ain't got a new house, baby. E'Tan just slapped on some paint and cleaned out the pipes. A new house would have been a bad thing."

"Well, it sure looks like it's new. Why, the roof is cleaner, the porch is wider, and the whole house looks like it sits farther back from the road."

"Damnit, Sarah." Ethan thrust a finger at me. "That's not a fair fight. Something could happen to me."

"Keeping my underwear is bad luck, *E'Tan*," I said, pressing my shoulder to his. "Watching your dick shrivel off would be payback."

The car lurched to a stop, and Mama hugged me. "Don't forget Mama loves you."

"I love you too, Mama. But I still know you're lying."

Ethan deposited Mama inside before leaving the porch in two leaps. He slid into the seat opposite me, telling Daniel to take the long way home before he raised the partition between the front seats and back.

"Finally alone," he said. "The old woman's great, but I like having you all to myself."

"Last night won't have a round two if that's what you're thinking."

"Get your mind out of the mud, Shakespeare. I just want to talk."

"I'm not up for deep discussions right now."

"Just a question. A small one. I promise."

Raising a finger, I said, "One. And it better not be deep."

"All right," he answered. "Why are you staying in a marriage you just said is falling apart?"

"Jesus, Ethan. You don't think that's deep?"

"What if it is? Tell me anyway."

I stared at the roadside, watching sunlight slice through the pines. "Let it go, Ethan. We were just kids when all this started."

"Yeah, but we're not anymore, so now you can answer. Why do you stay with him?"

"Let it go."

"Fuck letting go. Tell me."

My head snapped around. "All right, Mr. Bennet. And when I'm done, maybe you can tell me why a naked blonde was stuck to your chest fourteen years ago? Because I guarantee that this conversation wouldn't even be taking place if that hadn't happened."

Ethan stalled, fiddling with his collar and pulling his tie. "We weren't naked."

"You both had your shirts off. That's naked enough."

"What you saw wasn't what you thought was happening."

"So there was no half-naked blonde girl rubbing your chest?"

"Yes, but it's not what you think."

"Then what was it? You tell me what the hell I saw."

Ethan stared as if he'd gone mute. His breath went short, and I saw the trip in his throat as he swallowed, but the words seemed to catch as if trapped by some hideous grip.

"The girl," he stuttered, still staring, still choked, "she wasn't... a girl. Not like you think."

"Looked like a girl to me. Blonde, brown eyes, cackling at me as she ran. You both must have had a big laugh."

"We didn't laugh at you, Sarah. No one laughed."

"So, where'd I fall on the list?" I asked.

"The list?" He blinked, confused. "What list?"

"The Ethan Bennet list of summertime conquests. Where'd I fall on that list?"

"There was no list," he whispered. "No other girl. Only you."

"Except for the girl attached to your chest." I slid back, crossing my arms. "That summer didn't mean shit to you, did it?"

"That summer meant everything," he said. "If you'd stayed—"

"If I stayed, I'd have been stuck at the *Gazette* writing articles about trawler accidents while you dicked every waitress who lifted her skirt. I dodged a bullet marrying Blake."

"Dodged a bullet?" Ethan's eyes aimed right at mine. "You think you dodged a bullet with Blake?"

"You bet your ass I do. Thank God I had the good sense to run."

He looked toward the window and scowled. "Yeah, you ran all right.

Straight to a lousy marriage, a job you can't stand, and a kid who takes naps in a graveyard. I'd say that's working well for you, Sarah."

The cruelty of the statement propelled me, and I heaved from my seat, slapping him so hard my hands went numb from the force. The comb fell from my hair, and I knelt on it, ignoring the sting as I struck him again. Ethan's eyes flared, and he grabbed my wrist, enraging me further. I hit him harder, intending to keep hitting him until I noticed our hands drenched in tears. We shoved apart, breathless and trembling, like two prize fighters caught in their ring.

"You don't know anything," I said. "You don't know me or my marriage or my life. You don't know a goddamned thing."

"Holy Christ." Ethan pushed from his seat to my side. "I'm sorry, Sarah. I didn't mean that. I didn't mean any of that."

At any other time in my life, I would have opened that car door, leaped to the road, and never seen Ethan again, but something in his eyes made me stay. They were so brown, so wide, so bright, and sincere. Ethan was a lifeline I didn't know I would need, and I didn't dare lose it again.

"Oh, Ethan." Overwhelmed with the thickness of history we struggled to hold, I pulled Ethan into my arms. "Bits of you, pieces of us. It's not enough anymore, and I don't know what to do."

"You stay here with me," he said. "That's all you do, Sarah. You stay."

Thirty-Four

"Edward's in the solarium," Ethan said, closing the castle's front door after me. "We're having lunch in the greenhouse."

"The greenhouse?" I left my satchel on the bench and followed Ethan down the hall to the solarium. "You kept it?"

"Thing was too big to move. Glass was gone, so I restored the frame and threw vines on the roof. Made sense just to leave it."

"Edward must love that. I can't wait to see how he's grown."

"Sarah, wait," he said, resting his hand on the knotty pine door. "Edward's not the little boy who ran through this house when we were kids."

"Well, I didn't think he stopped growing at five, Ethan. No matter how he looks, he'll always be Edward to me."

"And if he looks like Buster?" he asked. "Because he does. His height and his voice. Hell, he even walks like him sometimes."

"You think because he looks like Buster, he'll be the same way? That doesn't mean anything."

"Maybe not to us," he said. "But what about the rest of this town? You know how folks are around here. One wrong step and those gossips would eat him alive."

"They wouldn't do that to Edward. Everyone loves him. They always have."

"I hope you're right about that. I really do."

Ethan opened the door, and a preemptive rendition of colors, scents, and odd, natural sounds rushed from every corner of the curving glass walls. Colorful light drained from the transoms, highlighting the path to two wicker chairs with a table and settee facing the water outside.

And in the middle, as if grown from seed, sat the greenhouse, bulky and wide. Missing its glass, only the roof and six heavy stanchions remained. Ethan white-washed it, tied it with vines and placed a honey oak table and chairs underneath.

"So much has changed," I said, taking the last cobblestone steps. "Has Abby seen this?"

"She saw it first. Edward and I sleep here sometimes. Still play the monster game too."

Laughter rose from behind the greenhouse, and a nurse emerged with the largest human being I'd ever seen. Edward didn't walk. He sauntered, gaiting the corner like a tanker cutting through waves. Magnolia branches combed through his curls, and he smiled at Ethan while tugging the hem of his shirt.

Ethan exchanged minor conversation with the nurse, dismissing her before waving at me. "Come closer, Sarah. Let him have a look at you."

"Edward. It's me." I approached Edward slowly, allowing him to study my much smaller frame. "Do you know who I am?"

Edward smiled, dragging his eyes from my hands to my face before offering a soft, single word. "Sarah?"

"Yes." I smiled and fell into him, clinging as tightly as my arms would allow. "You look like Abby, Edward. Don't let anyone tell you, you don't." I glanced toward Ethan. "He's perfect. Beautiful and perfect. Like an angel."

"Yeah. Like a six-foot-five, three-hundred-twenty-pound angel," Ethan said, inspecting the table and platters of food. "He's talking more. Coordination's better, but we're trying to get him to understand his own strength. Kid yanked the bumper off that old truck of mine like plucking twigs from a tree."

Edward wheezed in a laugh. "I fixed Ethan's car."

"You sure did." Ethan patted Edward's back, helping him into a chair. "Like it came off the showroom floor."

"Five settings?" The table shined with silver-trimmed plates, and I tapped one, adding, "Will I have to defend my career again?"

"Not with these people. Edward's doctor, Jackson Andrews, and his wife, Angela, are old friends. Big fans of yours too. You'll like them. Angela, especially. She's Italian, a retired Latin professor, and quite the dirty book connoisseur."

The door opened, and an older couple stepped from the landing.

"The front door was unlocked again." Jackson scowled as he strode toward us. "I realize locking doors in the South is a sign of a paranoid mind, but you've got to lock all the doors. Edward could wander off."

Ethan took Jackson's hand. "Sorry, Jackson. I'll remember from now on."

"*Mi amore?*" Angela studied Ethan's flushed cheek. "Your face is so red. Shaving?"

"Something like that." Ethan chuckled, rubbing his jaw. "Something like that."

"Ah." Angela smiled, turning to me. "This must be your razor."

Tall and thin, Angela's features were distinct to her European roots. She carried herself in natural regality. Long neck, long arms, long hair. Like the graceful movements of a dark-feathered swan. The chiffon dress and shawl she wore floated over her shoulders like fog hovered over the sea. She was winsome and sweet, and so like Lena, I couldn't help but adore her immediately.

"You're Sarah Thorn," Jackson said. "I worked with your mother at Memorial sometimes. Striking woman. Excellent nurse."

I thanked him as we all took our seats, and I couldn't help but notice how Jackson kept staring at me as if I were being studied or closely examined somehow. But, with his white-peppered hair and lively gray eyes, I hardly cared. He reminded me of a well-loved book, worn flyleaf and pages folded. No pretense involved. Just a good story. I liked him immediately too.

"Angela and I are great fans of your books." Jackson unfurled his napkin, draping it over his chest. "I've missed you greatly with nothing to read while I fish."

"Careful," I said. "Confessions like that get you shunned in this town."

"Nonsense." Angela scoffed, handing Edward a roll. "Your critics have no passion. You're a marvelous author, Cara. I've often wondered about the strength it takes to cage such a torturous will. The force of it. The need. How did you stop it from flowing?"

The question was more eloquently phrased than the usual, *Where did you go?* But her deftness of instinct, knowing like Mama, left me slightly unnerved.

"WhiteThorn needed my help," I said. "It was a good decision, really. I've had opportunities to work with extraordinary writers."

"And you have." Jackson lifted the lid on our bisque. "*Dancing on Third Street* was your gem, wasn't it? Publishing a book like that couldn't have been easy for WhiteThorn."

"There were challenges, yes."

"And its author?" he asked. "Writing that book must have proved challenging for Mr. Hatcaden too."

"Yes," I said, arranging my plate. "It was."

"Courage like that is unusual, you know. People so tortured rarely feel free to express the pain of their lives. It takes uncommon courage to do that."

"Some call John a coward," I said. "For hiding and for not coming out. They'd never dare call him courageous."

"Then they don't understand true courage." Jackson propped on his elbows, smiling at me. "True courage lies not in the act of being courageous, but in the sacrifice we make to do that which we must. Hatcaden wasn't telling a story when he wrote that book, he was confessing a terrible wound, and it changed people, Sarah. Moved them to see mental illness not as an anomaly of nature but as a feature of a sometimes-fractured human condition. A challenge of the human spirit to strengthen its own broken will. And that is a terribly courageous thing. I hope John Hatcaden knows this."

Nodding, I said, "Thank you, Jackson. I'll make certain he does."

"Your husband's brave too." Angela served Edward his trout. "Jack and I saw him on the news fighting protestors. Such a brave thing to do. Beautiful man."

Jackson laughed. "Excuse Angela's bluntness. Swooning over strange men on TV is a habit she can't seem to break. Please, don't take offense."

"Can't be offended by the truth. Blake has a reputation for defending his authors. He's not one to worry about consequences, which garners attention wherever he goes. He's impressive that way."

"And determined," Angela said. "What an adventure it must have been growing WhiteThorn from such humble beginnings. Like Ethan fixing old boats." Angela gestured to a boat at the dock. She shined like a portrait out there. A brilliant white hull, blazing red cabin, and teal waters lapping her sides.

"She's perfect, Ethan. Smaller than your usual boats. Did you build her?"

"Restored," he said, piling salad onto my plate. "She's a raised deck Express Coastal Cruiser. She'd run aground in Shell Beach. Abandoned."

"Abandoned?" I slumped, trading looks between the table and boat. "You found her?"

"Didn't have to find her," Ethan said, handing me my plate. "Never gave her up."

"Well, the name's ridiculous." Jackson spoke around a bite of his crab. "Why take time restoring that unique craft just to straddle her with an awful name like that?"

"Well, I think it's lovely," Angela said. "There's a mystery to it. That makes it exciting."

Looking at Ethan, I asked, "What'd you name her?"

"*Lemniscate Eius.*"

"That means *forever his*," Jackson blurted. "The man put a sign on that boat telling everyone he owns the damn thing. A bit redundant, considering your choice of career, son. But at least Angela's on your side."

"Jack's mistaken, in part," Angela said. "The word *eius* does mean *his*, but *eius* has multiple meanings. It also translates to *her*. This would mean the name of Ethan's boat could also be *Forever Her*." She smiled warmly at Ethan. "That's how I like to think of it. I like to think somewhere on that boat, our sweet Ethan, young and handsome, made love to a girl long ago, and he's kept her memory there all these years. He's hiding a love story on that boat, just waiting for her to return. That's why he used that word, *eius*, so its meaning could be shared."

"There's a romantic for you." Jackson dabbed his mouth. "Pure emotion without an ounce of practicality. Let's talk about Edward."

Jackson shifted the conversation to more pressing needs. He spoke about Edward's condition and the probable causes behind his delays, concluding the best answer was a lack of oxygen resulting from a difficult birth.

"Ida was a small woman," he said, reaching to pat Edward's hand. "Edward, a large child. She had trouble with Abby, too, as I recall. Both children were breech, and considering troubles at home, it's a miracle Edward survived." Jackson said Edward's prognosis was good, and then, turning to Ethan, he remarked with a curious claim. "Treatments have improved over the years. Not like when dear Helen was here."

"Helen?" I asked, looking at Ethan. "Who's Helen?"

Ethan blinked at me once before speaking to Jackson again. "Festival's all planned out. We'll have the auction on Friday, the street party Saturday, and Valentine's ball on Sunday. Everything's set."

Touching my arm, Angela asked, "Do you have a ball gown yet?"

"Not yet," I said, still studying Ethan. "I wasn't sure of the dates, and—"

"We'll need to get you one, then. I know just the place."

Ethan tied his hands in mock prayer. "Dear Lord, deliver this child from the evils of uptight business crap and into the righteousness of half-naked, tramp-wear like she wore when she lived here with us. Amen."

"He's joking." I flushed, smiling at Angela. "I never dressed half-naked down here."

"Did, too." Ethan patted his chest with both hands. "She had this red bikini top, all sorts of sin bulging out. Got me through puberty, that's for sure."

"We'd better leave now." Taking Angela's hand, I pushed from the table to leave. "He'll only get worse if we stay."

Ethan called out, "Find bottoms for that bikini top too. And if you can get it two sizes too small, that'd be terrific. We'd all love to see that."

God, he was filthy. And he made me laugh.

The weather was spring-like. Cool breezes on sidewalks, warm sun on the streets. Angela and I walked easily, winding through alleyways and shaded brick roads toward the better shopping downtown.

"This one." Angela angled me toward a fancy boutique. "Abelia's has wonderful things."

"Abelia's? My dress from last night came from here."

"I know." She smiled, stabbing the lock with her key. "I own Abelia's."

"Oh." Recalling the dress's brutal demise, I dropped my gaze to my shoes. "It was beautiful, Angela. Everything fit perfectly too. Even the lingerie."

"Why wouldn't it?" She winked. "Ethan picked it out."

We enjoyed our afternoon. It was light and carefree, and for a time, my mind eased from its structured confines, and I was a girl again, enjoying myself with a friend. Angela chose a gown for the ball. Crimson red satin, form-fitting with sheer sleeves, Belgian lace bodice, and a hem that haloed my feet.

"Who says redheads shouldn't wear pink?" Angela held a tight-wasted dress with a flared skirt. "We're breaking that rule with you."

We chose shoes, shorts, tops, and enough lingerie to hold me for weeks.

"You have enough to fill a large closet now." Angela gestured to the towers of bags. "Plus, whatever Ethan picked out."

"Ethan's already done too much," I said, zipping my skirt. "Buying my clothes wasn't necessary."

"No one tells Ethan what he can or can't do. He liked doing it."

"Being my friend is enough."

"Cara," she began, resting her arm on a rack. "A woman's friends know her face cream and favorite places to shop. Her husband knows her café and possibly her perfumes, but only a lover knows the fit of a woman's lingerie."

"We're not lovers, Angela. We're friends."

"Oh, I see." She nodded, spreading a scarf on a stand. "You know, I always thought it was the greatest sadness to assume that while the heart can be broken, it cannot just as easily be divided."

I glanced at her briefly before tucking my blouse. "Because it shouldn't."

"Perhaps. But our hearts love in unexpected directions sometimes, and when that happens, it's terribly hard to hide."

"We're just close, Ethan and me. We know strange quirks about one another, and that's all."

"I see it, Cara. Soft touches under the table and the gentle smiles you share. I see it when Ethan gazes at the boat he takes such precious care of yet rarely sails."

"Angela, please," I said, choking a breath. "Please don't make me talk about—"

"A man you love?" She smiled, hooking my arm. "Your heart is full of love stories. Let us start with the one on the boat."

An hour later, Angela became the only other witness to the details of my and Ethan's love story. I didn't tell her why it ended, leaving it only as a misunderstanding between two youthful hearts. She seemed satisfied with the tragedy of that.

"That's truly a love story, Cara," she said. "How could you ever have left it?"

And I answered simply, "I didn't."

Thirty-Five

That week passed quickly in Ethan and Edward's company. We lay on the beach, fished, and played together, splitting time between picnicking in the gazebo and sleeping under the stars in the castle's solarium. Ethan and I made love every day, and he'd ask me to call Blake in a final confession I wasn't yet able to make. Those were the moments his eyes would close, and he'd turn away as if thinking of something to say, but there was nothing more, and if there was, he kept it to himself.

After another dull visit with Abby, I returned to Mother's, tossing the keys onto the sofa before heading into the kitchen. Ethan stood by the backdoor, rummaging through a rusty, red toolbox, trying to fix the window I broke.

"And how's our Miss Abby today?" he asked, no doubt sensing my mood.

"Well, let's see," I said, opening the refrigerator and taking a soda from inside the door. "First, she talked about the weather, then Mama's *damn rats*. Then she went on about how Edward saw a pelican eating a snake last year. When I asked about Buster, she clammed up."

"Better stop pushing like that."

"I'm not pushing. I'm being direct."

"That's not being direct. That's pushing. You're a pusher, Sarah. Always have been."

"Am I? And what's it called when you're on the phone every day trying to get her out of jail?"

"That's called having connections." Ethan took my soda, popped it open, and claimed a long drag. "Just be careful when you talk with her. You can be forward sometimes, thinking stuff's going on when it's not."

"Like I'm paranoid? Is that what you mean?"

"I mean, be careful with Abby. Don't get agitated, or she'll shut us all out."

"Agitated." I spun on my heels, heading to Mother's room. "You sound like Blake right now. Just like him."

"Come on, Sarah. What's got you so worked up? Did Blake finally call you back? Is that it?"

Removing my shirt and shorts, I kicked off my flats and laid the pink satin dress on the bed. "Haven't spoken to Blake since Wednesday. How much time before the party? Is Mama at the park yet? She was bringing honey."

"She's there, and we have two hours." Ethan propped on the dresser, sipping my drink. "Is that why you're edgy? Because Blake hasn't called?"

"This isn't about Blake. I'm tired, have a headache, and I'm trying to—"

"Decide whether to go without underwear?"

"Really, Ethan?" I shrugged. "All right. I'll go without mine if you go without yours."

"No problem." He grinned, taking another long drag. "I haven't worn panties in years anyway."

I pointed to the soda and said, "Give me that drink, and I'll let you borrow mine."

"This drink?" Ethan asked, swigging again. "This soda's worth more than a pair of underwear."

"That's the only can left, Ethan. Give it to me."

"Nope." Ethan hiked the can as I jumped for it, rattling the dresser and mirror. "Now it's mine."

"Give me that drink, and I'll go without panties all day."

"Liar. What would poor Mama say about that?"

"She'd tell you to give me that drink."

"Hell, no." We laughed, fighting for that red and white can. "Sugary drinks are the nectar of the Southern gods. This one's mine. I earned it fixing the window you broke."

"You made me mad that day. That window broke because of you."

"Okay, okay," he said, pushing back. "Let me see you naked, and you can have what's left of my drink."

"That's my drink, and you saw me naked this morning."

"And now I want to do it again."

"Fine." I stepped back, slipping out of my panties and bra. "There. Now give me the can before I make you a victim in one of my books."

"Well, now you sound like Echo." Ethan set the drink on the dresser. "Wanna boil my nuts later too?"

"That depends," I said, hooking his belt loop and yanking him close. "On what?"

"On if that soda's still cold after we're done being dirty in here."

"Better get that stew pot ready, Miss Thorn."

"Oh, yeah?" I kissed him before pulling him down to the bed. "And why would I want to do that?"

"Because that right there," he said, sucking the curve of my neck, "is nothing but a dead-empty can."

"God, Ethan!"

It was wonderful being with him again. Ethan knew me as I had been, remembered me as I was, and he shared those memories in every touch, every kiss, and every breath he took from me. And in those moments trapped in his arms, I could pretend my mind wasn't breaking.

We lay there kissing, and Ethan uttered what had become a constant mantra at the end of our lovemaking. "Call Blake, Sarah. Tell him you're not going back."

"I can't."

He stared at me briefly before jerking away and snatching his jeans from the floor. "You feel warm. Better take something before we go out."

"Why can't I make you understand?" I sat up, dragging the dress from the foot of the bed and smoothing it over my lap. "We'd never survive if I stayed."

"Never survive?" He huffed, zipping his jeans. "Every time you open your mouth, I swear I hear Blake falling out."

"Blake's never treated me the way you think he has."

"Yeah. That's what Abby said about Buster."

"I don't sound like Abby."

"Yes, you do. Every time I tried moving her out of Buster's shop, she'd give some excuse about staying for Edward."

"Blake isn't like Buster. You always think the worst of him because you don't like him."

Ethan bent closely, bracketing his fists at my thighs. "The man's got you tied to his wrist like a dog. He tells you how to work, where to live, and how to breathe. You're so used to it you can't even see it anymore. Now, if I've misunderstood the situation somehow, do me a favor and tell me what part I got wrong because I'd love to know why I've spent fourteen years waiting for you to wise up."

Two raps rattled the front door, and we jolted apart.

"That's Mama." I stood, stepping into the dress and wriggling it over my hips. "Why'd you lock the front door?"

"I didn't. She just knows what we're doing in here, and that's her way of making us stop."

"Well, she's not going away." I dashed through the hallway and jerked to a terrified stop. "Blake?"

Thirty-Six

⟨⟨⟨⟩⟩⟩

Blake stood in the living room as I stumbled in from the hall. My hair was tangled and fell to one side, and the dress felt barely applied.

"Did I startle you?" Blake smiled, tossing his sunglasses and keys to the coffee table. Then he dipped closer and grazed a kiss on my lips. "I knocked once or twice but figured you might be asleep."

"That's okay. Why didn't you call?"

"Thought coming was best. Is your mom's car not working? There's a Mustang out front."

"A Mustang? Oh, that's... that belongs to—"

"That would be mine." Ethan strode in, tucking his polo. "We weren't expecting company, Blake. Nice of you to stop by."

Blake raised a brow toward me. "Ethan's here?"

"There's a broken window in the kitchen," I said. "He came to fix it."

"Perfectly innocent, old man." Ethan pocketed his hands. "Hope you didn't waste time for a quick break from New York."

"I came for Sarah. Thought she might need me."

"Sarah's doing great here with us. Mama's making sure she eats, Alicia got the house set up, and I'm—"

"Fixing windows?" Blake asked.

"Exactly." Ethan snapped a quick nod. "Captain Wonderful came to fix windows."

"From down the hallway," Blake said. "When the tools and window are here behind me?"

"Had to wash my hands." Ethan wiggled his fingers at Blake. "Got a little dirty earlier. Didn't we, Sarah?"

"Ethan, just go." I opened the door, and the room echoed with horns, bells, and muted, mixing music. "Tell Mama we'll meet at the park."

"Come to The Waterfront, Blake," Ethan said from the porch. "We're having an auction."

"Boats don't interest me, Bennet."

"Oh, I'm not auctioning boats. I'm auctioning Sarah. Might want to dust off your wallet." Ethan laughed before closing the door.

"Bennet certainly does get around," Blake said, opening his suit coat. "Doesn't he?"

"When something needs fixing, he does." Turning to the sofa, I picked up a cushion and began absently cleaning the room. "He was visiting and decided to repair the window while he was here."

"Is that what you're doing? Visiting friends?"

"Did you expect me to sit in jail every day? Yes, Blake. I'm visiting friends. Mama and Alicia came too."

Blake pulled a newspaper page from his coat, dropping it onto the coffee table. "Did Mama and Alicia dance with you too?"

The *Gazette's* front page blazed with colorful pictures of Ethan and me at Steadman's one week before. We were wanton and happy, with Ethan's hands on my back, my eyes pinned to his, and desire in our faces apparent.

"That was a charity dinner," I said, arranging pillows on the arm of the couch. "Ethan invited me the first night I came."

"Thought you came here for Abby."

"I did come for Abby. Nothing's resolved yet. There hasn't been time."

"How could there be? What with all the parties and window fixing going on."

"Where'd you get the newspaper, Blake?" I asked, planting my hands on my hips. "Going through the mail in my office now too? That's low, even for our wretched dynamic."

"Didn't have to look in your mail." Blake took my hand, crushing a small, folded note in its palm. "Someone was eager to share your itinerary with me. This note was inside the paper they sent."

Reading the note under my breath, I whispered, "Have a nice day." It was written on decorative parchment and had a smiley face drawn in a heart. "But who? Who would send this to you?"

"I dunno, Sarah. Maybe someone who wants you to leave your husband?"

Blake stood inches in front of me, snaking the tie from his neck.

"What're you doing?" I asked.

"Changing clothes. I'm invited to a party. Remember?"

"But you don't have any clothes."

"My luggage is on the front porch."

"Luggage?" I tipped to one side, peering out. "You have luggage?"

"Yeah," Blake said, fingering his belt. "I'm staying."

Thirty-Seven

I brooded on the sofa like a scolded child, listening to the laughter from the party downtown. Blake was dressing inside Mother's room. He'd taken a shower and came out briefly, shaking an Oxford and jeans from his bag. Blake kept himself toned through the years, and I watched water drizzling through hairs on his chest, trailing the infinite plains of his stomach and lower.

It was during those intimate invasions of space, that I'd recall our times together, remembering how that naked body moved over mine in the dark. And I'd ache for him in a way that held a sting of rejection so familiar, the desire was quickly dismissed.

The front door banged open, and Mama barged into the house.

"Where's your man?" she asked, darting in and out of the kitchen. "E'Tan said he come into town. Run, get him for me."

"Forget it, Mama. Blake's not in the mood to see you right now."

"That's a nonsense. Go tell him I'm here."

"He'll be out in a minute," I said, picking the sofa's frayed arm. "Once he's done thinking up ways he can kill me."

"That's an insulting appraisal, Sarah." Blake smiled at Mama as he walked from the hall. "Hello, Miss Nash. Nice to see you again."

"Lord, listen to that proper talk." Mama kissed Blake heavily, patting and squeezing his arms. "This is no monstrous man. This here's a good man. This here's a rare man. This ain't no monster at all."

"Stop stirring pots, Mama. You know I never called Blake a monster."

"I ain't said you did. Now, get washed up."

"Washed up for what?" I stood, smoothing my dress. "I'm fine."

"You ain't fine. You look like you rolled from the hamper, so get washed up."

Mama pushed Blake to the porch, closing the door at her back.

Front porch gossip was best witnessed standing beside Mother's bedroom window between the blue, tufted reading chair and the knock-off Tiffany lamp. So that's where I ran. I dusted the cobwebs from my usual spot, pushed the curtains aside, and pressed my ear to the screen. Mama's hands flew while Blake nodded gently in slow recognition of whatever she said.

That bothered me. The closeness of it. The risk of Mama drawing another unwary victim into her less-than-perceptible web. I scraped a brush through my hair and ran to the porch, cracking the door to the wall.

"What're you talking about?" I asked.

"Lord, child," Mama said. "What's got on you?"

"I don't like secrets, and that's what you're doing out here. Talking about me behind my back."

"She was talking about Abby," Blake said. "That's all."

"Did she tell you I think they're lying?"

"Yeah. She did."

"And did she tell you I think she helped Abby do it? I bet she left out that little detail, didn't you, Mama?"

"Stop it, Sarah. You're getting agitated, and you damn well know why."

"She and Abby are hiding something. Mama knows I'll find out, so she's lying to make me look crazy."

"You don't need any help doing that." Blake stood, helping Mama out of her chair. "Let's go before it gets late."

After reaching the park, and at her request, we left Mama under the shade of an oak. She preferred the fringes of social conformity, sitting at its side where she could watch, study its habits, and keep it for future use.

And Mama always found use.

Bayport's social undertow hadn't changed in my absence. Boats still clogged the waterway, vendors with colored displays still sold food and wares, and children chased one another along The Waterfront's playground and paths. The activity was exciting, but deep down, where only Blake and I knew, the pulsating crush of it frightened me.

"Miss Nash told me about Abby," Blake said as we walked. "You think they're lying about what happened that night?"

"Abby couldn't have killed Buster alone. She had help."

"You think Abby's taking the blame for a murder she didn't commit?"

"Or protecting someone who did."

"Like a conspiracy?" Blake asked. "You see a conspiracy involving Miss Nash and Abby?"

I stopped, shading my eyes from the sun. "Why are you talking like that?"

"Like what?"

"Like John Hatcaden's about to show up."

"I'm trying to get you to see the truth, honey."

"And what truth is that?" I asked, crossing my arms. "In all the five seconds you've been here, what truth do you see?"

Blake shrugged. "I see a woman who killed her abuser."

"Why? Because Mama told you she did?"

"Because that's what makes sense."

"Nothing about this makes sense. Buster didn't lay a hand on Abby. Not in years. She told me herself."

"Abby was used to it, that's all. Women like her ignore the signs until rage builds up and something snaps. Abby snapped."

I laughed at the irony before walking again. "For two men who can't stand each other, you and Ethan think alike. He said the same thing not two hours ago."

"Ethan's opinion is based on assumption, and mine's based on experience. I know how you think things are sometimes happening when they're not."

"Yeah, well, he said that too." I glanced at him once. "Which means you both think I'm paranoid. Also means you're both wrong."

"This is a high time, honey. You're flushed with fever. Headaches will start, then tremors. Take the meds, Sarah."

"Did you just come to cram pills down my throat? Is that why you're here?"

"I came because you'll need me."

"You saw me with Ethan," I said, dodging children casting their bait. "That's why you came."

His breath went short as he jogged to catch up. "That's true. I did. When I saw you with him, I knew I needed to try harder for you. For us. We need to find our way back to where we started."

"That's the problem, Blake. We never started at all. Besides White-Thorn, what connection do we have?"

"Love connects us," he said. "It's struggling, but it's real. You know it is. I love you, Sarah."

"That's one hell of a change. Last week you were measuring strait-jackets. Now you're in love and want to set things right? Talk about behavioral conflict."

Blake laughed, taking my elbow and guiding me onto a bench. "At least let me apologize for saying those things. I was upset and didn't want you feeling—"

"You don't want me feeling anything. That's why we have Hatcaden, right?"

"Hatcaden helps, Sarah. He helps you see the world as it really is."

"This is the world." I floated a hand toward the bay. "There's no sadness, darkness, or little gray pills. It's bright and happy. The sun's shining, and everyone's singing and hugging."

"Honey, look at the sky," Blake said, and we both looked overhead. "It's overcast. Gray. Look at the people. No one's hugging and singing. Your mind's exaggerating everything. This is a high time, and when it ends, you'll fall. Hard. You always do."

"At least I would have had it a little while."

"You can't, Sarah. Not even a little while. You need Hatcaden. You need me."

"Go back to New York." I stood, turning to head down the walk. "I know what I'm doing, and it's not something you'd understand."

"Yeah. I hear that's what Abby says too."

I spun quickly. "Don't pull that crap on me. This is nowhere near the same thing."

"The hell it's not. Two women aimed at some self-destructive path. And for what? What are you willing to lose?"

"That doesn't work anymore, Blake. My son's dead, and my husband's terrified of me. I have nothing left to lose."

I escaped down the pathway as the festival raged into life. Loud orchestras of horns, bells, and shouts rang out, forcing their way through the safety of trees and the distance between the pathway and the stage. I recoiled instantly, shielding my ears as the crowd bustled nearer, jostling and shoving in a wide human wake. Blake rushed to me, guiding us under a broad, shaded oak as the party surged.

There was foreign intimacy in Blake's sudden touch. There was no fear. No hesitation. No doctors or pills. His hands were smooth and slow, and they traveled the curve of my hips to my shoulders and neck and finally my face, where he covered my ears.

"Don't be frightened," he whispered. "I'm here now. I'm here."

Then his lips were on mine, and he told me he loved me, and the fear that had filled me was gone.

Thirty-Eight

The racket fell to a consistent thrum as the music quieted and the routine events began moving. There was a mic stand on stage with volunteers rolling equipment left to right and the shrieking of instruments buzzing in tune.

"Forgot how loud these things are," I said, slumping against the oak. "And there are so many people."

"Need to sit?" Blake held my elbow, steadying me. "Get out of the crowd for a while?"

"I'm all right. Holding me helped."

"No problem," he said, dipping close. "I was planning to grope you in a park someday anyway. Covering your ears came in handy."

"That was more than covering my ears. You held me just now. You don't usually do that."

"Don't I?" he asked, blinking at me. "What do I usually do?"

"What do you mean, what do you usually do? You give me a pill. Or call a doctor. Sometimes both."

"Well, not every time, Sarah. Sometimes I'm there and we—"

"You're never there," I said, wiping sweat from my neck. "Whenever you think I'm going to fall, you call for someone to take me away."

"Take you away?" Blake stared at the waterway and raked a hand through his hair. "Christ. All the times you told me you needed me, all the times you asked for my help. How am I only seeing it now?"

"Because you're too frightened to look," I said. "If you want to understand how awful it is, you'll have to stop being afraid."

"Cara." Angela pushed through a group of children licking ice cream drips from their arms. "A husband harboring his wife is a beautiful thing, no?" She smiled, offering a hand to Blake. "I'm Angela Andrews. Your talented wife's new best friend."

"And how do you know I'm her husband?"

"Television, of course. You were battling crowds like a soldier." She rested a hand on Blake's arm. "My husband says I was swooning over you. I wasn't, but as an American male, he's prone to self-entitled jealousy."

Blake laughed, gesturing to a Bennet Marine banner on stage. "Bennet Marine's hosting the auction?"

"Ethan's foundation is the featured charity," I said. "Festivals raise funds for non-profits, and the auction's part of that."

"Didn't realize Bennet had a foundation. What's it for?"

"For Edward." Jackson approached from the playground with Edward. "And anyone like him. The Bennet Foundation will ensure they receive proper care." Jackson gripped Blake's hand in a shake. "I'm Jackson Andrews, Edward's doctor. And you're Blake Bradley, fearless defender of the Hatcaden book."

"Ah, the library debacle. I gave that book more defense than Hatcaden probably needed."

"Hardly a debacle, young man. Imagine if London or Woolf had defenders like that."

"Their books weren't protested."

"Their sanity was. One side of their mind fighting the other. Cravings for death and all that."

Blake smiled. "You have an interest in bipolar writers, Doctor?"

"Only in what drives them. Interesting bunch, writers. The most brilliant often struggle with crushing emotional stress. People like you are important to them, even if they don't know it themselves. Never apologize for defending your author, young man. It's probably what keeps him alive."

Blake thanked him before turning to Edward. "Remember me, Edward? It's been a long time, and you were much shorter back then."

Edward searched Blake's eyes before whispering, "Michael?" Then he opened Blake's hand, dropping four carved animals into its palm. "Play with me."

"Oh, Edward, no," I said with a gasp. "This isn't—"

"Those are great toys you have there, Edward. Want to see mine?" Blake dug into a pocket, removing three matching toys: a bird, a cat, and a dog.

"Where'd you get those?" I asked. "Are those from Michael's..." There was no way to finish that thought. I knew what they were and understood where he got them, but I wasn't prepared for the *why*.

"They fall off," he quietly said. "I pick them back up."

"And you keep them in your pocket?"

"No," Blake answered. "Not all of them fit."

"Michael has army men too." Edward smiled. "He shares them with me at the beach."

"Would you like to play now?" Blake pointed to the playground bordered by palms. "There's room by the benches, and we'll talk about Michael."

Edward agreed, took Blake's hand, and led him toward the path.

"I'm sorry, Sarah." Jackson stepped closer to me. "The toys in Blake's hand belonged to your son?"

"They did," I said, watching Blake and Edward stroll by the swings. "When Michael was alive, Blake played with the boys at the beach. Edward remembered."

"Jack and I heard about your son's accident, Cara. That must have been a terrible time for you both."

"It was," I said, seeing Ethan cut through the crowd. "It still is."

"Hey, Shakespeare." Ethan shouldered between us and tugged on my hair. "Ready to be auctioned off?"

"Do I have any choice?"

"Nope." He laughed. "Too late to back out now."

"Then I guess I'm ready. Everything finished on stage?"

"Almost. Just getting the mics and speakers set up."

"Ethan, look." Edward dodged through the swing sets, holding his toys. "These are Michael's animals. Michael's gone now, so Blake keeps his toys."

Ethan looked at the animals and then back to Blake. "Guess they'll be safe with him, won't they?"

"I told him," Blake said to me. "Edward knows."

"Knows what?" Ethan asked.

"Nothing," I answered. "When's the auction start?"

"Few minutes," Ethan replied. "We've got time."

"I hope you don't mind being claimed by an old dogfish like me," Jackson said.

"Claimed?" I smiled. "I don't understand."

"Jack's bidding on you," Ethan said. "So's Evan. Can't have Bayport's favorite author stuck with strangers at the bidder's dance, can we?"

"Bidder's dance?" Blake asked.

"Highest bidding couple gets first dance at the Valentine's ball," I said. "Long dresses, black tie. I didn't know they added me too. They don't usually invite married people."

"We're debauched down here now." Ethan grinned. "Your reputation makes you a commodity, so I added your name."

"Why not bid on Sarah yourself?" Blake asked. "Instead of having your friends do it for you?"

"Well, that's a conflict of interest, old man. Featured charities aren't allowed to make bids."

"You never struck me as someone who cared about conflicts of interest, Bennet. Nice to know you observe at least some common rules."

"Oh, I observe all the rules. Just don't care if I break them."

Angela nudged Blake's shoulder. "Challenge Jack's offers, Blake. Bid on Sarah yourself."

"Maybe I will. It's been a long time since Sarah and I had a weekend alone together. Might be nice."

"Well, holy shit." Ethan laughed, slapping Blake's back. "Mr. Bradley dares entertain himself with the frivolity of the unwashed masses. We've got a fight on our hands, don't we, Blake? May the best man win."

"Best man won when he married her, Bennet. You're just too thick to catch on."

"Auction is starting." I snatched Ethan's hand. "We'd better go."

"I'll take care of Blake." Angela cuddled Blake's arm. "We'll stand by the stage where he can see you."

Ethan and I angled through the crowds toward the stage, and I scolded him. "Why'd you say all that crap about breaking the rules and unwashed masses? That only makes things harder for me."

"Just tell him you're not going back to New York. That's all you have to do."

"I can't do anything now. I want to get through the rest of this day and go home."

"Is Blake going too?"

"Yes, Blake's coming too. What am I supposed to do? Make him sleep in the yard?"

"That's what you should do, but I'm guessing you won't." We stopped by the stage, and Ethan pulled my comb from his pocket, plunging it into my hair. "Made you the damn thing; the least you can do is wear it." Then he leaped up the steps, taking long, angry strides across the stage.

"Two men pissed at me," I mumbled. "No wonder I'm crazy as hell."

Thirty-Nine

There were twelve auction lots, each of us gathered by the steps to the stage, primping and combing our hair. Charlotte was there, sneering at me from her group. She nodded in a cordial greeting, and I answered by extending my middle finger. That was classless, but the alternative would have bloodied my dress.

The competition was tough and included a cashier with breasts too large for her shirt, a realtor with a handlebar mustache, a dog groomer with great legs, and an assortment of nubile creatures whose perfection fell between the edges of scalpels and whispers of prayer.

Boobs went first at twenty-four hundred. Impressive, considering her chest rivaled Alicia's. The realtor caught a lower sum at fifteen hundred. Again, not bad, but his mustache wax cost more than that. The groomer gained a tidy sum of three grand. Her legs were perfect, and she was also worth more. Charlotte earned a paltry amount at two hundred.

No doubt she spoke.

With the rest of the lots quickly claimed, Ethan waved me onto the stage.

"And we've saved the best for last," Ethan said. "This red-haired beauty stands at a stunning five feet, seven inches tall. Her favorite food is Rolo's candy. She fights for Coca-Cola and seeks world peace by way of literary filth. What can we get for the brilliant writer and prodigal child of Bayport, Sarah Haley Thorn?"

My curtsey was followed by a quick royal wave.

"We start the bidding at," Ethan teased in a pause, "five-thousand dollars."

"Five-thousand," Jackson shouted, raising an arm. "Five-thousand dollars for my favorite writer."

"We have a bid from Dr. Andrews. Do we have fifty-five hundred?"

"Fifty-five." Evan stumbled in from the right, sloshing beer from his red party cup. "Fifty-five hundred for the girl who busted my nose."

The crowd laughed, and Jackson offered again, then Evan, raising the stakes as still others chimed in, gaining bids in increments of one hundred here, two hundred there. Ethan grinned, satisfied each time Jackson and Evan battled advancing bids.

Blake and Angela pushed to the front of the stage, where Blake smiled and crooked a finger at me. "You all right?"

"I'll live," I said, crouching with my knees in his face. "Just feel like a fresh piece of meat."

"No one says you have to do this, you know. You can always back out."

"And risk a headline telling the gossips their favorite smut writer ditched a charity event? No thanks."

Blake laughed. "What if you twirled or danced a little?"

"Being up here is awkward enough, and twirling would make it worse."

"Well, you're hardly a commodity just standing around. Give the bidders something to throw their money at. Stand right here and twirl once or twice."

Against my better judgment, I agreed. Standing over Blake, I raised my hands, tipped on my toes, and turned in tight pirouettes. The dress fluttered and waved at my knees, and Blake smiled, training his gaze on my thighs. There was something sensual about him. Like he held a secret and wanted me to know.

Then I did.

My panties. I wasn't wearing any.

I'd been twirling over my husband, completely naked beneath. I froze, clenching my thighs and gaping at Blake in ghastly, unsettled panic.

Blake laughed and nearly crashed into a giggling Angela behind him.

"Beautiful," he said, blowing a kiss. "You're beautiful."

Blake took the phone from his pocket while Angela inched to the front, her Italian romantic dying under the anticipation as bids rose higher.

"I'll give ten-thousand," Jackson shouted.

The crowd gasped and fell nearly silent.

"Dr. Andrews has us at ten-thousand," Ethan said. "Going once, going twice, going—"

"Two million dollars." Blake thrust his phone in the air. The words slashed through the crowd like a shot of hot whiskey. "Did you hear me, Bennet?" Blake hoisted himself onto the stage. "I said I'll give two million dollars to spend the weekend with my wife."

"What're you doing?" I asked, watching Blake approach. "Ethan, he's not serious."

Blake laughed. "If I wasn't serious, I wouldn't have offered."

"All bids close at the end of the ball Sunday night," Ethan said. "You're aware of that, right?"

"I'm aware."

"Are you?" Ethan gave me a brief, weightless glance. "What exactly are you aware of, Blake?"

"I'm aware I just ruined your weekend."

"Is that what you think? You think you ruined my weekend?"

"From the look on your face, I'd say that's exactly what I did."

Ethan smirked, stabbing the mic in its stand. "That's the problem with men like you, Blake. You live on the surface of things, thinking you know what's going on underneath, and you don't. Arrogance like that makes you blind. Makes you predictable too."

"Does it?" Blake grinned, tugging me close. "Can you predict what I'll do with Sarah once we get back to the house?"

"I predict you'll spend a few days playing give a shit husband of the writer you ruined, then you'll leave again, and I'll go back to kissing that little scar on the inside of Sarah's hip like I always do when my mouth's between her legs." Ethan leaned closer, adding, "How's that for ruining something, you arrogant fuck?"

Air keened from Blake's lungs, and he reared back, throwing a fist into Ethan's left jaw. Ethan rushed forward, and I pushed between them, bracing my arms at their chests. Jackson and Evan scrambled on stage, keeping the men apart as collective gasps faded into floating, awkward whispers.

"Come with me." Blake yanked me from the stage, and we forged over Branch Street's crowded intersections through the music and laughter of people blind to what was happening. Mama sat under the oaks, her sweet grass basket filled with crisp bills. We sped past like a whirlwind, and I saw her ease from the chair.

My wrist ached under Blake's grip, and my legs burned from near exhaustion as we entered Mother's house, and Blake pulled me inside.

"Him?" he asked, eyes stricken with gut-wrenching panic. "Before me?"

"Yes. Blake, please—"

"When, Sarah? When were you with Ethan before you met me? How close?"

"A month. Six weeks. Blake, I—"

"Jesus, Sarah, no."

"Blake, listen, please."

"Michael?" Blake wept, head bowed as a dawning thought broke open wide.

"Let me talk to you first. Let me—"

"Answer the question. Michael?"

Tears blurred, and I cried, letting a lifetime of lies fall away. I reached up, cupping Blake's cheek, admiring the shine of those beautiful eyes and the fluttering pulse of the neck I adored. Then I took a breath and gave the answer he always deserved to have.

"His."

"Jesus, God, you didn't." Blake stumbled backward, chanting that over and over again. "Jesus, God, you didn't."

He was rocking with his hands in his hair, dropping to the floor on his knees. Small grunts and pitched whines rose from his throat like the cries of a tortured dog.

"Blake, please. Listen to me. Let me talk to you."

His head shot up, and he lunged, grabbing my face and pushing me back to the wall.

"Why?" he whimpered, spit and tears tracing his lips. "I loved you, Sarah. I've always loved you so much. Why?"

This trembling creature changed from the confident, controlled man who once loved me into a furious mountain of smoldering, shattered grief. I could hear it in his cries, his soul slowly crushed beneath the weight of my betrayal. I could feel it. I could see it, and I couldn't make it stop.

"Do you know what I've done?"

"I've been so alone, Blake. So terribly—"

"The truth I've hidden from you?"

"Please, Blake. You pushed me away and—"

"The goddamn secrets I carry to keep you from falling apart?"

Rage took over, and Blake fisted my hair, kissing me deeply. I twisted, gasping for air and looking into the pain-filled eyes of a man I no longer recognized.

"Is this how he did it?" he asked, hand plunging between my legs. "Did you like it, Sarah?"

"Blake, don't do this."

"Did you do it right here in the house? How many times?"

"Blake, no." I choked, feeling every stinging breach of his hand. "Blake, please. You don't know what you're doing."

"I know exactly what I'm doing," he said. "I'm about to fuck my wife."

"Boy!" Mama slammed through the door with Angela curbing behind. "Girl, take this child to the car. She's coming with me for the night." Angela heeded Mama's orders and wrapped me in her shawl as Blake backed away. "Boy, rest your heart tonight, but come see me tomorrow."

"I won't be here tomorrow. There's nothing left for me here. There never was."

"Do as I say. The truth ain't like you see it."

"The truth? Does Ethan know the truth, Sarah? Does he know about Hatcaden? Will you tell him what really happened the night Michael was—"

Mama spun, raising her cane to Blake's throat. "That child's mind was broken by God Himself and held together by your will alone. Say anything more, and it'll shatter for good. You sure you want that burden?"

"Take her, Miss Nash," he said. "You take her, and you watch her, and you make sure I never see her again."

"You need her, boy. And she needs you. That's why God tied you up."

"God tied me to another lunatic; that's what He did. I'm done being God's watchdog. This one wants to die? Let her die."

Mama walked out before Blake slammed the door at her back.

An echoing crash folded into screams so loud, and so long they rose above the crowds in the distance.

"Let me go back," I cried. "Please, Mama Nash. Let me go back."

"And do what? Spill more secrets what should have died with your boy?"

"He can't be alone in there now. I need to apologize. I need to explain."

"There's a time for truth, and that ain't today," she said, tugging me hard by the arm. "Now get in the back of this car."

Mama and I slipped into Angela's car, and I draped on her lap, losing myself in the misery of what I'd done.

"Let it go, child." Mama rocked me, stroking my hair as I sobbed. "Tears remind us of the fires we make. This is your badness. And your badness should burn."

Forty

I stood in the doorway of Mama's backroom wrapped in a bathrobe with my hair dripping wet. The napping bed was a knot of sheets and blankets, damp from tears and the chamomile tea Mama poured down my throat the night before. Chamomile couldn't cure what I'd done. The bed's gunmetal footboard still squeaked when I sat on it, and I closed my eyes, consuming the odors of biscuits and eggs and the thrumming of bees in the yard. Mama was rocking on the porch by the window, humming her hymnals and shucking her corn.

"Those hymnals always made me feel better," I said, twisting the damp from my hair. "I've missed them."

"My singing ain't something to miss. You find that robe, baby?"

"Yes, Ma'am. I'm coming out."

"No, you ain't." Mama's rocker jerked to a stop, and I heard the crushing of tires on the drive. "Stay in that room and be quiet. Give me some time with this boy."

"Leave him alone, Mama," I said, parting the sheers. "He's heard enough."

"He ain't heard what I've got to say. Stay behind those sheers and don't come out. Don't say nothin' either."

Blake slammed the car door and crunched up the walk. "Where's Sarah, Miss Nash? She's not answering her phone."

"Girl ain't got her gadget, and if she did, I'd have tossed it into the marsh."

"Call her out here."

"Who you talking to, boy?" Mama stabbed an ear of corn toward him. "I got gators just itching for a breakfast like you, and no one would see if I did it."

Blake nodded, fiddling with his keys. "There's more I need to say to her. More I need to know."

"She ain't ready yet, but come sit here with me." Mama dusted the spare rocker's seat. "Got too many ears to husk on my own. Extra hands are a blessing today."

Blake gave in, stepped to the porch, and thumped the rocker on the sill as he sat. I could smell him. Hints of morning and late winter marsh, sweetened with the scents of cologne. Tender reminders I didn't dare touch.

"Did everyone know?" he asked, claiming a cob. "About Michael, I mean. Did everyone know?"

"We ain't gossips, boy. Only me and Sarah knew. No one else."

"That day on the beach, you set it all up?"

"I ain't set up nothing. I saw your face that day. How your eyes smiled when you walked into her room, touching her candies and pawing her things. You loved that girl before you ever took a breath. You were born to love her. You're God's whim."

"That's convenient for you, isn't it, Miss Nash? Pulling God from that bag of bones whenever you need an excuse? Sort of relieves you from any culpability when things go wrong."

"Nothing's gone wrong. God sent you that day for a reason, He just ain't finished with us yet."

"Not finished?" Blake turned in the chair. "Lady, do you have any idea what just happened to us? The pain you caused?"

"I ain't caused nothing. God gave me a child who needed help. I sent the help. That's what I saw, so that's what I did."

"You saw a girl you'd do anything for," he said, dropping his cob to the porch. "You saw a young, frightened, pregnant girl with a special mind, and you knew exactly what we'd do once I—"

"I saw a child crying about monsters and reaching for rescue. That's what I saw."

"And you sent me out there anyway. Even after you saw her like that?"

"Ain't talking about Sarah right now. That ain't who I saw in those bones."

"Then who, Miss Nash? Who screamed about monsters besides her?"

"You did," she said, looking at him. "Saw you in my bones that day."

"Jesus." Blake wept into the palms of his hands. "Don't do this to me. Not now. Not like this."

"You were brave, weren't you, boy?" Mama spoke gently, rubbing his back. "Holding your momma, telling her the monsters weren't real."

"Nothing could stop it. Nothing I did. Nothing I tried. I couldn't help my mother and I can't help Sarah. I can't—"

"That's all right, baby. This is your purpose. You're trying to fill it. That's what we're all meant to do."

Blake wept harder, and I covered my mouth, muffling my rising sobs.

"Sarah doesn't love me," he said. "She never did."

"That ain't one bit of true. That girl loves you like I've never seen love before."

"But I can't give her what Ethan does. I've tried."

"You ain't tried, baby. Not like she needs."

"What more can I do?" Blake sniffed, retrieved his corncob and stripped off its husk. "You know how it was after Michael died. I kept Sarah from hurting herself. Kept her safe. She won't take her meds, and when she does, she hates me for it. What does Ethan Bennet do that I don't, Miss Nash? You tell me that."

"He holds her," she said. "While you keep her. He lets her live, while you shut her down. He lets her remember a time when she wasn't afraid. With you, all she knows is fear. Your fear."

"I'm trying to keep her alive."

"You want to keep her alive then you need to set aside those fears and start loving your wife like a woman and stop treating her like some kind of wound."

"Loving Sarah is all I've done. Since that night on the beach... even now."

"But you never let her feel it. You got so scared after your boy was gone, afraid she'd see his face and remember things. You took too much. You just took too damn much."

"There are things you don't know, Miss Nash. Things you can't possibly—"

"Not seeing doesn't mean I don't know," she said, prodding Blake's chin. "Sometimes we need to loosen our hold on things, have faith in the love we feel and trust it's enough."

"Love wasn't enough to keep my mother alive."

"Love is always enough."

"Are you saying my father didn't love her?"

"I'm saying he was too afraid to love her the way she needed. He was too afraid to sacrifice."

"I saw my father," Blake said, ripping that husk. "I saw him cry for his wife, worry for her, and spend every minute of his last days feeling guilty for not keeping her from swallowing a bottle of pills. Don't tell me my father didn't sacrifice. He sacrificed everything he had."

"Not his fear," Mama said quickly. "He never sacrificed that."

Blake looked at her, a half-naked corn cob gripped in his hand.

"Real love is a movement of the soul, Cherie. There are no tender walks. There are no gentle steps. There are only leaps into dark, painful places where sometimes those we love become lost. Sarah's lost, boy. Forgive her. Take her in your arms and pull out the thing that haunts her. You do that and your heart will be settled, your mysteries solved, and your soul will answer its purpose."

They spent the next hour shucking corn and talking about sacrifice before Blake thanked her and stepped from the porch. I watched through the sheers as he stopped by the car.

"Last night," Blake paused, studying the weeds by his feet, "what I did to Sarah. Is she hurt?"

"Not on the outside, no." Mama stood and leaned on the railing of that corn littered porch. "But if you value the blood still warm in your veins, you won't rattle my baby again."

"That wasn't like me, Miss Nash. I'm not the kind of man who—"

"We know you ain't gone rabid. If you was rabid, you'd be dead by now. I'd have done that chore myself."

Blake nodded, flipping his keys. "I'll remember, Miss Nash."

"Good thing." Mama reached down and hiked a basket onto her hip. "Your kind would live longer if more of you did."

Forty-One

Mama's kitchen was crowded with breakfast items only dutiful Southerners served. Eggs, andouille, grits, and croissants adorned every platter and dish. Guilt killed my appetite, but Mama ignored that.

She poured a cup of dark roast, passed me a plate full of eggs, and said flatly, "Restore yourself."

There was no fighting the edict, so I stabbed a sausage and grabbed a croissant. "Thank you for talking to Blake, Mama. Leaving me will be easier now."

"He ain't leaving you," she said, scraping eggshells into a bowl. "Men like him need quiet words and a good night's sleep. He got those today, and he ain't leaving."

"Then he's crazier than I am."

"Don't use that word." Mama slapped on the faucet, squeezing two shots of dish soap into the sink. "Ain't no one done in this world till the good Lord tells us we are."

"Better tell that to Abby. She plans to die in jail with you holding the needle."

"Abby knows what she's doing. Best to settle our hearts."

"You mean let Abby die in prison for killing a man you would have killed yourself if you had half the chance?"

"Watch those wits, baby. Don't go dark."

"Why, Mama?" I shivered, feeling a fever bloom on my neck. "Did you throw bones today? See me go dark?"

"When my bones tell me their secrets, I listen."

233

"And yet you do nothing about it."

"That ain't true." Mama turned, wiping her hands on a rag. "When I'm led to do something, I do it."

"Is that why you pushed me toward Blake and not Ethan?"

"That was different." Mama stepped closer, caressing my cheek. "You starting a high time?"

"And Michael?" I asked, leering at her. "Did you see him that night too?"

"Lord, baby, don't pull down that thought."

"Michael said you were crying that day. Blake said you went to church."

"Wednesday's my worship. And I was crying for missing you at Christmas."

"You saw it, didn't you?" The chair fell to one side as I stood. "You saw Michael crushed under that truck, and you did nothing. You told no one."

"Oh, baby, no. That ain't how it works. God blinds us to—"

"What would you have said, Mama Nash?" My sobs came in short, throaty bursts. "Would you have told me to be watchful of Michael that night?"

"Jesus, you're trembling."

"Would you have told me to take my pills that week too?"

"Don't do this, Cherie. Sweet Jesus, don't—"

"Tell me, Mama. What would you say if you could go back and keep God from killing my son?"

"I would have told you it wasn't your fault," she said, snatching my face in her hands. "I would have said tragedy finds us, fate takes a turn, and sometimes, baby, sometimes children die. And when that happens, when we think we can barely struggle a breath, all we can do is fall to our knees and pray for the strength to move on."

Breath rasped from my throat in a scream, and I gripped her, remembering the riptide and its thunderous embrace. I thought of its chill, its silence, its darkness, and depth, and I ached for the solace it offered.

"Holy hell, what now?" Alicia kicked open Mama's back door. "Every time Sarah Thorn screams, someone's either dead, dying, or divorced. From what I've heard, it's probably the last."

"Want peppers on that tongue?" Mama kissed me and helped me into my chair. "Got a whole basket there by the stove."

"Hold your peppers, Grandma." The percolator rattled while Alicia filled up her mug. "Sarah knows I'm only teasing."

"Well, tease someone else. Girl's been through enough."

"All right, Grandma. All right." Alicia squeezed my hand before straddling a chair. "Angela told me what happened last night. You okay? Need me to do anything?"

"Nothing you can do." I sniffed, snatching a napkin and wiping my nose. "Thanks, though."

"That's a relief." Alicia patted the gun on her hip. "Damn shame shooting a perfectly good man like Blake Bradley. Too much paperwork to fill out."

"You here to take us to town?" Mama asked. "Need to get my honey jars packed if you are."

"Let me help." I stood, reaching for jars on the sill. "Should we take these?"

"Not those, baby." Mama laid a hand on my arm. "Those are for rats."

"Why would you feed honey to rats?"

"She means squirrels," Alicia said. "Grandma pours honey on cans, then ties them to her fence. That honey's poisoned."

"Hush up, 'Licia. It ain't like you're making it sound."

"No harm telling her, Grandma." Alicia sipped her coffee and smiled. "Those are poisonous blooms. Grandma's secret concoction."

"Well, that's dangerous." Violet-blue petals floated in gold as I tilted the jar to the sun. "Which flowers?"

"Glories mostly. Hard to believe something so beautiful can be so damn deadly. Right, Grandma?"

"I'm changing clothes." Mama ripped the jar from my hand and planted it on the sill. "'Licia? Go wait in the car."

"Sarah and I haven't visited yet. Get dressed while we talk."

Mama mumbled, flicked her necklace, and then turned to stride down the hall.

Alicia moved to the counter, freshening her coffee. "Dropped by your mom's place after Angela called. I grabbed you some shorts and a shirt. Figured I'd check on Blake really quick."

"How was he?"

"Gone. Bags too. Sorry to tell you this way."

"That's all right," I said, clearing plates from the table. "He came this morning, talking with Mama, and I figured he'd leave after that."

"What about you?" She nursed her coffee, standing by the kitchen's screen door. "Will you stay here or what?"

"Can't leave until Abby's sorted out. Then, I'm not sure."

"There's no sorting that out, Sarah. Abby's determined."

"So, you're on Mama's side now?"

"There's only one side, and that's Abby's. She knows what she's doing."

"How could she?" I asked. "Only thing Abby knows is that shop. She's never known freedom or happiness, and she doesn't know what it's like being in love, either. That's the saddest part."

"Abby knows love."

"How? From watching Buster beat the crap out of Ida? Abby doesn't understand what real love means. Sharing a soul with someone. Not to mention a bed."

"You're wrong, Sarah."

"How the hell am I wrong? For Christ's sake, she's never even been on a date."

Alicia spun and splashed her mug into the sink. "Abby's in love. She's felt it. She's got it right now. Understand?"

Her jaw went tight when she spoke, and I noticed the strain in her voice, the hitch in her breath, and the way her shoulders slumped when she turned. That's when I knew what she meant.

"Jesus," I whispered. "You must be going through hell."

Alicia shuddered, rolling her shoulders like a bridge on the verge of collapse. "Tell Grandma I'm waiting outside."

Alicia's pain was an obvious thing. Not in words, actions, or broad sweeping claims but in the bodily disbursement of grief. It showed in her gait, how she said Abby's name, and in the soft, martyred gaze in her eyes.

She was breaking.

"S'pose I should be more worried about that." Mama scuffed in from the hall.

"Worried about what?" I asked, pointing outside. "You knew about them?"

"'Course I knew. Been going on ten years or more."

"And you don't care?"

Mama sighed, retrieving a basket of jars from the shelf. "'Licia's stony inside. Tough in her heart like a man. I ain't seen her cry but three times in her life. Girl was six when her momma passed, and even then, she didn't shed but a tear. That always worried me. But when she clipped those chains on our Abby, put her in that car, and dragged her off that night, she cried so bad I thought her heart would drain out her eyes."

"Some people call it a sin, Mama Nash. They say it goes against God."

Mama nodded at Alicia and said, "Love that deep restores lost souls. There ain't no way that's a sin."

Forty-Two

The street party was the most riotous event of the festival. Music hung in the air, steaming pots of Low Country Boil crowded sidewalks, and every Branch Street business that could, threw open its doors to serve drinks. It was loud and boisterous, and, using Valentine's Day as their muse, people got raunchy as hell.

Mama didn't like it, saying, "Looks like Sodom threw up Gomorrah down here."

In a way, she was right.

"E'Tan's coming." Mama sat in her chair and rested ten amber jars at her feet. "That cursed car screams from a hundred miles off."

"I can't see Ethan right now," I said, peering down the street. "Not yet. I'm not ready."

"Secrets are living things, Cherie. Don't let yours jump from someone else's lips. You tell him about Michael before someone else does."

The Mustang veered to the curb, and Ethan leaned over the passenger seat. "I've been looking all over for you. You okay?"

"Considering I can't walk the streets without a bag on my head, I'm fine. How's your jaw?"

Ethan grinned, rubbing his chin. "My daddy taught me to take a hit way before Blake ever did." He reached over, opening my door. "Hop in. We're going somewhere."

"Where?"

"The Atlantic. We're taking our boat out today."

Mama yanked my shirt, whispering, "Tell him right now. All of it. Today."

"All right, Mama." I kissed her. "I'll try."

Ethan and I stared ahead as we drove, avoiding traffic and Bayport's ambling, half-drunken crowds.

"Heard Blake went back to New York," Ethan said.

"Nice to know Bayport's grapevine's still dripping with juice. Who told you?"

"Alicia. I went by your mom's house earlier, and she was cleaning up."

"Cleaning up?"

"Yeah. She told me what you did."

"What *I* did? But I didn't—"

"Don't act like you don't know." He laughed, waving at people crossing the street. "Ten thousand things you could have thrown at the guy, and you chose my toolbox. And through that window again? Alicia had a good laugh when she told me."

Recalling the crash as we left Mother's house made me thankful for Alicia's quick lie. She knew it was better that way, and she was right.

"Blake and I argued. I was upset."

"You're always upset about something." He angled a corner, pulling in front of the castle to park. "Just stop taking it out on that door."

"Let's go inside," I said, plucking threads from my shorts. "There's something you need to know."

"Not now." Ethan hopped from the car, and I followed as he took deliberate strides toward the dock. "Today, we're sailing."

"Let's go to the solarium first. We need to talk."

"I just told you, not now."

"But it's import—"

"Damnit, Sarah." Ethan spun, planting both hands on his hips. "What part of *not now* do you not understand? We're sailing, and I don't want to hear about your husband today. I did what I did because you needed a push, and I'd do it again if I had to."

"A push?" I trailed behind Ethan as he strode through the yard. "That was more than a push on that stage yesterday. You have no idea what you've done."

"Sure I do. I'm the one who did it, remember?"

"No, you don't. You don't know half of it because you won't listen to me."

Ethan slammed through the dock gate, kicking at buckets and winding up ropes. "I've spent fourteen years listening to you, Sarah. I've heard why you won't leave him, can't leave him, and refuse to leave him. I heard it was Michael and work and that it was *complicated, Ethan.* I've heard it all. So believe me when I tell you there's nothing you can say that can't wait a few hours. I know what you're going to tell me. I've already heard it."

"Ethan?" I leaned into him, pressing my hands to his chest. "What am I going to say?"

"You're about to tell me you're leaving again. That's what you do, Sarah. You leave."

"I'm not leaving you, Ethan. That's not what this is."

Tossing ropes to one side, he said, "Well, if it's something worse than leaving, you may as well keep it to yourself because I'm right on the edge of understanding Abby's motivation. Know what I mean?"

Smiling, I asked, "What would you like me to do?"

"Come sail with me. Don't talk about problems, husbands, or Mama's dark threats. Just get on that boat and come sailing with me."

"Off the edge of the planet?"

"If possible, yes," he said. "I'd like to fall over its edge."

We didn't find the edge of the Earth that day, but we found wind and waves that rocked us simultaneously as we danced on the deck in the sun. Our embraces were frantic, and I silenced my guilt, pulling Ethan down to the honey-stained boards, where I made love to him under the shadows of clouds drifting by. And Ethan moved over me, tender and slow, whispering the infinite strengths of a bond he thought could never be killed. But I knew it could. In the softest of ways. With the slickest of words. We could be killed with a whisper.

Forty-Three

Docking the Lemniscate was a tedious chore. There were ropes to tie, wood to rinse, and dishes in the galley to wash. Dishes were my punishment for spilling chum buckets over the deck.

"Why do I get stuck in the galley?" I asked, hearing Ethan climb down the hatch. "Whole place smells like fish, and it's stuffy here."

"Would you rather wash guts from the deck?"

"Chum buckets are preferable to dishes in ice water."

"Ice water?" Ethan stabbed a hand in the sink. "Water's warm, Sarah."

"Is it?" Realizing my fever, I withdrew the complaint. "Must have a sunburn. Everything's cooler once you've been in the sun."

"Sunburns are red. You're not red." He brushed a hand on my cheek. "You're flushed, though. You feeling all right?"

"Stop worrying. You sound like Mama."

"Hand's shaking too." Ethan pointed to the vibrating plate that I held. "Looks like the damn thing's about to fall off. What's wrong with you, Sarah?"

"Nothing's wrong." I turned quickly, stacking the dish. "That sandwich at lunch wasn't enough to ward off Mama's coffee from breakfast."

"You get coffee IVs, for God's sake. That's not from coffee. Let me see." Ethan reached for my hand, but I tucked it away. "Stop being a pest."

"You're not feeling well. You have a fever, you're shaking, and your eyes don't look right. I think we should take you inside."

"I'm not going inside. Grab me a soda, and I'll get something to eat at the party."

Ethan blinked at my hands before turning to open the refrigerator. The galley was quiet, and something about the moment prompted a question I held since Jackson first said the name.

"Ethan?" I asked. "Who's Helen?"

He coughed before answering, "Who?"

"Helen. Jackson mentioned her at lunch. Who is she?"

"Someone I knew as a kid." Ethan closed the refrigerator, handing me my drink. "Want a glass?"

"No glass. Do Jackson and Angela know her?"

"They did. Is it cold?"

"Yes, it's cold. Who is she? Does she live here?"

"Not anymore," he said, pulling the plug in the sink. He cursed at the water, watching it suck down the drain.

"Who is she?"

"Just a friend. No one you knew."

"We had the same friends. I don't recall Helen being one. Does she live here now?"

"She doesn't live... here."

"Where does she live? Bayport? South Carolina? On the planet? Why are you so—"

"She doesn't live at all anymore, all right? She died years ago, and I won't talk about her here in the middle of this lousy boat. One day I will, but not now."

He reached for the handrail and climbed through the hatch.

"That was her, wasn't it?" Tossing the soda aside, I chased him onto the dock. "The blonde by the boat. That was Helen."

"We're not doing this now." Ethan moved to the dock cleats, winding the boat lines in tight little loops. "It's too late to argue, and you're not feeling well. Stop pushing so hard."

"You think I push hard? You're the one telling me to leave my husband. You're the one sending him newspapers."

"Newspapers? I didn't send—"

"Don't you lie to me. You sent that newspaper and note to Blake in New York."

"Note? What note? What the hell's the matter with you?"

"The note to Blake. The one with the smiley face."

Ethan pointed over the yard. "Did you not see what happened yesterday? I smeared our affair in Blake's face while the entire town stood there and watched. Why the hell would I send him a note?"

"Because you're a bastard, just like I said." Stumbling away, I ran from the dock to head home. "Don't follow me. Don't call me. Blake was right about you. Everyone was."

Dashing down Branch Street, I careened through crowds, feeling the temperature rise on my neck. Exhausted, I closed my eyes and turned a corner to lean on a wall. The stench was pungent like hell opened its jaws in a yawn, and I realized where I'd stopped.

The butcher shop.

Forty-Four

Nothing changed in that dead-end corner of filth. Boxes and trash still littered the lot, and the stench of old blood stained the air. The back door handles were thick and dented, fastened with a deadbolt and chain that snaked to the ground.

The office window was narrow, but with the right angle, I could effort my hips through the rusted-out frame. Bricks lay like puzzle pieces scattered in the dirt, and I reached for one, rearing it over my head.

"What're you doing back here?" Alicia scuffed into the lot, holding a red plastic cup. She wore light denim jeans, an Echo Gumson T-shirt, and her close-cropped hair stuck out beneath a Bennet Marine cap. She looked like common street trash.

"What's it look like I'm doing?"

"Looks like you're planning to lob a brick through the window of a designated crime scene."

"What're you gonna do, Alicia? Arrest me for holding a brick?"

"For holding a brick? No. But I will if you break that window."

"Then finish your beer and make a bed next to Abby. I'm going in there no matter what."

"It's water," she said, dumping it out. "And I can't let you in there, Sarah. Not like that."

"I'm going whether you like it or not."

"Not without a witness, you won't." Alicia pulled the keys from her pocket, unlocking the chain. "Don't touch anything."

The door sounded pained when it opened; its hinges were creaking in loud, cracking pops, like breaking the ribs of a ghost. The back room was duskily lit, with sparks of dust reflecting whatever light filtered in from the windows in front.

"Can barely see anything," I said, kicking boxes aside as we walked. "Can we turn on a light?"

"Abby busted the lights."

"Abby did?" Alicia's answer didn't add up. The ceiling was twelve feet high, trespassed with ductwork, and unreachable for someone so small. "How could Abby do that?"

"She says she killed the lights, got Buster in here, and shoved him into the freezer when they fought. He probably died before sunrise."

"Abby couldn't shove Buster down the street, much less a hole he'd never go into alone."

I studied the room, taking in the ceiling and walls before setting my sights on the Perlick door, wedged open with crates.

"That's where Grandma found him," Alicia said.

"What was Mama doing in here?"

"Came to see if Buster would let her sell honey."

"Bullshit. Buster wouldn't do business with Mama unless he sold her rancid meat. She's lying."

Alicia adjusted her ball cap and shrugged. "Grandma bends the truth a lot, but only when it needs bending."

"Well, she's not bending it over Abby," I said, pointing to the Perlick. "Let me look in there."

"Room's bloody."

"Can't be any worse than before." I eased my head through the opening, peering through slivers of light. "This place always smelled like rotgut and death."

"Remember helping Abby open boxes in there?"

"Vaguely. Why?"

"She said you did the blood sister thing the day you tore up Buster's shop."

"Never tore up Buster's shop."

"Where'd you do blood sisters?"

Pointing behind me, I said, "There by the meat cases, why?"

"Just wondering how much you recall from that day."

"Enough to know I never attacked Buster Mills." I turned my attention to the freezer again. "Abby cut the latch?"

"Cut it off that day," she said. "Threw it into a marsh."

"And the latch didn't work after that?" I asked, gesturing to a sharp metal spike protruding waist-high to the right of the freezer door's edge. "Why would he keep pushing a sharp spike when he knew after the first stab it wouldn't open?"

"He'd been drinking all day. The coroner said hypothermia enhanced the effects of alcohol."

"Enhanced the effects?" I cringed, looking back at her. "He was stabbing himself, Alicia."

"You really care how that bastard died?"

"I care what happens to Abby if she doesn't tell the truth."

"The truth isn't in this freezer, Sarah."

"Then where is it?"

"Walking around town, bold as brass," she said.

I smirked. "What does that mean?"

"That means you should leave this alone. But if you need to satisfy your curiosity, look inside this hell hole and decide why that bastard did what he did because you're the only one who gives a damn why."

Alicia whipped open the door, and the stench of old meat filled the room. Blood covered everything. Corner to corner, wall to wall. Every silvery inch held rusty brown swaths like morbid finger paint art. Wire shelves lay toppled, and deep indentations dotted the door.

"He tried to beat his way out," I said.

"Looks that way. He was full of puncture wounds. Fingers sliced open, blood all over both hands and feet. Even his fat-ass hips. Dumb prick just kept stabbing himself."

"All his nightmares in one little room."

Stuffing her hands in her pockets, she said, "Buster Mills should have died in a bait well fifty years ago, Sarah. Abby only finished the job."

"That doesn't mean she should die for it." Broken bulbs dangled from sockets above. Shards of white like shark's teeth stabbed down-ward in jagged, menacing smiles. "This ceiling's over ten feet high. Abby couldn't reach that."

"She said she used a chair and an old oar handle."

"Where are they? The chair and the handle."

"Chair's in evidence, and she said she threw the oar into the marsh along with the latch and saw she used to cut it off. She can't recall where."

"Another lie." The floor shimmered with pieces of thick freezer glass. I crouched, picked up a nugget, and rolled it between my finger and thumb. "This glass is tempered. You know the force it would take to destroy indestructible glass?"

"Abby said Buster fell into those. Broke them when they fought."

"These cases aren't broken, Alicia. They're shattered. Abby couldn't have done this. Not on her own."

"Sarah, don't."

"Whoever did this was strong," I said, slapping dust from my hands as I stood. "And he'd never tell anyone because he wouldn't have under-stood what he did."

"We're leaving." Alicia dragged me out by my shirt.

"What happened that night, Alicia? Was Buster hurting Abby? Did Edward step in?"

"I shouldn't have let you in there," she said, fastening the lock to its chain. "Never should have called you back home."

"Then why did you?"

"Because Ethan made me, but you don't understand what's happen-ing here. Neither of you does."

"A jury would never convict Edward for protecting his sister. You know that."

"Abby doesn't care about a conviction. That's not what this is."

"You told me you loved her," I said. "This morning, at Mama's. I saw it in your eyes."

"I do love her."

"Then tell the truth about what happened in there. Tell her lawyer. She's innocent, and you're supposed to protect the innocent."

"All right, who?" She stepped closer, tearing the hat from her head. "Who do I choose? Who lives? Who dies? Who's destroyed? Because those are my options."

"What're you talking about, options? The only option is justice for Abby."

"This is justice, Sarah. Real justice. The kind where guilt's never questioned, and retribution comes at the same brutal price as the crime. That's the only justice Abby Mills wants, and it's a sacrifice she's willing to make."

"Abby doesn't know what she wants. She's protecting Edward because that's all she's ever known. But she can't. Not now, and not with this."

"Abby got justice, Sarah. It's done."

"Justice for what? Alicia, please. Tell me what happened in there."

She backed away, glancing behind. "Can't tell you that now. Promised I wouldn't."

"Promised who? Mama?"

"No."

"Who, then? Abby? You promised Abby?"

Alicia stopped and looked down the street with the sun finally setting and the party rising hard in the dark. "I have to go."

"Get me a meeting room at the jail tomorrow. I need to see Abby. I need to tell her what I saw here tonight."

Alicia nodded but said nothing as she escaped through the crowds by the park. St. Peter's chapel chimed six, and the skies grew darker as I headed down the aged brick streets toward home. My mind was ablaze, savoring all the worldly features made more sensual than even nature intended. The moonlight was brighter, the air was sweeter, and the throaty wails of lowly earthbound things called out in voices only I could hear.

My high time was ending. I was going to fall.

Forty-Five

⟨∞⟩

The cell phone rattled my pocket just after I closed Mother's door. I tore it free, seeing Ethan's name on the screen before hurling it hard at the wall. It felt good to break something. To tear it open, shatter its heart, and hear its pieces pelting the room. The kitchen phone warbled from its spot on the wall, and I ran to it, yanking the receiver free from its base and tossing it into the sink. The silence in the house was melodic, and I prayed to the heavens and called to the saints, pleading to set me ablaze.

Fireflies...

They came. Shooting like bullets from every crevice and crack, and I danced in them, sweeping, swaying, and crying for Michael, my mother, and every tender soul that I loved. I collapsed at the table, sweating and breathless, and remembered the battered back door. The glass was broken in uneven spikes, glinting silvery white against the glow of the moon. One pointed shard stuck out like a mountain peak.

"Like ice," I whispered, rising to touch it, caress it, to drag it over my wrist.

My eyes didn't blink. They never moved from that point.

The beautiful, damnable shine on that point.

I touched it, fondling the angles and razor-sharp curve before wriggling it loose from the frame. The surface was cool, and I flipped it, noticing the brightness of my gaping green eyes on the edge.

Michael...

My breath stopped, and I dragged the spike between my finger and palm, pressing it over my pulse.

"It gets better, Sarah Thorn."

Gentle whispers broke through the room, and Blake was there, staring at the glass on my wrist. He was unshaven but neat, and his faded black jeans and dark-colored Henley made him nearly invisible in the shadowy room.

"That's what I said at the riptide the first day we met, remember?" His voice was tender, and he lifted the glass away from my hand, setting it down by the sink. "You were beautiful out there. Nothing but lavender skies and waving red hair. Like something my mother dreamt up."

"Wasn't sure you were real," I said, watching him soothe the scrape on my wrist. "You don't usually get close when I'm like this."

"Well, I'm close now." He smiled. "And I'm real."

"Everyone thinks you left for New York. Why are you here?"

"I needed to talk to you."

Weeping, I asked, "About Ethan and me? About what I—"

"No, honey," he said, cupping my cheek. "About how I handled you that night. The things I said. You didn't deserve it, Sarah."

"You were right to be hurt."

"But nothing justified what I did to you. Nothing."

"I know, Blake. I know." Nodding, I listened as the shorebirds and peepers blended with my whispered words. "There was never a time I didn't love you, you know. Even after the lies and all the horrible words, I still always loved you so much. I want you to know that. I *need* you to know that."

"I do know that, Sarah. I do."

"But I'm so tired now, Blake." Tears fell as I blinked up at him. "Tired of not knowing what happened to us. Tired of fighting the dreams, and I can't do it anymore. Please, for your sake, go back to New York."

I tipped up and kissed him before escaping into Mother's room. Blake followed, flicking the light and drenching the walls in a soft yellow glow.

"I can't leave you now, Sarah. You just had glass on your wrist. I have to stay. At least for the night."

"There's no reason to stay. You were right when you said there was nothing left for you here. Our life was based on a lie and that lie died in a road seven years ago."

"Michael died, Sarah. Not you and not me. We're still here."

"We're not here, Blake. We're standing in the snow, watching our son fall under a truck over and over again. That's the last thing we saw before our lives fell apart, and we never moved on from that night. So don't think for one second we didn't die too. We did die, Blake. Right there with Michael. We just didn't fall in a road."

Exhaustion buckled my knees, and I folded to the floor as I screamed. Blake cursed, sweeping me up and laying me back on the bed. He pulled off my shirt and shorts, curled behind me, and wrapped us both in a sheet.

"Everything happening to you is my fault," he said. "And I'll stop it, Sarah. I promise I will. We've got to move on from that night."

I didn't ask in what way he'd remove the guilt that kept us apart, but Blake swore as he lay there, blending kisses with whispers on the back of my neck, that he would.

Forty-Six

I don't know how long Blake held me that night, but by morning, my tremors and fever receded, and I felt, as Mama would call it, restored. With the sheet draped around me, I padded the sun-streaked hall to the kitchen, hearing chimes from St. Peter's and hushed traffic noise from the street. Only ghosts of Blake's presence remained. The scent of cologne, damp towels on a chair, and the coffeemaker dripping its brew. Blake repaired the battered backdoor, taping the window and pulling the glass from its frame.

A serving of eggs sat on the table with a note that read, "Please, eat."

The plate tilted on an envelope with a lawyer's name on the corner and Blake's handwriting scrawled on the back.

"I need you to sign these," it read. "We need to move on."

There was a singular feeling of loss in those words. Different from physical death. Lonelier than guilt afterward. This was something new. Unique only to the moment when something long-suffering dies. We feel it leaving, and we know it must. We feel phantom pain in our hearts.

I ignored the breakfast of grief and dropped the envelope back on its plate. Thankfully, Abby's needs took precedence, so I slipped on a knee-length sweater dress, zipped the boots Angela insisted I buy, and left the house, still flooded in guilt. The distraction of outside events always worked to throttle my mind and driving to the jail proved helpful.

Voices floated from the corridor as I angled a hall, finding Ethan and a girthy older gentleman waiting outside the meeting room door. There was nothing particularly striking about the man, but his eyes were deep brown, and he watched me approach without blinking. Ethan was sleek and serious, hair slicked back and showing no pretense of our earlier contention. I hated when he did that.

"I need to see Abby alone," I said to Ethan. "Why are you here?"

"Came to see Abby, same as you. This is her attorney, Ward Elliot."

After offering Ward a sharp nod, I turned to Ethan again. "Where's Alicia?"

"Getting Abby. If you'd answered your phone last night, you'd know that. Where were you?"

Rummaging in my bag, I said simply, "In bed."

"Alone?" Ethan asked.

My head shot up. "Yes, alone. What the—?"

Ward interrupted. "This meeting was my idea, Miss Thorn. Sheriff Maynard said you'd be here today when we called to schedule our meeting with Abby. Since I needed to speak with you, I thought we'd take care of that now. I assure you this wasn't an ambush."

Hoisting my satchel, I said, "I grew up with Ethan, Mr. Elliot. He's like a guerilla fighter; all he knows is ambush."

Ward chuckled and guided us into the room. The space didn't differ from other days I'd visited Abby, but today, with Ward Elliot standing there, I felt entirely stalked. There was something savage about him. Threatening. With his rumpled suit and furious eyes, the man was primal in every sense of the word. He smelled of cigar smoke and leather and threw out intimidation like ordinary people exhale natural breath.

Intimidation was Ward's nature, and I don't think he much cared for the bullshit economics of normal human emotion.

Ethan held a chair out for me. "What's the mystery, Ward? Why the sudden urge to see us?"

"We'll tackle that in a minute." Ward grunted into a chair. "I'd like to pester Miss Thorn for a bit."

"You have something in common with Ethan," I said. "Pestering me is his life's ambition."

Ward laughed. "We share something too."

"Do we? And what's that?"

"Defending filth," Ward said. "Polite society deplores us for that."

"Abby's not filth, Mr. Elliot."

"Oh, no. Not Abby. There's not a speck of dirt on that girl. She's sweet, meek, and has the most innocent face of anyone I've ever seen. She's the perfect portrait of innocence. The Mona Lisa of noncommittal shame. Don't see that often, that's for damn sure."

"Abby's always been like that," I said. "Sweet. Naïve. Innocent of things."

"Uh-huh." Ward dropped a black, edge-worn briefcase onto the table. "Ethan said you know Abby better than anyone. That true?"

"I grew up with her. So did Ethan."

"But you're the closest to Abby. Her best friend, would you say?"

"Abby didn't have friends outside of us. She was shy, and her home life wasn't good. So, yes. I'm her closest friend. Why?"

"Ethan said you spent nearly every day with Abby when you were children. Is that true?"

"Practically."

"He says you spent a good deal of time in that butcher shop too. Is that also true?"

"Sure."

"In the freezer?"

"Sometimes," I said. "I'd help Abby unload boxes in there."

"What do you know about this?" Ward pulled a photo of the Perlick's door from his briefcase, sliding it over to me.

I picked it up and studied it. "That's the Perlick."

"Notice anything strange about that door?"

Looking closer, I said, "No, why?"

Ward leaned in. "What I'm going to ask will take some thought. Don't answer right away. Think about it. I want you to close your eyes, imagine that door when you were a child, and tell us what you remember. Can you do that?"

"I can try."

"When you saw this latch as a child," Ward said, tapping the photo again, "was it cut?"

"Cut?" I asked, looking at the scene.

"Think, Miss Thorn. Try to remember as much as you can."

Closing my eyes, I struggled to remember the shop. I recalled the window and cracked plaster walls, the filthy shelves, the acrid stench of blood and frost, and the rotten meat Buster sold to those too poor to pay for decent food.

I saw the tired eyes trapped in Ida's fearful expressions and Abby's cringing lips whenever Buster shouted her name. I saw the Perlick. The glistening ice and water drained into puddles, mixing with blood splashed from the carcasses he hung.

And I saw the door. The freezer door. Opened only enough to allow light while Abby and I shuffled inside, counting boxes until our fingers went numb. I heard her voice captured in my ear. A frightened, shaking whisper, warning me to leave before Buster got back.

"Jesus, Sarah?" Ethan reached over, taking my hand as I realized I'd started to shake.

"I can't see it," I said, dragging in a breath. "I don't know what happened in there. I can't remember."

Ethan burst up. "What is this, Ward? Sarah can't remember, so just ask whatever you want and get it over with."

"Sorry, Miss Thorn," Ward said. "I was hoping you'd confirm something before Miss Mills could deny it."

"Confirm what?" Ethan asked. "Do you have a point to make, or will we keep dancing around bullshit all day?"

"Your friend's a witness," Ward said.

"No, she's not. Sarah was in New York when Buster died."

"Ethan's right. I wasn't here. I didn't see anything."

"Sure you did," Ward said. "You just don't remember you do."

Abby pushed through the door, wide-eyed and panicked. "Ethan, go home," she said, holding her wrists for Alicia to open her cuffs. "Sarah came to see me today. You and the lawyer can leave."

"We're not done here, Miss Mills." Ward relaxed in his chair. "We've been having a chat."

"What about?" Abby shot Alicia a frown as she left.

"A door," Ward said. "We've been discussing a door."

Abby's eyes raced over the photos. "You can't do that. That's against the rules."

Ward pulled a file from his case, sliding it to Abby. "Ever heard of exculpatory evidence? That's evidence that shows a defendant might not have committed the crime for which they're being tried. The DA gave it to me, and he wants to talk to your friends now too. That means whatever he asks them, I'll ask them. That breaks those rules, young lady."

"They can't tell him anything. And there is no evidence. I threw it into the marsh."

"There's always evidence, Miss Mills. And there are always witnesses."

"Witnesses?" Abby sat down, watching Ward stalk her expression.

"Your statement says this killing was planned," Ward said. "That correct?"

"That's correct."

"The statement also says you cut the freezer latch before noon. Is that also correct?"

"Cut it that morning. Just like I said."

"With what?" he asked, raising a brow.

"A bone saw. That's in the statement too."

Ward heaved from the chair, pulled dog tags from his right trouser pocket, and tossed them across Abby's lap. "Know what those are?"

"Dog tags?" Abby stared at the dull bits of tin. "For the Army."

"Marines, actually. Those are mine. Wore them through two tours in Vietnam. Damnable place, Vietnam."

"I don't get it," Ethan said. "What's this got to do with anything?"

"It's got to do with proof, Ethan. And why we know your friend here is lying."

Abby sat up. "I'm not lying."

"Pick up those tags, Miss Mills. Tell us what you feel."

Abby shook her head. "No."

"Goddamn, you're a quick one." Ward snatched them, tossing them over to me. "What do you feel, Miss Thorn?"

"Metal," I said, fingering their edge. "Bumps from the imprints. Why?"

"Are they sharp?" Ward asked.

"Not at all."

"They weren't always like that. When we first get them, those things are sharp as hell. We'd scrape them on rocks or let them rub our skin bloody until they smoothed out."

"So?" Ethan asked. "So, what?"

Ward looked at Abby again. "Tell him, Miss Mills. Tell your friends what I'm driving at here."

"I can't tell them anything. I don't understand."

"You say you cut this latch?" Ward thrust the photo at her. "Forensics says you didn't."

"What?" Ethan pushed from the chair, moving to Abby. "What're you talking about?"

"Abby couldn't have cut that latch," Ward said. "Cutting brass with a bone saw leaves deep striations in the metal. Sharp and jagged edges. That piece on the door doesn't have those. Those cuts are old. Smoothed down like the blade on a serrated knife or the imprints on my dog tags. Worn from time, ice, and old-fashioned friction. Abby didn't cut that latch at all. No way she could have. That latch was cut at least twenty years ago, so unless she was an exceptionally strong little girl—"

"I did cut it. It's in my statement."

"The DA sees mistakes in that statement, Miss Mills. Obvious ones. And he'll take one hell of a look at you. He'll have a long talk with your friends here too. He'll turn your life inside out because that's his job. And because he's doing his job, I'm doing mine, whether you like it or not."

Abby tugged Ethan's arm. "Stop them, Ethan. They'll listen to you. Everyone always listens to you."

"He can't do that, Miss Mills. This is the district attorney's call, and he's seeing problems with your account of what happened that night.

He's compelled to investigate, and he'll follow the direction of evidence. That's his job."

"Then I won't cooperate," Abby said. "I waited until Buster was drunk, broke the lights, cut the latch—"

"That wasn't you, Miss Mills. That wasn't a frail little woman like you."

"The bone saw was sharp, and I—"

"How'd Buster get into that freezer?" Ward asked.

"I pushed him inside when we fought."

"How could you fight him? A monster that size."

"Buster was drunk. He was really drunk and—"

Then Ward threw out the one question which set fire to the room. Pounding the table, he said, "Where was your brother that night?"

Abby choked. "Edward?"

"Are you insane?" Ethan asked. "You think Edward Mills cut that latch twenty years ago? He was a baby, for Christ's sake."

"Not the latch," Ward said. "I'm talking about other mysterious things. Like the force required to push Buster Mills into a freezing hole, witnesses say he'd never have entered alone."

"The man was drunk." Ethan took Abby's hand. "Probably staggered in there himself, and Abby's confused."

"She's not confused, Ethan. She's protecting someone and lying about what happened. It's not unheard of."

"Unheard of, my ass. You know Edward was with me that night. It's in my statement."

"Edward was with you?" I asked, looking at Ethan. "Why didn't you tell me?"

"Because it wasn't unusual, that's why. I saw Abby at Mama's that morning, and she asked if I'd take Edward since Buster was drunk."

"Edward never left the house?" Ward asked.

"The kid runs through those halls like a linebacker, Ward. I think I'd have noticed if he left the house."

Ward propped on the table, crossing his arms. "You pull a lot of weight in this town, Ethan. People trust you, listen to you. I'd wager to guess they're a little afraid of you too."

"You're saying people trust me so much I can lie?"

"I'm saying you're feared just enough you'd never be questioned. That makes you one hell of an alibi, son."

Ethan stood straighter, cradling Abby close to his hip. "We're done for today. Abby's tired, and you're scaring her."

"Scaring her?" Ward huffed. "This is nothing compared to what she'll get with the district attorney. He'll tear through this piece of shit story like ripping tissue from a gift."

Abby pleaded with Ethan. "Make them stop, Ethan. Please, make them stop."

"He can't, Miss Mills." Ward bent closer, palming his knees. "Young lady, I'm smart. I'm tenacious as hell, and people are afraid of me because they should be. Whatever happened, if anyone else was involved, I'll defend them as fiercely as I'm trying to defend you, but you've got to tell us the truth."

"My brother is all that matters. I have to keep Edward safe."

"Was that it?" Ethan asked. "Did Edward see Buster hurting you and do something that night?"

"No. God. That's not it. This has to end now. Just tell them I did it. Please."

"We can't do that, Abby," I said. "We won't watch you die. Pick a better ending before someone else does."

"This is the better ending. The best I can give."

"For whom?" I asked.

"For the only people who matter, Sarah. Please, I'm begging you. Stop this with me."

Forty-Seven

Ward and I broke through the long bank of doors at the building's entrance. Ethan strode behind, so loud in his gait that the slaps of his shoes echoed all over the wide concrete steps.

"What the hell did you do in there, Ward?" Ethan asked.

"What you hired me to do. I'm defending an innocent woman."

"At the cost of her brother?"

"Abby's lying," I said. "We have to push her, or she'll die in a cell."

"She's right, Ethan." Ward turned at the foot of the steps. "This is the DA's call. Nothing we can do but create a new strategy now, just in case."

"The idea is to get Abby to change her plea, so she doesn't wind up in the chair. Now you've got Edward swinging right there beside her."

"She's lying, son. Her lies are obvious because the evidence is obvious, and the evidence points to her brother and someone strong enough to cut solid brass twenty years ago."

"So, who cut that latch?" Ethan asked.

"How should I know?" Ward shrugged. "Could have been her mother. Could have been Buster. Could have been the Easter Bunny or Christ himself, for all we know. Blaming anyone else would be better, but Abby doesn't. She blames herself for a crime where the evidence doesn't support her claim. So now the DA is asking why. Which begs your own question, who? Who cut that latch, and why would Abby lie to protect them?"

"I won't let Edward be hurt by any of this," Ethan said.

"I won't either. But a man was murdered. Brutally, I might add, and no district attorney will ignore a bloody case like this without looking under every contradictory rock they find. So, if you want a reason the DA is cramming your friend and her brother beneath the fine microscope of Bayport County's legal system, you run into that building and ask Abby Mills about that. You ask her why she turned a perfectly reasonable self-defense argument, which no DA on the damn planet would want to touch, into the shitstorm she created. And while you're doing that, I'll try to get her out of this building while producing an alternate strategy to defend her and possibly Edward Mills against anything the DA may dig up. All right?"

Ward gripped his briefcase, pounding through the lot as he left.

"Don't yell at him like that," I said, walking to the Buick at the end of the lot. "His client's lying. What more can he do?"

"Abby's lying, Mama's lying, I'm lying. What about you, Miss Thorn? You're the big storyteller here. Have any confessions you'd like to make?"

Reaching the car, I wrangled its keys from my bag. "What's up your ass this morning? If this is a leftover tantrum from yesterday, you can rein that in, Mr. Bennet."

"I went to your mom's house last night and saw his car outside. Blake's car."

"Yeah? He came to talk. So what?"

"And talking required crawling into bed with the guy?"

"We were sleeping." I opened the car door, throwing my bag on the seat. "And what'd you do, anyway? Sneak inside to watch?"

"There was no answer when I knocked, so I looked through the window and saw you lying together in bed."

"Spare me the righteous indignation, Ethan. You were no saint when I was gone. You never were."

"Well, you're right about that," he said, slamming the car door. "I lifted every skirt I was offered, but you know what I didn't do, Sarah? I never broke promises to anyone. That was your trick, lady."

"Promises?" I said. "I never promised you anything."

"Every touch was a promise. Every kiss. Every laugh. We've been to-gether our whole lives. If that's not a promise, then what the hell is?"

"What do you want from me, Ethan? Huh? You want an apology? You want an excuse?"

"How about explanations for once? What are you going to do? What happens after Abby's released? Will you go back to Blake? Will you stay here?"

He was right. I looked at the tree limbs, the rocks at my feet, and the roadway filling with cars, but there were no proper answers to give. "I can't tell you that, Ethan. Not now. Not yet."

"Forget it." He stuffed his hands in his pockets, turning his face toward the road. "Ball starts at seven tonight, and I'll be at your mom's place by six."

"The ball?"

"Yeah, Sarah. The ball. Don't even think about not going."

"Those dances are so crowded, and I'm not good with crowds anymore."

"We're not bucking tradition because you and your husband can't get your shit straight. One of you has to show up."

"All right," I said, nodding once. "I'll go. Where's it at?"

"Hampton House in Bluffton."

"Okay, okay." I sighed heavily, rubbing my eyes. "Blake and I made such a mess of things."

"Yeah, well, we're no better." He squinted, watching cars lining up at the light. "Every time we get together, one of us ends up bloody, bruised, or naked. Lately, it's been all three."

I couldn't help but laugh. "You're a pain in my ass, Ethan. You know that? An endless pain in my ass."

"Oh, I know," he said, reaching around to open my door. "I'm a horrible bastard of a prick."

Forty-Eight

❦

The aspirin in Mother's kitchen cabinet expired the same year she died. The tablets looked safe. Still round. Still white. No strange coloration. No battered dull edge. And after spending the morning surrounded by bars, leaving the house in search of safer options wasn't something I was willing to do. I filled a glass at the sink and decided poisoning was worth the risk if it meant soothing the headache tapping my strength.

It'd been years since I'd gone that many days without assistance from doctors and pills, and while I detested their presence in my everyday life, I'd forgotten how their vacancy felt.

Sadness consumed me, my guilt rose and fell, and I was weak. Worn from Abby's drama, Ethan's dark stares, and the potential for night-mares teasing my brain. Blake's fat envelope remained on the table, staring me down like a poisonous threat. The burger and fries I bought did nothing to lighten the mood, so pushing the end of my marriage aside, I sat at the table, choking down pride with my lunch.

Angela's voice floated in from the front. "Ciao, Cara," she said, open-ing the door as she knocked. "I've brought your gown for the ball."

"The gown?" I leaned, watching as she entered the house. "I was planning to get it today after lunch. No need to bring it yourself."

"Well, I needed a reason to come." Angela draped the dress on the sofa before sitting next to me. "I'm here to apologize."

"Apologize?" I asked, dragging one greasy fry from its box. "For what?"

"For the auction. The dress hugged your hips so tightly that I knew you wore nothing beneath. I told Blake he should take advantage and flirt with you. Had I known it would make such a mess, I'd never have told him."

"That wasn't your fault," I said. "If Blake and I didn't already have the ton of baggage we do, the day would have ended on a more positive note."

"Are you better today?"

"Not really," I said, tapping Blake's envelope. "Don't ask for details unless you want the waterworks again."

"What's this?" she asked, picking it up. "Are these—?"

"Divorce papers, yes. Haven't opened them yet. Figured the death of my marriage wouldn't go well with lunch."

"Oh, Cara. What will you do?"

"Not sure." I shoved my lunch mess aside, deciding I'd eaten enough. "Things aren't exactly simple right now."

"Ethan can help. He loves you so much."

"Loving me is one thing, and living with me is another. Blake's envelope is proof of that. I'll hurt Ethan if I stay."

"No, Cara." Angela shook her head and sat back. "Not having you might hurt him more."

"Believe me, I'm easier to live with in much smaller doses."

"Not for Ethan." She paused, looking down at her lap. "Sometimes the truth is more important than the trust to hold it. Don't you think?"

"Depends on what that truth is, I suppose."

Nodding slowly, she said, "The day we met during lunch, Jackson mentioned a young woman's name. Do you remember?"

"He said Helen, right? Something about treatments and—"

"Jack shouldn't have done that. Ethan made us promise never to talk about her. Sometimes Jackson forgets."

"Why can't you talk about her? Who was she?"

"Ethan's sister." She said it so quietly her lips barely moved. "His twin."

"A twin?" I sat up, getting as close to her words as I could. "He told me she died. Yesterday on the boat, Ethan told me—"

"He spoke about Helen with you?"

"Only because I asked. Ethan said she was someone he knew, and she died. That was all."

"I'm surprised he said that much." Angela shifted, fiddling with the trim on her scarf. "Losing his sister left a black spot for him. Ethan barely mentions her name."

"Why?" I asked. "What happened to her?"

Angela took a deep breath and said, "Helen was special. Darling and innocent. Like Edward. But she needed more help than her parents were willing to give. The state assigned Jackson to her case, but Ethan's parents were ignorant and superstitious. They didn't want to help her. They wanted her gone. It was so cruel, Cara. The cruelest thing I've ever seen done."

"Why?" I asked. "What'd they do?"

"Bull Street."

"Bull Street?" Stories of that horrible place came to mind. "That old mental hospital in Columbia? Ethan's parents sent Helen there? When?"

"Two months after their eleventh birthday. Men from the hospital were at the house when Jackson and I arrived. Ethan was holding Helen, fighting them off. They broke into that little boy's room, ripping those children apart like pulling wings from a butterfly's back. Ethan was sick with mumps, and his parents knew he couldn't help her."

"Jesus, that's when we met," I said. "My mother brought Ethan to Mama's that night. That's when we met."

"I know." She spoke softly, still picking that trim. "Jackson called Sheila after they took Helen away. Evan said his father pointed a gun in your mother's face, but she shoved him aside and ran through that house looking for Ethan. When Sheila found him, he was calling for his sister, covered in sulfur mud and terribly sick."

"Why didn't anyone say anything? All these years and nobody—"

"Those monsters ripped his sister away and sent her to that

madhouse while Ethan could do nothing to stop it. I still hear him screaming for her."

"Angela?" I slumped, seeing Ethan's pieces finally fall into place. "Was Helen's hair... blonde?"

"Like an angel's wings. But she was pale and thin, not dark and strong like Ethan. But their eyes were the same. Deep brown and wide open. And they had the same smile."

"Did she ever come home? When Helen was older. Did she ever—"

"Only once. Ethan wanted her back. Jackson said Helen wasn't a child anymore, and she'd be harder to help, but Ethan wouldn't listen. He loved Helen so much that he never saw the danger in bringing her home. Jackson gave in and signed the paperwork for Helen's release."

"How old was he then?" I asked, resting a hand on my eyes. "When Helen came home, how old was Ethan?"

"Twenty, I think. Maybe twenty-one. It was awful for him. Helen screamed, tore at her clothes, and fought anyone who got in her way. Ethan could do nothing to help, so Jackson took her back to Bull Street. Helen died from pneumonia the summer after Ethan started school. He never saw her again."

My mind thundered through images of that day by the boat. Ethan stood tall and unsure, locked between two women he loved, and didn't know which he should choose.

He had to choose Helen. *He had to.*

"We were just a mistake." I burst from the table, pacing back and forth by the sink. "Ethan and me, we were just a mistake."

"Loving Ethan isn't a mistake."

"I've got to make him let me go. Ethan's got to let me go."

"Ethan needs you, Cara. He loves you."

"He can't love me," I said, flattening my hands on the table. "He can't want me. He can't even be around me." Taking Angela's arm, I pulled her toward the door. "You should go now. Please, I need to think."

"I've broken something, no? A secret? A trust?"

"Nothing's broken. I needed the truth, and it was time someone gave it to me. Don't tell anyone what you told me today. We'll meet tonight at the ball."

Angela left, and I closed the door, hearing scuffs filter in from behind. "That Italian's got a big damn mouth."

"You heard?" I turned, finding Alicia with my cup in her hand. "All of it?"

"Most of it. Saw her car out front and figured I'd eavesdrop by the backdoor awhile."

"That's what you were trying to tell me at the hospital after Michael died. Ethan had a twin."

She smirked, took a drag from my straw, and said, "Obviously, Grandma disagreed."

"You should have told me years ago."

"Dredging secrets is a sin to Grandma. You know that."

"You tried at the hospital. Why?"

"Because I knew leaving Ethan without saying a word would kill him. It nearly did. He moved on well enough until all this happened with Abby, and he made me drag you back home."

"And you don't think being with me now would be worse?" I curved past her to the kitchen. "Why didn't you tell me when I came into town?"

"Because Grandma was right."

"For slapping you?" I asked, collecting my lunch mess and throwing it into the trash. "I'm about to do the same thing for all the bullshit around here. Want to tell me why Ward was asking about the freezer door too? According to him, I'm a witness."

"Can't tell you that either. Sorry."

"You're no better than Mama," I said. "Buried secrets inside bullshit promises."

"Can't tell one secret without spilling them all, and that's just what Angela started today."

"Well, somebody had to."

"You think so?" Alicia shrugged, sucking my soda again. "Wait for it, then. There's a storm blowing in, and you're standing in the middle of it."

"Is the badness coming, Alicia? Is that what this is? More of Mama's darkness and doom coming to slap us all down?"

"Coming?" Alicia opened the back door and stepped out. "Hell, girl, it's been here. We're just trying to keep a lid on it."

Forty-Nine

The gown was exquisite, slick, and shining as I smoothed it over my hips. "Like blood," I said, securing the comb in my hair. "Same color as blood."

Ethan chuckled as he shadowed Mother's bedroom door. "Well, I was going to say heaven's on fire, but if you'd rather go with something morbid like standing in a puddle of blood, I'll defer to your expert opinion."

"Ethan." I threw myself at him, practically climbing his chest. "I'm so glad you're here."

"Where else would I be?" He laughed. "You owe me money, remember? Don't wrinkle me, either. Mama took all day ironing this tux. She said the tailor's hands were arthritic clubs, and he couldn't swing an iron. I swear that woman makes a new enemy every week."

"You know I love you, right?" I looked at him, searching his eyes. "Tell me you know that."

"That's a rather inopportune question considering our current extra-marital predicament. Don't you think?"

"Tell me, Ethan. I need you to say it."

"Sure, I know. You've got a lousy way of showing it sometimes, but—"

"And you love me too. Right? You love me?"

"Jesus, Sarah. Yes. What's with the twenty awkward questions? If this is some sort of female test or trap or something I can tell you right now, I'll fail it."

"Why?" I asked.

"Why, what?"

"Why do you love me? Have you thought about it? Why do you love me?"

"Hell, I don't know. You're smart and pretty, and that red bikini always seemed to—"

"Ethan, please. I need to hear it. Why do you love me?"

Lifting a smile, he said, "Because I saw a girl on a beach once. She was fighting a monster so her friend would be safe. I watched her from the window of an old cracked-up boat and thought, if there was anyone I was meant to love, it would be that girl. I've loved her since. Is that what you wanted to know?"

"The girl on the beach. The one on the boat. You remember me like that?"

"Don't have to remember you like that, Sarah. That's who you are. All feisty and brave."

"Brave?" My eyes closed, and I rested my cheek on his chest. "I want you to have her, Ethan. The girl on the beach. The one on the boat. I want you to remember me just like I was. I want you to love me like that."

Fifty

The Hanson House was a grande dame of a thing. After serving as a Civil War hospital, she fell into ruin and then, like all Southern beauties neglected by time, reanimated through hammer and blade. Like the castle, curvaceous and white, the Hanson was larger, with wrap-around porches and long sweeping steps that fanned out from her glossy black doors.

The high-arched ceiling bracketed heavy relief, framing scenes of Southern life like Lena painted. Pelicans in flight, broad-leafed blooms, sunsets, and rises over placid teal waters loomed above as people soberly mulled underneath.

"Look at SB Thorn, raging in red," Evan said with a smile. He and Arnold stood in gentlemanly form as Ethan and I approached our table. "That dress should be cast as a sin, Sarah. You're beautiful."

"This dress should be cast as a torture device, Evan. I can barely breathe."

Ethan laughed, pulling my chair. "Be back soon. I'm off to rub elbows."

"Will you be long?" I reached out, clutching his arm. "Crowds bother me now. I can see they're all talking about me. They do it in New York too. I don't like it, Ethan. I'm not—"

"Take it easy, Shakespeare," he said, touching my cheek. "No one's lighting torches quite yet. Angela's on her way, and Evan and Arnold will keep you entertained. You'll be fine."

Ethan moved through the room with an effortless swagger, shaking hands and slapping backs as if he held no past. He was skillful. Filled with a jester's touch of humor and fanciful social acumen. It was a gift unique to self-made men with small-town powers, and Ethan practiced it well.

"Ciao, Cara." Angela claimed a chair, handing me a glass of Merlot. "Take this. It matches your dress."

"It matches my mood," I said, accepting the wine. I gestured to her black silk gown and the emeralds weighing her ears. "That dress is perfect, Angela. So elegant."

"Thank you, Cara. But your beautiful mind wonders about more important things than parties tonight. No?"

Sipping my drink, I said, "That obvious, huh?"

"Poets can never hide what lies in the heart. It shines through their eyes like a beacon."

"You're probably the only guest in this room who considers my books poetry."

She sighed, gazed dreamily over the frescos, and said, "*If the human heart could break in two and not die from its desperate wound, I would measure love equally and live hopelessly divided between God's sun and His beauteous moon.*"

The quote softened my mood, and I smiled. "Where'd you get that?"

"From you," she said. "Ethan found it scribbled on a tissue box when he moved from your mother's house. He had it etched in stained glass for my birthday one year."

"I wrote that after Mother died. Ethan finished the gazebo, and we had a picnic with Edward and Michael. I forgot about that."

"You've captured what true love is in those words. The delicate sadness of choice. I adore the honesty of it."

"It's hard to remember writing like that," I said, squeezing her hand. "I'm glad to hear it again. Thank you, Angela. Thank you."

The double doors slammed open at the front of the room, where delivery men pushed a bulky wooden crate through the hall.

"Looks like a dishwasher coming in here," Evan said.

"Too skinny for dishes." Arnold's eyes followed the path of the dolly. "And too wide."

Every guest within range watched that crate squeaking through the ballroom with Ethan guiding its route.

"Must be special." Angela craned from her seat. "I wonder what's inside."

"A collection of Echo Gumson merchandise." Evan raised his wine in a toast. "Plus, a stew pot to boil all our nuts in."

Evan and I laughed as Angela chastised our less-than-appropriate humor. It was a challenge for me and Evan to be anything more than provincial. Growing up without the benefit of well-heeled wealth, we were babes in the dwellings of lions. Although dressed in formal gear to dine with the natives, we were still, beneath the cloak of our fine gilded fabrics, undisciplined slaves of our natures.

The evening moved smoothly, with presentations made, announcements given, and Ethan running laps between table and stage.

"May as well be hauling nets for all the exercise I'm getting," he said, taking his seat.

"Any news on what's in the box?" Arnold asked.

"Not yet," Ethan said, sipping his scotch. "Directions say it has to be opened on stage. I guess we'll find out then."

Jackson's voice cracked over the mic. He announced Blake and me as the bidder's dance winners, thanked WhiteThorn for the donation, and welcomed Ethan and me onto the stage. Posted at either of Jackson's sides, Ethan and I supported a fake check while cameras flashed at our feet. The curtains split open to the left of the stage, and a broad, wrapped package was wheeled out on an easel beside us. It was wide and flat with a crisp white cover and a platter-sized seal on the front.

"That's a WT seal," I said, eyes racing over the room. "This is a cover reveal."

"A what?" Jackson asked.

"A cover reveal. We do them for press junkets and book signings. It's a publicity thing."

"What's it doing here?" Ethan asked.

"Being donated." Blake pushed through the curtains behind us. He was stern and determined, buttoning his tux as he walked.

Ethan glared. "Come to embarrass your wife again, Blake?"

"I'm here to help her, Bennet. Unless you want to end up on your ass again, I suggest you stay out of my way."

"Go back to New York, old man. Sarah's done being dragged by your leash."

"Is she done being dragged by yours?" Blake drew me in, checking the drift of my eyes. "She hates crowds, and you threw her into the middle of three-hundred people who routinely call her a whore. You're so caught up in your own pathetic glory you didn't even notice the fear in her eyes when she walked through the room."

"Let's leave," I said, clutching Blake's lapel. "We'll go to my mother's and talk."

"We're not going anywhere yet. We're making this donation, then I'll dance with you in front of this whole town. Let them sink their teeth into my neck for once."

Then Blake turned to the crowd, thrust his arms in the air, and brazenly shouted, "She learned the filthiest parts from me!"

High, stilted laughter and crashing applause burst out, blending with the waves of his voice and the pops of the cameras below.

"Blake, please," I said, tugging his arm. "Don't do this here now. It's all right."

"It's not all right, Sarah. Calling you a whore has never been all right." Blake paced slowly, glaring over the murmuring crowd. "Will it always be this way? Whispers in corners and eyes leering over my wife? Because if it is, I'd sure like to know so I can stop coming to a town full of hypocrites holding picket signs in one hand and signed copies of her books in the other."

The crowd instantly hushed, sipping their wine or spreading their napkins in laps. Their faces were all the same to Blake. He'd seen them at libraries, parks, and capitol offices where greedy ambition set fire to my books. Blake was a warrior in the art of defense, so satisfied with the requisite shame, he smiled as he always did and continued to throttle the room.

"My wife has an extraordinary mind and exceptional talent. As I watched her dancing at the auction, I couldn't think of anything to equal her courage, beauty, and the endless sense of wonder she sees in everything around her." Blake moved to the package, caressing its edge. "Before she died, Lena White-Bradley left her family an unfinished piece. A single stroke of Prussian blue against a plain white canvas."

"Blake, no—"

"In place of a financial contribution," Blake tore the papers away with one swipe, "WhiteThorn donates my mother's final piece, *Lena's Blue*, to the Bennet Foundation for Mental Health Research."

The crowd leaped from their seats, exploding into thunderous, cracking applause.

Rushing to Blake, I said, "You told Michael you'd never get rid of it. You promised."

"Michael's gone, Sarah. That painting won't bring him back."

"But the papers you left at the house. I thought—"

"They're here." Blake took papers and a pen from his coat. "Just need you to sign them."

"Put those away," I said, shoving back. "I'm not signing divorce papers in front of the town."

"Who says we're getting divorced?" He laughed. "They're letters of intent for the painting. I knew you wouldn't open the envelope, so I went to your mom's house and got them."

I snatched the papers and scribbled my name on the highlighted lines. "That wasn't funny, Blake."

Blake tipped closer and smirked. "It wasn't meant to be, Sarah."

"Quite the donation," Ethan said. "Might even call it an... ostentatious effort."

"Yeah, well," Blake slapped the papers into Ethan's left hand, "arrogant fucks have their moments."

Ethan tossed glances between Blake and me and then waved an arm toward the room. "Shall we sit?"

We joined at the table in stressful proximity. With Ethan on one side and Blake on the other, I felt suffocated, pulled like a toy between two wayward boys. They could tear me apart, share me, or get bored and walk away. Since neither bored easily–and sharing was *tragically* off the table–that only left one option: tearing me apart.

And that's what they did.

"The tribute was lovely, Blake," Angela said. "So romantic."

"Why, thank you, Angela." Blake snapped his fingers and signaled a waiter for bourbon. "Coming from an Italian, that's quite an endorsement."

"Seems you're breaking tradition this time, Blake." Ethan stared at his tumbler, absently swirling his scotch. "Sort of unusual for you to stick around more than a day or two. When are you leaving?"

"Thought I'd stay for a while," Blake said. "Take Sarah to the beach behind Miss Nash's old place."

"Beaches get chilly this time of year, old man. Staying warm could be a problem out there."

"Nothing a good fire won't solve. We've done it before."

"That was a long time ago," Ethan said. "Building fires out there is illegal now. Can't even harvest the wood. Sorry about that."

Blake stretched in front of me, challenging Ethan. "Guess I'll have to resort to something more physical. Thanks for the tip."

Ethan cursed while Blake sipped his bourbon, smiling in triumphant success.

"Just do it," I murmured down to my lap. "Each of you take an arm and rip me in half. Would that be easier? Would that be punishment enough for everything I—"

Jackson's voice struck out, announcing the bidder's dance, and the room went velvety black. Spotlights aimed at the chandelier, casting prisms of violet all over the floor.

Blake stood, took my hand, and lifted me out of the chair. "Dance with me, Sarah Thorn."

We walked to the center of the gray-marbled floor. My skin pricked alive with Blake's palm at my back and the glide of the dress on my legs. Violins floated against clean, tailored walls, echoing a familiar refrain.

"Is this?" I whispered, straining to hear. "Guns N' Roses?"

"They're singing about rain in November." Blake smiled. "Isn't that what Michael would say?"

"Why, Blake? Why this song?"

"Because you remember Michael when you hear it, and you need to, Sarah. You need to remember Michael again."

"You don't like me remembering Michael at all."

Blake stopped, rolled me into his arms, and said, "We're changing protocol."

We moved under colorful drips of light roaming our faces like shining, twinkling ants.

"Why are you doing all this?" I asked. "The painting. The song. Standing behind curtains and on Mama's front porch. You can't seem to find your way home."

"I did go home. Just not to New York."

"New York's the only home we have."

"Not anymore. Bought a condo on Hilton Head yesterday. Brand new building, right on the beach."

I stopped. "You bought a condo on Hilton Head? What the hell for?"

"Jesus, honey." Blake grinned and moved us again. "Whatever happened to Southern hospitality? If this town's no longer catering to strangers, it should change the brochures."

"This isn't like you. Spontaneous decisions aren't part of your makeup. Nothing happens without a strict plan."

"I have a plan. We're starting over. That's the plan."

"Was getting rid of the painting part of the plan too?"

"That wasn't part of anything," he said. "I wanted to win Sarah Thorn for the weekend, and I did."

"Giving the painting away wasn't right. You shouldn't have done it."

"We had to move on, and we couldn't do it with that thing reminding us of everything we lost. Everything that couldn't be saved."

"It's not a *thing*, Blake. It's Lena's painting. The last one she did."

"The last thing she did was kill herself," he said. "Every time I looked at that dark streak of blue, that's all I saw. I kept it for Michael, but he's gone now, and we can't bring him back. He would have wanted it this way."

"What about WhiteThorn?" I looked back at our table, seeing Ethan scowl from the rim of his glass. "How can you walk away from everything you built?"

"Everything *we* built. And I'm not walking away. I'll work here and fly back as needed. They'll survive well enough."

"And Hatcaden?" I asked, nudging down at Blake's hip. "Where is he tonight? Lurking nearby? Waiting to slap me with his usual dose of bullshit sanity?"

"Bullshit sanity?" He laughed again and pressed a kiss to my cheek. "That's a good one, honey. We'll have to keep it. But no. Mr. Hatcaden's home for the night."

"Well, I'm glad he's still part of your therapeutic regimen."

"You still need him."

"Then why isn't he here?"

"Because I'm here, and I love you. That's all."

I blinked away, seeing Ethan cornered by Charlotte. "Why can't I believe you?"

"Because I never gave you a chance. The thought of losing you blinded me to everything else. That's why you ran to Ethan. He gave you the life you wanted from me. The one I kept pushing away. And I'm sorry, Sarah. I'm so sorry I did that to us."

"We both made mistakes, Blake. I made them too."

"You'll be making another if you stay here with him. Ethan doesn't know you. Not like I do."

"All you know is the broken part," I said. "That's all you see."

"I know the part that hurts you. The part that tells you to hurt yourself. I know the part that'll stop you from telling Ethan why you could never stay with him."

"I'm telling him tonight."

"Will you?"

My head snapped up. "Why, Blake? You want me to hurt Ethan the way we hurt you?"

"I don't give a damn about Ethan Bennet, but if you stay with him, you know what'll happen. It almost happened last night when you—"

"I'm going to tell him," I said, watching Ethan march toward us. "Things are different now, and he needs to know the truth."

"Tell him about Hatcaden. He won't understand if you don't."

"I'm cutting in," Ethan said.

"That's up to her, Bennet."

I nodded. "It's all right."

Blake kissed the back of my hand. "I'm leaving after I check the painting. The new address is on your mom's kitchen table. I left it earlier."

"What's he talking about?" Ethan turned us once as Blake left. "What address?"

"The address where he's staying."

"He's staying here now? In Bayport? Where?"

"Would you stop it, please? He bought a place on Hilton Head and thought I should have the address."

"He's living here now? The bastard's playing house so he can shove it in my face."

"That's not what Blake's doing. He understands you, Ethan."

"Understands me?" Ethan scowled, stopping our turn. "Does he understand I'm in love with his wife?"

"He's always known that."

"Does he understand I can't breathe unless she's in the same room? Does he know that too?"

"Ethan, please. Just listen to what I'm trying to say."

"Come here." Ethan pulled me into a dimly lit vestibule, closing the door. "Leave him tonight. Come back to the castle and leave Blake tonight."

"I can't."

"Look at yourself." Ethan reached down, lifting my hand. "You're shaking all over. You're so afraid of him that you can't even think straight. Just leave him, Sarah."

"I'm not afraid of Blake. Blake's afraid of me, and he has a reason."

"That's just the crap he's been filling you with. Why would Blake be frightened of you?"

"Take me to the tide pool, and I'll show you tonight. I'll show you why I never left Blake."

"The tide pool? What for? What's out there?"

"Fireflies," I said, tilting a smile. "Lots of them."

"It's February, Sarah. There won't be any fireflies right now."

"There will be tonight. Take me to the tide pool, and I'll show them to you."

Ethan's eyes tripped over my face. My mysterious reasons for never leaving Blake were on the brink of discovery, and how could he live without knowing?

He couldn't.

"Let's go." A folded paper fell from Ethan's coat as he reached for the door.

"Wait." I picked it up and whispered the neatly inked words, *"Save a dance for me."* Written on gold leaf parchment, the note had a smiley face drawn in a heart. "Where'd you get this?"

"Charlotte Mason. I was about to throw it away."

"Charlotte wrote this?"

"Just now. Why?"

"It was her." I seethed, panning the crowd. "It was Charlotte Mason."

"Charlotte? What'd she do?"

"She sent that note and paper to Blake last week." I spotted Charlotte entertaining a group near the stage. She was laughing in that annoyingly stagnant way, clinging to the rung of social alliances and draining attention from uninterested eyes. "That paper's the same as the note sent to Blake. It was her."

"Sarah, wait. Let me handle Charlotte myself."

"There's nothing to handle," I said, hiking my dress. "It's time Charlotte Mason was put in her place." I was a blur of red streaking over that floor, fevered and trembling, reaching Charlotte as she lifted her drink. "*You cunt!*" I slapped that woman so hard that the glass flew out of her hand. Charlotte fell backward, stumbling into tables behind. "You filthy, vicious cunt!"

"Go back to New York," she screamed, sweeping wine and glass from her dress. "Go back to your books and your filth. Go back to Hatcaden and his grimy asylums."

"You like spilling secrets, Charlotte?" I lunged, feeling Ethan capture my arms. "Well, I've got a secret for you. Hatcaden's been here all night. He's angry and violent, and he's run out of patience with you."

"Sarah, stop." Blake thundered on stage, pointing at me. "Bennet, take her out of here. I'm tied up with the painting right now."

Ethan's mouth gaped, and he stared between Blake and me.

"Do it, Ethan," Blake demanded. "Take her to Sheila's, and don't leave her alone. I'll be there soon."

Aiming my anger at Blake, I said, "Take me out of here, Ethan. My husband can't abide public displays of my temper."

Ethan shouted to the crowd as we left. "If anyone here does business with Charlotte Mason, you'll never do business with me. I'll shut you all down, pack up your stores, and run you right out of this county."

We nearly leaped down the Hampton House steps. The moon was sliding between frosty gray clouds, and a cold, heady stench filled the air.

Ethan's lecture came the minute he started the car. "You couldn't stop at the cunt comment? You had to go slapping her too?"

"She's lucky I stopped with the slap."

"Your reputation's bad enough without the whole town watching you push a cow like her into a bunch of tables. What the hell's the matter with you?"

"Me?" I howled, pointing outside. "What's the matter with her? That woman hates my guts, Ethan. Why does she hate me so much?"

Ethan yanked the gear shift, skidding us onto the road. "She's pissed about the boat."

"The boat? What boat?"

"Our boat. The Lemniscate. Charlotte wanted to take it out, but I said no."

"That's all? The woman's pissed because you wouldn't let her ride the damn boat?"

"No," Ethan said, pressing the clutch and shifting the gear into third. "She's pissed because I wouldn't let her ride me."

"Let her ride ...?" A sudden snicker broke from my throat. "Charlotte wanted to—"

"That's exactly what she wanted. Came to the house with paint samples and threw me onto the couch. She was grabbing my shorts and pulling my hair. Like a wild cat clawing a tree."

"I'm sorry." I snorted, covering my mouth. "That must have... that must have been—"

"Awkward as hell. I nearly called a hotline after that woman left."

Grins and snickers gave way to hissing, shrieking gales of healthy, heavy laughter rocking between us and filling the car. We were children again. Fighting and laughing in a rhythm of familiarity so natural it defied all perils attached. That's how we were, Ethan and me. Two halves of the same shell.

And I would have to break it.

Fifty-One

The lot behind Mama's house was sand-swept when Ethan pulled in. We kicked off our shoes, and Ethan stripped off his jacket and tie, opened his collar, and rolled up both sleeves.

"Come on, Ethan." I swayed and laughed as I ran past the dunes. The air was crisp, the nightjars cooing, and the beach opened like white, winding ribbons in the dark. "Come to the tide pool. Fireflies are there."

"It's too cold for fireflies," Ethan said, stumbling behind. "Abby's the only one who fell for that obvious lie."

The tide pool reflected the silky night sky, and I hiked my dress, sat on the grass, and plunged both legs at its edge.

"Put your feet into the water, Ethan," I said, patting the grass. "There were more nibbling fish when we were little. Remember?"

Ethan grunted as he sat at my side. "I remember you stealing my candy and lying about fireflies we're supposed to see here tonight."

"If it weren't for you and Abby, I wouldn't have those memories at all."

"Is that why we're here?" he asked. "So you can remember things? Or because Blake told you to leave me, and this spot makes for a softer goodbye?"

"This isn't about Blake."

"It's always about Blake. We made our mistakes, but Blake kept us apart."

"Blake didn't keep us apart, Ethan. I did." I turned and faced him.

"I wouldn't have survived this long if you didn't love me. But things are different now, and I'll hurt you if I stay. I'll crush you, and I love you too much to do that to you."

"And I love you too much to let go." Ethan kissed me, laying us back on the grass. His lips were sweet and warm, stealing every ounce of courage I held only moments before. How could I let Ethan go? He was a part of me just as much as my own beating heart, and how could I leave us? How could I break my own heart?

"Get up, boy." Mama nudged Ethan's back with her cane. "Let her loose."

"Mama?" Ethan peered from my neck. "What're you doing out here?"

"No need to ask why I'm in my own yard." Mama poked him again. "Let her loose like I said. Time to clean the mess what I made."

"There's no mess to clean." Ethan pulled us up with a grunt. "Go back inside."

"Can't, baby. Time to manage our secrets."

"We're not managing anything. Now, go back to the house. You'll catch pneumonia out here in that shitty old robe."

Mama ignored him, taking a seat on the stump. "That was a badness what they done to you, boy. All you did was cry for your poor sister."

"Mama." Ethan lunged closer, pointing at her. "Don't talk about that. I told you to never—"

"I know what you said, boy. I know what you said." Mama sighed, resting her cane on the grass. "You stopped crying once our Sarah lay down. Lord, you were pretty little things. Like two tiny jewels, sleeping and breathing like you was joined at the heart. I threw my bones, thinking that's what God meant, so I let you be, but that was wrong. I should have pulled you apart that same day."

"Nothing's gone wrong." Ethan pulled me close to his side. "We just got off track, Sarah and me. When she comes back—"

"She wasn't meant for you, baby. It's time to let Sarah go."

"Let her go?" Ethan shrieked. "Back to Blake? The bastard controls everything she does, Mama Nash. Can't anyone see that? Am I the only one who sees that?"

"No, Ethan," I said, watching headlights slice the front yard. "Blake's not like that."

"That's your man, Cherie. Go to him now."

"Blake?" I asked.

"Yes, baby. I called him for when you go dark."

"Go dark," Ethan said, dodging his eyes between Mama and me. "What does that mean, *go dark*?"

Blake broke through the fog, reaching out. "Come with me, Sarah. You shouldn't be here right now."

"She's not leaving with you." Ethan took hold of my arms. "Tell them, Sarah. Tell them you're staying with me."

"Ethan, I can't."

"Yes, you can." He begged, giving a shake. "You're only saying that because Blake's here. Once he's gone, we'll start again. You were never supposed to leave me, Sarah. You were never supposed to—"

"You were gone for so long," I said, brushing damp hair from his brow. "You said you were fishing, but you were at Bull Street with Jackson. You were there bringing Helen back home."

"Bull Street?" Ethan jerked back. "Who told you all that? How'd you know?"

"When I saw you with her, I wanted to punish you. So, I did, Ethan. I punished you the worst way I could."

"Sarah, don't do this." Blake eased closer. "Don't tell him that now. Not like this."

"Leave her, boy. Girl's right to tell him. He'll never leave her otherwise."

"I'm not leaving Sarah at all." Ethan broke down, burying his face in my neck. "If you had waited for me by the boat, I could have told you the truth. I could have—"

"Listen now, Ethan," I whispered softly, floating the words on his cheek. "I need you to listen to me now."

"Sarah, please. Don't leave again. Please."

"I went to find you that day at the boat."

"I remember." He sobbed. "Please don't leave me again. Please."

"To tell you I sold my first story."

"Don't leave me here, Sarah. Don't let them take you away."

"And to tell you... I was pregnant with Michael."

"Michael?" Ethan jerked back, and for a moment, he struggled to speak. "Michael was...?"

"He was yours."

"No. That's not right." He shook his head roughly, spitting the words. "That's not true. I can't have children."

"You did have a child, Ethan. I was pregnant when I met Blake two weeks after I found you with Helen."

"But you wouldn't lie about something like that. Not to me, Sarah. Not to me."

"I did lie, Ethan. Michael was your child, and I never told you."

Ethan turned, pacing and breathing as the weight of it slowly cut in. "But when you'd come home, I could have... and when Michael died, I never... My God, Sarah. What'd you do? What the hell did you do?"

"When I saw you with Helen, I was angry and hurt, and I loved you so much."

"You loved me?" Ethan took a threatening step. "Did you just say you loved me?"

Mama gripped her cane as she stood. "Hold yourself, boy. You've had too much drink, and you ain't seeing the whole of this thing. Go inside and sleep. We'll sort this tomorrow."

"The hell we will. This shit's getting sorted right now." Ethan turned to Blake. "Did she tell you, Blake? Did you know you were raising my son?"

"Don't do this, Bennet. You've no idea what's happening here."

"Holy Christ!" Ethan howled, scraping his hands through his hair. "She lied to you too. She lied to both of us? Well, that takes some talent right there, Miss Thorn. Holy shit, I'm impressed."

"Ethan, please. I'm sorry. There was—"

"Everything was a lie, wasn't it?" Ethan tore the comb from my hair, skipping it into the tide pool. "Were you bored, Sarah? Were you lonely?

Did you fly down here for a few tidal creek fucks between goddamn book parties up there in New York?"

"We're leaving." Blake wrapped an arm at my waist. "Call Sarah once you've sobered up. Until then, don't come near her."

Ethan stepped in. "You're an even bigger idiot than I am, Blake. First, you married her. Then you made her famous. Then you buried a son that wasn't even yours. Talk about ostentatious efforts. Holy shit, there should be some Captain Wonderful medal for you, Blake."

"Sleep it off, Bennet. You don't know anything."

"I know she's a whore," Ethan said, low, sharp, and right in my face.

"E'Tan. You still that mouth before I call 'Licia out here and drag you off."

"She's a whore, Mama Nash. A lying whore who'd put any man between her legs as long as she got—"

"E'Tan!" Mama fumed, sweeping her hand across Ethan's jaw with a crack. "Don't make me help God in His efforts with you."

"His efforts with me?" Ethan swayed, holding the flush on his cheek. "What more could God do that Sarah hasn't already done? Christ, I was so damn blind."

"God does that, baby. God blinds us to things our hearts ain't strong enough to hold. God keeps us safe."

"How in the hell did God keep us safe?" Ethan paced again, wiping tears as they started to fall. "Was Helen safe gasping for air in that madhouse? Was Michael safe when God threw him under a truck?"

"There's a reason for everything, Cherie. We're not always meant to understand."

"I don't want to understand." Ethan dug the keys from his pocket. "All I've done is try to understand the mysteries of Sarah Haley Thorn. I'm tired of understanding, and I'm going home."

"She was young, Bennet," Blake said. "Frightened and young."

"What was I, Blake? What the hell were you?" Ethan scowled at me as he spoke. "She used us, old man. She pitted us against one another like two starving dogs in a ring while she watched for fourteen years." Ethan turned. "She can go straight to hell."

"She's been there, Bennet," Blake said, holding me close as I wept. "She's already been."

Ethan didn't hear what Blake said and if he did, he ignored it. I watched him walk away, tracing our steps in the sand until he quietly disappeared into the fog. I'd done what I needed to do. My heart was breaking, but it was an unavoidable pain that came with the necessity of hate.

There is clarity in the clean lines of hate. It's the divisive weapon that brings an end to obsession, no matter the love that survives. Where love lingers, hate will always press on. Ethan never would have left me had I not told him about Michael. God blinded him to my shattered nature, so I opened his eyes to my betrayal.

I loved Ethan Bennet. I knew I always would. I loved him enough to tell him the truth. I loved him enough to make him hate me for it.

Fifty-Two

〰️

B lake wouldn't leave me at Mother's that night, so we went to the condo instead. We reached the top-floor penthouse just after one. The moon was full, creating a hazy blue portal as we opened the door to the living room. Being new, the air was heavily seasoned with putty and paint, burying scents of the beach.

Blake's eyes followed as I made my way to the smoke-tinted windows framing the ocean below. I watched his reflection trapped in the glass. His movements were sensual. Softer and smoother, removing his coat as if shedding a layer of skin.

"What do you think?" Blake draped the coat on a plastic-wrapped chair.

"That it's white. Dead walls, stone floors. Gray and white kitchen. Like the penthouse back in New York."

"This is hardly New York. There's an ocean outside. No buildings. No people. Just beach, birds, and miles of moonlight and waves."

"The walls are empty," I said, spreading my hands on the glass. "It echoes in here, and it's cold."

"Furniture comes tomorrow. I brought clothes from your mom's house. Dishes, and some groceries. Plus, there's a bed down the hall."

"A bed?" I asked, slipping out of my heels.

Blake chuckled. "You expected to sleep on the floor?"

"I expected separate bedrooms."

"Do you want separate bedrooms?"

"No. That's not—"

"Sarah." Blake moved closer and took up my hand. "If you're uncomfortable, we can go to your mother's house. I'll sleep in your room, and you take your mom's bed, but I can't leave you alone tonight. You know I won't do that."

"That's not what I mean," I said.

"Then, what?" he asked, dipping to capture my eyes. "What is it?"

"I mean," I waited a moment, letting the awkwardness fade, "I thought *you* would want separate bedrooms."

Blake relaxed on the window and smiled. "No, honey," he whispered. "I don't want separate bedrooms. I never wanted separate bedrooms."

Lightning brightened the beach, and I stretched up, kissing Blake deeply. The kiss began small, then grew heated with his hand working the zippers on the side of my dress.

"We'd better stop." I breathed heavily and drifted away to the kitchen. "This is a little too fast."

"Teasing isn't necessary," he said, pushing away from the wall. "I'm pretty much a sure thing."

"Just being careful."

"Of what?" he asked, pulling his tie.

"Of you." I moved slowly, holding the hem of my dress. "Do you really know what you want?"

"I want you. Isn't that enough?"

"Not enough to buy a house in a town you don't like just to prove it. I don't expect anything from you, you know. I'm not even sure why I'm here."

"I wanted you with me. I wanted you close."

"So you can watch me?" I asked, peeking in cabinets and opening drawers. "I'm fairly certain John Hatcaden's waiting close by, just dying to slap me back into my proverbial straitjacket."

"Bullshit sanity?" He grinned and stuffed his hands into his pockets.

"Something like that."

"Well, I don't think we'll need him tonight."

"Are you sure?" I asked, and he trailed me down a moon-shadowed hall. "I see all sorts of wonderfully fatuous things tonight, Blake. Fire-flies, moonlight, stars on my skin. Why no Hatcaden?"

He stopped, resting a hand on the shiny brass knob of a door. "Because I'm not dressed for a wrestling match. Maybe later?"

"Perhaps," I said. "Is this the bedroom?"

"Yes, Ma'am. It is."

"And were you going to take me in there tonight?"

"If you'd like me to. Yes."

"Changing protocol in the bedroom now too?"

"The bedroom, the kitchen, the balcony outside. I'd like to change protocol in quite a few places tonight."

"Sounds athletic." I laughed, unbuttoning his shirt. "What exactly did you have in mind for us, Blake?"

Blake pulled me closer, hovered his lips over mine, and said, "All sorts of wonderfully fatuous things."

I don't remember our clothes coming off, or the moment it started to rain, but I could feel his body move over mine like a wave washed over my skin. I crashed beneath him, whispering his name with his mouth at my breasts and his hips pushing mine, urging us closer with each thrusting jolt. We spared no moment, gave no relief. We moved from room to room, surface to surface, speaking in secretive, coaxing whispers, begging for more of what the other one gave until the sun melted over the ocean outside, and we ceased our fevered movements in exchange for a tranquil, floating glide.

We gave absolution that night, Blake and me. We found common ground in a mastery of forgiveness for the worst transgressions two people can ever commit. We still held our fears and still felt the darkness, but now neither endured them alone.

Fifty-Three

Blake and I woke at a leisurely hour, made love once more, and spent most of the day caring for business needs. Blake made calls for work, I made mine, and in between, we wandered the beach or sat on the floor by the windows eating sesame chicken from boxes.

Blake bit a snow pea, giving his quizzical stare. "Feeling all right?"

"I feel great," I said, smiling in hopeful distraction. "Let's go to the beach and find shells for Edward."

"We need to discuss something first."

"Ah. The pills and doctors report." We stood, gathered our lunch mess, and tossed it into a box. "Our discussions always end with me taking pills."

"This isn't about pills," he said. "Not this time."

"There was a time when pills were the most important things in our lives. What's changed?"

"Me, Sarah. I've changed, but we can't do this right now. Not alone."

"Well, if it can wait, it should. I need to head to Mother's for clothes."

Blake gestured at my Levi's and blouse. "The things I brought aren't enough?"

"Oh, do you mean the shirt and jeans I'm wearing, the bra I wore when I was thirteen, and that useless pile of mismatched socks? No, Blake. Those aren't enough."

We both laughed, and Blake said, "Probably need more than an old pile of socks. Let me get my keys, and we'll go."

"Shouldn't you stay?" I asked, yanking my satchel out of a chair. "We have furniture coming today."

"Leaving you alone when you're not on your meds isn't safe, Sarah."

"But you've cured me." I wiggled my hands in his face. "See that? No tremors. No lights. Not even a headache, I swear."

He nodded slowly, drawing a thumb down my jaw. "Everything I've done, I did to keep you safe. Remember that, Sarah. Always remember that's true."

"I'll remember," I said, playfully kissing his chin. "I've always known that."

Although mild, the overnight storm left its presence on Mother's front porch. Pinecones lay scattered, palm leaves were blown, and a lonely willow branch stabbed in her precious azaleas as if thrown from deliberate hands. After entering the living room, I was relieved to find it unharmed. Earthy-soft scents bled through the kitchen as I made my way through the front. The storm blew open the wounded backdoor, leaving tangles of duct tape stuck to its frame. Tiptoeing through leafy pools on the floor, I pulled strips of tape from Blake's makeshift repair and stalled when I saw movement through the gazebo's webbed vines.

"Jesus. Ethan?"

Words vaporized as I trudged through the soggy backyard. Apologies. Excuses. Nothing seemed right, and my anxiety grew with each nervous step. The silence from the trees was surreal. There were no birds, crickets, or scraping sounds of hurried squirrel traffic. Just silence.

Ethan leaned on a stanchion, staring blankly at dangling moss. His jacket was gone, sleeves pushed up, and odors of alcohol seeped from his skin. He glared at my presence, silent and still, stalking my steps like a cat.

"Where's your car?" I stopped by the railing opposite him and plucked a leaf from a vine. "Didn't see it out front."

"Ditched it in a marsh last night. Alicia dropped me here. I needed to think."

"You wrecked the car? Are you all—"

"Don't ask if I'm all right, Sarah. Don't ask if I'm fucking all right."

"What can I say to you then?"

"You can answer my questions for once." Ethan shifted his stance. "When you got here two weeks ago, you wouldn't look me in the eye. Is it because I reminded you of Michael?"

I nodded, tearing my leaf. "He had your eyes. Brown and wide. They were your eyes."

"What about now? Does it hurt to look at me now?"

"A little," I said. "It's getting easier."

"Jesus, Sarah." Ethan turned, gripping the railing as the breeze pushed hair from his eyes. "You had so much time to tell me. All these years after that day by the boat."

"I know. I'm sorry. I just—"

"Stop saying you're sorry."

"But I can't say anything else. I tried explaining last night, but you wouldn't listen."

"Listen to what?" he asked, looking back. "Seems damn clear as it is."

"There are things you don't know. Things I never told you."

"What things?"

Faced with the rigors of the bare-naked truth, I could find no words to explain the disasters I'd caused. We listened to calls of distant boat horns and the brush of the leaves overhead, but there were no words I could find to defend the indefensible.

"So, nothing," Ethan said. "You can't say anything?"

"Ethan, I'm—"

"You used me."

"Used you? Used you for what?"

"What do you think? Lousy marriage, lousy husband. I was the stud horse stabled and waiting for your next ride. You're no better than Charlotte Mason."

"That's not true, Ethan. I love you. I've always loved you."

"When you love someone, you don't lie to them, Sarah. You don't take their child and betray them like that. Holy Christ, the same woman raised us. You'd think you'd have learned the same shit."

"What about Mama's lessons on forgiveness? Or did you forget about those?"

"It's a little soon to beg for mercy after lying for fourteen years, don't you think?"

"And when did you start walking on water, Ethan? Why didn't you tell me about Helen? You had just as much time as I did."

"Are you comparing this?" he asked, wagging a hand. "Is that what's happening here? You're comparing my family tragedy with your life-long lie?"

"It wouldn't have been a lifelong lie if you'd have told me about Helen."

"You took him." Ethan moved closer. So close I could smell body heat and the stale odor of Scotch. "You took my child out of vengeful, teenaged spite."

"You're right. It was spite. You hurt me, so I hurt you back. But everything changed after I came home, and we—"

"What?" he asked. "Started our sleazy affair?"

"It wasn't a sleazy affair." I leaped from the gazebo, heading back to the house. "At least not for me."

"Yeah, I could tell." Ethan chased through the kitchen and into my mother's bedroom with me. "Every time you went back to your husband, I could tell just how much I meant to you."

I dropped my satchel on the bed, turning to the closet for clothes. "Staying with you would have been a disaster."

"And there it is again, folks," he said, dropping a fist to the dresser. "Another declaration of the mysterious reasons Sarah Thorn does what she does. Never gives an answer. Hints are all we get."

"Hints are all you get." I tore blouses from hangers, stuffing them into my bag.

"And everyone else gets the truth? Why not me?"

"You're too self-centered." The satchel was heavy, and I hiked it over my back. "All you've ever known is you want something, never considering the price. Believe me, I come with a price."

"Oh, I paid that price, lady." Ethan followed my pace down the hall. "Don't tell me I didn't pay the price for loving Sarah goddamn Thorn."

"You paid nothing, Ethan. I kept you from paying it."

"You kept me from my son is what you did. There's no pain worse than that, Sarah. No pain could compare to that. Ever."

Stopping in the living room, I asked, "What's the last memory you have of us, Ethan?"

"Don't turn this on me."

"I'm not turning anything. Just think of it. The last memory you have of Michael or us. What is it?"

"I dunno," he said with a shrug. "Watching fireworks in the gazebo. Michael was on my shoulders. Why?"

"The last memory I have of our son was seeing his head crushed beneath the tires of a truck."

"Jesus, Sarah..."

"No, Ethan. You wanted a pity party, let's have one. Blake keeps me drugged, hoping I won't remember. Doesn't work. I see it every day. I see Michael's hand, the blood, and the big, brown eyes, wondering why. Why wasn't I holding him? Why wasn't I catching him?"

"Sarah, don't. Don't do this."

"You had the best of Michael and me. The best days. The best memories. All I see is the blood. All I hear are the screams. And I have the guilt too. I have the guilt of losing our son because God decided this little whim just wasn't broken enough."

"Broken enough? What—"

"You think betrayal's bad, Ethan? Try guilt. Guilt's worse, regret's worse, and so is fear. They're all worse than betrayal. And I made sure you never felt a single one of them. So, screw you and your drunken self-pity. You want me to go to hell? Hell's tame compared to where I've been. Hell's where people like me go for coffee."

"Sarah, listen—"

"Mop up the kitchen and lock my mother's front door, you self-righteous son of a bitch."

Then I slammed the door as I left. I wasn't comparing my betrayal with Ethan's loss; I was comparing his nature with mine. Both of us self-ish. Both were wounded. But where Ethan's padded sensibilities whined about what could have been, mine had witnessed its worst. So, I didn't give a damn about Ethan's pain after that. The man knew nothing of pain compared to our own because I made sure he didn't.

Fifty-Four

⊙⊷✖⊶⊙

Dragging my satchel through the door of the condo, I squinted through shields of coppery warmth. Blake's voice bled from the kitchen, and I jokingly said, "Please tell me you bought drapes for this place. I hear retinal transplants can be sort of pricy."

"Hello, Sarah." Jackson sat at a newly placed dining table while Blake acted casually, nursing a beer.

"Jackson." I stopped where I was, deciding to wait for the trap to play out. "Why are you here?"

"I asked him to come." Blake set his beer by the sink. "I thought he could help."

"Uh-huh," I said, throwing my satchel on a tall stack of chairs. "Well, thank you for coming, Jackson, but I'm afraid we're just wasting your time."

"And why's that?" Jackson asked. "Why do you think I've come?"

"Oh, please." I reached up, tightening my bun. "Don't insult me with meager therapies. I can spot a psychodynamic attack from a hundred yards off."

"Then you'll understand the question," he said. "Why am I here?"

"Why, you've come to assist with my daily dose of guilt, of course. Sorry, gentlemen. Mr. Bennet's beaten you to it. His just didn't come in a pill."

"I'm not here to medicate you, Sarah. That's not why I've come."

"Then why are you here?"

"To speak with John Hatcaden."

298

"Well, you can't," I said. "John's in New York and won't see anyone except Blake or me. Everyone knows that."

"But people have seen him, Sarah." Jackson stood, approaching me slowly. "His fans have seen him. His critics have seen him. The world has seen John Hatcaden." Jackson reached into his trouser pocket and removed a tortured copy of *Dancing on Third Street*. "I assume Hatcaden's signature would prove valuable. Would you mind?"

I looked into Echo's sad eyes. "Can't sign that book, Jackson. I didn't write it."

"Yes, you did. You published under the name John Hatcaden. Delete a few letters, scramble them up, and you get, *Doctor* John Frederick Joseph Cade. He championed the use of lithium for mental illness in 1948."

"You told him?" Horrified, I shoved around Jackson and stepped toward Blake. "After you demanded to keep the book underground, you told someone?"

"I didn't have to tell him, Sarah. He already knew. Ask him."

"Don't blame your husband," Jackson said. "Blake only told me you use Hatcaden as a sort of pet name for your medications and treatments. The rest I figured out on my own."

"You knew at Ethan's, didn't you?" I turned to Jackson again. "When we spoke during lunch. You already knew."

"Oh, I've known for years. Hatcaden's name was familiar, so I was able to figure it out. Echo Gumson was tougher. Had to play with it until, finally, there it was. *Mogens Schou*, the Danish psychiatrist. Also a brilliant man. The fact my colleagues didn't catch on makes me feel quite the superior snob."

"But we were so careful. No one knew outside Blake and me. How did you—"

"Mysteries are my hobby, you see. And when my favorite author went missing, I asked Ethan, and he mentioned you'd stopped writing to become an editor at WhiteThorn."

"Blake needed my help."

"Well, now you're insulting me." Jackson smiled, setting the book on a chair. "Human nature's my job, Sarah. Which is why I know writers like you can't stop. You're creatures of your gifts. That torturous will Angela was talking about. As a behaviorist, I found the change in habit curious, but it was the address that gave it away."

"Which address?"

"The Westward address," Jackson said. "Reporters were outside WhiteThorn's offices, hounding you for Hatcaden's location. Finally, you blurted, '3189 Westward Road.' Few would have thought to use such an obscure reference, but you delivered the number as if by rote. Using the imprint stamped on a lithium pill was terribly clever."

"Capsules," I murmured, pinching a finger and thumb. "The three-hundred milligram—"

Jackson reared back, laughing so loudly his voice thundered over the walls. "Well done, Sarah. Very well done. I quite enjoyed the chase. Quite enjoyed the fun. You are a treasure, aren't you?" His laughter mellowed, and he looked into my eyes, dropping his voice to a soft and careful whisper. "I watched Blake on television too. He was fighting protestors in front of the New York Public Library, ripping their signs, pushing them back, and taking those stairs three at a time to begin a verbal sparring match I'll likely never see again. My God, the intensity of it. The boldness and fearless devotion. He bridled that crowd, daring them to make just one more ridiculous proclamation against his author. I'd never seen such raw passion from anyone. That's when I realized, as I watched Blake standing there, so angry, so stricken, that wasn't a publisher defending a book. That was a husband protecting his wife."

"They were hurting her," Blake said. "The things they said. They hurt her."

"No doubt they were." Jackson nodded, lifting my hands. "Dancing on Third Street was your last. Written just after your son's death. You suffered terribly, didn't you? Blake did tell me that. You wrote for days in the hospital, pouring your nightmares into that book."

"I don't remember writing it. I only remember Michael falling into the road. Blake told me what happened. I can't remember the rest."

"I don't imagine you would. The human mind has a way of keeping us safe from such invasions."

"God blinds us," I said.

Jackson smiled. "Miss Nash?"

"Yes."

"Then we won't dare challenge it."

There was such kindness on his face. Such pity and cautious hope. It was in his silken voice, the curve of his smile, and the smooth texture of his bulky hands as they held mine so gently, so sweetly. As if caressing petals.

"You're bipolar, aren't you? Manic? Like Echo? Extreme highs followed by crashing lows? Risky behaviors and violent impulses. Hallucinations? You hold it back remarkably well, but I suspect there's more to this than what's been considered."

"There is nothing more. Blake told me what happened. He gives me the meds. I just need to take them."

"Medication won't help you with this. There's something you've blocked from that night. That's why I'm here. I'd like to take you back to the night Michael was killed."

"Blake won't let you. Other doctors have tried; Blake always said no. He knows how hard it would be for me."

"I've discussed this with Blake. This is necessary for your recovery, and he understands that now."

"Well, I'm not doing it." I pushed him away and stepped back. "I'm not watching Michael die on that road again. I already know what happened. I was there."

"Your mind carries a secret, Sarah," Jackson said. "It's harmful to you. It's telling you to harm yourself. You'll only continue to spiral if it's not plucked out."

"Blake, please?" I begged, rushing into his arms. "I don't want to do this. Don't make me go back to that night."

"I was wrong, Jackson. Sarah's not ready."

"Your wife's being tortured, young man. Her mind is tearing her apart, and you're the only one who can stop it. She needs to remember the truth."

"I do remember. My hand was on Michael's shoulder, but I couldn't hold on, and he fell. Blake told me what happened. He told me the rest."

"Blake told you a lie," Jackson said. "You buried the truth of that night. Your mind couldn't carry the pain of the memory, so your husband gave you one that you could."

I stared up at Blake. "What's he talking about? You'd never lie to me. You love me."

"Don't make me do this, Jackson. Don't make me hurt her."

"She's going to hurt herself," Jackson said, shoving a chair to one side. "Feel her hands. She has tremors. She can barely focus her eyes. She's starting an episode right now while you're standing there holding her. Help her remember that night, Mr. Bradley. For God's sake, help your wife."

Blake gripped my face, kissing me deeply in a single, desperate breath. Tears mingled on our tongues as he wrapped his fingers around my wrists, trapping my arms at his chest.

"This was my fault, Sarah. I only wanted you safe."

"Blake, let me go." Blake's fingers dug deep, and I pushed, squirming against him. "Stop it, Blake. Let go of my arms."

"Forgive me. Please, God. Forgive me." I felt the deep hum of Blake's voice and the beat of his heart as he drew me in tighter and started to give me the truth. "Michael didn't fall that night. Michael never slipped."

"Yes, he did. He pulled away and—"

"He didn't pull."

"He did, Blake. Michael turned, and my hand—"

"You pushed him, Sarah. You pushed Michael into that road."

"I pushed...?" A sudden shudder ran down my spine, and I blinked, trying to focus my eyes. "What'd you say?"

"Michael ran to the snow by the road. You grabbed him and pulled him off. You made him say the poem."

"The poem?" I looked away, flooded with images rising. "The riptide. I thought we were at the riptide."

"Your hands were on his shoulders. You said the poem, warning him about monsters."

"They were everywhere. The monsters were screaming. Calling for Michael."

"The truck backed up to the curb. You thought it was a wave."

"And... I pushed him?"

"You didn't know, honey."

"Into the road?"

"You didn't understand what was happening."

"Under the truck?"

"Sarah." Blake pulled me closer, feeling my body go tense. "It's all right."

"Are you saying—" There was no way to harness my thoughts. Couldn't gather the weight of it, the horror of what he was saying. "Are you telling me I killed him? You're saying I killed my own son?"

"You didn't know what you were doing, honey. You didn't know."

Adrenaline slicked through my veins like a torch. My heart raced, my chest ached, and my ears hummed with my pulse pounding through them, yearning to kill it all. I saw muted memories rising and spectral figures sliding into view as I remembered the night Blake protected me from.

The night when I murdered my son.

Fifty-Five

~~~

My mind opened cruelly, and I found myself in New York, staring down an icy Fifth Avenue corner. Blended sounds of Christmas carols and traffic horns floated in chorus overhead. The hurried passersby bundled against bitter frost, and the lateness of the hour dwindled the crowds to a straggling few.

Michael and I stood by the road, draped in shadows of tightly parked cars and tall mounds of ice-covered snow. He was laughing wildly, scaling their peaks.

The pain in my temple raced down my back, and I blinked, seeing cars morph into waves and icy black roads melt into miles of raging emerald ocean. I gasped, and the shoreline appeared in a single swath of blazing, enchanted movement.

"Monsters are here," I said, pulling him off the mound. "Come with me, Michael. Come to the riptide."

"No, Momma. We're in the city now. See all the buildings? See all the stuff?"

"They're coming for you." Panic fevered my skin, and I fell to my knees, tearing the scarf from his neck. "Say the poem, Michael. Say it."

"But there are no monsters. This is a high time you're having. Come back to me, Mommy. Come back to me now."

Creatures teemed from every corner of the shore. Their growls and howled cautions melted from the shadows, warning me to harbor my son, to keep him away from the madness they spread, and save him from our merciless curse. I told Michael I loved him, jerking him close and seeing Blake's face twisted in fear. He was far from us, pushing through pillars of driftwood logs and monolith white-ashen trees.

"They're coming, Michael. Swim to the riptide. You're safer in there."

"You're hurting me, Momma," he cried. "You're squeezing too hard."

"God blinks inside the fireflies," I said, kissing my son's tender lips, "and His tides lay us to sleep."

"Come back to me, Momma. Come back to me now."

Then I laid my hand firmly against the arc of his chest and pushed Michael into that road. He screamed, stumbling backward under the froth of that behemoth wave.

And then my son's face—my son's perfect face—so soft and so smooth like the breast of a dove, cracked open wide, twisting its features like a hideously tortured doll. Blood spilled from his eyes, tongue protruding in a grotesque curling cramp until his hands twitched and stilled, reaching for me with bloody bright smears melting snow.

Michael.

I pushed from Blake's hold, trembling, and trying to breathe. "How could you do it?" I said, pacing between the two men. "How could you keep that from me?"

"You were screaming, Sarah. No one saw what happened, and I thought if you remembered an accident—"

"That was no accident. I murdered my son. How could you let me live after that? Why didn't you just let me die?"

"Your conscience is innocent, Sarah." Jackson stood nearer, and I heard a *pop* in his hand. "In your mind, you were saving your son."

"There's nothing innocent about killing a child, Jackson. Blake should have let me die."

"I had to choose," Blake said. "I chose you."

"You chose wrong!" My nails swept the side of Blake's face, leaving three angry gashes down his jawline and neck. Blood drained into the crisp white cotton of his shirt, splashing droplets of red on his sleeves. "You let me live on purpose. To punish me. To watch me suffer."

Blake threw us to the floor, rocking the tall stack of chairs as we fell. He pressed on top of me, pinning my arms and tying my legs with his own.

I cursed and wailed, unable to stop. I told Blake I hated him. Told him his mother was right to die, and his father helped her do it. Every word, every syllable that clawed from my throat became an unstable weapon in my own mental war. Blake held me, one hand cradling my head, the other clutching my wrists as Jackson's needle stabbed my arm, and my body went limp under Blake's.

Everything felt silken after that. Sound condensed into joint lapses of captured breath and the throaty scrapes of Jackson's cough as he covered me with his jacket and Blake slid us toward the wall. Nothing felt natural; I couldn't see and hear beyond a twilight world of drifting thoughts and forgotten, dreadful beauty.

My father's hands appeared first. Shrimper's hands. Dark and scarred, wrapped at my wrists, dipping my feet into waves as I squealed. I remembered his deep and delicate voice telling my mother he loved us as he strapped a green canvas bag to his back and briskly marched to a plane. My head shifted in Blake's lap, following the cries of an anguished wife, flag to her breast, and I whispered, "My mother."

Shadows sliced over my glassy eyes, and when I blinked, I was on the beach. Blake was there, his bronzed skin blazed by the fire as our bodies writhed in their intimate movements. I felt his breath, his gentle, sliding stabs, and how his heart rocked against the dense press of my breasts.

"I'll love you forever," he said, crystal eyes shining on mine.

"Then I'll give you forever right now," I replied.

A sharp, cracking noise made me flinch, and I saw Ethan and myself as children again. "Mama says we're two halves of the same shell," he said, placing candy in my hand as I laughed. "Never pull us apart, Sarah Thorn. We'll die if you pull us apart."

A stinging bite hit the crook of one arm, and the scent of bitter blood brought Abby's teenage face into view.

"Sisters help when they're stuck doing chores," I said, and I yanked the Perlick door back to the wall. "Ta-dah!"

"No, Sarah. Wait—"

"Don't be scared, scaredy-cat." Reaching for a box, I bumped the door, and a sharp, searing pain scorched my hip. "Dammit." I winced, peering behind at a silvery spike. "What happened to the safety latch? Stupid thing feels like it's got icy teeth."

"Oh, Sarah. No," Abby whined. "Didn't I tell you not to open that door? Didn't I tell you to leave?"

"Stop worrying so much." I spat on my finger, thumbing blood from my cut. "Not like the world will end."

"But it might." With tears in her eyes, Abby lifted the box cutter and opened a gash in her palm.

"Christ, Abby. Why'd you cut your hand like that?"

"Who's your whim, Sarah Thorn?"

"You're my whim, Abby. And I'm yours. But why—"

"Remember this, Sarah." Abby reached for my shorts, dipping the waistband and grinding her wound into mine. "I cut my hand and your hip with a box cutter by the meat cases. We're not just whims anymore. We're blood sisters now. Forever and always. We'll always be sisters in blood."

"Sarah?" Blake's tender voice brought me back. "Honey? Can you hear me?"

"The door." My words were feeble, and I felt the straps of a gurney tight on my waist. "Tell Abby I remember the door."

"We're taking you out of here."

"Tell her, Blake. The sisters in blood. Tell Abby I remember the door."

"I will." Blake kissed me, touching my cheek. "Go to sleep now, honey. Just go to sleep."

And I did.

Fifty-Six

Coming through the fog of an unconscious jag was like enduring the spins of a wave. The chill bit first. There was a sting of bright sun, and then sound muscled into my ear. That's how it was after I'd emerged from what was to be my last excursion into mental darkness.

Afternoon light bled through the drapes, meeting my freshly raised eyes. Windsor chimes rang four o'clock, and I recognized my location just by the tune of their song.

"The castle," I whispered.

"That was one hell of a nap." Jackson flashed a penlight over my eyes. "Wish I could sleep like that."

"How long?" I rasped, clearing my throat. "How long this time?"

"Four days. Abby said you were waking, but I wanted to check on you first."

"Abby's here? How?"

"Girl changed her plea," he said. "Judge accepted and set her bail, which Ethan eagerly paid. He brought her home two days ago."

"I need to see her." I struggled to position my arms. "Help me get up."

"Settle down now, Sarah. Just settle down." Jackson pressed his thumb to my wrist. "Exams before tea parties. Visitors can wait."

"Why am I here?" I asked, melting back. "Why not the hospital or Mother's house?"

"Blake said no hospitals. Since your mother's home has about as much privacy as swings at the park, the only place left was the castle."

"Where's Blake right now?"

"In the hall. Poor man's been sleeping here on the floor, waiting for you to wake up."

"The floor?" I spied blankets and pillows piled on a chair. "I'm sorry, Jackson. Everything I did to you and Blake was awful. I know it was."

"Don't flatter yourself." He teased. "Nothing compares to Angela's outbursts when her morning café is brewed weak."

I managed a laugh, asking, "So, am I all right now? More normal?"

"Of course, you're not normal. Nobody's normal. What makes you think that?"

"Since Blake told me the truth, I thought I'd be more... normal."

Jackson wrinkled his brow and said, "Young lady, you've never been blessed with chastisements from a fatherly soul, and I've never been blessed with a daughter I needed to chastise, so why don't we do that right now?" Then he gathered his wares, settled beside me, and joined our hands on my lap. "There is no normal for you, Sarah. And there never will be. All you can do is resume proper therapy for your needs and learn to live the way everyone lives. Broken, but moving."

"Some are more broken than others, and I've always wondered why."

Jackson smiled. "We're no closer to answering that question than any other mystery fallen to earth. People like you are creatures of special design. Small bits of heaven God couldn't quite hold. None of us knows why we're here. We can only accept that we are."

"Bits of heaven, Jackson? Mysteries fallen to earth. Not very clinical. Is that what you tell all your patients?"

"Only two," he said. "You and a frightened young boy who once begged me to fix his poor sister."

"Ethan?"

"Yes." Jackson nodded. "He was ten."

There was a knock on the door, and Blake eased inside. He looked tired, scored from my nails, and his eyes held a foggy black underpinning as if they'd seen far too much.

"How is she?" he asked.

"A little weak. Give her time and a few decent meals, and she'll be prancing around soon enough." With a meaty slap to Blake's shoulder,

Jackson picked up his bag and added, "Help her write again, young man. I prefer reading smut while I fish."

Blake thanked Jackson, who closed the door as he left.

At first, we said nothing, only sharing quick glances and daring one another to speak. Blake tucked his hands into his pockets and walked to the fireplace, watching flames dance on the irons.

"This is why you didn't want to publish *Third Street*," I said. "You were afraid it might trigger memories of the night Michael died."

Blake gripped the mantel and sighed. "That book was the best and worst thing to happen to us."

"Protecting me was the best and worst too."

"What could I do?" He picked up a poker, stabbing at logs. "Watch you suffer in a madhouse? Let you die in a cell?"

"That may have been better."

"For whom?" he asked, setting the poker aside. He stepped to my bedside, taking a seat at my hips. "Everyone struggles, Sarah. Everyone battles their personal hell."

"Some have it forced on them," I said, resting my hand over his.

He sat quietly, folding a crease in the sheet. "No one forced me to do what I did. I made that choice on my own."

"But this is what MJ meant. When he told us about Lena's burden. This is what MJ meant."

"He was dying, honey. He didn't know what he was saying."

"Yes, he did. He was just wrong. It wasn't Lena's burden he couldn't remove; it was his. It was his pain he felt. His fear, his guilt. MJ died never knowing that, and I don't want that for you, Blake. I don't want—"

"What should I do? Walk away? Leave you alone with your guilt? What kind of man would I be if I did?"

"But everything I've done, Blake. Michael. My god, Michael. How can you look at me? Why do you stay?"

"Because Mama was right. I loved you before I ever saw you. And when I did see you standing in the water, fighting against anyone and anything that got close, I felt a sense of purpose I never had before."

"Love is more than purpose. That's not how it should be for you, Blake."

"That's exactly how it should be," he said, sitting closer. "I loved my mother, but she taught me I couldn't fight monsters. Lena didn't want my love because she was more afraid of living than dying."

"Her death wasn't your fault. Nothing Lena did was your fault."

"I only know that because of you. You taught me to love again, Sarah. Even when it came in bits and pieces. Even when I shut you out, you taught me to love you. You still let me try. You're the reason I live. The reason I breathe every day. There's no other purpose for love beyond that."

Blake saved us that night. Soft tales of forgiveness forged from a man so in love with me he burdened himself with horrors that never belonged to him. But there is no hiding the secrets we hold. Even when bandaged, they bleed. And if we're fortunate to be loved with such intensity, our wounds can be healed, our mysteries solved, and the remains of our lives given back.

The castle's lack of modern heat required primal efforts to stay warm. The fireplace's blaze dwindled to sparks, and I quaked beneath blankets, watching flames die against the window's assaulting drafts. I dragged from bed, intending to stuff pillows in cracks, but stopped when a voice rose from a darkened corner of the room.

"Go back to bed." Ethan pushed from the shadows of a Regency chair. "It's too cold for you to be walking around."

"Have you been here all night?"

"Just a few hours." With one hand holding mine and another on my elbow, he helped me back to the bed. Wearing a somewhat neater T-shirt and having less growth on his face, he didn't look as worn as Blake, but he was obviously just as tired.

"Why are you up?" I asked.

"Boat needs work. She's no good tied to the dock, and I feel like taking her out."

"Maybe you should wait. I smell storms coming in, and—"

"Is this why you stayed with him?" Ethan settled on the foot of my bed. "Because Blake understands what you need? Is that's why you stayed?"

"I'm in love with him, Ethan. That's why I stayed."

"And me?" he asked, searching my face. "Did you always love me?"

"Always." The answer fell quickly because it was true. "But I was hurting you. Whenever I came, whenever I left, I hurt you."

"You weren't hurting me."

"I was, Ethan. You know that I was."

"No," he said, aiming his eyes at mine. "You weren't."

We looked at one another, locked in a brief process of thought before I forced him to face the reality of what I'd become. I sat up, lifting my arms to reveal the scratches, bruising, and red streaking marks from the needles and tape on my skin.

"The girl you love isn't real," I said. "This is who she is now. She's broken. Struggling. And always chasing death. The girl on the beach, the one on the boat; she died long ago, and she's not coming back."

"There are doctors, Sarah. Specialists. I could have—"

"What could you have done?" I asked, sliding closer to him. "Ended up like Blake? Terrified of the woman you only wanted to love? I couldn't do that to you both. If I had stayed with you, everything we had would have died. *I* would have died."

"Every memory I have has you in it," he said, gently touching my face. "I can't help but love you, Sarah. I'll love you for the rest of my life."

"I'll love you for the rest of mine."

I kissed him once more, lingering my lips as he took me into his arms and lay me down in the bed.

"Stay under the quilts." He sniffed, tucking blankets under my chin. "Last thing I need is Mama talking about my old drafty house."

"She'd complain anyway."

"Probably," he said. "Got the chills too?"

"I'll be fine."

"Fine." He scoffed, lifting a corner of the quilt. "Why do women always say they're fine when everything's gone to absolute shit? Move over."

"Move over?" I lay there, blinking.

"What're ya dense, shrimper's kid? I'm not going to let you lie here and freeze. Now move your ass over."

Scooting back, I opened a wedge of space on the bed. Ethan's body was warm as he inched beside me, twining our legs and smoothing the covers.

"What's your name?" Ethan asked.

"Sarah Haley Thorn. What's yours?"

"Ethan Scott Bennet."

"You smell like scotch, Ethan Bennet. You used to smell like honey."

"Now, tell me the truth," he said, pressing his head to the pillow. "Were you trying to steal my comics that day?"

"Not at first, no."

"No? So what was the plan?"

"We thought you were dead, so the plan was to poke you. Then I was going to check your petie and steal your comics."

"That was your plan?" He chuckled. "To molest a dead kid and steal his books?"

"Well, it's not like you'd use them, Ethan. You'd be dead."

We laughed, and Ethan asked, "Remember what you told me that day?"

"You asked me to stay with you, and I said I would."

"And what'd you say after that?"

Softly, I whispered, "I told you I'd keep you warm."

"Well, you did, Sarah Thorn," he said, touching his forehead to mine. "You did keep me warm."

There was no more beauty Ethan and I could have gained in a lifetime of loving we didn't find lying there falling asleep. Our love was a radiant thing. Wild and free, and too untamed to capture in more than the briefest of moments. And what moments they were. Loving under twilight storms and sandy trenches laid bare by two broken hearts, not knowing why they loved but desperately needing its cure.

We shared a love story, Ethan and me. It was real. It was strong. And it lasted the whole of our lives.

Fifty-Seven

The following day brought a lightness I hadn't felt in years. Everything glowed with the promise that comes with the purity of redemption. The sky was blue, the sand was white, the waters moved like swaths of silken jade, and I was alive with every changing movement.

"Mama said to eat everything here." Abby brought breakfast to the solarium's sitting area, placing a tray full of eggs, toast, sausage, and fruit on the spindly glass table before dropping into a chair.

"That woman's gonna make me as big as she is." I scooped a forkful of eggs and held them. "Eat some with me."

"Eat some? I ate half just bringing it in here. You eat it."

"Where's Edward?"

"Nice try. Jackson took him fishing after checking on you. Is Blake still here?"

"Blake left for a run, then went to the condo for work."

"That man's been jumping between here and that condo all week. Why doesn't he work from Ethan's office?"

"Gosh, Abby," I said, casually popping a grape. "I can't imagine why Blake won't use the office of the man who had an affair with his wife. How odd."

"Oh, yeah." She giggled, drizzling honey on a thick slice of toast. "Not a good idea. No."

"No."

We shared our meal, and I looked to the sunrise, searching the ocean outside.

"He's done this before," Abby said. "Ethan, I mean. He'd take that boat out for weeks at a time. Usually, after you left."

"There's a storm coming in. I can smell it. I can feel it."

"He'll radio Alicia every day. He's fine, Sarah. Ethan's always fine."

"What about you?" I asked. "I heard you arguing with Ward this morning."

"If Edward's all right, I'll be all right. That's all I care about."

"Edward won't be all right if you're in jail."

"He won't be all right if you keep pushing things, either. He'll be worse off. I don't want this investigated, Sarah."

"Why? Was Edward with you that night?"

She shrugged and said, "I don't want to talk about that."

"Why not? We're already playing cat and mouse with the latch. May as well see who's gonna pounce first."

"Made a mistake with the latch," she said, smacking honey from her fingers and lips. "Who checks the age of metal, for God's sake?"

"Bayport County does, apparently. Guess you should have looked into that, huh?"

"Guess so. If I'd known, I would have said Ida or Buster cut it. No one would have questioned it then."

"Who cut it?"

Abby smiled, tilting her lovely dark head. "Blake told me you remembered the sisters in blood. About cutting yourself on the latch when we were kids."

"Did you tell him the truth, or did you lie and tell him you cut me with a box cutter?"

"Wouldn't have lied if you'd have left the shop like I said."

"Why lie at all?" I asked. "What difference did it make how I cut myself?"

"Made a difference to me. Mama would have skinned me alive if she knew you'd been in that freezer again. Especially that day."

"That day was no different than any other, Abby. Just Wednesday."

"But that was the morning Mama heard we were home." She reached over, scooping more eggs on her toast. "She came to the shop and told Buster she'd make him pay if he hurt us again."

"Did Mama know about the latch?"

"She knew, but there's a time for truth, and that isn't today."

"Who tore up Buster's shop?" I asked. "Who did that?"

"You did," she said, chewing her toast. "Buster nearly wet his pants when you threw the first jar. He jumped over the counter and hid under shelves when you threw the second. You crashed the third on the wall by his head, and he screamed so loud Alicia and Ethan ran from the park."

"Buster was afraid of the glass."

"Lots of things scared Buster. Just didn't know how much until then."

"What about this?" I patted my hip with the scar. "Couldn't remember the latch being cut when Ward asked, but now I do."

"Can't have you talking about that scar, Sarah. That's why I got out. Had to tell you not to talk anymore. Telling Blake was bad enough, but I can't have you dropping memories all over the street."

"Ward's going to ask about that latch again. If he doesn't, the DA will. What should I say?"

"Tell them you don't remember." Abby shrugged and then stood to pick up the tray. "Or tell them we did the blood sisters thing in the shop. Doesn't matter. If anyone asks, you'll just have to lie."

"And why would I do that? Why would I lie?"

"Because I asked you to lie. It's not like we haven't done it before."

"We were kids back then, Abby. Just children inventing a game."

"Games don't end because we grow up," she said. "They just get harder to play."

"Well, I'm not playing this one. And if you force me to choose between you and whoever cut that latch, I'll choose you."

"Damn it, Sarah." Abby slammed the tray to the table, spilling coffee and eggs on the floor. "Just because you don't understand my reasons doesn't mean they don't matter. If you love me, you'll do as I say."

"That's why I won't let you do this, Abby. Because I love you."

Mama burst through the solarium's door, gripping her cane as she tramped down the steps. "What are you two doing making such a racket in here? Sounds like a bunch of trash grabbers combing the beach." Her eyes zeroed in on the mess. "And who's throwing good food to the ants?"

Abby ran to her, pointing at me. "She'll tell, Mama Nash. She's going to ruin—"

"No, she ain't." Mama glared at me, patting Abby low on the hip. "Go finish my dishes. May as well give this girl answers before hell opens up and sucks her back in."

Abby's fiery eyes banked on me before she bolted up the steps, slamming the door as she left.

"I ain't cleaning that up," Mama said, skirting the mess. "I ain't made it, and I ain't cleaning it up."

"I'll clean it."

"You can't clean nothing being weak as you are. Abby did it. She'll clean it up." Mama claimed Abby's chair and looked out. "Sky's turning mean. Badness coming for sure."

"You talking about the weather, Mama? Or something worse?"

"Storms rip the heart of the world, child. What worse a thing could there be?"

"Some say murder's worse."

"Ain't nobody done any murdering."

"That's not true. Abby says she murdered Buster. And didn't you murder too? Gossips say you did. You killed your husband and daughter and got away with it, and now you think Abby can too."

"Those nags never got my story right," she said. "None of them knows the truth because I never told it. One day Abby's truth will be the same way. Some bit of storytelling dripped from the mouths of the wicked."

"What is Abby's truth?"

Mama smiled. "Now, you know that ain't mine to tell."

"So tell me yours," I said. "What happened to your husband, Mama? To your daughter? Did you do what the gossips say you did? Did you kill them?"

"I ain't killed my family. Their blood was weak like I said."

"That lie doesn't work anymore. You can't hide your past any better than I could hide mine."

"There's nothing to hide 'cos I ain't killed my family. Had an old dog once and had to put him down. Want to hear me tell about that?"

"A dog, Mama Nash? Or a man?"

"A dog," she said. "Showed up at the back door after my husband died. My daughter, Cissy, was happy with that. I was, too, for a while. But then, when 'Licia turned three, she come to me with her dress tore up, saying that old dog been biting at her. No matter how hard we beat that evil creature, he'd come right back, biting through each of us until he bit too damn much."

"So you killed him?"

"We put him down."

"Put him down," I said, tucking back. "How?"

"With a meal." Mama didn't move when the thunder cracked overhead, and I couldn't see her chest rise or fall with her breath. She just stared at the stormfront and the ocean outside, fingering the curve of that cane. "We lived in Breaux Ridge when he came. Little house on the edge of a salt marsh where a mushroom bed grew. They'd glow like starlight in the middle of the cypress whenever the moon was bright. 'Licia always wanted to pick those blue caps, thinking that was where the fairies lived, but I didn't let her. Those caps were special. Beautiful to look at, poison to touch. But there was one night I wrapped her hands in muslin and sent her out for those caps to make stew."

"You added poison mushrooms to stew? And he ate it?"

"Sucked down three or four bowls in an hour," she said. "Lapping it up till his eyes went black like two onyx buttons."

"That's how you killed him. Poison mushrooms?"

"Mushrooms like that won't kill a dog, but they will make them tame enough to follow along."

"Follow where?"

"Out the back door," she said, shifting her hips. "We walked him through the salt marsh, following the glow of the mushroom bed and the black candle Cissy held in her hand. He knelt in the center of those caps, reaching for Cissy like he was craven before an idol. She pulled up an old cypress root, cracking every limb he owned until she was too weak to swing, and he was too broke to move."

"Cissy beat him to death?"

"You don't beat a dog to kill it. You beat it 'cos it bites."

"Stop playing games, Mama. Tell me the truth."

"That is the truth. We let him howl till we saw them ferals moving through the brush. Then we left for the porch and sat in the rockers to listen."

"Ferals? What ferals?"

"Hogs," she said. "Wild ones. They come for mushrooms, but they'll eat whatever sits in their way."

"Oh, Mama Nash, no." I couldn't look at her. I blinked at the eggs still spread on that floor and the coffee still drizzling its path, but I couldn't look into the eyes of the woman who raised me. Who held me. Who loved me as much as her own. "No. No. No..."

"That dog screamed in a language only the devil could understand. We sat in our rockers snapping our peas until we heard nothing but the sounds of their teeth and the trample of hooves as they fed."

"And Alicia?" I asked, swallowing hard. "Where was she?"

"Playing with her paper dolls right by my feet."

"Jesus, she heard?"

"'Course she heard. We did it for her. One day she'd be grown, remember the pain and blood, and scream for a justice she never got. 'Licia has justice now, and her soul can rest free."

"Murder's a sin, Mama Nash. Or doesn't sin apply to women like you?"

"God understands things have to die, and good people have to do it."

"And me?" I sat up, gripping the arms of my chair. "Will God understand why I murdered my son?"

"You ain't murdered your boy."

"Calling it an accident doesn't change what I did."

"You ain't murdered your boy." Mama stood, slapping her cane on the table. "And talking like that's a badness to women and a blight on a good mother's soul. Don't say that again."

"Do good mothers kill their children?" My horror gave way to tears. "Does God understand women who murder their sons?"

Mama eased closer with an effortless glide. Her eyes didn't blink, her hand gripped her cane, and then she stopped at my chairside and lifted my chin on her thumb. "We saw monsters come after our children," she said. "You saved Michael when you gave him to God; I saved mine, sending the monsters. Those are the moments God understands most. He cries for our reasons and then looks away."

Mama's gaze was a lesson in primal defense. She held no remorse, nor did she carry any burdens of guilt. It was justice in its purest, most expedient form. And deep down, in those grim places where we harness our rages and greedy espousals of hate, we harbor a certain secret joy not admitted by the cultured few too arrogant to embrace the purity of that sort of uncomplicated vengeance.

Mama knew that purity. She understood its justice. And she embraced it with a clean and virtuous heart.

Fifty-Eight

Within days of Mama's confession, the brunt of the storms had arrived. Heavy gusts of punishing wind uprooted trees, vomited tide into streets, and blacked out generous portions of the county. Blake and Jackson gathered candles and flashlights, saved water in every available container, and secured the castle's grounds as best they could. After these assurances, there was little we could do besides wait.

Mama stayed with us, sewing and cooking. Abby kept Edward calm with the monster game, and occasionally, Blake and I hid away and just kissed. Our hands roamed freely, exploring deep, carnal spots, and just as the fire in our bellies fell lower, he'd pull away again, saying we'd need more privacy for what he wanted to do. That only made me want him more, but I think he knew that.

With its glass walls threatened by flying debris, we stayed away from the solarium. But at night, when everyone slept, I'd sneak in, looking through rain-slicked windows toward the ocean outside. I'd search black horizons, hoping to see a glint of brass or the white of a hull splitting waves. When that image didn't come, I comforted myself with visions of Ethan stretched on her deck, finding the stars in an unfettered sky. His frequent contact with Alicia settled my worries, but Ethan never said when he'd return and only offered stale promises of *in a few days* whenever we asked. By week's end, the worst of the storms subsided, and the sun broke through in wide spikes of light, brushing color over the gray until, as always, Bayport restored herself.

Voices mingled downstairs as I dressed. Tight whispers and footsteps ended at Ethan's office, and I heard the slide of the pocket doors slowly close shut. Peeking through the window, I found the Lemniscate floating at her dock. She was shining with dampness but looked sound, nonetheless.

I zipped my jeans and ran down the stairs, throwing open the pocket doors, saying, "Mama should whip you blind for—"

Bleak faces stared back. Alicia stood with papers in hand while Evan lingered beside Ward and Blake, standing behind Ethan's desk. Abby sat on the chesterfield, head in hands, and Mama entered behind me, muttering something about having made coffee.

"You here for Abby?" I asked Alicia.

"No, Sarah. Ethan."

"Ethan?" I studied each of them, crossing my arms. "What'd he do now? Streak naked across a schoolyard full of children? Honestly, Alicia. He's done worse."

"He's gone, Sarah," Alicia said. "Lost in the storm out at sea."

I hated those words. They were sharp, unemotional, and cruel in their depth.

"No, he's not." I nudged at the windows. "Boat's out there, tied to the dock."

"Evan brought her in." Blake pressed a hand to my back. "She was adrift, and Ethan wasn't there."

"But Ethan radios every day." I looked at them. "At ten o'clock every morning, Ethan calls Alicia at the station."

"Not for the last two days," Alicia said. "I sent a helicopter once the storms ended. They found the boat yesterday; she was waterlogged, and the radio was dead. Ethan's gone, Sarah. Caught in the storms at sea. You know how that happens out there."

"Not to him. Ethan was always in the water. He can swim for a long time. Maybe even—"

"Water's too cold." Evan shook his head. "And he was too far out."

"But Ethan's so strong," I said, falling to my knees beside Abby. "Isn't he, Abby? Tell them what a strong swimmer he is. Tell them."

"There's nothing to say." Abby sobbed, covering her face in her hands. "Ethan's gone. He's just gone."

Mama clutched her Bible, pleading with God and Christ to grant blessings for souls lost at sea. I couldn't stand the hypocrisy. The unending lessons of death, acceptance, and begging for strength during trials.

"What the hell are you doing?" I burst to my feet, glaring at her. "Are you praying about this?"

"We have to, baby. God gives us strength when we pray."

"Strength for what? Strength to move on after He's killed one of us off?"

"That ain't true, baby. God don't do things like that."

"Well, He did it with Michael, didn't He?"

"Sarah," Blake said. "This isn't her fault."

"Let her be, boy. Girl always suffered a battle with God; it's time she flushed out those pains."

"Well, I wouldn't have those pains if it weren't for God now, would I, Mama? That's what this is, isn't it? Our punishment for loving too little or loving too much?"

"God don't punish like that."

"Well, if He punishes us with bee stings, why the hell wouldn't He punish with death?"

"You ain't seeing this straight. We're God's blessed whims."

"We're not his whims," I said, snatching the King James from her hands. I lobbed it across Ethan's desk, scattering papers and pens to the floor. "We're not blessed, and I've got a stack of headstones that damn well proves we're not his favored children. You know what we are, Mama Nash? We're his prodigals. The ones who just piss him off. God doesn't understand the sins of His prodigal whims, and He doesn't look away when He sees them. You know what He does, Mama? He watches. God crouches up there with his claws at our throats, just waiting to bleed us all out. He's a monster, Mama Nash. A dog who's gone mad. You can't get more rabid than God."

Fifty-Nine

I'd never cried the way I did at Ethan's memorial service. It was a strange sort of rendering. I made no sound and gave no gesture. I just floated within myself, letting grief squeeze from my eyes like slowly bleeding fruit. The requisite circumstances of death occurred at the castle. There was the town gathering, the speeches, the little black dresses, and the placement of a blue granite memorial stone everyone said Ethan would have loved. That alone made me wince.

"Who in the hell would love their own headstone?" I could hear Ethan say. "What kind of bullshit is that?"

I took shelter on the castle's front porch until Evan ruined it. "Ward wants us in Ethan's office right now," he said, popping his head through the door. "Stop hiding out here and come in."

The thought of engaging in socially acceptable speech bothered me, but at Ward's insistence and having Evan make a second request, I girded my mettle and went.

Ward sat behind Ethan's desk with Abby and Blake in front while Evan took a spot on the Chesterfield.

"All right, Ward," Blake said, offering me his chair. "What's this about?"

Ward lifted a thick brown folder. "Ethan's will. He revised it the night Sarah fell ill. We can do this formally or just—"

"Just the highlights." I rested my head on my hand. "We're all pretty tired."

"Fine by me." Ward dropped the folder and relaxed in the chair.

"Ethan's left everything to Abby and Edward Mills. There are consider-ations for Miss Nash and Alicia Maynard, but Ethan left most of the estate to Miss Mills."

Abby gasped and sat up. "But I wouldn't know what to do with it all. And what about Evan?"

"Hell, I don't need it, Abby." Evan leaned over, tying his shoe. "I own half the business right now as it is. And I certainly don't need this old house. Dusty rat trap. That's why Ethan left it to you. He wanted you to have it."

"There's something else," Ward said. "Evan was to head the founda-tion, but Ethan changed that. Evan remains on the board of directors, but Ethan named Blake Bradley as chief executive officer."

"That can't be." Blake's eyes dodged between Ward and me. "You've read something wrong, Ward. That's not what it says."

"Read it yourself if you like." Ward nudged the folder to Blake. "Ethan's work carried risk. Years ago, I advised him to get his affairs in order before every excursion. Changes like this are incidental."

"But why would he add me and Edward like that?" Abby asked.

"You and Edward were always Ethan's beneficiaries," Ward said. "The only recent change was switching Evan for Blake."

"And he put me in charge of the foundation?" Blake husked a laugh. "Believe me, Ward, he wouldn't. There's a mistake."

"There's no mistake. Ethan called the morning he left, directing me to make that change. When I asked why, he told me to tell you one thing."

"What was that?"

"Keep her safe," Ward said. "Ethan told me you'd keep her safe."

"Jesus." Blake buckled, supporting himself on the desk. "What do I do with this? What the hell do I—"

"You can always refuse," Ward said. "No one's saying you can't."

"I'll do it." Blake turned to Evan. "But only if no one objects. Evan?"

"My brother wasn't one to make a bad choice." Evan stood, button-ing his coat. "He had his reasons for choosing you, Blake. I'm sure they were good." Evan stretched over the desk, shaking Ward's hand. "I've got to catch a plane back to Texas. Ethan Bennet might be gone, but his boats still sail."

Evan hugged Abby, prompting the first smile I'd seen from her in days.

"And now you." Evan took my arm, lifting me out of the chair. "Saw a girl on a beach one time. Red hair, wild eyes, terrible temper. She scared the hell out of me, but Ethan liked her. I told him girls like that are why God struck down Eden, and do you know what he said to me then?"

"No." I smiled. "What did he say?"

"He told me, 'Hell no, big brother. That girl right there is why God raised it.'"

My breath keened, and Evan hugged me before crossing the office to leave. His movements were tragic. There was permanence to them. And I knew, as his face disappeared behind those softly closed doors, we'd never see Evan again.

"Anything else, Ward?" Blake asked.

"Only the boat. Ethan's left that to you, Sarah. Do you agree?"

"I agree. Is that all?"

"As far as the will is concerned, yes." Ward stood, skirting the desk to stand before Abby. "Now, on to your mess."

"Can't it wait?" Abby asked. "Just for today?"

"There's no time. That storm put a hold on everything, but eventually that DA will come looking for your friend over here. We've got to straighten the details before he does."

"What details?"

"That latch, for one thing. First, you said you cut it. Now you say you didn't, but you're not sure who did. Nothing makes sense, young lady, so before the DA and his legal dogs dig for answers from your friend over here, we'll get those answers first." Ward swiped a notepad and pen from the desk, handing them to Abby. "Write everything that happened between the time Buster hit that freezer and the time they thawed him out. I want details."

"I told you what happened."

"No. You gave us a version of what happened. Let's fill in the blanks a little better this time."

"If I do this, they'll investigate further, won't they? My brother? My parents?"

"Young lady, are you not listening?" Ward leaned closer, cupping his knees. "We're not trying to keep them from investigating this case. We're trying to keep them from blaming you. The DA can only do this once, and he won't risk losing when a witness might recall that latch being cut by someone else twenty years ago."

"But I don't want it investigated at all. This has to stop with me."

"That won't happen, Miss Mills. There was a murder in this tiny town, and it's too damn bloody to brush under some prosecutorial rug. As your attorney, I'm bound to give you the best defense I can, which means I'll cross-examine investigators and ask Sarah about the latch. So, if whoever you're protecting is still walking above ground somewhere, they'd better come clean, or you'd better do it for them because that is a truth that'll never stay buried."

Abby stared through the windows at the ocean outside. "I thought I'd have more time."

"People in your situation usually do," Ward said, taking his briefcase from the floor by the desk. "And they're always wrong."

Blake saw Ward to the door, shaking his hand before returning to the office again. "Do you understand, Abby?" he asked, crouching beside her. "Everything Ward said, you understand?"

"I miss Ethan. He helped me with Edward, and I need him right now."

"We'll help with Edward. Sarah's here, and I'm here too. Whatever you need me to do, I'll do."

Abby sniffed and narrowed her eyes at Blake. "You're good at that, aren't you? Taking care of people? Keeping them safe? You made sure no one said anything bad about Sarah. That's what you do for people you love, isn't it, Blake? You protect them."

"Mama Nash calls it my purpose." Blake smiled, tapping Abby's hand with the pen. "Ethan would want you to do as Ward says. He'd want you to tell us the truth."

"All right." Abby nodded, let go of a breath, and scribbled her name on the pad. "Will you be here tomorrow?" she asked. "I want Sarah to take me to the beach, and I need someone to stay with Edward. Mama has trouble keeping up with him now."

"Absolutely. I'll take care of Edward."

"I know you will, Blake. I know."

Sixty

❦

Abby and I stood on the castle's front porch beside Mama. "Sky's growing mean," Mama said, pointing at the clouds overhead. "I want you both to stay home."

"Stop it, Mama." Abby scooted her feet into little green flats. "Nothing wrong with going to the beach in the rain."

Mama gathered us both in a hug, whispering prayers before heading into the house.

"She misses Ethan," I said. "She was up all night, cleaning everything. Maybe we should stay."

"And do what? Sit here crying all day? Ethan wouldn't want that. He'd tell us to go to the beach."

Abby's face brightened, seeing Edward thud down the stairs.

"Bring me shells, Abby," Edward said. "Yellow ones. The same as what's in your eyes."

"I'll get the biggest shells I can find." Abby kissed him, tucking in his shirt. "What do we say when a yellow shell's turned upside-down?"

"Peekaboo."

"And what do we say when it's turned right-side-up, and the yellow is winking at you?"

"I see you."

"That's right, Edward. Yellow shells are like my eyes, which means I'll be watching even when I'm not here, so you'd better behave."

Blake stepped out, handing cardigans to Abby and me. "Maybe

you should wait till the storms pass. Abby should finish the statement for Ward."

"Did it last night." Abby punched her arms through the sleeves. "There's an envelope on Ethan's desk."

"We won't be long," I said. "If the rain is too heavy, we'll come back."

Abby stretched up, hugging Edward. "Listen to Blake while I'm gone, Edward. He'll help you with things just like Ethan. Understand?"

Edward agreed, kissing Abby once before galloping back up the stairs.

"Thank you, Blake," Abby said as we stepped from the porch.

"Don't thank me yet." Blake laughed. "For all you know, Edward could be covered in chocolate and quoting Bart Simpson when you get back."

"I mean, thank you for being a good man. Without you and Ethan, I'd never know what a good man is."

Blake's shoulders slumped, and he gripped the back of his neck. "That's about the best compliment anybody's ever given me, Abby. Thank you for that."

Abby waved and blew him a kiss before hopping into the car. I'd never seen her so happy before. It showed in newfound energy and the elation steeped in her voice. She talked about Edward and the exciting things she had planned. She'd start by building a playground for Edward next to Ethan's stone in the castle's backyard.

"And I'll take him to the beach every day," she said. "I want him to dance on the shoreline like we did. Remember Sarah? Remember how we danced on the beach?"

"Always." I smiled, murmuring agreement as we rounded Oaks Bridge from the park.

"And Mama will always have something to do at the castle. She needs to come off that island sometimes. The mainland isn't all bluster and sin."

She quieted, and when I looked at her, she'd bowed her head to her lap. "Alicia," she whispered. "I have pictures of us and letters wrapped

332 ~ M. A. AIKENS

up in string. They're in a box in my left dresser drawer. I need to give her those now. Should have done that a long time ago."

And in a gush of unprecedented fervor, she arched from the window, calling to Ethan as the wind whipped hair from her face. "Thank you for saving your damsels, dear prince. You're the bravest knight in the world, Ethan Bennet. Braver than anyone else." Then she dropped to her seat, wind-blown and giddy. "Who's your whim, Sarah Thorn?" she asked. "Who's your whim?"

"You're my whim, Abby Mills. And I'm yours."

"You'll always have me, Sarah," she said, resting her head on the seat. "The best part of myself I can give."

Abby glowed with the promise of what lay ahead. Freed of the shackles of her once-wounded life, she paid no attention to the perils that faced her, looking ahead to a brighter beginning. The one Ethan assured her she would have.

Sixty-One

⟨❦⟩

The beach was breezy to the point of annoyance as the storm rolled closer to shore. Usually, I wouldn't have cared, but with the wind tying knots in the ends of my hair and the mist forcing into my clothes, our morning excursion seemed more like a battle for beachside survival and less like a leisurely stroll. Abby didn't notice. She skipped on the shoreline, shoes in her hand, absorbing the world underfoot.

"Let's go to Mama's and wait for the wind to die," I said, tightening the sweater. "I'm cold, Abby."

"A little longer." Abby pulled me down to the sand. "We have to make sandcastles first."

"All right, but only one. Jackson's coming for my session, and Mama will want to cram us with lunch. That woman's gonna feed us into our graves."

"Mama's wonderful. That's where you get your temper, you know. You get it from Mama."

"Since Mother didn't have one at all, that's probably true. Don't know why Mama puts up with me. Half the time, I end up yelling at the poor woman."

"Don't do that again," she said, patting sand into cakes. "Getting angry was always your way, but don't do it with Mama, and certainly not when she prays."

Guilt wrenched my chest. Abby wasn't one to sharpen her tongue, but when she did, it stung more than Mama's hard smacks on the ass.

"That was awful of me," I said. "You're right. I should be more patient with Mama."

"Patience is a struggle, for sure. I had to learn that too. Learn to wait for things. Learn to be patient."

"Ida and Buster were horrible people. You learned patience living with them."

"I learned patience making the poison."

"Poison?" My fist froze in a wet mound of sand. "You made poison, Abby? What for?"

"For Buster. Mama said we needed a lot because Buster was big, and collecting the glories took time."

"Glories? What glories?"

"Morning glories in Mama's backyard. Flowers and seeds. Mama ground them, wrapped them in muslin, and let them soak in her honey. Same jar. Same honey. Year after year. Old blooms came out, new ones went in."

"That's how you did it." I slumped, recalling Mama's blossom honey glowing like gems in a crown. "That's how you got Buster into the Perlick. He was drugged."

"Nearly messed up after Ida's cancer took hold. I ran to Mama's and tried to use the honey with Ida barely in the grave. Mama said two deaths in the same month would wag too many tongues. She said I had to be patient and wait."

"Where was Edward?" I asked. "Was he with you that night?"

"Wouldn't matter if he were. No one will know what happened except me, Mama, and now you. Alicia knows too, but we tighten our lips around her."

"Did Edward have any part?"

"He picked the glories," she said, tucking damp hair at her ear. "Mama wrapped muslin on his hands when he was little, and he'd strip those blooms whenever they popped."

"And the lights in the shop?" I asked. "How'd you break those?"

"With a chair and an old oar handle, like I said. I may be short, but I'm not an ant."

"Buster didn't see?"

"Buster always passed out by noon, so I had plenty of time."

"Who cut the safety latch off?"

"That's not mine to tell," she said. "Not that part, anyway."

"But the rest of it is?"

"The rest of it's mine, so yes." She swiped sand from her lap and sat back. "Want me to tell it?"

I answered soberly, "Yes."

"Buster liked his honey and biscuits after supper. That pig ate twelve of those things inside a minute, washing them down with that rotgut he drank. Once he was dizzy and nearly passed out, I called Mama and told her to come."

"Mama was there?"

"Of course, she was there. Mama wouldn't let me do that alone." Abby scooped sand into neat little mounds. "After she came, I went to the house and told Buster the power was out. He was wobbling and weaving, crazed from that honey so bad his eyes were nothing but black."

"Like two onyx buttons?"

"Onyx buttons?" She tilted a grin. The kind that told me she knew what I meant. Then she gave a slight shrug and patted her castle again. "Mama lit a candle so I could lead Buster into the shop. He was following along until the glass crushed under his feet. Then he went wild, screaming about scrimshaw, trying to find his way out. He bumped into walls, broke the freezer cases—"

"He was scared. The glass and the room. He was terrified."

"But that's what I wanted," she said. "I got close to his ear, saying I'd let him out of that well. Then I opened the Perlick as wide as I could. Those walls lit up like a star with that candle inside, and he cried even more. Blubbering and weeping, whining about being saved. He got all the way in, then I dashed around him and slammed the door tight."

"He couldn't get out?"

"Not with that latch broken off," she said. "Buster screamed, beating and kicking that door so hard I thought it would break from its hinge.

I told Mama it sounded like popcorn cooking. *Pop, pop, pop.* Real fast until, finally, it died."

"Why'd you do it, Abby?" I asked. "Why'd you kill Buster?"

"Because he deserved it."

"For beating you?"

"No."

"For beating Edward?"

She shook her head. "No. He never touched Edward like that."

"For rape?"

Abby stalled, biting her lip before she stared at the ocean and said, "I wouldn't kill Buster for something like that. I wouldn't kill Buster for rape."

"Then why do it?" I asked. "Why'd you kill him?"

"I have my reasons. Your world would change if you knew them."

"I won't tell anyone. Not even Ward. Please, Abby. Tell me why."

Abby eased closer, crushing the sandcastle under her fists. Then she pressed a kiss to my jawline and said, "There are mysteries beyond the hells we imagine. Secrets only the devil should tell."

I grabbed her shoulders and hauled her up from the sand. I wanted to scream at her, to shake the answers from her, but the words were trapped in my throat, afraid of the answers they'd get. Then she gave them. Not in screaming, wailing confessions but in the bend of her lip, the pulse of her neck, and the rip of the tears from her unblinking eyes as she silently begged me to stop.

"Who's your whim, Abby Mills?" I asked in a breath. "Who's your whim?"

"You're my whim, Sarah Thorn." She jerked me into her arms. "And I'm yours."

"Will you be all right?"

"We're all going to be all right." Then she lifted a smile before kissing me once on the mouth. "Now, go start the car while I collect Edward's shells."

I kissed her again before turning toward the dunes that lined the parking lot. Scrambling their peaks, I reached the car just as fog rolled in from the beach. It cloaked mother's Buick in a haze so thick it hovered inside even after I closed the door.

The heat blasted on with the turn of the key, and I held my hands against the vents to warm them. Abby's head bobbed beneath the edge of the lot. Then she blew me a kiss and lifted a portion of shells in her hand. I relaxed in my seat, waiting to see her scrape up the dunes.

She didn't.

"Abby?" I opened the car door, triggering its chime as I flattened a foot on the lot. Calling her name did little good, but I searched the shoreline expecting to see her carrying armloads of bright yellow shells.

Moving closer, I looked left, right, and then finally, down. Abby's sweater lay folded at the base of the dunes, a shimmering pile of shells stacked on top. An indent of footsteps dotted the sand, following the shoreline, toward the riptide, melting away in the waves.

She was gone.

Sixty-Two

We buried Abby at Shoreline beneath the same oak branches we dangled from as children. It was a simple affair. Unlike Ethan's service when the whole town came to grieve, Abby only had us. Mama made lunch at the castle. Jackson took Edward fishing to, once again, explain the mechanics of death, and Alicia was a different being altogether.

Her usually squared shoulders weakened, her cropped hair went uncombed, and she mulled about the rooms stalking in a foreign solemnity I wasn't sure she knew how to claim. She wasn't one to indulge in flexes of emotion, covering her pain with jabs of humor and teasing distractions. But there, holding letters from the woman whose love she'd secretly hidden away, she had no need for such useless defenses. She crept inside herself, dealing with her loss in the same fractal way a knight might mourn his queen. A dignified repose. Hidden, quiet, and strong.

Ward called, directing Blake and me to meet him in Ethan's office once we got home from Shoreline. We found him with his hands in his pockets, and his back turned toward the door. There was no greeting, and he offered no seat. Ward was silent, staring blankly through the windows and the water beyond.

"You needed to see us?" Blake followed me to the Chesterfield and sat down.

"Abby made changes to the will," Ward said. "They affect both of you, so I thought we'd take care of that now."

Looking at Blake, I asked, "What sort of changes? And when?"

"Last week. When I asked her to write what happened when Buster was killed."

"Didn't she do it?" Blake pointed to the papers spread on the desk. "She told us she left it right there."

"She did, plus a bit more." Ward turned, claiming the chair behind Ethan's desk. "Abby could do as she liked with what Ethan left her, and in her absence, she could leave everything to whomever she liked."

"That'd be Edward," Blake said. "Whatever Ethan left to Abby would immediately go to Edward, right?"

"That's true." Ward nodded. "But Edward needs special placement with people he knows."

"Like the Andrews?" I shared glances between Ward and Blake. "Edward knows them, loves them. Angela adores Edward."

"That's true too. And I've known Jack since grade school. Helped Angela with her business needs, and I can tell you how wonderful they are. But I can also tell you, they're not prepared to help Edward with the issues he might one day face."

"What are you trying to tell us?" I asked. "Are you saying the Andrews aren't fit?"

"I'm saying Abby's wishes are that her brother stays with you and Blake. She wrote a letter giving you custody of Edward."

"Jesus." I slid back, looking at Blake. "What should we do?"

"We should take him." Blake's answer was instant. "Abby knew Edward would be safe with us. That's why she did it."

"This town is all Edward knows," I said. "Do you know what that means? We'd have to live in this house. In Ethan's house."

"Edward needs us, Sarah. And we need him. We have to take him. Abby wanted us to." Blake turned to Ward. "What about the investigation? What happens now?"

"Closed. Spoke to the DA this morning. Abby Mills will become a rumor here now. Another cautionary tale of a woman who fought a monster and won. That's all."

"And you believe that?" I asked.

"What I believe is irrelevant, Sarah. I represent my clients according to the dictates of law. What I believe doesn't much matter to a system meant to be blind."

"But you're not blind, Ward. And I think it does matter to you. I think this case matters to you a great deal."

Ward pushed up, turning to gaze out the window again. "Blake, I'd like to speak to your wife alone. We shouldn't be long."

Blake stood and kissed my cheek before thanking Ward and leaving us alone in the room. The office was quiet. The clock ticked, the shorebirds squealed, and Ward rasped in and out as if struggling to breathe.

"I've defended evil men," he said. "I've sat beside thieves, rapists, wife killers, and heartless bastards that I could have gutted myself for knowing how black their souls were. But I swear, I could live this life ten times over and never see evil like Abby Mills saw." He looked at the desk. "There's an envelope in the top drawer over there. Abby left it for me. I need you to get it."

I stepped to the desk, opened the drawer, and retrieved an envelope ripped down the side.

"What is it?" I asked, flipping it once.

"Abby's confession."

"If this is Abby's confession, it can't tell me anything I don't already know."

"She told you she killed him?"

I nodded. "Same day she died."

"Did she tell you why?"

"She wouldn't say."

"Then you don't know what's in that letter." Ward reached down, snatched his briefcase, and tucked it under his arm. "I want you to read it. Right here, right now. Don't tell your husband, and don't tell the Andrews. And when you're done, take it to Mirabella Nash and tell her to burn it."

"Ward?" I asked, watching as he walked to the door. "Abby told me if I knew the truth, it would change me. Is that true?"

Ward breathed deeply and said, "I'm an atheist, Sarah. I don't believe in sin. I don't believe in redemption, and I don't believe there's any sort of heaven. But what Abby Mills wrote in that letter made me pray to God there's a hell and that Buster Mills is suffering damnation at the hands of the devil himself."

Then he stepped through the doors, leaving me to wonder how a man sharpened in war, a believer in nothing, could be brought to his knees in prayer.

Sixty-Three

A single piece of paper weighs 4.5 grams. Abby used five sheets to tell her story, yet the weight of the words made it immovable. In an instant, everything changed. Our childhood, once lustered, became dull and tragic. Our memories darkened; our innocence dimmed.

With the letter tucked down my dress, I smoothed my hair, wiped my tears, and left the office in a feigned effort of normalcy.

I found Blake on the porch, drinking tea. "Where's Mama?" I asked.

"Alicia took her home. Everything all right? What'd Ward want?"

"Just stuff about Abby. Mama knows more, so I'll run over to ask."

"Hey," Blake shouted as I stepped on the walk. "I'll love you forever, you know."

"Oh, yeah?" I turned, smiling with a slow backward pace. "Is that what gator tooth woman says?"

"No," Blake answered. "That's what I say."

Blake and I finally found peace, but something haunted our new beginning, and I needed to end it. Not for myself but for Abby. I'd give her the only thing she wanted in life... the death of her secrets so her brother could live.

Mama's little yellow house was golden once the sun grazed its roof. I entered slowly, recalling the warmth of our laughter and the honey-sweet scents of my youth. But it was different now. The rooms held shadows; the floors groaned, the doors cried, and as I stepped into the kitchen, my eyes settled on blossom honey, casting an orange glow over the walls. Mama sat on the stump by the tide pool, scattering biscuits to fish at its edge.

My legs were heavy, but I slammed through the screen door, wadding papers from my dress as I ran.

"Is it true?" I sobbed, falling to the grass at her feet. "What happened to Abby, is it true?"

"Got something for you." Mama sniffed, tugged the figure-eight comb from her apron, and pressed it into my hair. "E'Tan come back the next day and pulled it out of the water. He was going to give it to you himself, but—"

"Why didn't you tell me, Mama? Why didn't anyone tell me?"

"You couldn't know something like that," she said, dabbing her eyes. "Your poor little mind couldn't hold such a thing. But it's stronger now for the darkness you've seen. So now you can ask me, and now I can say."

"Edward?" I whimpered. "Edward is Abby's son?"

"He is, baby, yes."

I cried harder, grappling the folds of her dress. "Tell me now, Mama. Tell me what happened when Abby was twelve."

"Buster'd been at her," she said. "And when her body started heaving, with Edward growing inside, Buster tried to rip poor Edward right from that child's belly. Ida said he'd gone crazy that night. Stripped Abby down to nothing, dragging her, kicking and begging, into that filthy freezer where no one would hear her screams. First, he beat her, and when that didn't bring Edward out, that monster went about lancing her little insides, trying to reach Edward with whatever evil tool he could find. Bastard only stopped when he passed out. Ida brought her to me that night, bleeding down her legs. My baby was barely breathing, and I couldn't get her to speak."

Mama wept, pounding her thighs so hard I slid my palms underneath to keep her from bruising. "Go on, Mama," I said. "What happened then?"

"I told Ida to go jam that latch and shut that door so he'd die in the frost of that room. That worthless cunt stood there, telling me she wouldn't do it. I picked up my washing paddle and took to pummeling on her till she rolled over bloody on that porch where I strip down my corn."

"It's good you beat her, Mama," I said, mopping her cheeks. "I'm glad you did."

"I cleaned Abby as best I could. Gave her some whiskey and laid her down with our 'Licia. I whispered to her, promising Buster would die for what he'd done. Then I left for the shop to make sure he did. He was sprawled on that Perlick floor when I got there. I searched for anything to make sure he'd never lay another filthy hand on my Abby again. Then I saw those bone saws on top of a crate. I took the biggest I could hold, cutting that latch and shutting the Perlick, knowing he'd be dead by morning."

"You cut the latch? That was you?"

"Cut it and threw it into the marsh off Sam's Point Road. When I got home, Ida was gone. She took Abby with her and set that rabid beast free. I drove to the shop again. The sun was up, and your momma was there. Gossips told her Ida took a bad beating, so they jumped a Greyhound to Florida again. You were crying for Abby so bad your momma sent you with me for the day. We ate candy and played in the tide pool. Ethan come over and brought you some shells. Remember, baby?"

"I remember Mama. I do."

"Abby was free from Buster, so I tightened my lips, but when she come back with Edward on her hip, I went to that shop with my washing paddle, telling Buster justice was coming, and if he touched my Abby again, it'd be swifter than what I had planned. He laughed, saying he knew about the latch, daring me to call the police. I told him I didn't believe in justice like that. I said it just ain't brutal enough."

"That's why Abby didn't want it investigated, isn't it?" I opened the letter and stared at the words. "The police would find out about you cutting that latch, and they'd want to know why. Everyone would know about Edward after that. They'd never look at him the same way if they knew. Jesus, I forced her into that water, didn't I, Mama? I told her I remembered the latch. I did this, Mama. I left her no choice. She was—"

"This ain't none of your doing," she said. "Abby made her choices a long time ago. Her soul was tired. She was only waiting for a time when she could leave those burdens behind. Abby wanted Edward safe, and you gave her that, baby. You and your men. Her soul is at peace."

"Taking your life is damnation, Mama. That's what you told us."

"Abby didn't take her life. She gave it. She sacrificed so Edward could live free of the stain of his birth. No one will know the truth now. Only you, me, and that lawyer man."

Holding the letter, I said, "Ward says we're to burn it."

"Then that's what we'll do."

Abby's secrets died that night on the beach. Mama and I burned that letter by the shore, letting waves take its ashes out to sea. That was our final embrace of Abby and the last time we'd speak of the casualty of her life. From then on, we vowed to recount only the memories she and Ethan would want us to have. The bright ones. Those filled with springtime suns and looming August moons.

As the months advanced, molding into a more comfortable rhythm, we let go of the tragedies that precluded our happiness, allowing us to finally heal. I wrote again using Ethan's office, surrounded by the things he'd left and adding pictures of Michael beside them. My first book was the start of a series called *Castles*.

Unlike my previous works, *Castles* had no mysterious abominations, no horrors, and no licentious deeds. This was a fairy tale. The story of a girl and a knightly prince who sailed a magical boat, fighting monsters all over the world. Blake said I should use a pseudonym, fearing my SB Thorn moniker might drive the market away.

I smiled and said, "Fine. We'll use Abby Bennet."

Blake and Edward became inseparable. Fishing at The Waterfront or playing the monster game through the house. We did as Abby wanted, putting a swing for Edward beside Ethan's stone. We took him to the beach as often as we could, even at night where he'd hold my hand, dancing with me at the edge of the waves like Abby had done.

It was within this undaunted existence that I finally accepted my purpose in life, and it was a grand and magnificent purpose too. But it was never unique just to me. We were all creatures of special design, small bits of heaven God couldn't quite hold. We were the voice of the broken, the keepers of secrets, and the wings on a butterfly's back.

This is the testament of life. To sacrifice fear. To love unafraid. And to know heaven is but a mystery fallen to earth and that each of us had simply lived within its darkened shadows and burning light, being led by the whims of a wounded and desperate God.

About the Author

As a military brat, Margaret Aikens spent her childhood packing and unpacking books. She credits her love of writing to her father's collection of science fiction novels and to the blue-haired lady at the mobile library who gifted her a copy of *The Time Machine* in fifth grade.

Margaret holds certifications in website design from Florida State University and has worked as an SEO copywriter and content manager since 2008. Living in Beaufort, SC, for fifteen years granted rapt inspiration for her debut novel, *Whims of God*.

From Beaufort's soft, silky marshes to its moss-heavy oak trees framing the shore, Beaufort's primal resonance will always remain an integral part of Margaret's heart.

Currently, Margaret lives with her retired Marine husband in North Georgia's Appalachian foothills, where she's currently working on future novels.

Printed in the USA
CPSIA information can be obtained
at www.ICGtesting.com
LVHW090800020724
784424LV00002B/152

9 781737 420804